A Null for Hire Novel

By Terri L. Austin

Praise for Terri L. Austin

"Austin infuses her characters with relatable problems and hot chemistry that will keep readers turning pages." - *Publishers Weekly*

"Austin never fails to deliver engaging, complex and refreshingly unique characters whose journeys are full of smart banter and delicious chemistry."- *RT Book Reviews*

Books by Terri L. Austin

A Null for Hire Series
Dispelled
Disheartened

The Rose Strickland Mystery Series
Diners, Dives & Dead Ends
Last Diner Standing
Diner Impossible
Diners Keepers, Losers Weepers
Diner Knock Out
Diner Disfunction (Coming Soon!)

The Beauty and the Brit Romance Series
His Every Need
To Be His
His Kind of Trouble
His to Keep

Copyright

Disheartened

Copyright © 2018 Terri L. Austin
All rights reserved.

No parts of this publication may be reproduced, stored in a retrieval system, or transmitted in any form or by any means, electronic, mechanical, photocopying, recording, or otherwise, without the prior written permission of the copyright owner.

This book is sold subject to the condition that it shall not, by way of trade or otherwise, be lent, resold, hired out, or otherwise circulated without the author's prior consent in any form of binding or cover other than that in which it is published and without a similar condition including this condition being imposed on the subsequent purchaser. Under no circumstances may any part of this book be photocopied for resale.

This is a work of fiction. Any similarity between the characters and situations within its pages and places or persons, living or dead, is unintentional and co-incidental.

Cover art © Renu Sharma | www.thedarkrayne.com

EBook ISBN: 978-1-946066-02-2
Paperback ISBN: 978-1-946066-03-9

CHAPTER ONE

I stopped by my office that Monday afternoon to grab a protein bar. My last meeting ran long—negotiations for an arranged marriage between two shifter clans. Bobcats. By bringing the two families together, they'd strengthen their power base here in eastern Oklahoma.

Here's the thing about rural bobcats, though. They aren't old school, they're Old Testament. The bride has no say over whom she'll marry or where she'll live. Those details are left to the menfolk.

There's a reason why females are starting to outnumber their male counterparts. The males tend to die early. A lot of accidental deaths in that community. Go figure.

Now as I ran through the parking lot to my office, my mini umbrella offered little protection as a gust of wind blew cold rain sideways, biting at my face with icy stings.

Normally, Tulsa's autumns were temperate, spiked with warm days which eased into cool evenings. But this October had brought nothing but foul weather. The long summer drought had finally ended, but as usual, Mother Nature was a fickle bitch.

My office, housed in one of the older strip malls off Harvard Avenue, sat squashed between a day-old bread store and a second-tier insurance firm. There was nothing fancy about the place. Not the brown-gray nubby carpet or the mismatched furniture or the dingy walls. And seeing my former-assistant-turned-business-partner Sunny Carmichael behind her desk, wearing her usual uniform of a crisp white blouse and disapproving frown, did nothing to brighten the atmosphere.

I tossed my umbrella near the door and carefully pulled my Gucci bag from beneath my coat, pleased that I'd managed to keep it dry. My hair might be a wet tangle, and I was certain that last burst of rain hadn't done my makeup any favors, but the purse was safe. Priorities, right?

I placed my precious baby in the visitor's chair. "If this weather keeps up, we're going to need an ark."

"What are you doing here, Holly? You have another appointment in thirty minutes. It'll take at least that long to get all the way to Leonard."

"Settle yourself, woman. I just dropped by to grab something to eat. Text the client, let them know I'll be a few minutes late." I'd started work at seven that morning, and it was now almost eleven. Despite my repeated objections, Sunny kept booking back-to-back appointments, without a break. Going without food made me cranky. Clients, especially Norms, didn't like cranky, so I needed sustenance before trekking to my next job.

After I shook off my coat, I noticed we'd added a white five-gallon bucket to our collection. Must have sprung another leak.

I sighed. Deeply.

"We need to get out of this damned office before we float away."

"Don't be so dramatic," Sunny said. "A little water never hurt anyone."

"A little?" I walked over to the corner, and with the toe of my black Sorel boot, kicked the bucket. It was half filled with rainwater and I nearly sent a splash over the rim. The landlord treated repairs the same way he did deodorant—as optional. "If you think I'm going to spend this winter freezing my ass off in a wet office, you're crazier than you look. It's time to move."

"You're barely in the office. Hank may not fix everything but he prorates the rent for these little inconveniences."

Sunny was right about one thing—I almost always traveled to see my clients, not the other way around. Sure, we had the occasional pop-in, but it was rare. Still, we needed better digs.

I took a good, long look around the spartan room. Next to Sunny's desk was a battered side table that held a coffeepot and a can of powdered creamer. A plain clock adorned the wall above her head. A rusted file cabinet housed the printer. God, how depressing. No wonder Sunny was such a sour patch. If I had to sit in this gloomy room every day, I'd be one, too.

"It would be nice to have furniture that didn't come from the flea market." I touched the chipped edge of her wooden desk. "Thicker walls so we don't have to listen to Bill next door complain about his hernia. Most of all, we wouldn't be breathing in toxic mold."

Sunny pushed at her oval frames. "That mold myth has been blown out of proportion by the media. It's fake science. And we could always use the spare bedroom in your house. Not only would we save on rent, but you'd get a tax write off. Win-win."

Sunny invading my private space every day? Hell no. Only one of us would make it out alive. Probably me, because I fight dirty. Besides, I kept my handbag collection in the spare bedroom.

She grabbed her cell phone and typed something. "I'm sending you addresses. I squeezed in two more jobs today, so check your schedule."

Besides the office issue, my overbooked schedule was the main source of our contention these days. I'd never hurt for customers in the past. But since I'd recently helped my boyfriend, Inspector Cade McAllister, solve the murder of two young witches, business was booming.

Everyone who hired me wanted to hear details about the Black Magic Murders, as the Other community called it. I'd been keeping quiet about the whole situation, but the thrill of investigating was never far from my mind.

Being a null meant I was an anomaly. If you wanted to get ugly, you could call me a freak. Don't worry, I've been called a lot worse. And as a null, I breached the gap between the magical world and the mundane. I permanently sucked the mojo out of all spells, wards, good luck charms…you get the picture. Others—aka magical folk—hired me as a mystical bodyguard, usually for special events. I zapped Others' powers temporarily. Once they were out of my presence, their magic returned.

That included Cade, who was a sorcerer. Which made our dating lives a little complicated. But the fact that Cade spent most of his time out of town helped.

So far, our romance mostly consisted of hot phone sex and stolen weekends. On those rare occasions when we saw each other, I cut down on my work obligations and spent as much time with Cade as possible. When he left for his next job, I could barely think, let alone move. It was easy to put my doubts and concerns on the back burner. But after he'd been gone a few days, all those worries crept back and left me questioning what kind of future we might have. If any.

Not only did I nullify his power, but if Cade hung around long enough I'd shorten his life span. We had stuff to work out, questions that needed answers. But right now, I just wanted a break.

"Sunny, I need a few days off. I'm running on fumes and I haven't seen my grandmother in almost two weeks." Gran gave me an earful about it on the phone every damned day, too.

"I don't think so. If you take days off, we don't get paid. I like getting paid."

"We do very well," I reminded her. "More than enough to pay the bills and keep me in Gucci bags." I leaned over and picked up my new pale pink mini backpack, giving the quilted leather a loving stroke. "She joined the family last week. The other bags are a little jealous, but they'll come around."

"You're certifiable. The amount you waste on purses never fails to astound me. Anyway, if you want to entertain the idea of a new office—which for the record, I'm against—we'll need more capital. That means no days off. I'm working just as hard, you know, and you don't hear me complaining."

My brows skyrocketed. "Sunny, you bitch constantly." Besides obsessing about money, it seemed to be her only other hobby.

"I do not appreciate that language."

I didn't appreciate that stick wedged up her ass, yet I lived with it. Mainly because Sunny was damned good at what she did. She hustled for clients and always made sure the check cleared. But this was one battle I was determined to win.

"Fine. I'll keep working these crazy hours for a couple more weeks, and you'll look at available office spaces."

"Holly, you're getting extra business because of the murder notoriety. It's not going to last forever. We need to make hay while the sun shines—and don't take that as an invitation to use my name." She hit me with a withering glance. Her real name was Sunshine, bestowed upon her by her hippy parents.

My stomach let out a long, vicious growl. I couldn't argue about this anymore, not right now. I was already running late for my next appointment, and I needed something to eat.

Frustrated, I turned my back on her, walking down the short hallway to the bathroom. Unfortunately, she hopped up from her desk and dogged my heels.

"And no new furniture. What we have is perfectly adequate."

I slammed the door in her face, hoping she'd take the hint. No such luck.

"I got a call from a new client. They want you for a full day tomorrow," she said through the door. "It's out of town, so I charged three times our normal rate."

I leaned my hip against the sink. "Back off, Sunshine."

She muttered something as she walked away.

I glanced in the mirror and winced at my pale reflection. I was tired and it showed. I quickly reapplied some Buxom lip gloss and brushed a little blush on my cheeks. After whipping my long dark hair into a damp ponytail, I washed my hands.

When I tried to shut off the faucet, the plastic hot water handle twisted clean off. I attempted to shove it back in place, but it slipped out of my wet fingers, pinged off the wall, and fell into the toilet with a plop. Perfect.

I stepped back out into the hallway. "Sunny, there's a situation in the bathroom."

"Jiggle the handle a few times."

I didn't bother explaining. Since she loved this place so much, she could take tackle our new water problem.

Before leaving, I stopped by my inner office to grab a protein bar but got sidetracked by a large floral arrangement sitting in the middle of my desk. A riot of tulips, geraniums, and lilies ranging from pale yellow to reddish orange filled a hand-blown trumpet vase. That vase cost more than my little Gucci bag, I was certain of it.

This wasn't Cade's handiwork—unfortunately. "Master Sebastian?" I hollered to Sunny.

"Who else? They arrived first thing this morning."

Keeping a wary eye on the flowers, I grabbed a chocolate power bar from the top desk drawer and backed out of the room. I'd met the master vamp recently, and now it seemed he'd taken an interest in me. No, not sexually, because gross. The thought of getting banged and fanged at the same time gave me the willies. I wasn't sure what Sebastian wanted from me, and despite my disinterest, the flowers kept coming.

I really didn't have time to worry about him just then, so I relegated the vampire as another problem for another day.

I strode into the main room and shrugged back into my coat before whisking up my purse from the chair. "I'm out. The bathroom faucet's broken. You may need another bucket. See ya."

"Wait, what?" Then she shook her head and wagged her finger. "Listen, I'll text you the directions for tomorrow's job. It's almost two hours away. Reece Tolliver asked to speak to you directly, but I told her all work requests go through me."

Reece Tolliver.

I'd been reaching for the door handle when my entire body froze, my muscles locking down for a long moment. When I could breathe again, I slowly turned to face Sunny.

"What did you say?" My heart pounded hard and loud. Each beat seemed to echo around the small room.

She pointed to her dainty watch. "Holly, you need to go."

"Reece Tolliver called here. About a job?" An icy shard of anger tore through me, so sharp and raw, it took me by surprise.

Sunny studied me, her brown eyes narrowed. "I'm guessing by the look on your face the two of you weren't friends?"

"That's one way of putting it." More accurately, Reece had been my worst nightmare.

"Well, you're a professional. I'm sure you can manage to be polite. If you try really, really hard."

Swallowing past the bitter knot lodged in my throat, I walked toward Sunny's desk. "No. Absolutely not. I don't care how much you charge, I am not doing it."

She raised her chin in defiance. "As a partner, I now have an equal say in what jobs we take. Reece paid fifteen-thousand dollars and I refuse to issue a refund. Besides, her entire coven is going through some kind of magical disaster. She'll explain when you get to Moonlight Cove. That's the name of their community."

I leaned down, looked her in the eye. "I don't care what she's willing to pay. I couldn't care less about her explanations. Understand this, I will never work for that woman. And you may be a partner, Sunshine, but I'm still the talent."

CHAPTER TWO

I'd vowed to myself a long time ago that Reece Tolliver would never take up space in my head again, and I planned on keeping that promise. But it was easier said than done. As I sat in bumper to bumper traffic, memories from college kept drifting back. I thought I'd gotten over most of what happened, but just hearing Reece's name proved to me that I was more affected than I thought.

I breathed deeply, shoving down the feelings that surfaced, suppressing them. What good would it do to dwell on the past?

Because of the latest deluge of rain, the highway became a parking lot for twenty minutes. By the time I arrived at my destination, I was late. Not the best way to make a good impression, but it couldn't be helped.

A brand-new housing development needed my nullifying expertise. But as usual, Sunny had been sketchy on the details, so I didn't know exactly what I was walking into. More than likely the builder needed a "cleansing."

Sometimes, Norms simply wanted me to clear out bad energy—whatever that meant—or bless the space with some New Age sage burning. Yeah, it was bullshit, but who was I to deny clueless Norms a little comfort? I'd sprinkle a few herbs, create a faux ritual and boom, the home was cleared of evil intent. I gained a happy customer, Sunny added to her coffer and I paid my mortgage. For the record, that's what I called a win-win.

Glen Falls was a subdivision carved out of a heavily wooded area. I swung left onto a road that sliced through freshly dug piles of sandy dirt and rock. The rain had turned the street into a muddy bog, and my little Honda had a hard time gaining traction. With patience, I managed to slog my way up the slight incline.

In the distance, I caught sight of two finished houses across the street from each other. Several others were in the middle of construction. At one of the finished homes, three pickup trucks and one SUV congregated in the driveway. My awesome powers of deduction led me to conclude this was the meeting spot.

The two completed houses were fairly large. Five or six bedrooms most likely, spread between two sprawling stories, but almost no room between the homes themselves. I sure hoped the future occupants liked their neighbors, because once they opened their windows, they'd be rubbing elbows.

I parked in the driveway behind a red pickup, grabbed my umbrella, and made a mad dash up the long, curving walkway to the front door. The stone house reminded me of a fairytale cottage on steroids—quaint, but enormous—with gables over the windows and shutters made of aged-looking wood.

The front door stood open. Light shining from inside the house bathed the porch with a yellow glow. I shook out my umbrella and placed it with a cluster of others just like it.

"Hello?" I yelled, stepping through the door. I heard voices from within, and as soon as I spoke, they immediately quieted. "I'm Holly James. I apologize for being late. The weather and traffic…"

A tall man with more salt than pepper in his neatly trimmed hair emerged from the back of the house and walked toward me. His big boots squeaked on the plastic floor covering that protected the hardwood from stains. Wearing a wary expression, his cheeks had the rough, ruddy look of a man who spent a great deal of time outdoors.

He held out his hand. "Welcome. Stan McNeil. My construction company is in charge of building the houses here in Glen Falls. Come on in." After pumping my hand once, he let go, turned and backtracked, carefully keeping to the blue plastic runner, which was caked with muddy footprints.

I followed him into what I assumed was the kitchen, not paying much attention to the rooms we passed along the way. I was too busy keeping up with Stan's sturdy stride, my gaze glued to his broad back.

Two men and a woman stood, blocking the wide doorway. Stan positioned himself against the wall. Almost shoulder to shoulder, they obstructed my view of the room beyond. Though the three new people dressed as casually as Stan, in jeans and plaid shirts, the woman's makeup was flawless and her denim was distressed on purpose. One of the men had soft hands, an expensive haircut and a Rolex to class up his outfit. The watch might have been a knockoff, but I doubted it. He seemed like a guy who prided himself on affording the real deal. Also, he looked familiar, but I couldn't remember meeting him before. The other man bore a resemblance to the first, but his blond hair had been cut super short. His work boots were well worn—not for show. I'd be willing to bet he knew his way around a construction site.

Both men had light blue eyes and square jaws, but the man who looked familiar possessed sharper features. He was the one who broke away from the group and stepped forward, his intense eyes taking me in as thoroughly as I'd been studying him. "Dean Wyler." His handshake was warmer than Stan's had been, and he held on, seemingly reluctant to let go.

It finally hit me, where I'd seen him. This was the guy from the morning news.

"I've seen you on TV." Dean Wyler did a weekly segment on all things real estate—from architectural design, to room staging, to finding the right mortgage. He was sort of a celebrity—at least in Tulsa terms.

"Oh, that's just a little something I do on the side. My real estate and development business takes up most of my time. My family and I are partnering with Stan." He smiled, causing dimples to appear on either side of his wide grin. "We're glad you could make time for us. You come highly recommended, Ms. James."

News to me. Like I said, I did the occasional blessing for Norms, but most of my clients came from the magical community. "Who referred me? I owe them a thank you note."

He glanced back at the man and woman standing behind him. They both shrugged, while Stan remained stiff, arms crossed over his barrel chest.

Dean Wyler turned back to me, a look of adorable confusion on his face. "I'm sorry, I honestly can't remember. It'll probably come to me later." He gave me a flash of that bright, white, TV-ready smile.

Dean was a born salesman. His boy-next-door looks and friendly demeanor seemed genuine. I could see where people might find him charming, but he'd been holding my hand far too long for comfort. When I tried to subtly tug out of his grip, he finally released me.

Then Dean pivoted to the side and gestured at the man and woman. "Let me introduce you. This is my brother, Aaron. He works the construction side of our business. His wife, Amanda, owns an antique store and helps stage our houses."

I didn't really need their resume, but I gave them each a finger wave. Since I was already running way behind schedule, it was time to get this show on the road, but I still didn't know what these people wanted from me. "How can I help you today?"

Dean and Stan exchanged a long, uncomfortable glance, then the three Wylers turned and led the way into the kitchen-slash-family room. The entire area, including a cozy eat-in space and an informal living room with a massive brick fireplace, had been vandalized—like a wrecking ball had smashed through the room, demolishing everything in its path.

One of the refrigerator doors had been ripped off, thrown halfway through the far wall and was now embedded in the sheetrock. The fireplace and chimney bricks were broken and littered throughout the room, like they'd been ripped off and flung by a giant toddler. The rustic wooden beams overhead contained shards of glass. Probably from the large boarded up plate glass windows, if I had to guess.

Random cabinet doors had been reduced to splinters of wood. The light fixtures had been yanked from the ceiling, leaving the wires a tangle of red, black, and blue tentacles. And the stainless-steel oven door lay in the middle of the room, crushed like a soda can.

Amanda watched me as I picked my way through the rubble to examine the damage. What the hell happened here?

"Can you tell us what we're dealing with, Ms. James?" she asked.

"Call me Holly," I said absently and kicked a brick out of my way. "What makes you think I can help? Shouldn't you call the police?"

Aaron spoke for the first time. "Take a look at this." He grabbed a tablet from the cracked quartz countertop, turned it on. I walked toward him, and Amanda moved to make room for me.

He pressed the play button and I watched grainy footage of the room getting wrecked by unseen hands. The cabinets ripped themselves off the wall. The oven door went flying through the air, landing in a crushed heap. The four windows shattered, one after the other. Bricks flew across the room on their own. It was over in mere seconds. An invisible whirlwind causing at least tens of thousands of dollars' worth of damage.

Magic had to be involved here. But what kind?

I glanced up at Aaron. "Any outside footage?"

"Yes, but again, it shows nothing. No one set off the alarm around the outer perimeter of the houses. No cars drove through the worksite. We didn't see anyone running from house to house."

"Wait a minute. This happened to the other finished house, too?"

Amanda rubbed her forehead with a perfectly manicured hand. Blood red fingernails complemented her short dark hair and fair skin. Fatigue lines fanned outward from her large brown eyes. "The other completed house looks like this place. Trashed with no explanation, no video footage. The foundation for the rest of the houses are fine." She attempted to smile at Aaron, who rubbed a hand along her back.

"One partially built home did take a hit, though," Stan corrected. He leaned against the doorjamb, arms still crossed. "The walls caved in. Literally."

Why were some of the homes targeted, but not all? "Were any rooms other than the kitchen affected?"

"The upstairs doors were ripped off their hinges," Stan said. "Some damage was done to the bathrooms. But the kitchen seemed to be the central focus."

"Oddly, most of the lights in the bedrooms and hallway still work," Aaron said. "Why do so much damage here, but leave the upstairs light fixtures intact?"

Amanda heaved a sigh. "I'm just glad I hadn't brought over any furniture yet. Especially that armoire. Took me weeks to refurbish it. I'd have been devastated if it had ended up like this." She tipped her head toward the debris littering the floor.

My brain spun through the possibilities. I'd seen imps do mild damage to homes, especially when their nests had been disturbed by construction equipment. But those slimy little beasts were barely sentient. They created mischief like throwing silverware on the floor, hiding keys, that kind of thing. They weren't capable of this hardcore devastation.

"Do you guys have any enemies?"

Dean gave a halfhearted shrug, but Aaron was more forthcoming. "Of course. Our competition would love to see us fail. 3W—our real estate company, is doing very well."

Amanda cocked her head as she gazed up at him. "Aaron, come on. I can't imagine any of our rivals would do this. It feels…personal."

"No, it's business, plain and simple," he said. "Any one of those sons-of-bitches could have done it."

"How?" she asked. "We agreed, this"—she waved her arm wildly—"this has to be something…unusual. No one was on the video, remember?"

Aaron shoved his hands into his pockets and strode to the broken refrigerator, forcefully kicking a brick with the side of his foot. "Snyder hates us. He could have paid someone to do this. Somehow."

Stan nodded in agreement. "This is what I've been saying. Liam Snyder would pull this kind of stunt in a heartbeat. And he has ties to the mob."

"If this were a hit job on the development," Dean said, "why not just burn the houses down? This is all so elaborate and strange."

Taking the mob out of the equation, I agreed with both men. This was a focused hit, not some random act of magic. Someone—some Other—wanted to hit back at the Wylers or Stan or the development itself. A witch or a sorcerer could have pulled this off easily enough. A telepath could have done it, too—but could he or she have accomplished this amount of destruction without getting near the house or being seen on the video footage? I didn't know enough about telepaths to answer that.

I wished to hell Cade were here. This would be right in his wheelhouse. Not only was he an Investigator, he could read magical signatures—mystical DNA—left behind by the perpetrator. According to Cade, all magic leaves a trace, a pattern unique to the practitioner.

Dean tugged on his earlobe, his expression sheepish. "Do you think this could be the work of a poltergeist or something like that?"

Stan huffed, rolling his eyes in disbelief.

"Well, it's always possible," I said. Except that it wasn't. Poltergeists didn't exist. Ghosts were real, of course, but they couldn't pull enough energy to do this kind of chaos. Mostly, they got stuck in a loop, staying long past their expiration date and living moments of their lives over and over. No, I suspected a spell of some sort. That made the most sense.

"Could we have built the houses over a sacred burial ground?" Amanda whispered, clutching the silver pendant at her throat.

Welcome to America, Amanda. This entire continent was one big burial ground.

I met their gazes head on. "As you know, I'm just a psychic." I managed to say the word without choking on it. "I'm intuitive to certain…energy frequencies. But I have a friend who's an actual medium. I'm going to call him, get his take on this."

Before meeting Cade, I would have just nullified the houses and walked away, leaving everyone to sort out their own shit. But since I was now dating a Council Investigator, the responsible thing would be to call someone and get a second opinion.

"Oh, for God's sake," Stan sputtered. "This is ridiculous. Someone came into these homes and did this. A person, not a spirit. Someone who knows how to cover their tracks on camera."

Dean placed his arm on Stan's shoulder. "I understand your doubt, but if that were true, why not just hack into the system and erase the footage?"

"Just give her a chance, Stan." Amanda crossed her arms, then turned to me. "How soon can your friend get here?"

Since Cade was out of town, I'd have to go with Plan B: Mick Raven. He was the only other sorcerer I knew on a personal level. But Mick was also Cade's oldest friend and most hated enemy, so it complicated things. I knew Cade wouldn't want me to call on Mick for a favor, but desperate times and all that.

"I'll see if he's available. Will you excuse me for a moment?" I pulled my phone from my bag and walked back through the house to the front porch. I wavered only a moment before dialing Mick's number.

He answered after the first ring. "Well, this is a surprise, darling. A most welcome one. How have you been?"

Mick spoke with an unidentifiable accent, a seductive one that caressed words, spinning them into an enticement. He could read my grocery list and make it sound hot. The fact that he looked like some kind of sexual demi-god didn't hurt either. But I wasn't tempted to go there. Cade was all I wanted, and frankly, more than I could handle.

"Great. Hey, you can read magical signatures the way Cade does, right?"

He paused for a moment. "Why are you asking?"

"I'm in the middle of something, a job. I suspect magical mischief, but I can't be sure."

He laughed, low and rich, the sound striking a chord low in my belly, curling through my chest and up my neck. Even the man's laugh was sexually charged. But Mick could turn that seduction act on and off like a switch. He was well-practiced, and the flush on my cheeks proved it.

"You are never boring. But I am curious as to why you're calling me and not your beloved. Wouldn't he be more adept at this than I? He's the professional, after all."

"Well, yes. But since he's out of town—"

"Quite the contrary, Holly. In fact, Cade is sitting across from me as we speak."

CHAPTER THREE

I was so shocked I couldn't speak. How long had Cade been in Tulsa? Why hadn't he called? Cade and Mick hadn't been friends in years, yet he'd stopped by Mick's club, The Raven, instead of coming to me. That stung like hell.

"Holly," Mick said, "are you still there?" Smug bastard. I could tell by his amused tone he enjoyed knocking me for a loop.

Cade's rough voice rumbled in the background. A moment later, he was on the line. "Why the hell are you calling Mick, Little Null?"

"Were you going to let me know you're back in town? Or just slip in and out without giving me a call?" I patched over my pain with indignation. Then another thought hit me. "Have you done this before?"

"Yes, no, and no. I'm here with Mick on business. Just tell me what's wrong."

"How long have you been in town?"

"A few hours." Wrong answer.

As of yesterday, he'd been in Utah. He could have called before he hopped on a plane. But he hadn't.

I'd known from the start that Cade's job took precedence over everything else. Even me. Dealing with it in theory was one thing. Feeling it played out in real time was another.

Okay Holly, time to rein in the crazy. Before my mind started spinning out and I turned into that girl, the pathetic, insecure one who kept her boyfriend's balls on a tight leash, I stopped talking.

"Holly, tell me what's going on. Now." Where Mick enticed, Cade demanded. Right then, it rubbed me the wrong way.

"Don't start issuing orders to me, Sorcerer. I'm not your lackey."

He paused for a second, and when he spoke, his tone was stark. "It's been a real long day, baby."

Cade rarely gave me details about his cases. The fact that he'd just now let his guard down even a smidge—in front of Mick—told me he was dealing with something major. I immediately softened.

"I need you to read a signature for me. I'm on a job where two houses were destroyed last night. I don't know if it's a spell from a talented witch or a telepath with a hatred of model homes, but something is off."

"Give me the address." When I did, he assured me he'd be there in thirty minutes, then hung up.

"Welcome home, McAllister."

Before heading back inside, I ran out to my car and dug out the supplies I kept in the trunk. I poured the remainder of my Evian into a spray bottle, mixed in a few essential oils and after pricking my finger, added several drops of my blood to the concoction. No, this wasn't part of the fakery. My blood was a nullifying agent—a permanent one as long as it wasn't washed off. But now that I thought about it, would any bodily fluid work? Spit or sweat—pee? Disgusting, but something to ponder.

Back inside the house, the Wylers and Stan trailed after me, gathering around like a pack of antsy dogs, peppering me with a dozen questions. Why did I say prayers in Latin? What had I put in the spray bottle? How long would the blessing last? Was I sure the invisible vandal wouldn't come back and break their pretty house again?

I turned on them. "Shh. Please. I need to concentrate." Not true, I was just tired of their yapping.

I sprayed the doorways and windowpanes, chanting a few prayers of protection I'd learned for such occasions. Once I circled my way back into the kitchen, I said, "Make sure you don't wash this off. That's vital to the process."

They all glanced at each other with a mixture of doubt and curiosity. Then I lit a sage stick and waved it through the house, muttering under my breath, stopping at random spots. This part of the routine was bullshit since I didn't have magic backing me up, but Norms loved it.

I walked back down the stairs, the quartet clomping behind me, when I noticed Cade standing in the entryway. The overhead bulbs illuminated a circle around him, lightening his pale hazel eyes.

I paused and we stared at each other for a long moment. Just looking at him temporarily robbed my brain of oxygen, made my heartbeat kick into overdrive.

Cade's impressive height and muscular body demanded attention whenever he entered a room, but it was his powerful, dangerous presence that made people quickly avert their eyes. There was nothing subtle about McAllister. He was all hard edges and sharp angles.

Dark stubble covered the bottom half of his face. A shiny, white scar on his right cheek peeked through the bristle, adding another feature to his tough guy persona. But it wasn't just a façade. There hadn't been much joy in Cade's life for a very long time, and that pain etched its way into the grooves on either side of his grim mouth.

His blue T-shirt was plain, no writing. He had five more just like it, in various shades of faded. He wore a casual olive-green jacket and, from beneath the collar, I caught the barest glimpse of his tattoo—a dragon with red, green, and gold scales flowing along the side of his neck. Dark denim clung to his thick, muscular thighs.

His dark hair had been freshly buzzed sometime in the past week, and he'd recently soaked up some rays. His sun-bronzed skin created a perfect foil for those eyes. Eyes that heated with desire as they drank me in, from head to toe. My entire body felt hot, tingly.

I missed McAllister, his scent, his strength. And that familiar expression on his face—it was completely carnal, full of delicious sexual promise that he never failed to deliver.

As I stood there, the frustration and hurt I'd felt earlier drained away. I traipsed down the rest of the steps, the burning sage in my hand creating wafts of smoke as I descended. "Hey."

His jaw tightened as he looked me in the eye. I didn't need the words. I knew he'd missed me, too.

I joined him and started to make introductions. "This is the man I was telling you about, C—"

"Christopher Mitchell." Cade stuck out his hand, shook with the Wyler brothers, Amanda, then Stan.

I blinked at his use of an alias, but it made sense. Especially in dealing with Norms. If they didn't know his real name, they couldn't track him down in the future.

Dean headed toward the kitchen. "Let me show you the worst of it."

Cade motioned for me to walk in front of him. Even as he followed, I could feel the heat rising off him. McAllister ran hotter than other people.

In the kitchen, I tossed the sage stick in the sink and flipped the faucet on. Thankfully, the water still worked. As the smoke dissipated, I watched Cade roam the room, taking in everything just as I had. He walked to where the refrigerator door remained lodged in the wall. Reaching out with one hand, he touched it, though he wouldn't be able to get any reading off of it since I'd destroyed any magical signatures that might have been present.

He glanced at me. "Have you examined the other house?"

"No, I was leaving it for you."

He gave a brief nod and looked to Dean. "Show me."

Dean's mouth opened and closed at Cade's blunt command. "Sure, yeah. Of course."

"Don't you want to see the video footage?" Aaron asked.

Cade barely glanced at him. "No." Then he left the room, waiting for Dean to catch up.

Amanda's eyes widened. "Well, he's not all warm and fuzzy, is he?"

"He's more like a drill sergeant," I said.

"And he actually speaks to dead people?" Her forehead pleated when she raised her brows.

"Yeah," I lied. "All the time."

Aaron's mouth flattened into a straight line. "I'm going with them." He strode out of the room, apparently not wanting to be left out.

Stan leaned back against the cracked countertop, ran a hand over his face. "I can't believe we're doing this."

"It's fine, Stan," Amanda said. "If it doesn't work, you can say 'I told you so' all you want." When his expression didn't change, she added, "And I'll buy you a bottle of that rotgut you like."

He gave her a half smile. "Deal."

I excused myself again and walked to the front of the house to call Sunny.

The phone barely finished ringing before she answered. "If you're calling to apologize for your rude behavior," she said by way of greeting, "don't waste your breath. I told Reece you'll be there tomorrow at ten o'clock."

"I'm not apologizing, and we've been over this. Maybe you should get your hearing checked."

"Then what do you want?"

I explained that this job was far more complicated than we'd been led to believe, and I needed to reschedule my next couple of appointments. After I hung up on her protests, I stood under the eaves for the few minutes it took Cade to leave the house across the street.

He strode toward me, each step accentuating his long legs, his solid muscles. He seemed impervious to the rain, which had slacked off. Dean, however, carried an umbrella as he fought to keep up with Cade's fast gait. Aaron lagged behind, his expression grim.

When Cade reached the porch, his gaze cut to me, telling me nothing. He held open the door and jerked his head, motioning for me to enter first.

I retraced my steps back to the kitchen. Amanda and Stan stood side by side, whispering. When they saw me, they jumped apart.

"Oh, you're back," Amanda said, her voice a little too loud, too bright.

Stan tugged on his earlobe and kept his eyes on the tips of his boots.

I wondered what I'd just interrupted. A good old-fashioned gossip session or something more personal?

Cade, Dean, and Aaron tromped in behind me, making the large room feel suddenly small.

"Well?" Amanda asked. "What's the verdict?"

"Poltergeist. No question." Cade stood with his legs slightly apart, his shoulders thrust back, as if daring the Wylers to question his conclusion. They wouldn't. Norms loved the idea of a poltergeist. And if they were fictitious creatures, so what? It'd give these people a story to chew on for years to come.

Dean nodded, satisfaction gleaming in those baby blues. "What do we do, Christopher? Holly sprayed the house with holy water, but will that be enough?"

Oh yeah, I'd also told them my Evian had been blessed by Father Jimenez that very morning. I might be going to hell.

Cade finally glanced at me. "Holly's as good as they come. If she told you she's taken care of it, I believe her." He pulled his wallet from his back pocket and whipped out a card. "But if you have any more trouble, call me." He shook hands with the men first, and when he got to Amanda, she captured his sleeve with her crimson-tipped fingers.

"Can I get a quick reading? My mother…"

This was awkward. Cade may be an uber-powerful sorcerer, but he couldn't communicate with the dead. Hell, he barely spoke to the living.

When Cade gently gripped her hand with both of his, I watched in fascination. "It's not that simple, Amanda." He looked her in the eye. "I don't sense any female presence around you right now, and I'm not in the proper head space to call on a spirit. I need a lot of meditation for that. I do get the sense that you're thinking about a change. You're torn in two, and the indecision is weighing you down." My God, he sounded so grave, so sincere, I almost believed it. "Trust yourself. Don't worry about trying to satisfy anyone else." Then he dropped her hand and stepped back.

Tears filled her eyes. "Yes. Exactly. How'd you know that?"

Cade cleared his throat. "It just comes to me."

I stepped forward then, gave them all a smile and produced my own business card, one that stated my name, number, and labeled me as a consultant. "Thank you for letting me work with you today. I'm going to clear and bless the other house before my next appointment."

"I'll come with you," Cade said.

Dean clapped his hands. "Excellent. I'll walk you out." He led the way to the front door and held it open for Cade and me. "Thank you both. If there's ever anything I can do for either of you—"

Just the words I'd been waiting to hear. "Actually, I need a new office space. Could you recommend one of your realtors?" Sunny would be angry that I'd done this behind her back, but her nose was permanently out of joint, so what difference did it make? We didn't have to commit to anything, and it wouldn't kill her to look at a few places.

Dean's face changed from friendly to speculative, his sharp features reminding me of a fox. "Are you looking to rent or buy?"

"Rent."

"Tell you what, I'll make some time next week and handle you personally." Dean smiled, that same grin I'd seen on TV countless times. One that accompanied the PR slogan he recited every week: We won't be happy until you're home.

"That'd be great. Thank you, Mr. Wyler."

Dean placed his hand on his chest, his skin pale against his dark flannel shirt. "Dean, please. You chased off a poltergeist today, Holly, and I'm very grateful." He pressed his lips together, stifling a chuckle. "Wow. That may be the craziest thing I've ever said. But I'd be honored to help you find a new office."

Cade placed a guiding hand on my back, scowled as he nodded at Dean, then led me down the walkway to my car. We didn't talk as I opened my trunk. He grabbed my supply bag and followed me toward the house across the street. Before opening the front door, I glanced back to where Dean stood. He gave a little wave before disappearing inside the first home.

Cade's hot body radiated tension. Though only his fingers touched me, I could feel that trapped energy like an electrical current, shooting sparks through my back, and straight to my nipples. They hardened almost painfully.

I walked through the door and flipped on the light in the entryway. One bulb from the chrome fixture still worked. The rest laid shattered under my feet.

Unlike the last place, this home had an open concept, so the damage was front and center. The living room and kitchen had been torn apart. Even one of the beams separating the dining area from the living room had been broken in half.

"Something weird is going on here. I was right to call?" I turned to face Cade.

He said nothing. The tendons in his jaw twitched—his only display of emotion. Before I could take my next breath, he'd dropped my bag, kicked the door shut with one foot, and wrapped his hands around my waist, lifting me off the floor. Then he had my back against the door as he pressed his hard body into mine.

He peered down at me, the look in his eyes wild, almost feral. My insides melted, heat trickling from my belly downward. With just a glance, this man could take make me wet in seconds. And he hadn't even kissed me yet.

"Hey," he whispered.

"Hey."

We stared at each other for a long moment. I'd never grow tired of looking at that face. It wasn't handsome. Cade's features were interesting, hinting at secrets and dark desires lurking past the stony expression he showed the world. But sometimes, like now, that tough exterior relaxed the tiniest bit. Enough to let me see what was going on beneath the surface.

He didn't just want me, he needed me. And the feeling was mutual.

"Do you have any idea how much I've missed you?" His low growl sent shivers through me. "I hate being separated like this."

He'd already reduced my body to liquid heat, but his words had melted my heart, too. Wrapping my legs around his waist, I stroked his cheek, the stubble coarse against my palm. I let my finger drift over the scar marring his jaw. "I missed you, too. So much, Sorcerer."

He kissed me then, his tongue swirling against mine. He tasted faintly of peppermint. His delicious, exotic scent—cloves and spice and something uniquely Cade—surrounded me.

Thrusting his hips forward, he ground his cock against my core. I jerked in response, and he grew even harder.

No matter what else happened between us, this always felt right. I came alive under his touch. I loved the heavy weight of him, the way he folded me into his body. He made me feel cherished, protected. McAllister stirred something primitive inside me every time we came together.

I ran one hand over his short hair, the other hand curved around the back of his neck. He cupped my breast, squeezing with just the right amount of pressure. The ache between my legs grew stronger, a rhythmic throbbing that beat in time with my pounding heart.

Cade's kiss became rougher, more demanding. A branding. A possession. He nipped at my bottom lip until it stung, then sucked the tip of my tongue. Neither one of us liked it gentle.

I ground against him, trying to get some relief. I didn't merely want him, I craved him like an addict craves their next fix.

Then Cade thrust his hand beneath my sweater, working his way under my bra to caress my bare breast. I let out a deep moan of pleasure against his mouth. Just as he pinched my nipple, his phone rang.

CHAPTER FOUR

Taking a shuddering breath, he leaned back, still holding me against the door. "Fuck it. I'm not answering." He squeezed my breast again, a little harder this time.

The phone kept ringing.

As I gazed into his eyes, I saw desire warring with reason. He closed them for a second, then lowered me to the floor. "Goddamn it."

Turning away, he pulled the phone from his pocket and stalked across the room toward the busted kitchen. "What?" he barked.

I let the door hold me up for a few seconds, because my knees were weak. Desire still surged through me. It would take a minute for my heart to stop pounding, my nipples to stop aching.

I gave Cade his space as he prowled the kitchen, with its wrecked countertops and cabinets. The refrigerator door remained intact but was dented, as though it had been punched by a giant.

Cade's shoulders stiffened as he listened. "Yeah, all right. Thanks." He hung up, then kicked a broken piece of quartz countertop out of his way.

When he still didn't say anything, I asked, "What do you think is going on here?" Feeling more centered, I made my way toward him, carefully stepping around large shards of glass and wood fragments. "It has to be a spell of some kind."

Stan, or one of his crew, had patched the broken windows with particle board, but the smaller windows near the ceiling were still intact. Weak light from the entryway wasn't enough to chase away the dark, but that dim glow cast a patchwork of shadows stretching out along the floor and walls.

"Why him?" Cade asked.

"What are you talking about?"

"You called Raven." He stepped up to me, his boots crunching over broken glass. I'm on the short side of petite, so I had to crane my neck to glance up at him. His face was unreadable in the dim light. "I don't like it."

Yeah, I knew this would eventually come up. "I would have called you. If I'd have known you were in town. You came back to Tulsa and didn't bother to give me a heads up. I don't like it." His eyes narrowed as I repeated his own words back to him.

"I was working."

"I realize."

He pushed the edge of his jacket back with one hand, settled his fist on his hip. "Okay, I should have called. Figured I'd show up at your place with takeout and a bottle of that crappy wine you like. Surprise you." He glanced away, as if the admission embarrassed him.

All my irritation fizzled away. "Fine, I forgive you. This time. And my wine is delicious, for the record." Who didn't love Pinot Grigio?

"He'll put a wedge between us, if he can. I don't trust him."

It took me a second to catch up to his conversational curve ball. "Ah, Mick. He can't bother us if we don't let him. And he did help save your life."

He huffed. "Yeah, and that asshole will never let me forget it."

"Do you trust me, Sorcerer?"

"Of course." He dropped his hand from his hip and slid it around my nape, tugging me toward him. "Course I do."

"Good. Because I don't care how suave or handsome Mick is, or the fact that he has really great hair—"

His left eye twitched. "Is there a point you're trying to make here?"

"The point is, I don't want him. I only want you." I slid my fingers up his chest, lightly raking my nails over his pecks. He made a deep growly sound in the back of his throat. "Only you, McAllister." I stood on my toes and kissed his scar. "And now that you've seen this situation for yourself, who should I have called?"

"Me. Even if I'm out of town, I'll have someone I trust come out and examine the scene." He leaned down and gave me a swift, hard kiss.

"Okay."

"Good. Now, let's discuss that asshole outside."

I stopped petting his chest. "What asshole?"

"The one you were flirting with."

"Have you had a recent head injury or something? I have no idea what you're talking about."

"Oh, Dean," Cade adopted a falsetto tone, "I've always wanted my own personal real estate agent. How kind of you."

I burst out laughing. "You're a lunatic. That wasn't flirting. That was victory. Sunny has been fighting me on everything, including renting a new office. I haven't been able to persuade her, but maybe Dean Wyler can."

"Mmm. Looked a lot like flirting from where I stood, but maybe I really am a jealous bastard sometimes."

I cupped my ear. "I'm sorry. I didn't hear you. Say that again."

He gave my ass a pat. "I don't like to repeat myself. And you were right about this place. Something is off here. The magic is all fucked up."

"What do you mean?"

"Normally, I see colors, textures linked to spells. But this house and the one across the street are black and gray." He stopped, pressed his lips together as if he were searching for the right words. "There's no pattern. No consistency. A jumble."

"Just chaos?"

"Exactly."

"Have you ever seen anything like it before?"

"Today, as a matter of fact. The black and gray chaos was very similar to this, like a tangle of wires, all knotted together. Makes no sense."

"Where was this?"

"Near Longtown, on the lake."

"Have you ever seen anything like it before?" I asked.

"Never." That wasn't encouraging.

I stepped out of his arms and walked around the room. "Do you think your case could be related to this vandalism?"

"I have no idea. But it's a damned odd coincidence if it isn't." He glanced around the room once more. "Either way, I'll figure it out eventually. Let's finish up here. I still have to meet with Herb." Herb Novak was the MME for this area—Medical and Magical Examiner. If Herb was involved in Cade's latest case, that meant homicide.

"Another murder?" I asked.

"Unfortunately." He looked exhausted as he ran a hand over his cheek. "A brutal one."

"The murder scene had this same kind of jumbled pattern?"

"The body did. Victim, female, was found floating in Lake Eufaula. Probably dead for a few days but being in the water it's hard to pinpoint a time of death. As for the actual killing site, we're still looking for it."

"You sure she didn't die in the river?"

He pinned with a look. "Oh, I'm positive." There was a lot he wasn't saying, so naturally, I had a million questions. But Cade didn't talk about his investigations. He considered it privileged information. Still, if the murder was related to what happened here in these model homes, that made it my business too, right?

"Could she have been murdered here?" I looked around the room, horror settling over me at the thought.

Cade reached out and grabbed my hand. "No. There would be blood. A hell of a lot of blood. These homes may have the same chaos pattern, but my vic wasn't killed here, trust me."

I squeezed his hand before letting go. After having just tracked down a vicious murderer a couple months ago, I wondered when Tulsa had become such a hotbed of brutality. It made me uneasy, and I was suddenly very glad that Cade had nagged me about getting a gun. Even with all the extra clients, I'd managed to hit the shooting range once a week. As McAllister pointed out, I may render Others powerless, but they could still beat my ass the old-fashioned way.

I brushed away a feeling of foreboding that settled over me and glanced at Cade. "Want to help me banish a poltergeist?"

He shook his head. "Norms."

"I know, right?" I darted to the front door where Cade had dropped my bag, then brought it back to the kitchen. Fortunately, the faucet still worked even though the sink had been smashed into a dozen large pieces. I filled my spray bottle, added oils, and ripped off the Band-Aid from my finger before pricking it again.

"What the hell are you doing?"

A couple of drops of blood spilled into the bottle. "Whatever damaged this place might come back. My blood will keep that from happening." I stuck on a fresh bandage and hauled out another stick of sage. After lighting it, I handed it off to Cade. "You can follow me around with this."

"What's the point? Smudging won't help, Little Null. You're not a shaman."

"No, but the Norms will smell it. They like a show."

Cade followed as I walked through the house, spritzing the doorways and window sills.

"You haven't told anybody else about your blood, right?" he asked.

"Not on purpose. But the night you were kidnapped, it was mayhem. People ran everywhere, bullets were flying. I'm not sure who overheard me mention it. I wasn't exactly being subtle, though."

He stopped in his tracks. "So Master Sebastian could be aware that your blood nullifies magic? Shit."

It had occurred to me that Sebastian's interest in me could be blood related. Not as a beverage, but to use against his enemies. Which was yet another reason I'd been avoiding him. The thought of being chained up like an animal and drained slowly struck me with a deep terror that echoed through my entire body, all the way to my toes. I'd rather die than be a blood slave.

"Has he contacted you recently?"

I kept my back to Cade, continued spraying all entryways into the house. "He sent flowers again this morning."

"I'll contact him tomorrow. Make sure he understands you're not interested in his gifts or anything else."

I stopped spritzing and spun on my heel. "No." I gestured with the water bottle. "This is my fight, not yours."

Even in the dim, gray shadow I could see his eyes harden. "Bullshit. You think I'm going to sit back and let him intimidate you, harass you? Does that sound like me?"

"When you speak, you have the power of the Council behind you." The Council was in charge of keeping Others in line, but the vampires were an autonomous group who policed their own. If Cade got in a pissing contest with Master Sebastian, it could prompt some kind of standoff between the Council and the vamps. That wouldn't be good for anyone.

"Please, Cade. If this escalates from flowers and gifts to something more sinister, I'll let you know. We'll handle it together. Okay?"

He rotated his neck, then blew out a long breath. "It's just easier when I handle shit on my own."

"Funny, I was thinking the exact same thing." I ignored his scowl as I resumed my work.

When I finished the house, Cade shouldered my duffle bag and held the front door open for me. The rain had picked up again. "Damn it," I said. "I left my umbrella across the street."

"In the house?"

The trucks and SUV were gone, and the lights had been extinguished. I spied my little black umbrella in the corner of the porch, under the gable. "It's still outside. I'll run and get it."

Before I could finish talking, Cade had trotted to the end of the driveway and extended his hand. "Veni," he said, his voice loud enough to be heard over the pounding rain. He always used Latin for his spells, but English worked just as well. Sounded less impressive, though.

I held my breath, excited to see magic in action for a change. But instead of the umbrella flying into his hand, a bolt shot from Cade's fingertips. The umbrella made a whooshing sound and exploded. Orange flames burst upward from the black material.

Cade ran out into the street, shouting something I couldn't understand. I assumed he used a spell to try and douse the flame, but once again the spell backfired, and the umbrella shot toward him like a missile, aiming straight for his head. Cade hit the pavement just in time, and the fireball landed in the middle of the driveway.

I ran past it and joined Cade in the street. He'd already jumped to his feet, was scraping the mud from his wet hands. His brows pinched together. "What the hell was that?"

I touched his shoulder. "You okay?"

"Yeah."

We walked slowly toward the umbrella. The flames had been extinguished by the rain, and only tattered remnants of material remained, reminding me of bat wings—if the bat had been zapped in an electrical storm. Water sizzled off those blackened metal stretchers, and the smell of fried chemicals hung in the air.

Cade and I both stared at it as though it might jump back up and attack once more. But the umbrella simply lay there, looking all innocent and pathetic.

I crouched down, tilting my head. Water flowed down my collar, making me shiver. Not only from the rain, but from Cade's spell going haywire.

He hunched beside me and reached out to flick the umbrella. "This chaos, whatever the hell it is, transmuted my spell."

"You mean it backfired?"

"The magic backfired, because something corrupted my spell. It's like my own magic attacked me."

"I don't understand. I nullified both houses." I blinked water out of my eyes and stood. "What's morphing your magic?"

He glanced up at me, his pale eyes troubled. "I have no fucking idea, Little Null."

CHAPTER FIVE

Bertram Flourish, attorney at law, was what Gran called a dandy. He wore suits that cost thousands of dollars and fit his trim frame to perfection. His jewel-toned shirts always complemented his perma-tan, and he never had a dark, wavy hair out of place. He was equally fastidious about the law.

Bertram was also a male siren.

Here's the problem with legends, myths, and fables—you can't trust their veracity. The old tales have been told for hundreds of years, the erroneous details passed down so many times people take them at face value. Sirens, for example, aren't just female. And sure, some of them sang haunting songs that lured sailors to their deaths, but they're not all killers. Bertram used his persuasive powers of speech to sway judges and juries to his side of an argument.

He kept me on retainer for cases that might become contentious. I couldn't say I liked him, because behind the smooth baritone voice and the natty suits, he was a cold, calculating shark. But I did respect him.

After Cade and I had parted ways, I drove straight to Bertram's office, my clothes and hair still damp, uncomfortably clinging to my cold skin. I consoled myself with a cup of hot tea, which helped stave off the goosebumps.

I sat alone in the corner of Bertram's plush conference room, thinking about what had happened at the model homes. Cade's spells twisted, behaving in a way that didn't make sense. And what was this black and gray jumble he saw? In my imagination, it looked like scribbles that a child might draw. Loops and curves backing up on themselves, over and over again. Why hadn't I permanently nullified the magic that had caused all the chaos in the first place? That confused me the most.

I killed magic. Period. I didn't slow it down or change it. I ended it—plain and simple. I wasn't like Sunny, who was immune. She saw through glamours. Spells just fell right off her, as if she were surrounded by an invisible shield. But when I came in close proximity to magic, I ended it. And once a spell was shattered, it had to be recast. Therefore, whatever affected Cade's spells this afternoon wasn't magically induced. It couldn't possibly be.

So, what else could screw up spells, make them backfire, and turn on their caster? I wondered how it tied into Cade's murder investigation. He'd never seen this kind of jumbled pattern before, but he'd encountered it twice in one day. This wasn't happenstance.

My brain turned it all over without coming to any conclusions when the door of the conference room opened. Bertram nodded at me, then ushered in five goblins. In my presence, their glamours fell away, showing their true countenance.

I was taller than all of them, and I'm only five-foot-two. Their grayish-green skin appeared wan, almost sickly under the bright fluorescent lights. Their eyes, in varying shades of yellow from pale citrine to deep mustard, were overly large—roughly the size of lemons. The goblins reminded me of cartoon characters. Each had a bulbous nose, and long, crooked fingers punctuated by pointed, filthy fingernails. Oh, and because I nullified their glamours, all five were naked and unashamed. Let's just say the eyeballs weren't the only parts of their anatomy that were oversized.

The female stepped in first. She bore a few warts on her nose and sneered at me with fleshy lips. A male schlepped beside her, his rounded gut jiggling with each shuffled step. He had a cottony tuft of white hair sprouting from his huge, pointed ears. Another male and female strode in behind them.

For some reason, I sensed they were younger than the first pair. Maybe because they walked a little faster and had fewer liver spots. The last goblin swaggered in. He wore accessories—the real deal, not a glamour trick. A twisted gold chain, as thick as a cattle rope, hung around his neck. A sideways trucker cap barely stayed perched atop his oblong head. Instead of hostilely flashing his brown, pointed teeth at me—as the rest of them had—he sported a grill embedded with diamonds. A hip hop-loving goblin. You don't see that every day.

Goblins had one passion—their hoard of precious metals and shiny jewels. They worked the mines back in Europe and Asia, stealing whatever they could get their hands on and squirreling it away. Nowadays, they targeted rich people, and weren't above killing in order to add to their stash. They could literally suck the breath out of a human being, making a death appear like a simple heart attack.

I wasn't sure why they were all here in Bertram's office. Sunny, as usual, hadn't given me any details.

As everyone settled around the oval conference table, its gleaming wood surface reflecting the overhead lights, Bertram shuffled something. Parchment, maybe? When he began speaking legalese, I tuned out and glanced down at my phone.

Sunny had sent six texts, each more emphatic, insisting I take on Reece Tolliver as a client, because her entire coven was in the middle of some kind of unnamed crisis. Sunny even sent directions to Moonlight Cove. Out of morbid curiosity, I clicked onto the map and noticed that the coven happened to be situated on the banks of Lake Eufaula. Where Cade had found his murder victim.

Wasn't that a hell of a crazy coincidence? Seriously, what were the odds of finding a body with a weird magical pattern so close to a coven that was in the middle of a mystical crisis? Had to be about a bazillion to one.

I rubbed my forehead, my mind racing. Had the coven's spells gone wacky, the way Cade's had? Maybe the coven had something to do with the murder. Cade would say that was a big leap, but I believed Reece Tolliver was capable of anything.

In college, she and her little witch-bitch minions made my life a living hell. For four, long, miserable years, she waged a campaign to get me off campus. She wasn't the only Other who wanted me gone, but she was the ringleader. Starting with freshman orientation, I had my tires slashed, my room ransacked, my possessions destroyed. That was only the beginning.

By the time I graduated, I'd had to change my phone number fourteen times, because Reece kept posting mine on various escort sites. I had to seek restraining orders to have them remove my name and photo, only to see my information pop up on ten fetish sites the next day. It was a never-ending cycle.

And the kicker? Everyone on campus thought I had a raging case of untreatable herpes.

Bullying was a lame word for what Reece and her kind had done to me. Not even Norms would befriend me, because the few who tried received the same kind of harassment I did.

I thought about dropping out, changing schools. But tucking tale and running wasn't my style, despite the fact that Reece did everything she could to diminish me. I didn't let her win. I was too damned stubborn—or prideful, as Gran called it.

I blinked, pulling my mind from those hateful memories. A high-pitched shout from one of the goblins caught my attention. I glanced up as the older goblin woman hissed at Bertram.

"Read it again," she demanded.

"I'm sure you heard it right the first time, Matilda."

"Again," she yelled, her scratchy voice rising an octave.

Bertram cleared his throat. "I, Harriet, matriarch of the Mullen clan, leave my entire hoard to my grandson, Gordon. The rest of you get nothing. Not a damned gold coin."

Ah, a Will reading. Goblins could live thousands of years. Grandma's stash must have been huge, possibly worth hundreds of millions.

I glanced out the window and watched the rain fall, as my mind drifted back to Moonlight Cove. It made sense that

Reece and her coven lived on Lake Eufaula, considering she was a water witch. I didn't know much about them, except that their magic was linked with the moon.

I pulled out my phone and looked up Moonlight Cove, not expecting to find much more than possibly a Wiki article. Instead, I saw a sophisticated website touting the virtues of a planned community with its own school and several businesses, including an online store and farm-to-table restaurants.

The witches had created some kind of resort town that catered to summer fun on the water. Even more surprising, they opened their doors to take in short-term renters. Covens didn't like outsiders, so I didn't know what to make of it.

When I heard screams and gasps, I glanced up from my phone. The goblin clan, with the exception of the hip hop lover, began talking at once. Their voices grew louder and squeakier with each word.

"There's more," Bertram said, rapping his knuckles on the table. He glanced down at the parchment and continued to read. "I'm ashamed to call you family. You're all horrible, small-minded, lazy sons-of-bitches. Matilda, you were a terrible mother to these children, so I mainly blame you. By the way," Bertram continued, shifting in his chair, "I know it was you who stole my prized black enameled cat broach, the one with emeralds for eyes. I have never forgiven you."

Revenge from beyond the grave. Nice touch, Granny.

Eager to find out more about Moonlight Cove and whatever evil Reece was up to, I let the goblins hash it out and continued to read from the website. I clicked onto the photos, showing town picnics, canoe trips, and fireworks. Very Americana.

I tried to access the online store. As I waited for it to load, I tuned in to the drama at the conference table.

"Why does Gordon get everything?" the younger male whined. "I was always nice to Grandmother."

Bertram smiled, but his eyes were cold. "If you'd allow me to continue without further interruption, I'll tell you." They all scowled at him but quieted down. Bertram continued to read in his smooth, melodious voice. "Ernst, you pathetic little ass kisser. Do you think I'd let you have my fortune, knowing you'd use it to pay for your wood-sprite whores? Never!"

Granny was as salty as hell.

My phone still hadn't loaded the page, so I looked up Reece's social media profiles instead. Surprisingly, she didn't show anything personal. All her pictures and posts tied back to Moonlight Cove and its special events. Coming up this month, a corn maze and a pumpkin patch. How thrilling.

I wasn't buying this version of Reece. A wholesome, strawberry blonde stared back at me from my screen, her blue eyes shiny and friendly, inviting people to come out to Moonlight Cove and bring their family for a day of fun. It had to be a scam.

I looked at more photos, read the captions. For some reason, Moonlight Cove was trying to appeal to Norm clients. Were they renting vacation homes to Norms as well? If covens didn't like Others invading their space, they'd hate having mundane folks come into their community. The water witches would have to hide their magic, act like regular human beings for weeks on end. Something about this didn't add up.

Reece Tolliver was up to her old tricks. She had an angle going, and I was going to find out what it was. And if she was involved with Cade's murder victim, I would personally drag her ass to the Council myself.

I shut off my phone and slipped it back in my bag just in time to watch Bertram close his folder and look at every goblin. "In a nutshell, Gordon gets it all. Any questions?"

Instead of voicing her protest, Matilda heaved herself over the table and tackled the goblin with the grill—Gordon, I assumed. He fell with his chair, and his trucker hat went flying across the room. His mother lay on top of him, smacking his face with one hand and choking him with the other.

I glanced at the rest of the family, expecting one of the goblins to jump in and help Gordon. But they all sat there, staring with their big, stupid yellow eyes. Ernst, the ass kisser, crossed his arms and grinned. Even Bertram looked on dispassionately, then picked up his phone and started texting.

What the hell was wrong with these people? Not people, I reminded myself. They were Others. They played by their own rules, did whatever the hell they wanted. Just like Reece Tolliver.

Matilda finally stopped smacking Gordon, but only so she could use his chain like the rope it resembled. She twisted it in both hands, tightening it around his throat until his face turned purple. Still, no one made a move.

All morning, I'd been thinking about my hell years in college and the abuse I took. Maybe that's why I decided to break one of my own ironclad rules. I never got involved in these Other squabbles. I wasn't here to police their behavior, just make sure they didn't use magic against one another. But as sweat broke out on Gordon's broad face, I realized I couldn't just stand aside and watch this woman strangle her own kid. It wasn't right.

I hurled myself out of my chair and flung my upper body and arms at Matilda, knocking her off Gordon. She now lay on her side but didn't let go of the chain. She adjusted her hold on the necklace, refusing to let go.

"Not your business, null," she screeched. As I sat on the floor, winded, she hoisted herself to a sitting position and straddled Gordon once more.

His dark yellow eyes started turning orange. He opened and closed his mouth like a fish but couldn't catch a breath.

Matilda was small, not weighing much. Certain I could overpower her, I moved behind her, and sliding my arms around her torso, pulled backward. Then I realized I was grasping one of her leathery boobs.

"Ugh." I removed my hand and put her in a headlock instead. I used every bit of strength I had to pull her off Gordon, forcing her to let go of the chain.

After a few seconds of struggling, Matilda released the necklace. I wasn't sure Gordon was even alive, but then he sucked in a breath and began coughing. While I watched him, I'd loosened my hold on Matilda's neck. Big mistake.

She spun on her knees and grabbed me by the hair, ripping strands from my ponytail. And she wouldn't let go. I reached out and swiped at her face, raking my short nails across her cheek as hard as I could.

"Bitch," she yelled and lashed out with her free hand.

I managed to avoid getting my eyes ripped out by pushing on her chest and shifting my torso at the same time. She didn't let go of my hair, and she managed to tear through the fine wool of my sweater, scraping one of her dirty nails across my shoulder.

"Shit!" Pain lanced through me. It was enough to fuel my adrenaline. When she lifted her hand to scratch me again, I punched her in the throat so hard, my knuckles burned.

She finally let go of my hair and used both hands to clutch her throat. She gasped for air the way Gordon had a moment ago.

I pulled my arm back, ready to sock her in one of her yellow eyes, when an enormous man in a black suit and skinny tie stepped between us. He took us each by the arm and hauled us off the floor. Once I was on my feet, he let me go, but he kept a firm grip on Matilda.

As I gazed up at him, I noted his protruding brow. His cheeks looked as if they'd been carved from stone, and his sharply pointed ears twitched. He picked her up by the back of her neck as though she were a puppy and carried her, kicking and screeching, from the room.

Bertram strolled over and offered me a handkerchief to staunch the flow of blood on my shoulder. "There was no need for you to play the hero, Ms. James. I don't pay you to get involved in skirmishes."

"Thanks." I dabbed at the scratch. It wasn't deep, but it stung. Strands of hair fell onto my face, and I blew them away as I wobbled back to my corner chair.

After another minute, the table of goblins rose from their seats, glaring at me on the way out. When they cleared the door, Bertram glanced down at the floor were Gordon lay, still trying to catch his breath. His face remained as purple as a ripe plum.

"I'll get everything sorted, Mr. Mullen. You can expect your Grandmother's inheritance by next week."

With shaky hands, I took the elastic band from my hair and retied my ponytail. My head hurt, my scratch ached, and one of my favorite sweaters had been shredded beyond repair. It was a Helmut Lang. Seriously tragic.

While I continued to apply pressure to my war wound, Gordon climbed to his feet and grabbed his trucker hat, placing it back on his head. He didn't respond to Bertram. He was too busy staring at me with those big, goofy eyeballs.

"I didn't need saving by no null bitch. I can handle my own shit, yo."

"You're welcome, asshole." I stood and pulled on my jacket, then tucked my phone in my pocket before heading out the door.

Bertram held up a hand. "Just a moment, Ms. James. Since you saved Mr. Mullen's life, he now owes you a boon. Goblins don't like debt." He slid a canny glance toward Gordon. "Isn't that right?"

The little creature hissed at me, flashing his ridiculous grill. I realized the diamonds spelled out the word GDOG. This kid was the best of the goblin bunch? No wonder Granny Mullen was so bitter.

Bertram retrieved the parchment from the folder. "Sign here, acknowledging your debt, Mr. Mullen. We'll just go ahead and make this nice and official while we're all here." He held up an expensive looking fountain pen with a sharp, gold tip.

Gordon walked to the table with something less than a swagger this time. He took the pen, pricked his finger, and signed in blood. Then he flashed two fingers at me. "Deuces."

Once Gordon—excuse me, G-Dog—had left, Bertram said, "You'd better get that scratch seen by a doctor. Goblins are filthy creatures."

"They're also your clients."

"Yes, and they pay very well. But that doesn't negate the fact that they lack a certain attention to hygiene." He shuddered almost delicately, though he never lost his neutral expression. "If you hadn't been here, I hate to think what would have happened to my office. As I'm sure you know, goblins have a penchant for violence."

"They could use a few etiquette lessons," I agreed. "Can I ask you a question?"

"Of course."

"You said he owes me a boon. What kind of boon?"

"Theoretically, you could ask for anything. Money, a favor, all of his hoard. If you asked for the latter, you'd be wealthy beyond your imagination, Ms. James."

"Not interested." Not unless Gordon's hoard contained Birkin bags. Then I might be seriously tempted.

"Well, whatever you decide to ask for, do it quickly."

"Why is that?"

Bertram's smile wasn't reassuring. "Oh, you'll find out. Good day, Ms. James."

CHAPTER SIX

I was hungry, hurting, and in need of a shower. I smelled of goblin, which reminded me of sloppy joes for some reason.

When I arrived home, my driveway was empty. I'd sort of hoped Cade would be home by now. I wanted answers about this afternoon's magical breakdown. And I wanted him. I'd had a little taste earlier and it wasn't nearly enough.

Which brought me around to a prickly question. When Cade came into town, he always stayed with me, but now that he was here indefinitely would he be more comfortable at his own place? Staying at his own house made sense, but it left me feeling hollow. I selfishly wanted him here with me, but his work came first. That's just the way it was.

I walked up the front porch steps and twisted my head back and forth, working the kinks out of my neck as I unlocked the front door and wondered which I should do first—drink a big glass of wine or hop in the shower. Both at the same time? Multitasking. I liked it.

A loud thump of speakers drew my attention to the street. A silver Hummer slowly drove past my house, and when the window lowered, music filled the air. Something about bitches ain't shit.

I fully turned, staring at the car as it slowed to a stop. Whoever was inside was here for me. And since I'd made my fair share of Other enemies over the years, I decided to be proactive.

With my heart hammering, I reached in my purse to pull out my gun—a sweet little semi-automatic. Couldn't remember the brand for the life of me, but it was hot pink and shot nine-millimeter bullets. That was all I needed to know.

With my thumb on the safety, I began to slowly pull it from my bag. The car's interior light flickered on, and G-Dog waved. Just like that, all the anxiety drained away, along with the tension tightening my muscles. Annoyance replaced the fear that had seized me and I stomped across the yard toward his car, tucking the gun back into the bottom of my bag.

"What up, null?" he said over the booming music.

"Are you following me?"

He flashed his gold grill. I wasn't sure if he was grinning or grimacing. So hard to tell with goblins. "Boon. Name it."

"No. Go away."

"I got things to do, mama. Don't leave me hanging like this. Tell me what you want."

"It's been an hour, Gordon."

His upper lip pulled back at the sound of his given name. "I'm G-Dog, you feel me? Think about it. I'll be seeing you." He threw me the deuces sign again, rolled up his window, then drove on.

Perfect ending to a perfect day. That little dipshit knew where I lived. Even though he was more of a pest than a threat, I didn't like the fact that he'd been following me around town. Hell, maybe I should just take his hoard, buy Sunny out of her half of the business, and go on a relaxing island vacation. After all this rain, I could barely remember what the sun felt like.

While that had a certain appeal, taking another man's—goblin's—treasure wasn't my style. Sunny was my partner now, for better or worse. And after the first three margaritas and a long nap, island life would bore me silly.

I walked back to the house and flipped on the lights in the living room. The soft blue walls and chintz chairs always gave me a sense of calm. Even after a day like this one.

I decided a shower was mandatory, especially after getting another whiff of Gordon, so I headed toward the master bedroom and shimmied out of my clothes. When I got down to my bra, the strap was stuck with blood to the scratch on my shoulder.

I stepped in the small master bathroom and carefully peeled the material from my skin, opening up the wound once more as I stared at it in the mirror. The scratch itself wasn't deep, but the skin surrounding it was red, irritated. I cleaned it up with hydrogen peroxide before ditching my bra into the hamper. Unfortunately, the sweater had to go in the trashcan. Rest in peace fuzzy, pink friend.

I flipped on the shower and let the water warm up, then took my measure in the mirror. I noted the dark circles beneath my eyes—only partially due to mascara, which had melted off in the rain. My hair was a frizzy nightmare. A long nap did sound nice.

The endless days and evenings spent with Others, being a damper for their magic, was beginning to get to me. Yeah, the money was fantastic, but lately I had a feeling that something was missing from my life.

When I'd worked with Cade, solving the murder of those two witches, it had given me a sense of purpose I'd been lacking for years. What he did mattered and I'd been a part of that, if only for a minute. I liked it—questioning people, bouncing ideas back and forth with McAllister, offering up theories. I was good at it, too. But the chances of Cade letting me wiggle my way into his latest investigation were zero to none.

Unless I took on Reece as a client. But even if I went to Moonlight Cove and snooped around, I didn't know what to look for, who to question. Without any info on the murder or the victim, I'd be swinging in the dark.

I climbed into the shower and stood under the hot water, letting it soak into me. I washed my hair, then my body, being extra gentle with the skin on my shoulder.

After scrubbing away the goblin cooties, I stood facing the shower head—my eyes closed, face tipped upward, as I relaxed and released the tensions of the day.

When a knock sounded at the bathroom door, I squeaked and automatically clutched my breasts for some dumb reason.

Then Cade pulled aside the shower curtain, a small smile gracing his lips.

"Hey baby, I'm home."

I dropped my hands and turned to face him. He immediately noticed my shoulder, and his smile faded.

He reached out but stopped just short of touching the wound. "What happened?"

"Goblin trouble. No big deal."

His cold eyes met mine. "I want a name."

"You know what I want, Sorcerer? Hot shower sex."

The frost in his eyes melted as his gaze tripped down my body. Then he began stripping off his clothes. "We're not done with this conversation." He kicked off his boots and socks, then shucked his worn jeans and boxer briefs in one swift motion. His cock was hard, ready. "I'm not that easily distracted."

I was. I'd already forgotten the thread of our conversation.

When he stepped into the shower, I gripped the base of his shaft, using it to pull him closer. His skin, already so warm, heated even further at my touch.

Bracing his hands on the shower wall, he caged me between his outstretched arms. I continued to stroke him slowly, twisting my hand at the head of his cock, rubbing my thumb over the center of its tip.

Cade leaned his head down, pressing his forehead to mine. "Can't take much more of that."

"I know, but I missed the feel of you." I wanted to touch the rest of his body, take my time as I let my hands roam over his rippling muscles and smooth, tanned skin. But the need between us was too urgent just then. I hadn't seen him in three weeks. It felt like an eternity.

I stood on my toes, licking his left pec where the dragon tattoo began. I traced its path with my tongue, up his shoulder to the side of his neck. The scales slithered across his wet skin.

Then Cade took charge. He gently grabbed my wrist, forcing my hand away from his erection. "Do you have any idea how much I've missed you?" he asked, his voice raspy and thick with lust. Tucking his hands beneath my ass, he lifted me, pressing my back against the shower wall.

While the water had warmed the white and gray tile, it still felt cold against my spine. I arched into him, my breasts rubbing against the solid muscles of his chest. Flames from his dragon scorched my right nipple, and his cock prodded my hipbone.

Cade glanced down where our bodies touched. "Fucking beautiful. Every last inch of you."

I leaned my head toward him, nipped the hollow of his throat with the edge of my teeth. At the side of his neck, I watched his pulse flutter.

He let go of my ass with his right hand to cup my breast. My nipples were still achy from this afternoon. When he plucked one between his thumb and forefinger, I hissed in pleasure. "Cade." He twisted it, causing a rush of delicious sensation to dart from my breast to my pussy. "Now. Please?"

He didn't always give in when I pleaded with him. Sometimes my desire made him drag things out, denying me an orgasm until I trembled with need. But our time apart had apparently made him as desperate as I was.

Letting go of my breast, he leaned down and kissed me, his tongue sparring with mine as he gripped his cock and lined it up with my entrance. In one slick shove, he sank firmly inside me.

Turning my head to the side, I groaned into the curve of his neck. "Yes."

"God, you feel good." He began moving. Each measured thrust was slow, forceful.

I curled my fingers, digging them into his back. Whatever doubts I may have about our future, Cade and I had this. I'd never felt this kind of connection with anyone else. Our entire relationship could be measured in weeks, but I felt as if I'd known the sorcerer my entire life. He felt right.

I closed my eyes, losing myself to the sensations. I was close to spiraling out. Cade must have been there, too, because he picked up speed, his hips pistoning faster, harder, tipping me over the edge.

When I came, I rested my head on his shoulder, biting my lip to keep from crying out. Ripples of pleasure burst through me, filling me until I couldn't breathe. Couldn't think.

Cade came while I was still reeling. His thick cock pulsed inside me. He clutched me tighter, his fingers digging into my ass. I'd probably be bruised tomorrow, but I didn't care.

As I slowly came back down, Cade remained buried inside me. We held onto each other silently, and I savored the closeness. It felt good to be in his arms, like I belonged there.

He moved one hand to cradle the back of my head. "Love you." I'd never grow tired of hearing that.

"Love you, too, Sorcerer."

We stayed locked together until the water cooled. I shivered, and he set me down to turn off the taps. Then he reached past the curtain to grab a thick, ivory towel from the rack on the wall.

Cade looked into my eyes as he knelt before me, his big body taking up the entire stall. His chin grazed a spot between my breasts, his stubble lightly abrading my skin, sending a fresh wave of goosebumps up my spine.

I stayed pressed against the wall as he took his time drying me. First my legs, then my hips. He rubbed small circles over my belly before covering my breasts. He kneaded them, the cotton gliding over my still-sensitive nipples, making them tingle all over again.

Keeping eye contact, he lifted his head to swipe his tongue across one breast, pulling the nipple into his mouth, sucking. I locked my fingers behind his head, pulling him closer. But Cade was in control of himself now, and this time when I urged him forward, he pulled back, breaking contact.

His eyes were more green than gold as they took me in, his gaze darting over my flushed face. He stood in one graceful motion, and grabbing my hips, spun me to face the wall. Wrapping the towel around my hair, he squeezed out the excess water. "Now tell me about the goblin who attacked you."

CHAPTER SEVEN

Cade was like a dog with a damned bone. Which was probably what made him such a good cop.

I explained what happened in Bertram's office. The goblin rumble and my role in it.

"It wasn't your place to get involved. Since when do you care if Others go at each other?"

"Since today, I guess. She was tearing at him with her bare hands, Cade."

He now used the towel on himself, so I faced him and watched as he rubbed his body, his muscles flexing and bunching under his skin. His abdominals contracted with each swipe. God, what a show. I could honestly watch him do this for hours.

He flung the towel over his shoulder, then reached for me, his hand trailing over the scratch. "Never put yourself in the middle of a fight again. Please." He said it calmly, his voice pitched low. He'd probably rather issue a command and be done with it, but he knew me too well. I bristled at commands, so he was going with the velvet glove approach. I appreciated the effort.

"Next time, I won't jump into the fray." Probably.

His finger traced the angry, red skin around the scratch. He stared into my eyes for a long moment, as though trying to convince himself that I was telling the truth, then finally nodded. "Good."

Arguing with him, reminding him that I could handle myself wouldn't do me a bit of good. Cade's protective streak wasn't rational, it was emotional. After his sister's death, McAllister took his role as protector very seriously. I understood why and I loved him for it. Even if it was sometimes chafing.

He stepped out of the stall, and I climbed out after him. I threw on a pair of underwear and some pajama pants. Still topless, I led the way to the main bathroom and pulled out the first aid box from the linen closet, then hopped up on the counter.

Cade followed a minute later. He'd pulled on his jeans, but left the fly unzipped. He wasn't wearing underwear, and the sight of all that bare skin made my mouth water. He sported a farmer's tan—his neck, face, and arms darker than the rest of his torso.

"Was it warm in Utah?"

"Hotter than it should have been for this time of year."

I reached out and fingered the line of demarcation on his bicep. "I'm jealous. I miss the sun. It's been nothing but gray skies here for weeks."

He leaned into me, pressing his bare chest to mine. Placing one hand on my hair, he tipped my head back and kissed me. "Maybe in January we could take a trip. Somewhere warm."

"Really? Where?"

He rubbed his nose against my cheek, breathed in my scent. I closed my eyes and arched my back, pressing my breasts further into his chest.

"Anywhere you want, Little Null." He straightened but remained standing between my legs. "Right now, let's get that scratch taken care of."

If I were anyone else, he could simply weave together a spell and take care of my wound in seconds. A more serious condition might require potions or herbs and possibly a complicated incantation. Instead, I handed him the antibiotic ointment.

"This is called first aid. I'll walk you through it." I gave him a wink.

"I think I can figure it out, thanks."

"I'm just saying, you haven't had much practice doctoring people. So, you probably don't know I should get a lollipop after you're through."

"I've got something else you can lick."

"Is it cherry flavored?"

He huffed, which was a full-blown guffaw in Cade-speak. "Sit still and let me concentrate."

With infinite care, McAllister tended to me, applying the ointment and then taping a piece of gauze over the swollen scratch. It was starting to throb a little.

"In all seriousness, I think you should see a doctor." He threw away the gauze package and placed everything else back in the box. "Goblins are filthy. They live underground, for fuck's sake. Go first thing tomorrow. Get it checked out."

"If it gets any worse or looks infected, I will." I reached behind me and opened the medicine cabinet. I grabbed the Tylenol, popping two in my mouth, swallowing them dry.

"Just get it looked at." Placing his hands on either side of my legs, he lowered his torso to look me in the eye. "I'm not asking."

So. Freaking. Bossy. "It's adorable when you think you're in charge of my life." He started to scowl, and I brushed one hand down his smooth chest in order to distract him. "I'm starving, McAllister. Please tell me you brought food. All I've had today were a couple pieces of toast and a protein bar."

"Goddamn, you're stubborn." He blew out a breath and stood. "I brought home sandwiches from that barbeque place you like."

"And curly fries?"

"Do I look stupid to you?" His eyes narrowed, daring me to answer.

I kept my mouth shut and dashed to the bedroom to pull on a long-sleeved T-shirt. I also grabbed the shirt Cade had been wearing earlier and threw it at him as I hightailed it to the kitchen.

I decided to forgo the wine and grabbed a couple of bottles of beer from the fridge while Cade unpacked the food from two white sacks on the counter. The smell of tangy smoked meat filled the air, and my stomach let out a rude growl.

We settled around the small island and tucked into the burnt end sandwiches. Heaven on a bun. He'd also brought along coleslaw to go with the curly fries. I gobbled everything like someone might snatch away my plate before I could finish.

Neither Cade nor I spoke until we were through, then I eased back on my stool and wiped barbeque sauce off my fingers. "You know, I'm curious—"

"Here we go," he muttered, then sipped his beer.

I ignored him and carried on. "Where did you find the victim's body? Where on the lake, I mean."

He set down his bottle, leaned his arms on the island's granite surface. "I really don't want to talk about the case."

"Ah, that's too bad, because I might have a lead for you." I hopped down from my stool and began gathering wrappers and napkins, shoving them into the white sacks. "But if you don't want to talk about it…"

I made a move to throw them away when Cade wrapped his hand around my upper arm. "We're not playing games. Tell me what you know, Holly."

"It may not be important to your case. But I won't know that until you tell me where you found the body." I smiled pleasantly when he flashed his teeth in annoyance.

He dropped his hand with a sigh. "This is privileged information."

"What do you think I'm going to do, post it on my timeline?"

Cade and I participated in a stare off for a few seconds, then my eyes started watering. I blinked first.

"I'm serious," he said.

"You're always serious. Just tell me where you found her."

"I already mentioned that she was found near Longtown. Best we can figure, she was probably killed and dumped in McIntosh County. The deceased had been submerged possibly for a couple of days. We believe the body floated south before getting caught on a sandbar. She'd been sighted by a drone sent out by Water Control. They reported it to the police. Our guy at the station caught it and flagged it. Now, why were you curious about where we found the victim?" He leaned back and crossed his arms over his chest, staring me down like the interrogator he was.

"Wait a minute," I said. "Why do you suspect the death was Other related?"

He closed his eyes for a few seconds. "I'll tell you in a minute. First, I met with the Council today."

When he didn't say anything more, I tossed the trash away. I climbed back on my seat and stared at him. His expression told me nothing.

"They'd like me to extend an invitation to you. With spells backfiring and the strange patterns I saw today, they believe your skill set could be useful."

"They want me on hand in case spells go awry?" He nodded. "Do they have any clue as to what might be happening?"

"Nope. Part of my job is to figure it out."

"And they want me to help you on this investigation—the murder and everything?"

His lips thinned as he finally looked down at the table. "Yeah. Officially this time. On the books."

My stomach fluttered as excitement shot through me. I desperately wanted to work on another case with Cade, but I wasn't blind to the fact that the Council wanted to make this "official" for some reason. I'd spent a lot of years staying off their radar, and for good reason. Council members did little but line their own pockets and play power games. Just like Norm politicians, they couldn't be trusted.

"What does that mean, on the books?"

"You'll be an employee of the Council, same as me. And they'll have a say over what you do and how you do it. The Council will basically have you by the proverbial balls."

He was right to worry. In no way should I become involved in Others' official business. Gran had been warning me for years that my null for hire biz would draw the Council's attention. She wasn't being overly protective. Neither was

Cade. After all, it wasn't that long ago nulls were killed at birth. As far as I knew, I was an endangered species of one.

Even with all those doubts ringing in my head, I still wanted in on this case. I'd be helping Cade catch a murderer, participating in something meaningful.

Cade continued to watch me. He knew I was going to accept.

"Sunny will like getting paid this time," I said. "But of course, we'd need to put some real boundaries in place. I won't be beholden to the Council. No strings."

Cade scoffed. "Good luck with that. Once you're in, there's no going back. You know that, Holly, so think about this long and hard. They'll do whatever they have to in order to get your cooperation. This time you get paid. Maybe next time they threaten Sunny. Or Gran."

"Over my dead body. They're coming to me, Cade." My gaze flitted over his harsh features. "You tried to talk them out of offering me this job, didn't you?"

"Of course I did. The shit I deal with is ugly, Holly. My world is ugly. I want to keep you away from that, and if that makes me an asshole, then I guess that's what I am."

I stood and moved to him, rubbed circles along his back. He shuddered a little beneath my touch. "I don't think you're an asshole for wanting to protect me. But I'm tougher than you think. I really can take care of myself. I've been too busy to get a manicure." I held up the short, unpolished nails as proof. "But I still make time to go to the shooting range at least once a week. I'm getting good at it, Cade."

He turned and pulled me to stand in between his legs, bracing his hands on my hips. "You're the one good thing in my life." He sounded ragged, almost desperate. "I don't want to lose you, too. And if you keep getting involved in Others' shit, you're going to get hurt. This murder I'm working on is horrifying. The vic was a Norm, Holly. A defenseless girl."

I clung to his shoulders. "I'm not defenseless. The killer used magic, which I nullify."

"No, he didn't just use magic. He tortured her in human ways. He brutalized this poor girl."

I froze, taking in his words. Tortured her in human ways. I swallowed, my mouth suddenly dry. "What did he do?"

Cade scooted his stool back and stood, then left the kitchen without a word. I followed and watched as he dug into his messenger bag. He pulled out a folder. "I'd do anything to keep you from seeing these, but I know you want in on this case for whatever misguided reason." I opened my mouth to protest, but he kept talking. "This kind of thing, once you see it, it's in there." He pointed to his temple. "It never lets go." He handed me the folder. "Be sure."

"I am."

"Want me to stay with you, discuss everything while you look through it?"

If the murder was as hardcore as Cade had said, and I didn't doubt him, I wanted to read through the file alone. I needed to prove to him that I could handle this.

"I'll be fine. I'm sure I'll have questions afterward."

"Never doubted that for a minute. I'll just bring my stuff in, get started on my laundry, if that's okay."

"You're staying here?"

He stilled. "I can stay out at my place, no problem. Didn't mean to presume."

I flung the folder onto the sofa and tugged on his arm. He remained unyielding until I used both hands, then he took one step toward me.

"I want you here, McAllister, but my presence comes with a warning label. What I'm trying to say is that if you don't want to stay with me, if you need access to your power, I understand."

His shoulders lowered almost imperceptibly. If I hadn't been attuned to his every move, I'd have missed it. "I'd like to stay here, with you."

I smiled up at him. "Okay, good."

"Go read the file." He ran his hand down my face, stroked my chin with his thumb before heading out the front door.

I took the file to my bedroom, shut the door, and sat on the bed with a stack of pillows behind my back. I flipped open the file for Jane Doe and stared at a photo of the victim's body.

She'd evidently been pulled from the sandbar and laid out on the rocky shore. And what the killer did to her made me forget to breathe for a second.

At first, I couldn't even process what I was seeing, then the details came into focus. The girl looked young, maybe late teens. It was impossible to guess anything more, because her face was so bloated from being in the water. She'd been gagged with a rope, her wrists tied behind her back. She bore a horizontal gaping wound under her ribs.

My vision wavered, but I forced myself to study each photo. Jane Doe was covered in symbols—they'd been carved into her skin and looked vaguely like runes that had been distorted somehow.

Her body bore evidence of bruising. Her face, torso, and thighs were discolored. I turned past the rest of the photos to read Herb Novak's autopsy report.

He used the word "incision" to describe the knife wound, but I thought that was imprecise. To me, an incision was something a doctor performed. It was clean and neat. Professional. True, this woman's chest had been sliced open, but this was no clean cut. According to Herb, he noted places where it looked as if the killer hesitated, didn't go deep enough, then course corrected and shoved the knife so far into her chest that it nicked her spine.

Next, the killer ripped the heart from her chest. While she was still alive.

CHAPTER EIGHT

My stomach roiled at the thought of it, and the dinner I'd just eaten threatened to make a reappearance. I swallowed convulsively, taking deep breaths until the nausea passed.

Who could do this to another human being? For what purpose? Taking the heart, carving the symbols into her body, it had to be some kind of elaborate ritual. Not just a murder— but an act of pure evil.

I had a feeling Jane Doe wouldn't be our last victim. This killer was just getting started. The ritual itself was far too elaborate and took a lot of planning.

I flipped back to the photos, stared at the face of the young woman. What must she have felt during her last moments before death? Even though Herb had found a shit-ton of ketamine in her system, she still must have been terrified. How could she not be?

Then I remembered Herb's special gift. He was a post-cog, meaning he could touch a body and get flashes of the last few seconds of a victim's life. If Jane Doe had been feeling a strong emotion, he'd have sensed it.

I flipped through the file, looking for his findings. I skimmed through until I found Herb's handwritten notes:

When I attempted to get a mental picture of the victim's last moments, it was as if I hit a brick wall, both literally and figuratively. I could see nothing of her thoughts. I had no understanding of her emotions before death. Instead, I was seized by a headache so violent, I vomited before passing out. Inspector Cade McAllister reported that my pulse had slowed to thirty beats a minute. Once I regained consciousness, my resting heart rate returned to normal. The headache, however, remained throughout the day. No spells or potions were able to lessen it. I did not try to repeat the experience of viewing Jane Doe's last moments. I must note for the record, nothing like this has ever happened to me in over one-hundred-seventy years as a practitioner.

That black and gray jumble—the chaos Cade had spoken of—must have been what caused Herb's magic to fail. Not just fail, his post-cog powers turned on him, making him pass out.

Then I remembered Reece Tolliver and Moonlight Cove. I wondered if their problems were similar. I still hadn't told Cade about their close proximity to the body because we'd gotten sidetracked by the Council's offer.

So, what was the link between the model homes, the dead girl, and the coven—if the coven was indeed infected? I could see why Cade had been reluctant to link the murder with the vandalism. The two didn't go together, but yet they had to be related somehow. We just needed to figure out how.

I put that thought aside for later and finished reading Herb's notes. Despite Jane Doe having been in the water for a few days, he managed to retrieve DNA from inside her body. Though he didn't detect any signs of tearing, he didn't rule out rape, but she'd definitely had sex. No word yet on whether the DNA could be linked back to someone with a criminal history. Herb would perform a DNA test just like the Norms, and since this case was resistant to magic, it would take a few days.

I turned back to the photos, bracing myself for what I'd find and studied the close-up shots. A lot of rituals contained a sexual component—fertility rites, goddess worship, pagan celebrations of spring, harvest and new moons. Most witches didn't add sex to their celebrations, but it wasn't a totally foreign concept.

Jane Doe had also been branded on her abdomen, at the base of her spine, the sole of her left foot, and the palm of her right hand. Four different markings on each spot. In Herb's opinion, the symbols had been carved into the skin with a sharp, hot knife, but he didn't know the significance nor had he ever seen those exact designs.

I started at the beginning of the file, flipping through the photos, not allowing my eyes to land on her face or the knife wound in her chest. Instead I focused on the symbols. They reminded me of bastardized runes but could be gibberish for all I knew.

I grabbed my phone and took pictures of each one. I looked at them from different angles, but still couldn't make sense of them.

I heard a knock on the door and jumped in surprise. Cade walked in and strode to the bed, stretching out beside me. "What do you think?"

"I want in on this case. I might come in handy, especially after reading what happened to Herb. If I'd been on hand, I might have been able to nullify the headache."

He sat up, propping himself against the headboard. "You don't need to do this, Holly. You have a thriving business. Getting in deeper with the Council—it's a bad move, baby. You know I'm right. Not to mention the dangers of searching for this psycho." He waved at the file. "What if something happened to you? Your Gran needs you. I need you." He grabbed my hand, entwining his fingers with mine. "Do you really need this evil shit inside your head?"

I knew beyond a doubt that when I closed my eyes I would see Jane Doe again, her slashed torso, her bloated, blueish face. But this wasn't just a diversion for me. In the big picture of life, goblin Will readings weren't important. Finding a killer, bringing him to justice—what could be more vital than that?

I sighed, and pulling my legs beneath me, turned toward him. "When we went hunting for the Black Magic Murderer—"

"Not you, too." He glanced up at the ceiling. "I hate that name."

"The point is, I used my lack of magic for good. People talked to me because I was a null. A completely unimportant person in the Other world. I can do that again. Besides, I liked working with you."

He peered down at me, one brow arched. "I thought you liked your job. Keeps you in handbags. That's what you're always telling me."

"It does. But I'd like to contribute more. And yes, these photos are terrifying. I'm not going to be able to get them out of my mind. But I want to help, and more importantly, I can take care of myself."

Cade unfolded his long frame from the bed and stood, thrusting his hands into his pockets. "Thing is, you got lucky on that last case, Holly. You stumbled your way through. You're not trained. You're a—"

"If you say liability, I'm going to kick your ass." He'd called me that once before. I rose to my knees on the mattress, facing him. "I didn't just luck out, Cade. I was instrumental in that case. You're welcome, by the way."

"Don't kid yourself, sweetheart. I would have broken that case without your help."

"I know that. Because you're a good investigator. But I did help. Look, I know you're worried I'm going to end up like Shayna." Cade's sister visited him when he was on a job, even though it was against protocol. Because they'd broken the rules, she'd been killed by a pyromancer, and Cade wore the guilt of her death like a mantle of shame and failure.

"Shut up. I mean it. Don't mention her again."

"I'm not Shayna."

"That's for damned sure."

I couldn't breathe for a minute. My eyes burned, but I refused to show that weakness in front of him. I blinked back tears that had gathered in the corners of my eyes, then lifted my chin in defiance. "Fuck you, Cade."

I grabbed the folder and climbed off the bed. I needed some space before I said something I couldn't take back. Before he said things I wouldn't be able to forgive.

I walked to the door, but Cade reached it before I did. He placed his hand across the doorjamb, barring my exit.

"I'm sorry. That came out wrong." His eyes were wary now, not angry. "Shayna was a sorcerer like me. But she wasn't powerful. When that asshole started the fire, it burned so hot and fast she died instantly. I'm not sure she could have cast a spell strong enough to save herself, but she never even had the chance.

"Still, Shayna had magic, even weak magic, in her arsenal. But you? You could be hurt by a million other things." He snatched me by the shoulders, pulling me close. "You're so fucking vulnerable. You could get killed crossing the street, and there's nothing I can do about it."

Cade squeezed a little too tight. The goblin's scratch flared to life, and I couldn't stifle a groan. "Cade, my shoulder."

He immediately moved his hands to gently cradle my face. "That's a perfect example, right there. You got hurt today. No healing spell is going to help you. It could get infected. Norms die from infections. Simple infections. Tell the Council to go to hell, Holly."

When his parents died, Cade was in his early twenties, his sister still a teenager. Then a few years later, Shayna died, too. All that loss molded Cade into the hard man he'd become. He normally didn't speak of his emotions or fears, but he was doing it now.

He held my face, his eyes imploring me to let this go. I placed one hand over his. "Someone killed this girl in a horrible way and dumped her body, like she was nothing but a piece of garbage. My mother might be out there Cade, lying in an unmarked grave. Just another nameless victim. I want to help."

He dropped his hands from me and sighed. "I get it. I don't like it, but I do understand. If you do this, we stick together. And I have rules."

"Of course you do." I peeked up at him. "Out of curiosity, did the Council have to vote on me or something?"

"Yeah. They weighed the pros and cons of asking for your help. It was a split decision."

"How did Wallace vote?" Wallace Dumahl, my paternal grandfather. I met him a few months ago for the first time. He introduced himself, then immediately asked me for a favor. It wasn't exactly a tender Hallmark moment.

"Wallace didn't attend the meeting. I'm sorry."

I forced a smile. "Don't be. He's hiding the fact that I'm his granddaughter. No surprise there."

I returned to the bed and opened the file, scattering the photos over the comforter. Cade made a quick trip to the kitchen, grabbing another beer for himself and a glass of wine for me. He settled next to me on the bed and adjusted the pillows behind him.

"Tell me what you're thinking," he said.

"After a couple of days, don't the fish usually start, you know, nibbling on a body?" I repressed a shiver at the thought. But as I glanced at the photos again, I didn't see any bite barks.

"We noticed that, too. Herb even made a reference to it in his findings."

"I haven't finished reading his report. Why wouldn't the fish touch the body?"

"I have no idea. One of the many weird things about this case."

I pointed to one of the photos, a detailed look at the slash made in Jane Doe's chest. "Why take the heart?"

"Rituals involving sacrifice, fealty, or allegiance, always mention the heart. But Aztecs and Mayans are the ones who ripped it out this way. As to why this killer is doing it, I'm not sure. And before you can ask, I don't know what the markings mean either. They look like runes, but none I've ever seen. Almost a cross between runes, Linear B script, with a little cuneiform tossed in for good measure."

I gave him a side-eye. "You just made half those words up, didn't you?"

"I studied ancient languages in college. I'm smarter than I look, Little Null."

Cade didn't often talk about his past. But since he opened this door, I planned on peeking inside. "A cop with a degree in ancient languages. Interesting."

"I didn't always want to be a cop."

"What did you want to be, then?"

"A professor."

I never saw that coming. Then I pictured Cade behind a lectern, wearing glasses and a wrinkled long-sleeved shirt rolled up to reveal those powerful forearms. He'd probably have on a pair of tight, faded jeans, too. The visual made me smile.

"I wanted to go on digs," he continued. "Study artifacts. That was my dream."

"Really?" I could see it: Cade in the desert, squinting against the sun. His hazel eyes somber as he poured over a broken piece of pottery. Still investigating, still intense about his rules, but absorbed in an ancient mystery rather than a current one.

He nudged his shoulder against mine. "What, you don't think I'd make a good prof?"

"I do, actually. I would have crushed on you so hard."

The corner of his mouth kicked up. "Yeah?"

"Totally. So, what made you change your career path?"

He glanced back down at the crime scene photos. "A lot of things." And just like that, the door slammed shut and I was back out in the cold. It was hard, but I refused to pry. Not today, anyway.

"All right, so what is this Grade B language stuff?"

"Linear B script. Oldest known Greek writing." He picked up a photo of the symbol burned into the girl's palm.

"Why burn them into the skin?"

"Don't know. In the past, branding was often used as a punishment or a sign of ownership."

I gathered all the photos and stacked them together, then glanced at Herb's autopsy notes. "Ownership. Sacrifice. Is someone doing this as an act of worship?"

He grabbed his beer from the nightstand. "I have no clue what's going on in this freak's mind. What god or goddess would he be appealing to? Seems like a mishmash of ideas, cobbling together a bunch of different rituals, different symbols."

I glanced through Herb's notes, skipping past the scientific stuff I didn't understand. Then I read what had been found inside the victim. "A rock was placed in her mouth before the rope. What kind of rock?"

"A stone you'd find anywhere near the lake. I don't know why. An offering upon entering the otherworld, maybe? Who the hell knows?"

"Well, this is just getting more and more bizarre."

"Keep reading. You're not done yet."

I didn't like the sound of that, but I kept perusing Herb's notes. Jane didn't have any distinguishing marks on her body. No strange moles or birthmarks. No tattoos. No track marks from shooting up. And her fingerprints weren't found in any database, which meant no arrest record.

But Herb did find a blackbird's feather stuffed in her chest cavity.

I glanced up at Cade. "A feather? Like the Egyptians?" I actually knew this one from my college class on ancient civilizations. The Egyptians removed the heart and weighed it against a feather in the afterlife. The feather represented innocence. "Why stuff it in her chest, though?"

"Another good question. Or maybe this is all part of an elaborate fantasy dreamed up by some nut job."

I was beginning to agree. Perhaps the killer used all sorts of references to create his own death ritual. It obviously meant something to the killer, but what?

Cade leaned his head back against the headboard. "Weren't you going to tell me something earlier? Something about a lead?"

I slapped my hand over my forehead. "Oh my God, yes. Sorry, I kept getting sidetracked." I closed the file and grabbed my glass of wine. "A girl I knew from college called the office, wanted to hire me. Something is going on with her entire coven. She's a water witch. Lives on Lake Eufaula. The coven owns a place called Moonlight Cove."

Cade whipped his phone from the pocket of his jeans, his thumbs flying over the screen. After a moment, he showed me a map. He pointed to where the dead body had been found. "We think she floated southward from here. And Moonlight Cove is here. No more than ten or fifteen miles apart."

I took the phone and glanced at it. "Have you heard of this place?" I scrolled through the ads and found the official website. "It's not just a coven, it's a planned community. They have an online business and take in summer residents." I handed Cade his phone.

"I've heard of them. They have a resort type of thing going there. I'm kind of surprised you didn't know that."

If it involved Reece Tolliver, I couldn't have cared less. "I've never dealt with this coven."

"From what I understand, they're quite profitable. What, exactly, is happening out there? More fucked up magic?"

"Sunny was short on details, as usual, but she said something about nullifying the entire coven. So, maybe?"

He rose to his feet and started tapping on his phone. "Details, Holly. Call this woman you knew in college and get details. I'm texting my people to see if they know anything."

The thought of calling Reece made my stomach clench tight, and I immediately felt ashamed of my reaction. I'd just spent an hour looking at these horrifying death scene photos. If I wasn't going to be intimidated by the Council, I sure as hell wasn't going to let the past keep me from doing what I needed to do. Reece was nothing but another resource, and possibly a link to Jane Doe.

"I'll get her number."

Cade's phone rang and he began issuing orders to some poor soul. I left him to it and retreated to the living room. I called Sunny, and she wasn't happy to hear from me. Quelle surprise.

"What do you want?" she sniped.

"What did Reece Tolliver tell you about her situation? Give me specifics."

"Does this mean you're going to take the case?" Her tone was only slightly less hostile.

"That's what it means."

"Hang on," she said, "let me check my notes."

"Are you still at the office?"

"I told you I've been working long hours, too."

I felt properly chastised. Sunny more than pulled her weight in the business. She always had.

"Okay," she said, "Reece called at seven this morning, said something was, and I'm quoting here, "corrupting her coven's magic." She needed you to nullify them ASAP. I wasn't about to cancel today's clients, so I told her you'd be there tomorrow."

Shit. If Reece's coven was experiencing what Cade went through when he tried to cast a simple spell on that umbrella, they must be putting out fires left and right. Both literally and figuratively.

"Give me her number?"

I added it to my phone as Sunny rattled it off. "Thanks."

"Wait. What changed your mind?"

"Cade and I are trying to solve a murder. The body was found close to the coven."

"You're helping in another investigation? Not for free, you're not," she said.

"This one is sanctioned by the Council."

"Then I'm going to send them an invoice."

"I want you to do more than that. Have Bertram draw up a contract. I don't want to be on the line for more than one job. No loopholes."

"For once, I agree with you. Each investigation should have its own contract, limited in scope, defining your role in detail. And I'm charging them a great big fat fee because I'm going to have to clear your schedule." I heard her tapping on the keyboard. "But think long and hard about getting in bed with the Council, Holly. We've always been careful to keep out of their crosshairs. Seems like you should at least give it some serious thought before jumping in with both feet. If things go wrong, they may even blame you. That could destroy our business altogether."

I hadn't even thought of that angle. "I won't allow myself to be some poster girl for their mistakes. Besides, Cade and I make a good team. Everything will be fine."

"Famous last words."

"Try to stay flexible with my schedule. I don't know how long this will take. Could be days, or it could be weeks. I might find some time to squeeze in my regulars."

"Got it."

After I hung up, I stared at Reece's number for a moment. Taking a deep breath, I dialed. She answered on the second ring, sounding every bit as arrogant and snotty as she always had.

"Who is this?"

"Holly James." I was trying for cold and professional. Instead, I sounded hollow, unlike myself. "I hear you're having trouble with your coven?"

"It's about time you got back to me. What took you so long?"

Good thing I wasn't expecting an apology for all those years of harassment, otherwise, I'd have been sorely disappointed. "What seems to be the trouble, Reece?"

"Didn't your assistant fill you in? It's FUBAR around here. Something's happened to our magic."

"Sunny is actually my partner."

"I actually don't care, James. I have bigger things to deal with right now."

"Can you give me details, please?"

She blew out a breath, sounding frustrated. "I don't know how to make it any plainer. Our magic is fucked up. We can't cast spells without them spinning out of control and taking on a life of their own. When we try and fix them, it makes the situation worse. I have three dead witches on my hands and others are suffering. We need help now, not tomorrow morning. Now!" Her voice rose the longer she talked.

"Three dead? What happened?" My issues with Reece and the past became just that—in the past. The coven was evidently another contaminated magic zone, and this time there were casualties. That was a hell of a lot bigger than my college drama.

CHAPTER NINE

"Were you always this stupid, James? Their spells backfired and killed them. Do. You. Understand?" She spoke slowly, like I was an idiot.

"I thought you might fill me in on the type of spell." You foul bitch. Okay, so maybe my anger wasn't entirely in the past.

"How the hell would I know? It's been crazy here. Everyone's in a panic."

If this strange activity was tied to Jane Doe's murder, it might give us a time of death.

Cade walked silently into the room. With his arms crossed, he listened to my side of the conversation.

"When did all this start?"

Reece didn't respond right away. Then she said, "Late Saturday night, early Sunday morning? I'm not exactly sure."

"If things were so bad, if three of your members died, why didn't you call immediately?"

"My coven leader isn't convinced you can help. Furthermore, she doesn't want you out here nullifying our entire town if this is a temporary situation."

"And what makes you think this is temporary? Has anything like this happened before?"

"Look, I'll answer all your questions later. Just get your ass out here and help my people."

I glanced at Cade, whose expression was implacable. He gave me no indication of what he might be thinking.

"Yeah, I'll be there soon." When I ended the call, I asked, "Did you hear any of that?"

"Caught some of it. Three dead bodies?"

"And more who are hurt. Started late Saturday night or early Sunday morning. The coven leader thought it would stop on its own. If the murder is tied to the magical infection, maybe that's when Jane Doe was killed."

"We can't assume anything at this point. The two might be isolated events."

I didn't buy that theory for a second. A bizarre ritualistic murder happened only miles from where a coven's magic went haywire? It had to be related.

He rubbed a hand over his head. "We're going to have to take the coven into quarantine and get this shit straightened out."

"Do you think one of them might know something about the murder?"

"We'll find out." He walked to the front door and slipped into his coat. "You might want to get dressed in something warmer. It's going to be a long night."

Turned out, I didn't need anything warm. As we drove out of Oklahoma, the rain stopped and the temperature rose several degrees.

As we headed toward Arkansas, the two-lane highway took us through teeny tiny towns, where slower speed zones made me twitch in frustration and all-night gas stations were few and far between. God, I hated rural routes, but it was still the fastest way to get to the Other prison. Or the holding cell, as Cade called it.

When we finally arrived, I'd been expecting a jailhouse, a secure building in the middle of nowhere. Instead, Cade drove through the outskirts of Little Rock until he pulled up to an underground cave beneath the Ozark Mountains. There was a bunker buried under the earth, magically enhanced but with state of the art Norm technology, as well. The Council must believe in covering all their bases.

He drove toward the cave, to a gated opening. Security lights flooded the night as Cade stopped at a check-in point. He flashed his badge at a guy dressed in black fatigues, who also happened to have an AK-47 strapped to his back.

"That's an unusual weapon for an Other to have," I whispered. Cade remained silent.

The guard peeked through the window, glancing at me, then at Cade's ID. "We've been expecting you, sir. Drive on through." His hard gaze drilled into me before handing Cade his badge.

"Are you sure it's okay that I'm here?" This was the second time I'd asked that question. The first time, he'd ignored me.

"Holly, it's fine."

"But it feels weird, like I'm invading Other Headquarters or something. I must be nullifying wards and sigils that keep the riffraff out and the monsters inside. In case you're wondering, I'm the riffraff."

Cade glared from the corner of his eye as he drove forward, past massive metal doors and into the underground labyrinth. The tunnels branched off in every direction, spreading out as far as I could see. "This place is guarded with magic and mundane security. And it's so goddamned huge, you won't be nullifying even a fraction of it. Besides, this area is classified, meaning wards and sigils are reset every day."

I squirmed in my seat, staring at the squat columns which, along with the ceiling, had been plastered white. The floors were gray concrete. Lights bounced off small puddles of water that collected near the walls. "Exactly how huge?"

"Miles."

Signs pointed the way. Sections A, B, and C split off to the left, where Cade made a smooth turn. There were no other vehicles that I could see. It was as if we were alone in this underground cave, with its mushroom pillars and heavy, humid air. If I got lost down here, I wasn't sure I could ever find my way back out.

At a dead end, Cade hopped out of the truck and walked to a random control panel, plugging in a code. An invisible door, one that masked itself as a cave wall, slid open. We drove down yet another deserted tunnel. After a few minutes, he stopped in front of a metal door labeled Section A-23.

"This is it. They'll be here soon. I think we beat them by at least an hour."

"I imagine it takes a while to ride herd on an entire coven?" I knew it was a prudent step, but it seemed a little tyrannical to me. There were historical precedents for rounding up average citizens and separating them from the rest of society—none of them good.

He cut the engine. "This isn't something we do lightly. Holding a group of Others, suspending their magic, is serious business. As soon as we clear up this magical infection or whatever it is, we'll let them go home."

"Right."

I climbed out of the truck and shrugged out of my sweater. I wore a gray long-sleeved T-shirt underneath. The cavern was as muggy as a steam bath and carried a dank, musty smell along with a hint of exhaust fumes.

We walked toward a metal door, which Cade opened with yet another code. Inside, he flipped on a bank of switches. Light flooded a space larger than a football field. There were bunk beds. Hundreds and hundreds of them. A flat pillow and a thin, green blanket topped each one. Two narrow lockers were crammed between the beds. Home sweet home.

"How many people are you expecting?"

"Around two-hundred. Come through here." Cade strode to the right and entered a maze of offices, all with glass walls to grant a view of the holding cell beyond.

"What will you feed them?"

"They'll be given packaged meals—MREs—like the military uses. Hopefully, they won't be here for more than a couple of days. There are board games, decks of cards, and toiletries in the lockers. They'll make do."

I trailed after him through the office to a small kitchenette. He started a pot of coffee, shrugged out of his jacket, and placed his messenger bag on the small round table.

"You say this type of thing doesn't happen often, but you seem familiar with the setup, McAllister."

"Been through it once or twice. Not with a large number of people, but with my prisoners. In smaller holding cells, naturally. But the layout is the same." He grabbed a couple of mugs from the cabinet, filled them with coffee and doctored mine with powdered creamer and sugar automatically.

"Thanks." I took a sip, my mind still turning over the murder and what I'd read in Herb's report. "Herb said he's going to test the DNA found inside our Jane Doe. Can he tell if he's dealing with a Norm or an Other?"

"Unfortunately, no." He leaned back against the counter. The stubble on his cheeks and chin seemed thicker now, darker. His eyes were bloodshot, his shirt wrinkled from being worn all day, then wadded up on my bathroom floor during our shower encounter. I wondered how often he worked under these conditions.

"When was the last time you slept?"

"A couple of nights ago." He quirked one brow. "I'm fine. Don't fuss or the other sorcerers will make fun of me."

#

Cade underestimated the water witches' arrival. Almost two hours later, they stumbled in—grumbling, confused, and in some cases, royally pissed. Cade and I stood by the door, gazing at them as they straggled in single file.

Five guards armed with rifles fanned the room, taking posts at various perimeters. It seemed like overkill to me. Besides, the witches couldn't use their magic to break out of here. The coven's power was gone, not just because I was in the room. It had been mystically bound once they cleared Moonlight Cove. Their magic would be hobbled until we found out what was corrupting their spells.

They didn't look like troublemakers, either. The people who trailed in were families with children and grandparents. They congregated around the vast room in small groups.

A few people were wheeled in on stretchers by gun-toting paramedics. One of the gurneys held a little girl, no more than eight. Her mother, a petite woman, looked as though she'd been through the wringer. Her face appeared almost gray and pinched with worry.

She stood by the stretcher, smoothing the little girl's blonde hair back from her face. As far as I could tell, the child was unconscious. I wondered what had happened to her. To all of them. What kind of devastation had the backfired spells caused? I'd seen what happened in the model homes. Multiply that by two hundred and you'd have Moonlight Cove.

Cade and I planned to inspect the place tomorrow. I'd clear out any spells that might still be in play, even though I wouldn't be able to nullify the contaminated zone. We also wanted to look for clues as to why this happened in the first place. And if we could link the coven to Jane Doe, all the better.

One older woman strode in by herself. She was obviously the leader. I could tell by the way she carried herself—chin high, back ramrod straight. Her short hair was pure white and brushed away from her face. She may not have been beautiful, but she was striking. Cold blue eyes surveyed her new surroundings, but her face remained impassive. As she walked toward the center of the group, everyone stood back a pace, giving her space, their attention fixed on her.

Reece stepped into the room last. She hadn't changed a bit, but then what did I expect—she was an Other. She might be twenty-five or two hundred for all I knew. Her strawberry blonde waves were a little shorter than they used to be, but her skin was still pale, flawless.

She wore comfortable clothes, but those ripped, frayed jeans came with a designer label, and her black suede boots carried a red Louboutin sole. Casual yet expensive. She'd always had good taste.

Glancing around the room with her brow furrowed, she finally spotted me. Her green eyes narrowed as she marched to where I stood. She stopped two feet away, her gaze flickering over me from head to toe. By the sour purse of her downturned lips, she still found me lacking.

Cade tensed beside me. I could feel it radiating off him in waves. He was already on high alert, but Reece's obvious animosity had him on point, ready to defend me if need be.

"You double-crossed me, James."

"Reece. You look good. Well, better than the last time I saw you." Graduation day. Her pert nose had been broken, blood streaming down her pointed chin. My knuckles were bruised for a week, but it had so been worth it.

She bared her teeth at me. "My entire coven is suffering, but you wanted payback instead. You small-minded bitch."

"Go back with the rest of your people." Cade hadn't moved. He hadn't even raised his voice. But his tone was coldly vicious.

I placed my hand on his arm. "I got this. Can we take the office for a minute?"

His gaze slid from Reece to me. His chest heaved as he took a deep breath. Then he dipped his chin in assent.

Reece eyed him with distaste and followed me into the office. The door barely shut before she began lambasting me. I simply stood there and let her vent.

"I should have known you'd pull something like this. You called the Council on us." Her green eyes reminded me of brittle blades of grass after a hard freeze. "According to your reputation, you take any job that comes your way. You'd even whore yourself out for a kid's birthday party. But because of our history, you couldn't keep your mouth shut, could you?"

I still said nothing.

She paced back and forth, hips swaying in her skin-tight jeans. Then she stopped, facing me in the small hallway. "What, did you want an apology?" She spit out the word, like it was a vile tasting pill she couldn't quite choke down. "Boo hoo. I was mean to the null," she mocked. "Get over yourself, James." She flung an arm toward the window where water witches gathered in a tight group, watching us. "This thing with my coven is bigger than your hurt feelings."

Growing up, Gran had taken great pains to find a town that was free of Others. Until I hit the college campus, I'd never encountered one—Gran being the exception, of course.

I didn't recognize them—everyone was a Norm to me. But they knew what I was immediately. I stripped them of their powers, their spells, their glamours. And in return, they went on a hate campaign, spearheaded by Reece.

Because of all the stress, I barely passed my classes that first year. When I came home for the summer, Gran and I had a long talk. She wanted me to transfer to a smaller college, but I refused. It was the first time we had a serious argument, and though we lived in the same house, we didn't talk to each other for weeks. It was awful.

During that break, I took self-defense classes and practiced the techniques every day. I returned to school determined to take my life back. The harassment didn't stop, but I got tougher, fought dirty. I learned to protect myself.

Now as I watched Reece, those old feelings of dread and anxiety that I'd always associated with her weren't there. I'd been so worried about meeting her again, yet I didn't feel the slightest bit intimidated. Maybe because she didn't have a band of bitches backing her up. Maybe because I was viewing her through the eyes of an adult. Or maybe I'd grown numb to the slights and insults over the years. Others may hire me, but they still didn't like me, and they made that plain on almost every job I took.

Reece was just another witch who resented my null status.

"Let's clear this up. And listen closely, because I'm only going to say it once. I didn't call the Council. But what happened at your coven might be part of something bigger, more widespread. You're here until we can find out what's making your spells backfire, and then you can go home."

Her pale brows rose, and she barked out a laugh. "You're an idiot. You don't actually believe that, do you? The Council is going to try and take our lands, our business. We'll be lucky to get out of here alive. Why do you think our leader, Adeline, was hesitant to call you in the first place? She was trying to keep this quiet."

Cade believed the coven would be free to go home once we'd cleared this up, and I had no reason not to trust his judgment. He'd worked with the Council for years. He knew what they were capable of, and he didn't sugarcoat the truth. That wasn't his style.

"Believe what you want, Reece."

I glanced through the window, where Cade stood keeping an eye on me. I waved him in.

He strode through the door and his presence immediately sucked the oxygen from the room. He was in a pissy mood.

"We need to interview your coven. We'll start with you." He barely glanced at her as he moved past both Reece and me, heading down one of the hallways to a room that held a table and four chairs.

I pivoted and followed Cade, sitting next to him on one side of the table. It took almost a full minute for Reece to join us.

Jane Doe's file sat on the table in front of him. He plucked out a photo, a close up of her bloated face, after Herb had removed the rope and rock from her mouth. "Ever seen this woman?"

Reece barely glanced at it. "No. What's this about? I thought you were going to sort out our coven's magic problem. What does that have to do with a dead woman?"

"That's what we'd like to know," I said. "Look at the photo this time before you answer."

Reece's green gaze flitted between Cade and me. "What is this, a tag team event? You're working with an Investigator?" Her lip curled in disgust. "And you're together, aren't you? I can tell by the way you look at him."

She leaned forward, arms on the table, and nailed Cade with a condescending glare. "Why would you even touch her? You've got to be powerful to work for the Council, and yet you're letting her emasculate you. Magically speaking."

Cade tapped the photo. "The woman. Look at her."

With a sigh, Reece studied the picture. "No. I've never seen her."

Cade took the picture back, tucked it into the folder. "Tell us what happened at Moonlight Cove. Everything. From the beginning."

Apparently, shit hit the fan in the wee hours of Sunday morning. "Something happened within the coven. I don't know why, but every spell, incantation, and ward went wrong. Very wrong. Everything is, I don't know, rebounding." Exactly what had happened to Cade.

"By around four a.m. Sunday morning, Adeline called a meeting and forbade us to use any magic until we could figure out what happened. But she didn't know how to fix it." Reece stared at her clasped hands, her brows pulled together. "We couldn't keep the young ones from casting, and it made everything worse. Then we started taking inventory of all our members. David Bowman drowned—in his shower. We think he cast a spell to heat the water. Arlo and Susan Landry are both dead. We don't know what spell they'd cast, but they hacked each other to death with kitchen knives. They were happily married for eighty-six years. Two of our houses have burned to the ground when the owners tried to light candles." She rubbed at her thumbnail.

If this hadn't been affecting other areas, like Jane Doe's dead body, I would have suspected a hex. But to curse an entire coven would take a shitload of magic.

"Does the coven have enemies?" Cade asked.

"We have no beef with any other covens." She continued to gaze at her hands, and her careful wording told me she wasn't being completely honest. What a shock.

"What does your coven leader think is the cause?" I asked.

"She doesn't have any theories either."

After a few more questions and zero answers, Cade dismissed Reece. He waited until she cleared the door before speaking. "What's the history with the two of you?"

"Bad blood from college."

"You should have told me."

I leaned back in the metal chair. "Would you have cut me out of the questioning?"

He didn't answer. "Don't keep anything else from me, Holly." He turned toward me, and I saw the anger in his eyes. "I don't like being at a disadvantage."

"There's nothing else you need to know."

Next, Adeline Stevens walked in. Though her clothes were simple, she wore them well. Her pale blue sweater was made of virgin wool and designed with an asymmetrical neckline. I recognized her black, chunk-heeled Chloe boots because I'd spied them at Saks a few months ago. Understated, yet tasteful.

With her head held high and her aquiline nose in the air, she gracefully slid into the chair. She looked me over, and I could see where Reece got her sense of superiority. This woman had it, too. As though she were a queen, lowering herself to interact with the peons. But as she cocked her head at an angle, I recognized more than just the same mannerisms that Reece possessed. There was something in the tilt of her blue eyes and the angle of her jawline.

"How are you related to Reece?" I asked.

"She's my niece." Adeline's voice was surprisingly scratchy and low. I expected something more regal, not an Oklahoma twang. "What does that have to do with this interview?"

Cade leaned back in his chair. "You're here to answer our questions, ma'am." He looked at me, then dipped his chin toward the folder.

I pulled out the photo of our murder victim. "Have you ever seen this woman before?"

She glanced at it for a few seconds. "I don't know. Is she a Norm?"

"She is," Cade said. "Maybe she rented a summer cottage?"

"Who knows? They all look and sound the same to me. Oh, how they squeal, and chatter, and cause a ruckus every summer. I'm just glad when Labor Day is over and we can all get back to our lives."

"That's very unhospitable of you," I said. "Why have Norms come to Moonlight Cove if you can't stand them?"

"Didn't Reece tell you?" Adeline pulled her lips into a sour twist. "It was her brilliant idea."

CHAPTER TEN

Cade played it cool, crossing his arms over his chest. "I want to hear your version."

"I was against it from the start," Adeline said. "Taking on Norms for the summer seemed a disastrous idea, but Reece had a plan. She talked enough of the coven into going along with it, and it's paid off. I can't fault her for that. Nevertheless, it's degrading."

That high and mighty Other attitude rubbed me the wrong way. "You're their leader. You could have nixed the plan?"

"Like I said, there was merit to the idea. I may hate it, but I'm old. Reece has modernized our coven, started a profitable online store, etcetera." She gestured with one slender hand. "I may not like it, but that doesn't mean it hasn't been good for my witches."

"It's fairly unusual that a coven owns an entire town," Cade said. "What else are y'all doing out there besides renting cabins to Norms?"

She became almost immobile, except for her eyes. She blinked three times in rapid succession. "I don't know what you mean."

"I mean, Ms. Stevens," Cade said with a snarl, "you have a school, several businesses, and your own damned police department. That costs a hell of a lot of money." He uncrossed his arms and braced them on the table. "I don't think you got there from an online business and a few summer rentals."

I could have sworn she stopped breathing, but then she elegantly shrugged. "I'm telling you, that's what happened. Our online store sells all sorts of organic ingredients. We've established a nice little enterprise for ourselves."

"No ma'am," Cade countered, "you're running more than a cottage industry. You've got a multimillion dollar business. All from selling organic herbs? I don't think so."

I hadn't realized the coven was that wealthy. I hadn't really thought about it, but Cade was right—it would take a lot of money, a lot of tax dollars to have their own town and all those facilities.

Cade stared Adeline in the eye. "I want a list of all your clients, both online and those who've stayed at Moonlight Cove." Being on the other end of his stare, I knew how intimidating it could be. But now Adeline appeared unruffled.

"That's not my department, I'm afraid. You'll have to ask Reece for that information."

"What do you think is going on with the magic at Moonlight Cove?" I asked. We'd gotten way off topic. I wanted to find a link between Jane Doe's death and the coven's magical contamination.

"I have no idea. I consulted my books, but I couldn't find anything similar happening before." Adeline turned to Cade. "When can we go back home?"

"When we figure out why your magic is backfiring."

She fixed her cold blue gaze on me. "I thought that was why we paid you twenty-five thousand dollars, to nullify the town. Practically extortion, if you ask me."

I gave her a bright smile. "But I didn't ask you. And no, I can't nullify whatever is infecting your magic. I can only nullify the spells that have gone wrong. I did that when you walked into the holding cell. You're welcome, by the way."

Her face fell, and she appeared a dozen years older. "You mean you can't fix our magic?"

"No."

I didn't like this woman any more than I liked her niece. That didn't mean I wanted their coven to suffer. If I could remove whatever was infecting their magic, I would.

"When did you first notice something was wrong?" Cade asked.

"I got a call early Sunday morning, around two, I think. Several of the coven members were having problems. When they tried to perform a spell to correct what had gone wrong, it only made things more complicated."

Exactly what Reece had said. And the same thing happened to Cade, and even to Herb Novak when he tried to use his post-cog powers on Jane Doe.

Cade dismissed the old woman. She appeared a little less regal than when she'd walked in. Our answers had shaken her.

"They don't know what's going on either." I stood and stretched my legs.

"No, but I'm not buying that online store bullshit for a second."

"What do you think they're really doing?" I reached my arms up over my head. According to Cade's watch, it was after three a.m. It had been a long day for me, but much longer for him.

"Don't know—yet." He stood and grabbed the folder. "Let's go get some sleep."

"What about the rest of the interviews?"

"I have a feeling they're all going to say the same thing. They don't know what happened, the spells backfired. I'll have some other inspectors come in and interview them. We can look through the transcripts later. Right now, I need some rest."

"Are we staying here, in the bunker?"

"Holding cell, and no. We'll stop at a hotel, get a few hours of shuteye." He held open the door, jerking his head for me to precede him.

When we stepped out of the offices and into the holding cell, quiet descended on the group. The coven turned to stare at us.

Cade stepped away from me and addressed them. "Everyone try to get some rest. Interviews will continue tomorrow. If anyone has information that will help clear up this situation, let us know now."

A few voices piped up, but not with helpful answers.

"When are you going to let us leave?" one woman yelled.

"You have no right to keep us here!" That came from a tall man in the back, his voice echoing through the cavern.

Then they all began speaking at once, shouting their complaints. Cade just rolled his eyes and placed his hand on my back, ushering me to the door.

A small woman trotted up to us. She was the woman I'd seen earlier, the one accompanying the little girl on the stretcher.

"Excuse me." We turned in her direction, but she had me in her sights, not Cade. "I wanted to thank you. You saved my daughter's life."

I plucked at the neck of my T-shirt. "I didn't do anything. Really."

"Yes, you did. I'm grateful." She cast a glance over her shoulder. "I'm Maddie. There are certain things—"

"Maddie," Reece called from across the room. "Annabelle needs you."

Maddie's eyes grew wide, wary. Without another word, she turned and hustled back to the group. Reece stood tall in the center of everyone, her gaze piercing right through me.

Apparently, Reece could still inspire fear—even for those within her own coven.

#

Cade and I stopped by an all-night pharmacy and grabbed essentials: water, toothpaste, toothbrushes, deodorant, and a couple of clean, cheap T-shirts. I also grabbed a travel size bottle of face wash and moisturizer. Then we headed to a hotel to get a few hours of sleep.

When we reached our room on the third floor of a Holiday Inn near the highway, Cade dumped the plastic bags of toiletries on the dresser.

"Are you going to tell me about Reece?" he asked.

I dug out the face wash and took it to the bathroom. "Nothing to tell. She was a bitch then, and she's a bitch now. What do you make of Maddie? She might know something."

His boots made a thud on the floor in the main room. "I don't know. She just seemed grateful and a little on edge. I would be, too, if they wheeled my unconscious kid in on a stretcher. What I really want to do is get my hands on their client list, find out what the hell they've been doing with Norms out there."

After a quick wash, I slapped a little lotion on my face. When I came out of the bathroom, Cade was already undressed and tucked into bed. The white sheet covered his man bits, but his chest was bare. He raised his arms above his head and stared at the ceiling.

What a sight. He had no idea how good he looked, all rough and manly, his abs on display. The dragon's bright colors rode his chest, and even though I was tired, I could be persuaded to stay up a little longer.

"I'm so fucking exhausted," he said, his eyes meeting mine. Then he lowered his arms and held out one hand. "Come here."

Cuddling would be okay, too.

I stripped down to my panties and crawled in next to him. The sheets were rough on my skin, but Cade was warm, his body smooth and perfect as he wrapped his arms around me. He shut off the light and I must have fallen asleep immediately.

The next thing I knew, Cade was dressed, sitting on the side of the bed with a cup of coffee in his hands. "Wake up, Hols. We're going to meet Herb this morning at Moonlight Cove."

I sat up, rubbed my eyes, and took the coffee from him. As I sipped it, I watched him cross the room to the desk. His laptop screen held his complete attention.

"What are you looking at?"

"Just going over the coven's site. They sell all sorts of natural homemade remedies along with herbs and tinctures. They claim to help cure everything from digestive issues to a lagging libido. They're big with the essential oils. This shit is expensive, too. Not enough to purchase a town on the lake, but enough that they'd all be very comfortable."

"Yeah, they're hiding something. Reece has always been shady."

He turned in his chair. "Still holding out on me?"

I finished my coffee and shrugged. "Why did you become a cop instead of an archaeologist? You never gave me a reason."

He turned back to his computer without saying a word. And the point goes to me, sir.

I threw aside the covers and headed for the shower. Once I'd used all that was left of the tiny bottle of shampoo, I climbed out, wrapping my hair in one towel, my body in another.

Cade was on the phone when I slipped into the room to get my clothes, but he clocked me. His eyes heated as he took me in, his gaze lingering on my barely covered breasts. I was certain we didn't have time for that this morning, so I turned my back and shimmied into my clothes from yesterday. Over my long-sleeved gray shirt, I pulled on the new oversized red T-shirt that reminded me of the one I'd worn in high school gym class. Definitely function over fashion. Le sigh.

As Cade continued his conversation, I retreated to the bathroom and brushed my dark wet hair into a ponytail, then added a little makeup from the bag in my purse. I stood back and viewed myself in the mirror. Not stellar, but it would have to do.

When I walked back into the room, Cade was ready to go. "Wish we had time to linger." His voice took on that deep timbre, the one that made my nipples hard.

"Me, too. I guess I'll have to settle for breakfast."

We stopped at a Waffle House. Cade ate enough for three men. Then we headed back to Oklahoma.

During the trip to Lake Eufaula from Little Rock, I spent the time talking to Sunny. Bertram had sent over a contract. I signed electronically and texted it back. Once that was done, I looked online for the symbols that had been carved into Jane Doe's skin, but came up empty.

Next, I looked up the Wyler's arch nemesis, Liam Snyder. He, too, was a land developer, buying and selling off parcels of farmland for residential homes. "Hey, can you have someone look into Liam Snyder? The Wyler family think he's connected with the mob. Which means he's probably rich enough to hire a witch for a little revenge vandalism."

"And you think because the area has contaminated magic, the vandalism went haywire?"

"It's a possibility I'd like to eliminate."

"I'll check into it," he promised, picking up my hand and stroking my palm with this thumb.

After we stopped for lunch at a sandwich shop and filled the truck with gas, I twisted in my seat to face Cade. "You're looking into all the missing persons in the area?"

"Of course. So far, no Jane Doe."

"And what about the symbols?"

"I sent photos to one of our language experts. She didn't recognize it either, but she's doing some research."

"What can I do?"

"Go through the file again, see if you can find anything new. Start using that imaginative brain of yours to put together theories."

"Theories you'll shoot down?" I teased.

"You have your strengths, and I have mine." He nearly smiled. I could tell because his scowl lessened ever so slightly.

I spent the rest of the ride digging through the file once more, looking for anything I'd missed. Unfortunately, nothing jumped out.

Once we grew closer to Tulsa, the weather turned crappy and cold again. I grabbed the sweater I'd ripped off the night before and tugged it on. Cade turned up the heater when I started to shiver.

We drove south past Tulsa for another hour and forty-five minutes. A bridge over the Canadian River separated Moonlight Cove from the farming community of Eufaula. Once Cade turned off the main road, we hit a winding bumpy track that cut through an apple orchard. But it didn't look like any orchard I'd ever seen. Everything about it was...wrong.

Cade must have noticed at the same time I did, because he slammed the brakes so hard that if I hadn't been wearing my seatbelt, my head would have bumped into the windshield.

"Sorry, Hols." He patted my thigh, but his attention focused on the orchard.

The tree trunks had been stripped of their bark. Peeled as cleanly as a banana, left naked and unprotected. Acres of stripped trees, free of foliage and fruit. The branches were another matter. They were dark, the bark still in place, but strangely twisted. They reminded me of arthritic fingers, misshapen and deformed as they stretched out and overlapped with other branches, forming a canopy. All of them linked together, as though they were holding hands. I'd never seen anything like it.

"What is that?" I asked.

"Stay here." Cade left the engine running as he exited the truck. He hopped the wooden fence and entered the orchard. He had to duck his head in places, because the branches were too low. After a minute, he disappeared.

A Bob Seger tune played softly on the radio, but I found it annoying. I switched it off and rolled down my window. "Cade!"

He didn't answer.

The sight of the trees linked by gnarled branches and the haunting clouds in the sky made me shiver. I bounced my knee up and down. I'd give him five minutes, then I was going after him.

He only had fifty seconds left when he finally emerged from the orchard. He ducked and weaved as he made a path through the bare trees.

When he climbed back in the truck, I noticed a line of blood on his forehead. I reached into the console and grabbed a tissue. When I pressed it to his head, he blinked and finally looked at me.

"That was fucking weird."

"What?"

"The branches. It was like they bent toward me as I walked. Goddamned oddest thing I've ever seen. That didn't happen up here by the fence line. You must be nullifying it, but as I walked through the orchard, the trees—it felt like they were watching me."

CHAPTER ELEVEN

I dropped my hand from his head and glanced through the open passenger window. "Want me to walk through there, nullify the entire thing?"

"No, I just want to know what the hell is going on here." He slammed the truck into gear, and I rolled up my window, shutting out the cold.

Though he drove slowly over hills, dips, and sharp turns, I could sense the tension in him. The normally unflappable Cade was a little shaken.

"What about the black and gray chaos pattern? Did you see it again?"

"Oh, yeah. Everywhere. It twisted through the trees and around the branches themselves. Like a wild tangle of electrical cord."

"The model homes. A murder victim. And now a coven. Does any of that make sense to you, any links at all?"

"Not yet."

The road finally straightened and the woods gave way to fields. Acres of a carefully harvested corn maze stood on the left side of the wide road, a pumpkin patch sat on the right. Would have been a good harvest, too, if the magical infection hadn't hit.

The pumpkins weren't merely rotten. It appeared as if they'd exploded like bombs, leaving the field a mass of pale orange guts and seeds. The corn maze looked as if it'd been felled by a steamroller, every single stalk flattened, bending away from the road.

"The crops must have been enhanced with spells."

Cade said nothing but continued driving as I gawked from one side of the road to the other.

"Hey, stop."

"What's wrong?" He eased to a halt.

I unlatched my belt and hopped out, wading through the flat corn. It crunched beneath my boots and I kicked at a stalk. The ears were black and rotten. Made my stomach clench a bit.

Cade followed. "Holly. Wait up."

There was a smell in the air. Like dead fish. I held my hand over my mouth and nose. "What is that?"

He lifted his head in the air. "Maybe whatever is killing off their crops killed the fish in the lake. Smells like it, anyway."

I nearly gagged. "That's awful."

"What are we doing out here?" With his hands shoved in his coat pockets, he glanced down at the ruined corn.

"Where are the birds? These fields should be thick with crows." I pointed over my shoulder. "Look at all that pumpkin meat, just sitting there. Easy pickings." But the air was heavy and still, no squawks above or rustles under the corn. "Where are the squirrels and mice? Even the animals don't want this stuff."

"I didn't notice. Should have."

"The same way the fish didn't feed on Jane Doe's body." I looked back at the destroyed fields, trying to figure out what else was bothering me.

All this produce. Then it hit me. "Water witches aren't usually known for their farming skills. So, what's with all the crops?" Water witches skewed toward fertility, and the moon played a huge role in their magic—the pull of the tides and all. They were strongest near a water source. All these crops seemed out of character, but then again, I wasn't an expert.

"Maybe they figure since they own the land they might as well put it to use," Cade said. "It's a good question, though. You ready?"

I took one last glance at the pumpkins. There was a feeling in the air, a sense of wrongness. That was the only way I could describe it.

With a shiver, I climbed back into the truck. We drove past the fields for another couple of miles before we encountered an enormous wrought iron gate. It'd been left open, so Cade drove right through.

The buildings were blocked from view by tall, thick holly bushes on either side of the road. But when Cade turned a curve, the community came into view. The pictures online didn't do Moonlight Cove justice. Pure small-town Americana. They'd recreated it perfectly.

Early twentieth-century bungalows and two-story gabled farm houses, all newer construction, remained faithful to the original concept—at least from the outside. White picket fences framed each yard, and cobblestone walkways separated one row of houses from another.

"It's like a movie set," I said.

"Maybe the nostalgic touch appeals to the Norms?"

A corn dolly hung on every front door. Don't let the name fool you. They weren't actually dolls at all. By taking the last of the harvested corn stalks and braiding them into a noose, our fore farmers hoped the dolly would bring a good crop the next year. They'd burn it on Halloween—Samhain, for those magically inclined—and say a little prayer of thanks. Out of tradition, Gran still made them every fall. She taught me how to make them when I was a little kid.

For a group of water witches, Moonlight Cove sure seemed to be very grounded in earth magic.

Cade hit Main Street. There in the center of town was an old fashioned five and dime store. The glass windows had been decorated for autumn and showcased the store's wares such as wool throws, school supplies, plaid thermoses, and an assortment of yarn. It all seemed authentic, as if the town had been frozen in time somewhere around 1950.

"These people do leave the coven occasionally, right? Where are all the cars?" I asked.

"I was wondering the same thing."

Something had interfered with the magic here. Something malignant, powerful. And smelly. As the wind carried another whiff of that foul scent, it infiltrated the truck.

Cade drove slowly along Main Street, which contained a few coffee shops, a pub, a barbershop, and a boutique. On one side of the street, a candle store and an all-natural shop selling soaps and lotions took up a nice chunk of real estate. A little wine bar stood off by itself. The chalkboard sign out front stated the daily specials, made from fresh produce grown on the Moonlight Cove farm.

"Maybe this is where they're making their money. Maybe tourists pay through the nose for this quaint little adventure," I said. Everything was within walking distance. The whole town must encompass only five to eight miles.

This place would be a perfect getaway for the upwardly mobile set who liked crystals, fishing, and watersports. The homey atmosphere would appeal to people looking for an old-fashioned family retreat before heading back to their McMansions.

I pulled my sweater up over my nose as I took in the public buildings. The Town Hall and library were connected. The light brick two-story school stood next door.

"Where's Herb?" I asked.

"Adeline's house. Figure we'd start with the coven leader." Cade seemed to know where he was going. We hooked a left at the theater, which bore an old-fashioned marquis sign. Currently playing: The Lion King and Back to the Future. Not much of a variety, but very wholesome.

Cade finally hit a cul-de-sac that held five houses. The one at the center was huge compared to the other smallish bungalows we'd seen. It boasted craftsman columns, a wide porch, and diamond-shaped beveled windows. And what a shock—another corn dolly hanging on the front door. Herb's white van was parked on the street out front. I'd noted a lack of driveways, as well as cars.

Before Cade and I could hop out of the truck, Herb emerged from his van. He wore white overalls and oversized glasses. White, wavy sprigs of hair sprouted around his head in a horseshoe pattern, leaving the top of his head bald.

I waved. "Hi, Herb."

"My dear, dear null friend. How are you?" He hustled up to me, hand outstretched. "So, we're on another hunt together. And such an interesting killer this time." He grinned, making his ears wiggle slightly. "Are you up to the task?"

"Um…"

Cade strode to stand beside me. "Did you search the coven leader's house?"

"Yes. Although she has an extensive library, there was no smoking gun, so to speak."

"What are we looking for, exactly?" My job was to nullify the wild spells that had gone awry, which meant hitting every home and building in town. But as for evidence, I still didn't know what we hoped to find.

"Anything unusual. Anything matching the odd symbols." Cade dipped his chin at Herb. "I'm going to go take another look around Adeline's. You drive Holly through town. Stop at all the places where people died or were hurt. See what turns up."

My eyes narrowed as I focused on Cade. "I thought we'd search together." Code for: don't leave me alone with Herb. Cade just shrugged.

As we stood on the narrow cobblestone sidewalk, the sky opened up. Large, cold plops of rain fell around us. I had put on my coat, but since Cade had fried my umbrella, I had nothing to protect me from the elements. It didn't seem to bother Herb, who was glancing up at the sky, grinning as the rain splashed against his glasses.

"I don't imagine we'll find much," Cade said. "Don't forget to nullify the warehouse by the way." He pulled a piece of paper from his pocket, unfolded it. It was a map, the kind tourists get to guide them through a theme park. "That should be here, on the edge of town, past the rest of the crops. Can't have magically tainted products going out to Norms or we'll have a real shit show on our hands."

"Fine." I pulled my collar up, secured the top button of my coat.

Cade slapped Herb on the shoulder. "Mind your manners, Herbert."

"Of course. I'm delighted to have Holly join me today. I've so many questions about your null powers."

I shot Cade one last evil eye before climbing into the van with Herb, who tried to start the engine with a flick of his finger. His brows furrowed in confusion, then he laughed. "I'll have to get used to having you around all day." He unzipped his coveralls, yanked them down, then patted both pockets. "I seem to have lost my keys."

I snatched them from one of the cup holders. "Here you go, Herb."

"Thank you! I have to wonder, is it difficult for Cade to lose his powers every time you're together. How do you two manage to work that out?"

It was going to be a long day. "Why don't you ask him?"

He started the engine and blinked at me. "Oh, I have. He won't give me any details. In fact, he was quite tightlipped about the whole thing," he said, almost cheerfully.

"Do you have any idea what's causing magic to misfire here, and on Jane Doe's body? What's the link, Herb?" As we drove into town, I studied each house. The gardens had died off in the cold weather, but the yards were well maintained and free of dead leaves.

"I suspect," Herb said, "the killer was at each location. But that's just a hypothesis. As to why the killer's presence infects magic, I still have no idea."

Was the killer one of the coven? Maybe. He or she would have walked all over town, talked to neighbors, attended to business. And all the while, infecting the magic of everyone in Moonlight Cove. But what did that have to do with the model homes? Why wreck kitchens and wreak havoc on household appliances? That's what kept tripping me up.

"It's as good a theory as any, at this point," I said.

"Until we have proof, it's just that. A theory." Herb pulled to a stop in front of a two-story narrow house painted light blue with white trim. He tapped his window. "A couple was killed here." He plucked his phone from his pocket and glanced at the screen. "Arlo and Susan Landry."

The couple who'd been married almost a century. The couple who stabbed each other to death.

As we exited the van, a strong breeze rushed by, bringing with it the needle sting of rain and the smell of decaying fish. God, that smell. "What are you going to do about the dead fish?"

"From what I understand, our people at the EPA have staved off an investigation and are keeping it out of the press. As soon as we're done investigating, we'll clean it up."

Others infiltrated every stratum of society from the alphabet bureaucracies, news rooms and pulpits, all the way up to the halls of government. This helped keep a lid on anything magical that might come to light and steered Norms toward a more suitable conclusion. Although some Others allowed Norms to see a hint of their power—psychics, healers, mediums, for instance—they were minnows in the magical world, eking out a living like everyone else, and they took pains not to be too accurate. Otherwise, the Council would take notice, and no one wanted that.

I trotted past Herb to the covered porch. I assumed he had a key or something, but he reached past me and opened the door.

"They keep their doors unlocked. There's practically no crime here at the coven."

"Except this double homicide." I led the way inside, and immediately smelled the coppery tang of blood.

It matted the gray area rug and had spilled onto the hardwood floor. Reddish brown smears and splatters coated the white curtains and the pale gray walls.

I closed my eyes and swallowed a few times, trying not to imagine what had happened here.

Herb prowled around the room, peering into the kitchen. "This must be where it started. There's significant splatter along the cabinets and countertop." He turned and glanced back, his eyes twinkling with excitement. "Nothing like this has ever been recorded. If magic is behaving in a way that even you can't nullify, we've got quite a discovery on our hands."

His enthusiasm left me more nauseated than before. "I need some air." I sped quickly through the front door and slammed back into the van, waiting for Herb.

I thought about what he'd said, what I'd seen when Cade tried to perform magic outside the model homes. The magic—the spells—mutated. Magic wasn't causing the spells to mutate. So, what was? What was interfering with magic to make it behave this way?

Herb came back a few minutes later, less enthused than he had been. "I didn't find anything out of the ordinary. Nothing useful at all." He started the van and grinned at me. "Maybe at the next house."

According to Herb's notes, our next stop was David Bowman's. The man who'd drowned in the shower.

"What killed the fish, Herb? The crops I understand. The coven obviously used spells to boost their harvest. But surely they didn't use magic on the fish?"

"That's a good question." He pulled to a stop and dug into the pocket of his coverall to retrieve a small leather notebook with a pen attached. He opened it up and jotted something before turning to me. "You always have the most interesting questions, Ms. James." Then his eyes grew distant, cool. "You're quite fascinating, you know. An anomaly. I'd still like to learn more about your power."

Good luck with that, you crazy old coot. I hopped out of the van before he decided to dissect me then and there.

The temperature had dropped again and each time I exhaled, my breath hovered before me like a specter. The cold, wet air stung my lungs, made my nose run.

Without waiting for Herb this time, I walked into the house and glanced around. He followed me, shaking his head like a dog, trying to dislodge the water coating his thin strands of hair.

"Did you perform an autopsy on the dead coven members?" I asked, glancing around the living room. All very tidy and filled with manly, leather furniture.

"Yes, I spent all night examining them. I was unable to use my post cognitive abilities to view their last dying moments. Very disappointing."

He tromped up the stairs, and I followed. He peeked in a couple of rooms, coming to a stop at the bathroom. It wasn't large, just a small pedestal sink, toilet, and tiny shower with a glass door.

"Apparently the shower stall became this man's coffin. His skin was scalded, most likely by trying to magically adjust the temperature, which backfired on him. But the cause of death was by drowning."

I shivered. "Ironic, huh? A water witch drowned to death."

"Hmm, yes."

Herb peeked into the medicine cabinet, and I left him to it. I trotted back down the stairs. I planned on going to the van but spied something out of the corner of my eye.

Above the hearth, a wreath made of dried foxglove and basil had been propped against the mantel. There was nothing pretty or decorative about it—the color of the leaves had been leeched out by the drying process, leaving them a dull green.

I walked to the fireplace and picked up the wreath, turning it around in my hands. It was smaller than a steering wheel. What was interesting was that both basil and foxglove were used in protection spells to ward off evil.

I sniffed it, smelling only the sweet tang of basil. Why would David Bowman need protection from evil? And what kind of evil were we talking about here? An irritating neighbor or something more serious?

I walked into the kitchen and in the corner of the breakfast nook, a small altar had been erected on a wooden table. It looked similar to Gran's, with its cornucopia and fall gourds. But David had added river stones and a beautiful chunk of uncut moonstone. Dark blue shone in its depths. Nothing strange here. All witches had altars, even Gran, who no longer practiced the craft.

I glanced around the small kitchen and noticed a bouquet of fleabane—a wildflower daisy—had been dried and bound with a jute string. It hung from the latch on the window above the sink. Again, not that odd. Witches hung herbs as talismans to bring good fortune. Fleabane was used to get rid of insects, including fleas, of course, but a more esoteric use was to rid the house of harmful spells and ill intent.

When I was a little kid, I obsessively read Gran's grimoires. Fleabane was a common ingredient in potions and talismans to ward against evil. Was it a coincidence that this man had a wreath of foxglove and basil, as well?

I heard Herb shuffle down the steps. "Are you still here, Ms. James?" He poked his head into the kitchen. "Let's not waste any time. Onto the next site, dear null."

"I'll be there in just a second." I whipped out my phone and texted Cade.

Found signs that David Bowman put up protection against evil. Have you found anything?

Before leaving David's house, I stole his compact red umbrella standing by the front door. Sadly, he wouldn't be needing it anymore.

CHAPTER TWELVE

Next, the tedious work began. Herb and I parked on the street near the holly bushes and traveled from house to house. Technically, I could have just walked up to the door and nullified whatever wayward spell might be lingering, but I wanted to check each home, see if any other coven members were worried about warding off evil.

I noticed that several of the residents grew wild onions in pots near windows. Maybe they used it for cooking, but again, it was often used for protection. Almost every altar I came across contained dried tormentil—a yellow ground rose—which could be used for the same reason.

As I walked into more houses, I spied fleabane hanging above doors and windows. And of course, every home had a corn dolly hanging from the front door, as though it was standard issue.

While I had no proof, my gut was telling me this coven had been doing something underhanded. Whatever the water witches were up to, had it corrupted their magic? And why were they so worried about protecting themselves from harm?

We found the two houses that caught on fire. They were beyond repair. Thankfully, the rain helped keep the fires from spreading. It made me sad to realize these people lost everything by casting a simple illuminating spell, though.

We walked the streets, visiting house after house. At first, I outpaced Herb. I knew what I wanted to find in each residence, but he was peeking and pawing through the homeowners' things, looking for—well, I wasn't sure what he was looking for. But by the time we made it to Main Street, he was keeping up with me.

He stopped at a small café and peered through the window. "According to my notes, this is where the girl was found."

"What girl? Do you mean Maddie's daughter?" The woman who approached me at the holding cell, the one who thanked me.

He glanced in his notebook. "Yes. The girl's name is Annabelle."

"What happened?"

"Apparently, the child awoke in the night and claimed her legs were restless. Her mother cast a small spell on the girl to settle her down."

"And it backfired?"

"Yes. Poor little thing started running and couldn't stop. When the mother tried to correct the situation, she began to run backwards. The mother and aunt had to throw themselves on the girl to keep her still."

"For two days?"

"Yes," he said, tugging on his earlobe.

Leading the way inside the café, I weaved around the maze of empty tables. The lingering scent of coffee beans filled the main room. It was a nice upgrade from the dead fish smell permeating the air outside.

We didn't find anything downstairs, other than a clean kitchen and pantry. There were no wild onions or dried foxglove anywhere. Upstairs, the small apartment was tidy except for a quilt thrown on the floor. But a sour stench of urine mixed with sweat filled the room. Probably from Annabelle. Poor thing.

Maddie said I'd saved her child's life, but I only felt shame twisting my stomach into a knot. I should have come to Moonlight Cove immediately but ignoring Reece had been more important. I'd wanted to punish her for being such a bitch. In reality, I'd been punishing the members of her coven.

I tried to shake the feeling, but it wouldn't let go. Even if Reece had called me Sunday morning when all this happened, I still would have shunned her. Reece was a terrible person, yes, but I wasn't exactly a saint.

Herb roamed the tiny living room, giving the tan sofa and chair a quick glance, and peeked into the drawers on the side table.

I walked to the small altar in the corner of the room. Just the usual—gourds, a chaff of wheat, and a small, fancy bottle of water with a cork stopper.

I wandered to the window facing Main Street and pulled up the blinds. A sprig of rue hung upside down. Its yellow flowers had faded to brown. An herb with a musty fragrance, it was known to be toxic unless handled very carefully.

It was also used to ward off evil.

"Herb."

"Yes?" My body jerked at the closeness of his voice. He stood right behind me, hands clasped behind his back.

"Do you know which wards the coven used? Anything specific?"

His fluffy white brows skyrocketed. "You know, that's an excellent question. I never thought to ask. I assumed they warded against the usual—ill-intent, theft, generic spells of protection on the land and inhabitants." He unclasped his hands, flicked the rue. "But this plant is used to expel a specific evil." He tipped his head toward me. "Demonic mischief."

I sputtered a laugh, then remembered Herb had no sense of humor. "Demons?"

"Mmm, yes. But more commonly, it's used to cure earaches."

Lord knew I had earaches growing up. Gran would make a poultice of ginger, garlic, and warm olive oil. It smelled awful, but it worked. Maybe Maddie used rue to soothe Annabelle's ears. Or maybe a ritualistic murder happened not far from here, and Maddie was trying to protect her home from the evil it would bring.

We left the building as the rain continued to fall in icy sheets. The umbrella provided some protection but my clothes were damp. Our little drives to and from each street had been so brief, the van's heater never had a chance to kick in. Goosebumps covered every bit of me.

Herb climbed behind the wheel and started the engine. He whipped a white handkerchief from his pocket and wiped his glasses.

"Could an enemy cast a spell of this magnitude?" I asked. "Maybe another coven wants Moonlight Cove to fail?"

He drove across the street and parked in front of the wine bar. "If you'd asked a few months ago if someone could be that powerful, I'd have said no. But you and I have seen things… Now, I just don't know."

I spent the next few hours hitting the businesses, the school, the tiny Town Hall, and the theater. I didn't see any more plants that warded off evil. Maybe it was a cultural thing in the coven, something handed down from generation to generation, and had nothing to do with the murder or the magical mishap.

As Herb drove east, away from the populated part of town, I thought of the interview Cade and I conducted with the coven's leader, Adeline, last night. She'd been against allowing Norms to come for the summer, but Reece and the majority of coven members wanted to make changes. Norms would bring in some money, maybe even a nice chunk of change. But Cade said the coven was worth millions. So, what was the benefit of opening their doors to Norms?

I finally leaned my head back. Herb drove along a gravel road that bisected a huge field that had recently been plowed over. It went on for acres, as far as I could see.

"They use all this farmland?" I asked.

"I believe so," Herb said. "They boast fresh ingredients in all of their food here. Will my driving through this lane be sufficient or will you have to go row by row?"

"I think we'll be fine driving this route." At least I hoped so. I still had to go through the warehouse. I was cold, tired, and ready for this day to be over.

Herb drove the gravel road between the plowed fields, and I caught site of the warehouse down the hill. As we drew closer, what lay beyond it captured all my attention. It was the largest greenhouse I'd ever seen. Victorian in architecture, it had to be at least three stories tall, jutting into the sky like a wedding cake made of ice. I could barely take my eyes off it. Even when Herb parked the van next to the warehouse and jumped out, I sat there, just staring.

Gran had always kept a garden—almost a full acre. From the time I could walk, I'd helped her plant, weed, water, and harvest it every year. Spending time with her there was one of my best memories. She also kept an herb garden. She taught me how to make salves and teas and herbal concoctions. No magic required. I rarely made those home remedies for myself, but I could. Just give me a pinch of fresh herbs like feverfew and peppermint, add a cup of vodka, and after a few weeks you had yourself some pain relief with a little kick. But honestly, it was just so much easier to keep a bottle of Tylenol in the house that I never bothered.

"Ms. James?"

Herb brought me back to the present. The warehouse.

I once more opened my stolen umbrella and dove through the rain. Inside the warehouse, I found the lights near the door and flipped them on.

Hundreds of shelves stood before us, lining both sides of the building with a wide row in between. Every shelf was neatly packed with product. Some contained bottles of liquid and others held boxes of packaged dried herbs. I wandered through the rows and plucked a good luck charm from a box of hundreds. It was made of hematite and stamped on one side with a brass pentagram. Factory made, straight from China. That shit didn't need to be nullified.

I walked to the back of the warehouse where long tables were set up and filled with jars of dried herbs, alcohol, and shea butter—elixirs and lotions. One table bore a dozen hot plates and large stock pots. At least the coven made their own home remedies, as they claimed on their website.

Herb's shoes squeaked on the cement floor as he followed me. "They have quite a little business here, don't they?"

No matter how much money they made with this store, it couldn't possibly add up to a multi-million-dollar empire. I knew bullshit when I smelled it. Whatever Moonlight Cove was up to; however they made their money—it wasn't in this room.

"Let's hit the greenhouse, Herb."

"Lead on, my dear."

I cut through the back exit, across the wet grass. The moment I opened the door of the greenhouse, moist, heavy air filled my lungs, along with the smell of rot and thick, rich soil.

Row after row of plants filled the shelves, black and dead in their terracotta pots. I spied common plants like Lady's Mantle, which helped ease menstrual cramps. Maca root—good for people with chronic fatigue, but it also increased fertility in women. That made sense, considering the coven was comprised of water witches. The moon and its phases had always been linked to women's cycles and fertility.

In the center of the room, two Meyer lemon trees, their fruit withering on the branches, shot fifteen feet in the air. It should smell wonderful in here—full of sweet, delicate floral scents. Instead, it smelled of decay with an underlying hint of mold.

On the far side of the room, all sorts of exotic blooms had grown here before the curse wiped them all out. Mandrakes and kadupuls and fire lilies—again, all plants that aided in fertility. Though the green house was huge—by greenhouse standards—there weren't enough plants here to harvest and sell online. Were these plants used for the coven only, or did the Norms who came to rent houses in the summer benefit? Maybe that's what Moonlight Cove was really selling—a chance at fertility.

I walked along the rows of dead flowers, touching some of the plants. I stopped at an orchid, brushing my hands across the rippled, brown petals and thought about my theory. Desperate couples would come here and pay a hell of a lot of money to up their chance of pregnancy. But no amount of herbs and tinctures could guarantee that outcome.

Maybe they didn't have to. Perhaps a couple that had tried everything came here looking for one last chance to have a baby. Was the coven cashing in on Norms who'd be eager to try anything to have a family?

I thought back to those online photos of fun in the summer sunshine. Families huddled together, gasping over fireworks. Couples enjoying a farm fresh dinner at the restaurant. The old-fashioned atmosphere of the town itself. Add in the herbs and juices and special charms to help aid in fertility. I could see where that would pull in Norms who were searching for something, anything to help them get pregnant. But still, did it make them millions? No, it wasn't adding up—literally.

Herb stood next to the other wall. "Ah, Ms. James. Come. Look at this."

I hurried to his side. "What is it?"

"Caleana major. It's never been propagated. The very existence of it relies on a fungus growing symbiotically along with the flower. A fungus found only in the outback of Australia."

"What's it doing here?"

"That is the question. Very interesting indeed." He straightened and glanced around at the other plants. "They've cultivated some very old specimens here. Look at this."

I bent down and studied a dead petal folded in on itself. "What is it?"

"Melampyrum cristatum, I believe. Parasitic, naturally."

"Uh huh."

"It's said that one seed can cause a man to lose his libido for up to a year."

My eyes widened at his chipper expression. "Why would they want to propagate that?"

He waved his hand and a plant fell to the floor, smashing the pot and scattering dirt all over my wet boots. "Oh, sorry. Don't you see? All these plants are utilized in the aid—or in at least one case, the hindrance—of fertility."

"I know."

"I didn't see any of these rare flowers or seeds in the tonics they're selling in the warehouse."

"Nope. I think they're giving them to the vacationing Norms who come here every summer."

Herb's bushy brows rose, causing wrinkles to crease his wide forehead. "That's rather ingenious."

"Kind of." Why not publicly tout the fertility angle, though? Come to Moonlight Cove, have a relaxing stay and up your chances of pregnancy with our natural herbs. Nothing wrong with that. So, why did Adeline act so cagey about it?

As I pondered, I got a text from Cade. I let him know we were in the greenhouse and he promised to meet me there soon.

I looked up from my phone and glanced out the far window. That's when I finally spied a parking lot in the distance. "So, that's where they keep their cars."

Herb stood beside me, smelling of the peppermint he'd just popped in his mouth. "Ah," he said, sucking around the candy, "at least that's one mystery solved, eh, Ms. James?"

He clapped me on the shoulder. The one with the scratch. I grunted softly and walked back outside.

By the time Cade arrived, Herb and I were already in the van. The heat dribbling through the vent didn't make a dent in the cold gripping my body.

Cade pulled his truck next to me and rolled down his window, so I did the same. "Find anything?"

I explained my fertility theory. Cade's eyes narrowed as he listened.

"Sounds like a plausible scenario," he said. "We need to question them about it and get that list of the Norms who've stayed here."

"What have you been up to?"

"I've been at the treasurer's house all day, trying to open encrypted files on the coven's main computer." Even with the rain creating a veil between us, I could clearly read his frustration. That scowl was back in full force. "Couldn't use a spell to crack it, not if I didn't want the damn thing to explode or worse. I've got the computer with me. Herb and I need to head back to the lab. I'll hand this off to the experts. Can you drive the truck home?"

"You don't want me to go with you? Question the coven some more?"

"Nah. It's going to be another long night. I got a report from my colleagues who interviewed them this morning. The coven didn't give up a thing. I have a feeling I'm going to get more of the same. You might as well go home and get some rest."

He climbed out of the truck, the computer tucked under his arm. Then he opened the van's side panel and placed it on the seat. "I don't know whether this thing was encrypted by magic or by technical means."

I held up my hands and made a sweeping motion. "It's hereby nullified." I turned to Herb. "Bye. Thanks for driving me around today." Then I hopped out of the van and into the truck before Cade could change his mind about letting me drive it. I played with the seat adjustment and fiddled with the mirrors.

Standing in the freezing rain, Cade gave me at least forty different instructions for how to handle his baby. "Take it easy in this weather. There's a lot of power under that hood. Don't be afraid to give it some gas though if you need to change lanes. But not too much gas. The blinker is here"—he reached past me to point out the obvious—"and make sure you use it."

I finally rolled up the window as he delivered a lecture on windshield wipers, and I drove off with a honk of the horn. As I glanced in the rearview mirror, Cade bared his teeth. And for the first time that day, I smiled.

CHAPTER THIRTEEN

When I was only a few days old, Brianna, my nineteen-year-old mother, showed up at Gran's house with me in tow. She was supposed to be safely tucked away in a Texas college, attending football games and sneaking into bars using a fake ID. Instead, she'd met my sperm donor, Samuel Dumahl, and gotten herself knocked up instead. When Sam found out he'd fathered a null, he ghosted her.

After spending one night with Gran, Brianna left me behind. She took her suitcase, purse, and car. Then she disappeared.

Gran maintained that Brianna wouldn't leave me behind—not permanently. Something terrible must have happened to keep her from coming back. After all this time, I suspected something awful had happened, too. Then again, Brianna was good at hiding things. She'd had an older boyfriend and a secret baby, all the while reassuring Gran that college life was great.

Whether Brianna wanted me or not, I had a hole in my life that would never go away. A yearning to find her, whether she was dead or alive. She'd given birth to me, in spite of what I was. I must have sucked the magic out of her from the beginning. And if she didn't know in utero, she'd known I was a null the moment I was born. Yet instead of handing me off to strangers, she hand-delivered me to Gran. On some level, Brianna had cared about me.

I still didn't know much about my father, other than the fact that he came from a wealthy enchanter family. He died recently, leaving behind a wife and three kids. Legitimate ones. Samuel never acknowledged me in life, but after his death he left a letter to his father, spilling the beans about my existence. I'm still not sure why he didn't continue to keep it a secret. Did he feel guilty about ducking out on his parental responsibilities? That's something I'd never know.

What little I did know about Sam, I discovered through my grandfather, Wallace, who was nothing more than a smooth-talking politician. He came off like a Southern gentleman, but like all soulless political types, he hadn't delivered on his promise. In return for helping him with a favor, Wallace swore he'd do everything in his power to find my mom. I'd only heard from him once in the last several weeks. He'd been ignoring my calls and texts, refusing to acknowledge our agreement. Like father, like son. I wasn't surprised, but I couldn't help feeling disappointed.

Still, in spite of being abandoned by both of my parents, I had a happy childhood with Gran. She showered me with love and acceptance, making the ultimate sacrifice to give up the craft in order to raise me. I owed her everything.

After getting saddled with me, she bought a 1920s farmhouse in a small community devoid of Others. The old house came with tall ceilings, narrow rooms, and a few stained-glass windows. Gran kept some of the character of the original house—the crown moldings and hardwood floors—then added her own personal touch that included a lot of country blue and handmade quilts.

Now as I drove down the long gravel driveway, I tried not to think about Wallace and his broken promise. I didn't want to talk to Gran about it, not tonight. I never should have gotten her hopes up about finding Brianna. That was a cruel thing to do.

Though the rain had abated on the trip from Moonlight Cove, I was still a little bleary-eyed from not getting much sleep the night before and from walking in the rain all day. Also, the scratch on my shoulder ached like a bitch.

Once I passed the white picket fence, the farmhouse came into view. The tight fist of anxiety I'd been feeling all day loosened its grip on my chest, making it easier to breathe. A feeling of contentment settled over me like it did every time I came home.

I parked and walked up the steps of the wide front porch, passing a border of hearty mums still in bloom, despite the cold snap we'd had. Rusty red and buttery yellow added a pop of color to the dead grass.

I hadn't told Gran I was coming, but she sensed me. She may not practice the craft anymore, but the moment I hit the porch, she'd feel her inherent magic shut down. I imagined it was like a sudden power outage during a thunderstorm. One second the electricity was on, the next it was gone, leaving only darkness behind.

I stepped through the front door just as Gran walked out of the kitchen, a thin, white tea towel draped over one shoulder.

"Oh, so you remember where I live? I thought you'd forgotten the address."

"I'm not here two seconds, and you're already giving me grief, old woman?"

As I shut the door behind me, she crossed the few remaining feet and pulled me into a long hug. She smelled, as always, of herbs and vanilla. The herbs were from her various teas, tonics, and bath satchels. The vanilla-scented perfume was all Gran.

She'd be seventy in a few months but appeared no older than fifty. She'd have looked much younger if she hadn't spent the last couple of decades around me. I took years off her life—literally.

Gran's dark red hair came courtesy of L'Oréal. She took pride in her curves, preferring low cut blouses that flashed more than a hint of cleavage and skintight jeans that hugged her hips. Gran wasn't afraid of being noticed. In fact, if people weren't staring at her, she'd take serious offense.

I hugged her back, suddenly missing her more than I thought possible. After tangling with Reece yesterday, I hadn't realized how much I needed this—the warmth and security of home.

"Love you, Gran."

She pulled back, gazing at me through leopard print glasses—the woman was a sucker for animal prints. "What's wrong?"

"Nothing. Can't I just be glad to see you after two weeks?"

"Not this glad." She took a step back, eyeing me from head to toe. "Come on in the kitchen. I'll make us something to eat, and you can tell me all about it."

I could never hide anything from her, and it didn't have a thing to do with magic. Gran could sniff a lie like a detection dog sniffed out heroin. Why she hadn't picked up on my mother's secret lifestyle, I had no idea. Maybe Gran had been too busy with her coven at the time. Maybe she'd wanted to give Brianna some room to spread her wings. Either way, Gran didn't make the same mistake with me. Instead she buckled down, treating me like I was on the witness stand over every minor incident. I sometimes resented it, especially when I was younger, but I always understood why she was so protective. Since I'd always been a pretty good kid, her powers of perception were wasted on me.

I hung my coat and purse on a hook by the door, then shadowed her into the blue and white kitchen with its goose print wallpaper. I hopped up on the Formica countertop and watched as Gran stood at the stove, stirring a simmering pot of something that smelled delicious, savory. One of her soups probably, made with vegetables from her own garden.

"Beef stew," she said, as if reading my mind. "I'll throw some biscuits in the oven, and then I want to hear about your situation." She gazed at me over the top of her glasses, her dark blue eyes serious and penetrating. "All of it, missy. You hear me?"

"Yes, ma'am." I gave her a jaunty little salute. "I'll go wash up."

I left her to it and trotted upstairs. I washed my hands and fixed my hair. Then I drifted down the hall to my Gran's bedroom.

"Can I borrow some clean clothes?" I yelled.

"Help yourself," she called back.

I had to dig through her cheetah and leopard leggings to the bottom of the drawer where I found a pair of boring, gray sweats and changed into them. The warm clothes felt like heaven, and they smelled of vanilla and fabric softener.

With my damp clothes over my arm, I headed back down the hall, pausing at Brianna's room. Gran always kept the door shut. She'd never forbidden me from going in, but she didn't encourage it either. So as quietly as I could, I opened the door and crept inside.

It was like entering a time capsule. Or a shrine. Gran had faithfully recreated my mother's room exactly as it had been in their old house, as if Brianna might return tomorrow. The walls were painted a pale yellow. White curtains fell over her window, gauzy and covered with embroidered daisies. She had only one poster on her wall: the cover of Dr. Seuss's Oh the Places You'll Go. Seeing that always brought tears to my eyes. I didn't know what Brianna dreamed of as a girl, but I doubted she'd seen it come to fruition.

According to Gran, Brianna had been whip-smart. She was quiet, but funny, and loved school. I approached her small book shelf, as I'd done so many times before, and as my fingers trailed over the paperback spines of Jane Austen and the Bronte sisters, I pegged my mother as a romantic.

I shifted my attention to her dresser. The items collected there didn't have a speck of dust on them. Gran was fastidious about it, coming in here at least once a week to dust the furniture and sweep the hardwood floor.

I glanced at the half empty bottle of perfume that smelled like baby powder. It was another romantic choice. Pink and fluffy and subtle.

Leaning forward, I scanned the pictures Brianna had tucked into the mirror's frame. Photos of her and a couple of her friends. I plucked one and studied it, smiling at my mom's long curly hair. She looked so young and innocent, my heart ached.

"Dinner's ready." Gran stood in the doorway, watching me.

"Sorry." I moved to put the photo back in place.

Gran waved one hand. "Keep it." I'd never taken a photo of my mom from the house. Those were Gran's memories, and I didn't want to deprive her of even one. But now, I hesitated, looking at the picture one more time.

"Are you sure?"

"Of course." She stepped into the room and stood at my side. "That was her best friend."

"Amber, right?"

"Yes. That girl had a wild streak. I'm not sure what Brianna saw in her. There were never two more dissimilar people, but you couldn't pry them apart."

My mother wore a thin gold pendant with a diamond studded heart. "Did you give her that?"

Gran took the picture from my fingers, peering down at it. "We had that made after your grandfather died. I took the stones from a pair of his cuff links." That was something about my mother I hadn't known.

Gran heaved a sigh and shoved the photograph in my hand. "Let's eat." As she left the room, I noticed her blinking back tears, and I felt guilty for stirring up old memories.

This time, instead of tucking the picture back on the mirror, I hung onto it and slipped it in my purse which was hanging on a hook in the entryway. Then I dropped my damp clothes by the front door before joining Gran in the dining room.

She'd already set the table. The stew smelled delicious. She'd also opened a pot of local honey for the hot biscuits.

Before sitting down, my eye was drawn to the corner of the dining room where Gran kept her altar on a sideboard. Though she no longer celebrated sabbats, she still kept an altar as a tribute to her heritage and a way of giving thanks.

I wandered over to it, taking in the chalice, made of green glass and filled with a little bit of water. The table held a large chunk of smoky quartz along with a fat, white candle, an athame—a ceremonial knife with a carved, wooden handle—

a gray feather, and a small cornucopia filled with decorative squash. Fire, air, water, and earth—all faithfully represented. A braided corn dolly hung on the wall above the table. I reached out and touched the crisp, dried corn stalk, thinking back to Moonlight Cove.

"What's wrong, Hollyhocks?" Gran asked.

I sat down at the table, placing a napkin over my lap. "Tell me about water witches."

She lifted one brow, penciled dark red to match her fiery hair. "Why the sudden interest?"

As we ate, I told her about the contaminated spells and what I'd found at Moonlight Cove. I finished with Reece Tolliver requesting my help. At the name, Gran's spoon hit the side of her bowl.

"What possessed you to work with the likes of her? That girl nearly cost you an education, not to mention all that damage to your self-esteem. If I'd still been practicing, I would have put a hex on her." She leaned back, crossing her arms over her chest.

"There's more."

"Heaven help us, how much more?"

I explained about Jane Doe and her proximity to the coven, mentioning only that Cade suspected magic might have been involved in the death. I completely left out my role with the Council, because there was only so much a null could take in one day, and Gran would have some very strong opinions.

"Hmm," she said, relaxing her arms and taking a bite of stew. "That's a lot to unpack."

"What made their magic go all wonky like that? And what's with all the crops and the corn dollies?" I grabbed another biscuit from the bread basket, spread a thick layer of honey on top.

"People plant crops, Holly. Witches especially. Between herbs and flowers for potions, it's not unreasonable. And what else are they going to do with all those acres?"

Okay, maybe I'd put too much importance on Moonlight Cove's land-loving ways. "But the crops had been bespelled. And what about all the wild onions and Fleabane and rue?"

She lifted one shoulder and pushed her bowl out of the way. "Again, what's so strange about warding off evil? A lot of old witches do that out of habit. Just like sprinkling salt on the threshold or carrying an acorn in your pocket for good health. Just old witches' tales, but people still do them."

Perhaps. But I was still convinced something more was going on—besides my theory about helping barren Norms with their fertility problems. I shared my ideas on that subject, as well.

She took off her glasses, twirling them by the stem. "They're a cloistered bunch, so welcoming in Norms…that doesn't sit right. There would have to be some kind of motive behind it. Water witches and fertility go hand in hand, so that makes sense. But I'm more interested in the spells backfiring. Do you know if the coven had contact with an undine?"

"I don't know." I hadn't thought of that possibility. An undine was an elemental spirit associated with water. Offer her gifts and sacrifices, and she'd bring good fortune. "I didn't see any sign of it, but then I didn't go down to the beach. Too many dead fish for my taste."

"Finish up here and we'll consult the books," she said. "Though I doubt we'll find anything about this strange magic situation."

God, I loved consulting the books. Along with her grimoires, Gran also had biographies on the history of her family and ancient tomes about the powers of Others. I used to pour over those books as a child, seeping in every bit of knowledge I could. Perhaps my mother and I weren't that different after all. We just had different taste in what we liked to study.

Gran took the dishes to the kitchen and I gave the table a quick swipe, scooping up crumbs. Once more, I glanced at her altar and felt that familiar pang of guilt. I'd taken so much from Gran—her daughter, her powers, her way of life.

Was I doing the same thing to Cade, taking too much, altering his life, and not for the better? He kept assuring me that it would all work out. Why didn't I believe him?

"Hurry up, girl. Time's a-wasting," Gran yelled from the living room.

Snapping out of my musings, I walked to the kitchen and tossed away the biscuit crumbs. Next, I grabbed my phone and the little notebook from my purse. I wanted to write down all of my impressions of Moonlight Cove, everything I could remember from this afternoon, even if it seemed insignificant.

Gran sat on the shabby sofa in the living room surrounded by old books, their leather covers crinkled and cracked, their thick pages yellowed with age. The musty scent smelled as much like home as Gran's chocolate chip cookies.

"Water witches," she mumbled, thumbing through the pages of the oversized book in her lap. "Don't have many of those in Oklahoma, so all I know is what I've heard through the grapevine. Their lot tend to stick together, as there's so few of them." As she turned the pages, I caught glimpses of hand-drawn pictures and old-fashioned lettering.

Gran hummed under her breath and I wrote my recollections, including all the plants I could remember. I jotted down particulars on the messed-up spells, as well.

I wrote so much, my hand began to cramp. Gran was engrossed in the book she held, her eyes narrowed as they swept across the page.

Once I finished writing, I started thumbing through the book nearest me. A thin, long grimoire of spells that required some serious skill on the part of the practitioner. I noticed that quite a few involved blood.

"Blood makes a spell stronger," I said.

"Mmm hmm." Gran didn't glance up from her book.

"But what if you used your own blood instead of animal blood?"

She closed the book on her finger to keep her place. "It would be more powerful, naturally. When blood is willingly sacrificed, the magic absorbs it. Like the difference between regular gasoline and rocket fuel."

I thought about Cade's murder victim. She sure as hell hadn't given herself willingly. "What if it's taken, not offered? Like a sacrifice?"

CHAPTER FOURTEEN

"Well, that's a whole different story. That's black magic. You don't just walk away from that, not without it destroying your soul. Some will pay that price, of course, but you know all this, Hollyhocks. What's going on in that head of yours?"

"Nothing, really." I was hoping to find something I could pinpoint, some cause for the spells going awry. I absentmindedly rubbed at my shoulder. Touching it, I winced at the pain. "A goblin scratched me yesterday. Can you look at it for me?"

She dumped the book on the table and stood. "For goodness' sake, why didn't you say something earlier? Come in the bathroom and let me see."

I climbed to my feet and trailed after her. I'd never admit it to her, but sometimes it was nice to be fussed over.

I took off the gray sweatshirt and lowered my bra strap while Gran gathered all of her supplies, most of them homemade recipes handed down from her ancestors. The doctor was a last resort in our household. I could only remember going once to set a broken arm. If magic worked on me, I wouldn't have had to wear that cast for six long, itchy weeks.

Gran peeled away the gauze Cade had taped to the cap of my shoulder the night before. She tsked, gently prodding the skin. "It's red and angry. What the holy hell were you doing messing with goblins?"

I explained my work situation, and she just rolled her eyes. "Don't ever get involved in a family dispute. You'll always take the brunt of it, because no matter what, blood sides with blood."

"Yes, ma'am." She applied a poultice of honey, garlic juice and crushed goldenseal. It stank as it stung my wound, sending fire through my nerves. After a few moments, though, the burning sensation eased off a bit.

Gran slapped the jar of salve into my hand. "Day and night. You'll smell, but you'll heal." Then she patted my cheek. "And try to stay out of trouble for a change."

That was something I couldn't promise. "Day and night. Got it."

After she finished doctoring me, she made me drink a tea concocted of feverfew and raspberry leaves. Then she settled back on the sofa with a tumbler full of vodka and cranberry juice.

"Why don't you ever make these remedies in cocktail form?" I asked, sipping the tea. Between that and the poultice, my shoulder was feeling better already. "I could use a feverfew margarita."

"Because I like to torture you." She grinned and held up her glass in a silent toast.

"Sadistic old woman." She just cackled.

I set my cup aside and found the photos I'd taken of the markings on Jane Doe's body. I zoomed in on them, so she wouldn't notice the background. "Ever seen anything like this?"

She took the phone and adjusted her glasses. "No. Looks like a rune gone wrong. All those straight lines, then suddenly a squiggle that doesn't belong." She swiped through all the branded marks. "Was this found on Cade's dead girl?"

"Yeah. Keep it under your hat."

"Who would I tell, my quilting circle?" She peered at me over her glasses, her gaze lingering on my face. "Wait a minute. You're involved in this murder, too, aren't you?"

Here we go. "Involved is such a strong word. More like consulting."

She tossed my phone on one of her grimoires. "Are you tangled up with the Council again? Assure me you wouldn't be that stupid."

I could have lied, but what was the point? She always knew when I wasn't telling the truth, and then I'd catch hell about that, too.

"I have a contract. One time only. Sunny's charging them through the nose."

She sat silently, staring at the empty fireplace. Her lips slashed into a frown that accentuated the lines on either side of her mouth. After several long minutes of silence, her gaze shifted to me, even though her body remained still. The sorrow I saw on her face nearly broke me. I'd disappointed her. Again.

I knew that my decision to work for the Council would make her worry. I expected she'd lecture me, telling me how foolhardy I was. But that sad expression tinged with acceptance nearly brought tears to my eyes.

"If this is the path you choose, there's nothing I can do about it. I've said it all before, but I'm just wasting my breath, aren't I?"

I moved to sit next to her on the sofa. "I remember everything you taught me, Gran." I picked up her hand. She didn't resist, but she didn't curl her fingers around mine, either. "Cade and I are in this together. He has my back."

She said nothing, but the vibrant woman I'd always known seemed to shrink before my eyes. "If you continue to play with fire, you're going to get burned. Maybe not this time, but eventually."

"We don't even know this dead girl's name. She was tortured, killed, and dumped in the lake. Treated like she was nothing, Gran. That's not right."

She slowly turned her head to look at me then. "And you wondered if the same thing might have happened to your mother?"

I nodded, unable to trust my voice. If I spoke now, I'd start crying.

"All right then. Help Cade, but please, come back to me in one piece." Gran squeezed my hand so hard, my fingers ached.

#

We searched the books for another couple of hours but didn't come up with any cause for the magical infection, nor did I find any reference to the markings. Not that I thought I would. I was beginning to suspect that everyone was right: the markings were made up, as was the ritual. And what that had to do with spells rebounding, I had no idea.

When Gran caught me dozing behind a grimoire, she sent me off to bed. But once I entered my bedroom, with its purple walls and Keith Urban posters, I felt awake enough to call Cade.

The good news: his tech guy decrypted the computer. The bad news: it contained nothing but a list of stock from the warehouse.

"I've been at the holding cell all night, questioning these people. So far, they're not giving anything up. I've been thinking about your theory, though, and I believe you're right. The witches help Norms get pregnant. But there's nothing illegal or unethical about that."

"Then why are they hiding it?" I asked. "Why not hand over a list of their clients? If they weren't doing anything shady, they'd help with the investigation. There's something they don't want the Council to uncover."

"Exactly." Frustration edged his voice, making it deeper, gruffer. I pictured him, eyes narrowed, stroking his scar with one finger.

"What do you think they're up to?"

"I have no damned clue, Little Null."

"Maybe Jane Doe is on the list."

Cade let out a long sigh. "Maybe. But until I can confirm that, I'm not making any assumptions."

Right. Rule number eighty-seven in Cade's guide to investigating: never assume. "What's your next step?" I traced my finger along the quilt covering the bed. Gran had sewn it by hand. Squares of purple and lavender with pops of dark green.

"I have a team. We're headed to Moonlight Cove tomorrow and we're going to tear that fucking place apart. From top to bottom."

I'd wanted to be involved in every aspect of this investigation, but the weatherman was calling for more rain. My fingertips were still pruney from today. "Do you need me there to help?" Please say no.

"Not really, but you can come if you want." Not the most gracious offer, but then this was Cade we were talking about. The fact that he'd included me at all was progress.

"I think I'll stick to my schedule. That'll make Sunny happy. But call me when you find something?"

"Will do." Then he paused. "By the way, what are you wearing?"

"Gran's old sweatpants and wool socks. It's very sexy. You're really missing out, McAllister."

Cade let out a rare laugh. The sound of that deep rumble made my toes curl. "Night, baby. I'll call you tomorrow, let you know what's going on."

"Love you, Sorcerer."

I was feeling sleepy, my heart lighter than it had been when I'd arrived. A night of Gran and grimoires would do that for me. But if anyone could ruin a moment of tranquility, it was Sunshine Carmichael. When I called her, she wasn't in a good mood—which was pretty much business as usual.

"What?" she demanded.

"I'm not investigating with Cade tomorrow, so I can keep my morning appointments, at least."

"I'm sure they'll be thrilled." I heard clacking in the background, meaning she was still in the office.

Sunny had always been a hard worker. She tackled all the details I hated, like making schedules and paying taxes. I felt a little guilty that she was stuck in that damp, moldy office all day, every day. "Thanks for all the hard work you put in, Sunny. You do a great job."

"I know, and frankly, I don't need you to pat me on the back for it."

What had I been thinking, offering kudos? Words were wasted on Sunny. She only wanted appreciation in the form of cold, hard cash. Benjamins, preferably.

"By the way," she said tartly, "you never told me you met Dean Wyler."

"I haven't had the chance, but yes, I met him. He was very nice, very toothy."

"Don't be dismissive. You always do that. The man is a genius when it comes to real estate. Did you know he and his brother started flipping small houses before he became a realtor? Now look at him. He's on TV every week and he's been quoted in national publications."

"What publications?"

She let out a huffy sigh. "I don't know exactly, but according to his bio, he's been quoted."

Someone was crushing in a bad way. "He said he'd help us find a new office."

"I talked to him today. You should have told me to expect his call."

I tried to picture Sunny flustered and blushing. It was hard to imagine. I'd seen her interact with handsome men before and she'd always remained unruffled, but I'd never seen her in the presence of a hometown celebrity. Even Sunny was vulnerable to Dean Wyler's charms.

"Did he send any good listings?"

"Not yet. He invited us to a cocktail party tomorrow night."

"That's short notice. Please tell me you declined?" I really didn't have time to make chitchat with strangers. Cade and I had a murder to solve.

"I accepted for both of us. And you are going."

When I made Sunny a partner, I should have stipulated she remain a silent one. Big mistake on my part. "Fine. I'll give it an hour, but then I'm out."

"We'll see. I'll send your itinerary for tomorrow." She hung up without saying goodbye.

Graciousness wasn't one of Sunny's gifts. Nor was patience or simple phone etiquette. She'd have made a great prison guard, though.

As I undressed, I glanced around my room at the pictures I'd tacked on the walls—photos of my friends from high school. I'd been in pep squad and debate club. I had a dozen girls I would have considered my close friends. Girls I haven't talked to or thought about in ages. After graduating, we'd all gone our separate ways, as people do. Friends borne out of convenience, but still providing that feeling of comradery, of shared memories and inside jokes.

I missed having girlfriends. The only girls' night out events I attended these days were job-related. I'd thought I'd find my tribe in college, friends I'd have for years to come. Look how that turned out.

I crawled onto my old twin mattress, beneath the floral sheets and the soft quilt. I'd never been one of those people who had my life mapped out at a young age. In the hazy future, I saw a husband. Probably kids. A job I liked. Nothing special. Just an ordinary life. I'd never expected to spend all my time surrounded by Others, much less fall in love with one.

Life's a real kick in the pants, sometimes.

CHAPTER FIFTEEN

When I awoke the next morning, I wondered where I was. But once the whiff of coffee and the smoky tang of bacon tickled my nose, I remembered. Gran's house.

I glanced around the room, catching a glimpse of gray skies through the slats of the blinds. Just another beautiful fall day in Tulsa. God, how I wished the sun would peek out, if only for a few hours.

I sat up and stretched my arms above my head. The scratch on my shoulder felt a little tight, but much better than yesterday. The throbbing pain was gone, thanks to her garlic and goldenseal treatment.

After making my bed, I threw on the borrowed clothes from the night before and padded down to the kitchen. Gran stood at the stove, flipping bacon. Today, she wore pink and black zebra print leggings and a long-sleeved black T-shirt. She flicked me a glance behind purple cat eye glasses. "Good morning."

I grabbed a mug that matched the 80s wallpaper—lots of geese with a country blue bow. As I sipped, I tried to gauge her mood. Finally, I just asked, "Are you upset with me?"

"I'm just concerned." She turned back to the bacon, the line of her slender shoulders tense. "By the way, have you heard from your grandfather?"

I'd been hoping to avoid this topic. And it was hard to think of Wallace Dumahl as a grandfather. He was a stranger to me. "No. I'm sorry, Gran."

She waved off my apology. "Not your fault. I didn't expect he'd find any answers, not really. Your mother is gone. That's just something we're going to have to accept."

We had accepted it. Until I'd brought a glimmer of hope back into our lives.

"Gran—"

"I did a little more research after you went to bed, looking for anything with those symbols."

"And?"

"I didn't find squat. I'm wondering if whoever burned them into that poor girl's skin created those symbols out of whole cloth."

"Cade and I wondered the same thing. It's like the killer used bits and pieces from different cultures."

She transferred the bacon onto a plate lined with paper towels to absorb the grease. "Whatever it is, it's evil." She turned to me. "You're trying to do something good, something important. I understand that, Holly, I do. But please be careful."

I put my mug down and walked to her, pulling her into a hug. "I promise I'll be safe." Even as I said the words, I knew I had no business making such a vow. I'd try my best to not take unnecessary risks, to be smart and follow Cade's lead, but there were no guarantees in life. Gran and I both knew that, but I lied anyway. Lies were often more comforting than the truth.

#

Take a teenage air witch who couldn't manage her powers, a low-level sorcerer with road rage issues, an uber-weak telepath, a vegan bone caster, and a healer with a deep hatred of her fellow man—and you had my standing Wednesday appointment. Dr. Fishbein, an empath psychologist who kept me on a monthly retainer, corralled this crew every week, trying to help them with their issues.

Dr. F. sat in his chair, legs crossed at the knee. The double chin always seemed out of place on his long, narrow face. His most notable features were his ears and nose—both huge. His light brown eyes were his best quality. They radiated kindness. This man cared deeply about his patients. And their privacy.

Still, he couldn't allow Carrie, the angsty witch, to accidentally whirl up another micro tornado. He'd had to buy new furniture and replace the building's roof. His insurance premiums jumped two-hundred percent. I was a much cheaper alternative, but of course with me here, Dr. F. couldn't use his magic to soothe his patients' frayed tempers.

Carter, had been raving about people who refused to use their turn signals for the last ten minutes. Dinah, the healer, finally told him to shut the fuck up. Using those exact words.

"Remember people, this is a safe space," Dr. F. said in a calm voice. "Let's use positive language, encouraging words."

"We were all thinking it." Carrie, the witch, rolled her eyes and picked at her nail polish. It was black, like her hair, clothes, and attitude. "If you don't like sharing the road, just take the bus, dude."

Carter pointed at her. "That's what I'm talking about. It's that kind of attitude that pisses me off." He'd been accused of using his magic to cause two separate accidents on Norms who'd cut him off in traffic. He'd been sent to Fishbein by the Council, and this was his last warning. If he pulled that stunt again, his license would be revoked and he'd be sanctioned. No magic for six months plus a stiff fine.

"Drivers bother you?" Dinah practically spit out the words. "Huh, try sick people. They're all so whiny and self-involved." As she sneered, her voice took on an exaggerated, mocking tone. "I was playing with fire spells and got burned. My sons got in a fight and one ruptured an eyeball. My husband cracked his skull when he got drunk and rammed his head through the doorway. Fix it, Dinah. Fix it, fix it, fix it. That's all I hear, day in and day out." She sat back in her chair, crossing her arms, angling her body toward the door. "And if one more person complains about my choice of music, I'm going to lose it. It's my office! I have rights, too, don't I? Blue grass soothes me."

Dr. Fishbein turned to her, his voice as calm and gentle as a cloudless summer day. "Dinah, you most definitely have a right to your space. But you also have to think of your patients' needs. What if you listened to your music at home? Or in the car, after a long day at work?"

"Why should I have to make all the compromises? Answer me that!"

"God, you're pathetic," Carrie said, as she continued to chip away at her nail polish. "They're paying you. Stop being a dick already."

Deon, the telepath, cleared his throat. "I don't think that type of name calling helps our situation." Deon could send a bicycle rolling a couple of feet or move a salt shaker across the table with some very intense concentration, but that was the extent of his powers. Until he got angry—then he tended to blow things up. Houses. Power stations. Cows. Most of the time he was pretty easygoing, but every once in a while, his fuse ignited, and pow! He was here to get a handle on that.

"Agreed man. Let's keep the trash talking away from the group." Andrew, the xylomancer (in fancy speak, that's a bone caster), sat quietly, stroking his chin pubes. He smelled of skunk weed and wore T-shirts made of hemp. Andrew's parents sent him to Dr. F to encourage him to embrace his magic, but he still refused to touch animal bones.

I sat outside the trust circle, in a corner of the room. As the meeting continued, I read over my notes about the murder case. Sadly, there weren't many. Then I studied the hand symbol found on the victim and began doodling it on one page. I turned it in different directions, tried to make sense of it, then drew it a few more times.

"What's she writing?"

The room became quiet. I lifted my head to find them all staring at me.

Carter stood, hands on his hips. His beefy gut caused the buttons on his yellow shirt to pull slightly. His round face had turned bright pink, all the way up to his sandy hairline. "Are you writing about me? Because this group is confidential."

Dr. F. turned around in his chair so that he could see me. "As you know, Holly is on hand to make sure things remain calm in the group. And you're right, Carter, everything we say here is confidential. Holly, can you please tell us what you're working on."

I sighed. Deeply. I held up the symbol I'd been drawing. "Just a little artwork." I flashed my pages to the group.

Carter hitched up his pants. "Well, how was I supposed to know? She sits over there, all quiet. A flipping null," he mumbled.

With an expression of faint disappointment, Dr. F. turned back to the group. "I think that's all for today. Next week, let's try to come up with some ways to express ourselves so that everyone here feels safe, okay?"

Shuffling ensued as they hauled their chairs back to the long conference table by the wall. As they trailed out the door, Deon moved toward me.

"Hey."

He'd never said hello to me before, let alone singled me out for conversation. I stood and slung my rose gold Tory Burch bag over my shoulder. "Hey."

"Are you getting a tattoo or something?" He gestured toward my notebook.

"Why?"

"I've seen that design before."

I froze, barely able to breathe. Could Deon hold a key to these symbols? Calm. I needed to act calm and not grab him by the shoulders and shake the information out of him.

"Really? And here I thought I'd found something unique." I flipped open my notebook, showing him what I'd doodled.

He studied the markings. "Well, I've seen it once before. Some girl at The Raven had it tattooed on the palm of her hand."

"Ouch." I feigned a wince. "I was thinking about the forearm."

"Good luck. See you."

"Deon?"

He turned back.

"Do you remember what this girl looked like? I'd kind of like to see how it turned out, find out what tattoo artist she used."

"Some little blonde chick. Don't remember much about her other than the hand."

"And when was this? Was it recently?"

His eyes grew wary. "I don't know. Maybe a few weeks back."

"Who was she with?"

"I…I don't know. I just saw her hand." He turned and hurried out the doorway.

I trotted after him, shoving Dinah out of my way. "Wait. She wasn't a Norm, was she? Was she an Other?" I hissed the question down the hall. Most of the people in this professional building were Norms themselves—dentists, chiropractors, accountants. I didn't want to out the magical community with one careless slipup.

Deon didn't turn around as he disappeared through the double glass doors, but Dinah rounded on me.

"Do not touch me, null." She pointed her finger in my face. "I don't like to be touched."

"You're a healer, Dinah," Carrie said. "That's your whole point in life."

I said nothing and walked past them, barreling through the doors, hoping to catch up with Deon. But as I strode through the parking lot and fumbled with my umbrella, I caught sight of his Nissan sedan turning the corner and zipping onto Harvard Ave. Damn.

But I might have a clue on my hands—if I could find this girl.

Could she have been involved in the murder? Hard to picture a woman having the strength to carve up Jane Doe, rip out her beating heart, and drag her to the river. But Tattoo Girl could have been involved in the ritualistic aspect.

Also, Jane Doe had dirty blonde hair. What if Deon had seen our victim? The killer could had branded her to cover the tattoos. That was an interesting idea.

As I turned to walk to my car, I was brought up short by Gordon the goblin. He stood so close to me that when I glanced down, I caught my own reflection in the gold medallion around his neck. It was almost as big as a hubcap.

He wore a baggy Tommy Hilfiger tracksuit and a black, knitted cap on his oversized head.

Gordon had taken me by surprise. If he'd been an enemy wanting to harm me by non-magical means, he could have easily done so. Between the sound of the rain and my mind's preoccupation with tattoo girl, I hadn't even heard him approach.

"Jeez, Gordon. You scared the crap out of me. How long have you been standing there?" I took a step backward, nearly slipped on a slick spot on the asphalt, but righted myself.

"Call me G-Dog. What's your boon, yo? I need an answer, like now."

I really hated it when people snuck up on me. When a goblin did it, it creeped me out even further.

"I'll call you when I figure it out." I didn't have his number, but so what? I didn't need a boon. What I needed was the identity of Jane Doe, and Gordon couldn't help me with that.

I moved to walk around him, but he stepped in my path. "Don't work that way, mama."

"Well, I don't know what to tell you...G-Dog, but stalking me like we're in a Lifetime movie isn't cool."

His protruding brow wrinkled. "I don't watch that girly shit. Anyway, what'd you do to my moms?"

"What?"

"She can't work her spells no more, which means she can't protect her hoard. She's like, wicked pissed, man. She got a hard-on for you, null. You best watch your back, for reals."

Mama Goblin, what was her name—Matilda?—couldn't perform magic. Only one reason for that: she must still have my blood under her dirty, disgusting claw. Which meant she hadn't washed thoroughly since she scratched me. Eww. I nearly shuddered from revulsion, wondering what else might be crusted beneath those filthy nails. I felt a sudden urge to rip off the bandage Gran had applied this morning and pour an entire bottle of peroxide over the wound.

Gordon just stared at me with those eyes the color of lemon custard and waited. But what could I tell him? I sure as hell didn't want Matilda coming after me, yet I couldn't reveal that my very blood was a nullifying agent.

"Not my problem. Tell your mother if she comes after me, I carry a gun. And I won't hesitate to use it." Big words from a woman who'd just been caught with her metaphorical pants around her ankles. I needed to be more observant of my surroundings.

This time when I began walking toward my car, Gordon didn't move to stop me.

The wind tugged at my ponytail and the rain slashed sideways. The temperature had dropped several degrees in the hour I'd been inside Dr. Fishbein's office. Now, slick spots coated the parking lot.

Tulsans didn't do well with freezing temperatures. Do you turn in to a spin? I could never remember.

As I walked gingerly to my car, careful not to make any fast moves that might land me on my ass, I noticed small icicles hung from the trees lining the street. The bare branches glittered like Christmas ornaments.

Once I hopped into my car and cranked up the heat, I called Cade. I wanted to tell him about the tattooed girl from The Raven. After all, he'd made such a big deal about always calling him first. When he didn't answer, I left a message.

As the car's heater kicked in, I sat in thought. What to do, what to do? Call Mick and suffer Cade's anger, or sit on this key piece of information?

CHAPTER SIXTEEN

I parked outside The Raven, expecting to see several cars in the lot—Mick's employees. He'd invited me to come to the club and interview his staff. But other than a black SUV with tinted windows next to the entrance, the lot was empty.

From the outside, the four-story brick building appeared to be abandoned. Every window had been blacked out. You'd never suspect that inside was a den of iniquity for Others. As long as they followed Mick's rules, they could do as they wished. Not that it was a wild orgy or anything, but public sex wasn't exactly frowned upon either.

When we'd spoken on the phone, he'd been accommodating. Mostly.

"Holly." Mick had answered, saying my name as though it was his favorite flavor. "Two calls in one week. I am honored, darling. Truly."

"I've got a question for you."

"And I may have an answer," he purred. "Or not." His voice alone could make a girl feel a little tingly below the equator. Mick Raven oozed sex. From his looks, to his sensual movements, to his self-assured attitude. Everything about him promised a good time between the sheets. He should have been born an incubus instead of a sorcerer, but maybe it was better for the female population that he hadn't been.

"A girl came into your place with a tattoo on her palm."

"Mmm. Did she? And who is this girl?"

"That's what I want to know."

"Ah, this is related to Cade's murder case, is it not?"

"It is."

"And why is Cade not asking me this himself? He seemed very distraught the last time you called. I don't think he likes the two of us conversing."

"And you enjoyed torqueing him about it, I'm sure."

"Holly, you have the wrong impression of me."

"Do I, though?"

"I don't wish to upset your beloved. He seems so terribly…possessive. I'd find his jealousy most tedious, but if it doesn't bother you…"

McAllister had warned me that Mick would try to put a wedge between us. That either man thought I'd fall for this bullshit was an insult on many levels.

I decided to call Mick's bluff. "I'm guessing you don't personally have the information I need. Why don't you give me the names of your bartenders and servers? I'll contact them directly. That way, I won't have to bother you, and you won't have to worry about making Cade angry."

He laughed—a deep, rich sound that raised the hair on the back of my neck. My nipples may have hardened just a little. Traitors.

"Come to the club, Holly. I'll be waiting."

Now I sat in my car, my windshield wipers slapping at the sheets of rain. As I worked up the energy to get back out in the deluge, the door to The Raven opened and Mick stood framed in the entryway.

I was struck anew by his unearthly good looks. His eyes were the color of bitter chocolate. High cheekbones and a strong jawline gave him an air of haughty nobility, but those carved lips added a dimension of sexual allure that would entice any woman with a heartbeat. Straight black hair framed his tawny face. His dark gray suit was high end, probably custom-made because it fit him perfectly—from his broad shoulders to his trim waist. He paired it with a crisp white shirt, sans tie.

Mick crooked his finger at me and his lips lifted in a slow, seductive smile. Here we go, straight into the lion's den.

I shut off the engine, grabbed my purse and the umbrella. Though I was only eight feet away from the door, I popped it open before climbing out of the car and ran to where Mick stood.

He took my umbrella and stood aside, allowing me entrance into the club. "Come in and get warm." As I walked past him, I got a whiff of cloves and cedar and some intangible male scent.

"Where is everyone?" I glanced around the darkened club. "If you lured me here under false pretenses, Mick, I'll be forced to kick your ass."

The door shut behind him, hiding his expression in the shadowed archway. "Would I do something that underhanded, Holly?"

"Of course you would."

He bent down and whispered in my ear, "Is it that difficult being in my presence? Because I delight in yours."

Mick flirted with me for two reasons: to annoy Cade and to try and get a rise out of me. I didn't take it personally.

"Why did I think this was a good idea?" I muttered.

"Admit it, darling." He straightened. "You like me. Just a bit, yes?"

"So arrogant." Gran swore it was inherent to male sorcerers, buried deep in their genetic code. Maybe she was right, but couldn't they at least try to keep a leash on the cocky attitude?

I rubbed my hands together to generate some warmth and gazed once more around the silent club. It was always strange to be here without topless girls dancing on the daises or see the bar teeming with people.

"Seriously, when's the staff getting here? I assume they really are coming."

He placed his hand on my lower back as he stepped around me and headed behind the bar. "Coffee?"

He was going to play this his way. My impatience would probably only encourage him to keep messing with me. "Yes, please."

"Cream and two sugars." His dark gaze trailed over my face.

He remembered that small detail, which disturbed me more than his flirting. It meant he was paying attention.

"Come. Sit." He poured coffee from a brewed pot under the bar, added two packets of sugar and grabbed a pint of cream from the small fridge.

I trudged toward him and slipped onto a barstool. Tightening my hands around the plain, white mug, the heat seeped into my palms. That felt delicious. I took a sip, letting the strong coffee warm me from the inside, too.

"To answer your earlier question," he said, "my people are on their way. I texted everyone after you called. I am, however, quite shattered that you don't trust me."

"I'm sure you'll get over it."

He flattened his hands on the bar and leaned toward me. "Tell me, have you ever wondered what would have happened if you'd met me first?" For once, there was no trace of amusement in his eyes.

"Met you before Cade, you mean?"

"Mmm hmm."

"Never," I answered in complete honesty.

"I have. I've thought about it quite often, Holly. Things would be different."

"I doubt it. Plus, I'd still nullify you and all this." I jerked my head toward the dancefloor. I'd blown through his soundproofing spell and wards by walking through the door. "I'd have been a novelty for you. Nothing more."

"Perhaps at first." His gaze captured mine. "But there is something here, between the two of us. Deny it all you wish."

I didn't lower my eyes as I set my mug on the bar top. "It's not me you're after. You just want Cade to suffer, because you're still angry with him." Mick had been in love with Shayna, Cade's sister. When she died, Mick blamed Cade and their friendship ended.

At my words, Mick dropped the urbane expression I was used to seeing. Behind it lay an intensity that frightened me.

Those dark eyes hardened, allowing me to see the predator beneath the veil. Then in a blink, he appeared normal again.

"What does this tattoo look like?" That sophisticated, self-assured smile was back in place, as if the change never happened.

I tried to pretend all was normal and, with trembling fingers, pulled out my phone. I attempted to calm myself as I sorted through the pictures, finding one of Jane Doe's palm and handed my phone to Mick.

"Do you know what this symbol is?" he asked, his eyes on the screen.

"No. Do you?"

He placed the phone on the bar. "I've never seen it before." He straightened and crossed his arms. "Does having a symbol tattooed on the palm carry some special significance?"

"I'll have to find this girl and ask her."

"Then that is what we shall do. Send me a copy of that photo."

I did and also showed him a picture of Jane Doe. When he didn't recognize her either, I sat in silence, sipping my coffee. I kept my gaze on the bar, not wanting to catch another glimpse of Mick's scary side.

I'd always sensed that beneath the animosity Cade and Mick had toward one another, their friendship could be salvaged. But after seeing his expression a moment ago, I wondered if he hated Cade. Truly hated him. Yes, he'd helped me save McAllister from a certain death a couple of months back, but Mick could have done it for his own reasons.

As I sat pondering, two men walked into the club, shaking out their umbrellas and propping them in the corner. One had shoulder-length, blond hair and huge gym muscles. The other was leaner with a light brown fade haircut and full beard. The Viking and the Hipster. They each shrugged out of their jackets and stamped their feet on the floor mat.

I watched them closely. Their winces were almost imperceptible, which told me Mick had prepared them for me. When Others were unaware of my presence, they got this funny look on their faces, a cross between pain and confusion. I personally had no idea what it would be like to suddenly lose magical powers, but from what I'd observed it seemed to disorient Others.

"Sam and Titus, this is Holly James." He waved them over.

We forewent the handshakes and nodded in greeting. "Thanks for meeting me today." I had my notebook out and ready. I pointed my pen at the Viking. "Are you Sam?"

He nodded, shoving his hands deep into the pockets of his jeans.

"You're a bartender?"

Again, with the nodding.

"Do you speak?"

"Yeah. Sorry." He shifted his light blue gaze around the bar, finally settling on my knee. Okay, then.

I held out my phone and zoomed in on the symbol in question. "There was a girl in here recently. She had this tattooed on the palm of her hand." I flashed it at both of them.

Hipster…Titus, took my phone, careful not to touch my fingers. "Doesn't look familiar." He held the phone in front of Sam.

"No, I've never seen it."

Mick walked out from behind the bar and sat on the stool next to me. "Thank you, gentlemen." When they continued to stand there, Mick said, "Go find something useful to do."

They walked toward the back of the club and disappeared behind the staff door.

"I don't think Sam likes having a null here."

"Then Sam can go fuck himself. This is my house."

"What is he anyway? Sam."

Mick tilted his head, a slight smile gracing his lips. "Can't you guess?"

"Nope."

"He's a werejag."

"Ah." Jaguar shifters tended to be loners, and they were few in number. "Still, seems an odd job for a werejag. I thought bartenders were supposed to get chatty with the customers."

"They see him as a challenge. Drives the patrons crazy, trying to crack through that stoic veneer. He has no trouble finding companionship every night, though."

A petite woman stepped in next. As she slipped off her coat, she revealed a lithe dancer's body. Which suited her, since she was one of the gogo girls. Her name was Angela, and she'd never seen the mark, nor did she remember the woman in question. She, too, disappeared at the back of the club.

I unsuccessfully stifled a yawn.

"Are you bored with my company?" Mick asked.

I didn't answer, because five more employees trailed in, one after the other. Another bartender and four waitresses. They didn't remember seeing my girl, either.

Once they scattered, I rubbed my forehead. "What about video footage?"

"I only keep it for a week." He slid his arm along the bar, his fingers barely touching the back of my sweater.

I straightened, breaking contact. "She supposedly has blonde hair." If I didn't uncover any clues here, Cade and I could go back and question Deon, maybe get more details or at least a better timeframe of when he saw this mystery woman.

Another server walked through the door. She'd bleached her hair white and added pink streaks around her face. She didn't smile as she approached us, but she didn't throw off any hostile vibes either.

"Cat, this is Holly James."

"Hi." She actually held out her hand, willing to touch me.

I shook with her. "Nice to meet you. Thank you for coming in."

"No problem. I could always use the extra hours." She shot Mick a side-eye.

I flashed my picture. She studied it, squinting her blue eyes. "I don't remember this exactly, but a girl did come in with something inked on her palm."

I tapped down a flash of excitement. I still needed a name.

"She was sitting in my section." Cat pursed her lips, her gaze on the ceiling before glancing at Mick. "Maybe a couple of weeks ago?"

"Was she with anyone you recognized?" I asked.

"No, sorry. I only remember her because of the tat. They fade, you know, when you get them on your palm. The ink won't hold."

"Why is that?"

"The skin grows faster on your palm. It's kind of a waste of money, if you're looking for something permanent."

Mick slid his arm from the bar top and leaned toward Cat. "Would you recognize this woman if you saw her again?"

"Maybe." Cat shrugged. "Probably? A lot of people come through the doors, and I only remember the regulars."

"Thank you," I said. "You've been a big help."

"You're welcome."

Mick stood and buttoned his jacket. "I'll make sure you get more hours in the upcoming weeks."

She grinned. "Thanks, boss." She turned to me and waved. "Nice to meet you." Before she slipped out of sight, she turned back. "Oh, there's one more thing I remember. She was a Norm."

Cat suddenly had Mick's complete attention. Though his posture remained loose and relaxed, I could feel his interest. It was almost tangible. "How can you be sure?"

"I've gotten good at reading the signs. She didn't view me as a snack. And she didn't act all superior, either. Totally a Norm." Then she was gone, disappearing in the shadows of the club.

It finally dawned on me why Cat had acted so casual with me—she was a Norm, too. I should have figured it out sooner. No telltale expression of nausea or panic. No hostility. Just an open, friendly reaction.

"She knows about Others? How did that happen?" I asked.

"She came from an unusual household. Her father sold grain alcohol spiked with fentanyl." Some vamps loved that stuff. Because their systems metabolized alcohol at an incredibly fast rate, vamps discovered that grain alcohol could provide only a short-term buzz. Combine it with synthetic drugs and that high could last three or four hours. From what

I'd heard, most didn't bother, because the feeling was so fleeting. But some got hooked, just like Norm addicts.

"Her father sold exclusively to vamps?"

"Yes. Cat grew up around them. She's quite comfortable with Others."

"But isn't that dangerous? For her I mean, being around all these predators?" A fair segment of the Other population was more monster than not, taking what they needed from humans before discarding them. I could name a dozen types that would look at a human girl and want her for food, sex, or both. What she wanted wouldn't matter.

Mick's eyes glittered dangerously. "Are you suggesting I can't take care of my people?"

Had I dinged his ego? Too bad. "This isn't about you, Mick. Others don't always think about the consequences, especially close to a full moon or when they're hungry. We humans are disposable." I grabbed my purse, tucking my phone inside. "If one of your patrons decides to break your rules, Cat could wind up hurt. Or worse."

His face became very still, very cold, making my stomach muscles quiver a little. I'd never want to be on the receiving end of Mick Raven's wrath, that was for damned sure.

"Do you know why my club is so successful?"

"Because Others can come here and be themselves."

"Yes. And in doing so, they've made an implicit decision to abide by my rules. If they break those rules, they're punished. By me. I don't accept excuses, and I don't give second chances. Make no mistake, I take care of what's mine, Holly." He looked into my eyes, and his own grew so dark, they were almost black.

Was he implying that I was his to protect, or had I misread his comment? Either way, I needed to get the hell out of here.

I slipped into my coat, and my shoulder twinged at the site of the scratch. I slung my bag over my good shoulder and made tracks for the exit. Mick followed, keeping up with me, his quick steps graceful, controlled.

We arrived at the door at the same time, and as he reached past me to open it, his chest lightly pressed against my back.

Even through my sweater and wool coat, I could feel his body heat. That must be a trait all sorcerers shared.

I darted outside and stood under the narrow metal awning and spun to face him. "Thanks for your help."

"Anytime. Day or night, I'm at your disposal."

"If you find out any more about the girl, you'll call Cade, let him know?"

"No, I'll call you."

"Fine. Whatever." I took two shuffling steps backward.

He stepped outside and stood in front of me, his toes bumping mine. "Do I make you nervous, Holly?" He reached out and ran a finger down the column of my throat. "Your pulse is fluttering madly."

I smacked his hand away. "Goodbye, Mick." I turned, determined to shut him down once and for all.

But before I could take a step toward the parking lot, frogs started falling from the sky.

CHAPTER SEVENTEEN

I gasped and jumped back, bumping into Mick. He placed his hands on my shoulders to steady me.

"What the hell?" I whispered.

Frogs—most of them no more than two to three inches long—landed on the ground, my car, the employees' cars, Mick's SUV. A sickening little splat accompanied each one, and there were hundreds. As far as I could see frogs littered the ground, the parking lot, and the road leading to The Raven.

Mick's hands tightened on my shoulders. My scratch screamed in protest and I moved away, absently rubbing the spot as I watched the bodies pile up. Mounds of greenish-brown frogs. The rain continued to pour down, too, coating their bodies, making their skin glisten. Dead shiny frogs as far as the eye could see.

"What's going on?" I asked, turning to glance back at Mick.

With narrowed eyes, he watched them fall. "I've heard of this happening, but I've never seen it in person. Waterspouts, like tornadoes, pick up fish or…frogs, I suppose. The clouds blow them away and gravity does the rest."

"But there are so many."

The employees appeared and huddled behind us, staring through the open door of the club. We watched for more than ten minutes. Finally, the frogs eased off, and only rain fell from the dark gray sky.

"This is some biblical plague shit," Cat muttered.

"No," Mick chided. "Just a natural nuisance."

For several minutes, I remained rooted in place. Every step I'd take would have me stomping on dead frog bodies, squishing them under my boots. My stomach heaved at the sight. Sooner than later they'd start to smell, too.

"Come back inside," Mick said, tugging on my sleeve. "I'll have my people shovel them into a pile."

Numbly, I followed him back into the club. "You read signatures, don't you? Like Cade?"

Mick cocked his head, his eyes narrowed on me. "Why?"

"There's been some weird phenomenon going on. Magical mix ups, spells being infected. I was wondering if the frogs had a weird signature, too. Just covering my bases."

Mick called Sam, Titus, and his busboy Mark to sweep the frogs from the parking lot. "I'll go look once their done. Cade is better at reading signatures. If a spell is strong, I can see vague patterns."

"Thank you, Mick." I parked on the barstool once more and pulled out my phone. I called Cade again, but he still didn't answer. I didn't bother leaving another message. Then Sunny's ringtone sounded. I liked to change it up every once in a while. This month it was Walking on Sunshine.

"Well, I've had to rearrange your schedule. Again. I've gotten four calls in the last two hours. More spells are backfiring."

"Where, exactly?" I asked.

"One close to Tulsa, two in Eufaula and two in Henryetta."

Did that mean the infection was starting to spread? If so, how—and furthermore, why?

"Shoot me the details and I'll see you in the office later."

It took forty-five minutes for the guys to scrape up the frogs and dump them on the far side of the parking lot. Then Mick walked outside. He stepped back in the club a few minutes later, his wet hair plastered against his head. His face was stark and pale. As he approached me, I read the concern in his dark eyes.

He offered his hand, helping me down from the stool. Help I didn't need, but I wasn't going to fight him. "Let's go to my office for a moment."

His employees still lingered near the door, staring out at the mountain of frogs, their expressions ranging from curious to worried.

I trotted up the stairs behind Mick. The second floor of the club held semicircular booths with scarlet curtains that could be closed for privacy. All sorts of naughty things went on up here. I'd witnessed a few myself on previous visits.

I shadowed Mick through the maze of dark hallways leading to his office, where he flipped on the light and made a beeline for the small bar. He poured himself a measure of whiskey in a cut glass tumbler.

The huge room was darkly furnished and masculine, like its owner. A wooden desk dominated the space, and I caught a hint of the thin cigars Mick preferred.

Usually he savored his whiskey, but today he drained the glass in one swallow, then turned to me. "Do you want one?"

"No. Tell me what's wrong."

He poured himself another drink and swirled it in his glass as he prowled around the room. He glided to the seating area in the far corner, then pivoted. "What is going on Holly? You call it an infection, but I saw distinct patterns—" he shook his head—"no, that's the wrong word. Not patterns, really..."

"Was it something like a black and gray scribble?"

He looked up at me, surprise stamped on his face. I had a feeling nothing caught Raven off guard, but this had. "Yes. Exactly. What is it?"

"I don't know. But thank you for checking. I'll add this to the growing list of places that are infected. And you can't cast a spell here in the club or the parking lot. Whatever this is will warp your magic into something bad. Trust."

He stalked toward me. "What does this have to do with the murder Cade is investigating?"

"I don't know. You'll have to ask him."

He glared at me, his face blank, but anger burned behind those dark eyes.

I shrugged my purse up on my shoulder. "I don't know what's going on Mick. If you want particulars about the murder, you'll have to talk to Cade."

"Aren't you also working on this case? From what I've heard, you are sanctioned by the Council."

I shouldn't have been surprised Mick knew. He had his finger on the pulse of the Other world, but still, I was annoyed. "If you already know, don't ask. And even if I am working for the Council, I'm not telling you the details of this case. You want information? Give me the name of the girl with the tattoo on her hand. Now, I have to go."

He set his glass on the desk. "Where?"

"Eufaula and Henryetta. I told you, magic is backfiring. Just promise you won't use your powers when you see those black and gray squiggles." I moved to open the door, but Mick was there in an instant, slamming it shut.

"I'll go with you."

"Uh, no. Not a good idea." Not only would it make Cade see red, but I didn't need backup for my null business.

"I think it is." A hint of anger was still there, glimmering in his gaze, but it was starting to fade.

"Forget it, Raven. All I have to do is show up and the spell is nullified."

"Ah, but you said yourself that I shouldn't attempt magic if the, what did you call it, squiggles, are present."

"True. Whatever is subverting magic in the first place is still in play. And it's un-nullifiable. If that's a word." I was pretty sure it wasn't.

"Why is that? You nullify all magic. Why wouldn't you nullify whatever is causing the magic to mutate in the first place?"

"Because it's not inherently magical?"

"Then what is it?"

"That's the million-dollar question." I stared at his hand still on the door, keeping me locked in the office. "I have to go."

"You will call me after you nullify these infected spells."

I scoffed. "And why would I do that?"

Something in his expression changed, became sharper. "Because I said so."

I shook my head. "I have one bossy sorcerer in my life, and you're not him. If you're worried about this infection spreading, call Cade."

He placed his free hand on my arm. "You are my only concern, Holly. If you are hired to nullify these spells but Others still cannot use magic, you are going to have some very unhappy clients on your hands. They may take their frustration out on you."

I hadn't thought of that but being unpopular with Others was what I did best.

"I'll be fine. And you'll call if you find out the name of the girl with the tattooed hand?"

"I will." His hand slid to the doorknob and he opened it for me. "Be safe, darling."

#

The roads downtown were a mess. Several cars ran off the road because of the frog freefall. I skirted vehicles and took as many backstreets as I could. And yes, I ran over those creatures, their tiny bones crunching under my tires. I turned up the radio to cover the sound.

Once I got out of downtown, the roads cleared. Apparently, the rest of Tulsa remained frog-free. Only parts of downtown had been affected.

I plugged the first address into my GPS. It was near Leonard, not far from the Wylers' model homes. Maybe a couple of miles as the crow flies. The rain slowed me down considerably and taking the back country roads did little to help make up time.

I finally pulled up to a brick ranch surrounded by acres of soybeans. And from what I could tell, the soybeans were dead and black, like the corn at Moonlight Cove.

I knocked on the door and a woman in her forties answered. Her dark hair looked as if she hadn't brushed it today, and she wore sweatpants and a faded gray T-shirt.

"The null. Finally." I heard female voices in the background, screaming at each other. She halfheartedly waved me inside. "Things have been crazy. Come on in."

I walked into the small living room. A recliner had been upended and all the cushions from the sofa hemorrhaged stuffing. I followed the woman to the kitchen but stopped walking when I spotted wet towels covering the tiled floor.

"The washing machine broke and the dishwasher has been spewing water all morning."

"Did you try to fix them with a spell and it just made everything worse?"

She glanced at me, eyes wide. "Yeah. How did you know?"

"What's the story with your crops out there?"

"They're just…dead. Too much rain maybe?" Doubtful.

She scrubbed her pale cheeks with both hands. The sound of girls fighting continued from the hallway to my left. "Come with me."

She sidestepped me and headed toward the voices. She opened the door to a bedroom with matching twin beds. The room was painted hot pink and accented with black and white zebra stripes on the lampshades. Two girls, barely teens by my estimation, were in the middle of a standoff. They stopped screaming when they saw me, both wearing expressions of confusion.

"Hey, it's gone," the woman said, placing a hand on either of their chins. "You're all cleared up." She turned back to me. They hit each other with an acne spell this morning, but it was nothing like I'd ever seen. They were covered in boils. When I tried to reverse the spells it got even worse."

The shorter one jerked her chin from her mother's hand and pointed at her sister. "That's because she started it. Bitch."

The taller one smacked the younger's hand away. "You're the bitch." Then they tried to bespell each other once more. It didn't work, because hello, null in the house.

I slouched against the doorjamb. "Here's the deal, kidlets. You're in an infected magic zone." They, along with their mother, stared at me with unblinking eyes. "That means your crops are dead because you put a spell on them. Spells are backfiring because you're in this zone. That's why your appliances aren't working and your zits turned nuclear. So, no more spells. No more magic. Not until the Council can figure out what's going on. Avez-vous compris?"

Evidently, my poor French wasn't the least confusing part of my speech. Rounding on me, they all began speaking at once.

"What do you mean, infected magic?"

"No more spells. Are you kidding?"

"Can't you fix this?"

"Crops?"

"What are you talking about?"

I held up one hand. "Listen carefully this time. All around town, magic is corrupted, like a computer virus on your laptop, only it's messing up your spells and not your files. Magic is backfiring. So, for the time being, no spells. If you do, and I have to come back out here, it'll cost you double."

The woman threw up both of her hands. "Then what are we supposed to do? How are we going to get along without our magic?"

"Pretend you're a Norm. Think of it as roughing it. But with electricity and indoor plumbing."

CHAPTER EIGHTEEN

Back in the Honda, I glanced at my phone. Still nothing from Cade, which was very annoying. I plugged in the next closest address, which happened to be in Eufaula, not a stone's throw away from Moonlight Cove. Maybe I'd stop by there after I nullified my next two clients to see how Cade was getting along.

I turned on the radio and listened to the news, detailing the strange frog situation. They, too, blamed it on a waterspout tornado. Of course, no radar had picked up that strange weather pattern anywhere in the area. Also, in the news, a weird trend in and around Tulsa had been taking place. At least a dozen unusual animal births had occurred in the last few days. Cats with two faces. Goats with two heads. Conjoined calves. Colts with five legs.

Something strange was moving through my town and I didn't like it. I wondered if it started with the murder, or if the death of Jane Doe just happened to coincide with the magical infection and subsequent natural craziness. I had a feeling they were all intertwined, but how?

After another hour on the road, I made it to the small town of Eufaula. Its only claim to fame was the lake. People came in droves all summer to fish, swim, and ride their wave runners. During the fall, it reverted back to a small farming community.

My GPS led me to yet another farm where the crops were dead—again, soybeans—and the homeowners lives were falling apart around them. I walked in and gave them the same speech. They threatened to call the Council and demanded to know why their magic wasn't working. They also weren't happy that the null they'd hired for five-thousand dollars didn't come with a guarantee for future mishaps. Mick had been right, this could turn ugly.

My next client, Tammy of Tammy's Tresses, kept a shop on the main drag. Tammy was having a bitch of a day. Not as bad as her customers, though. Tam's spells caused one of her clients to lose all her hair, and an older woman now resembled a skunk. Not just her hair, her entire body was covered in black and white fur. Every time Tammy had tried to fix the problem with another spell, it'd made things worse. And to top it off, a skinny teenager now sported the biggest afro I've ever seen. And since her hair was bright red, I could barely stop myself from making Annie jokes.

When they discovered that I simply nullified the spells but couldn't reverse them, they weren't pleased, to say the least. I gave them my little spiel about not casting any more spells and an angry Tammy tried to corner me with a pair of scissors, demanding her money back. But she was no match for me. In one quick move, I knocked the scissors out of her hand and gave her a one-armed shove. Then I hightailed it out of the shop like my ass was on fire.

I hated to admit it, but Mick had been right. People were scared and angry that their magic was on the fritz, and I made an easy target for their frustration.

Once I drove out of town, I pulled over on a side street and checked my phone one more time. Cade had called and left a message:

"Sorry I didn't answer sooner. I'm headed back to Little Rock. Don't know when I'll make it home."

Well, that saved me a trip to Moonlight Cove.

#

Henryetta, Oklahoma used to be known for its coal mines, but since those closed down long ago, its main draw was the addiction rehab facility and the bull riding school. I was sure there were other things the town was known for, but as I skirted Lake Henryetta for my next appointment, all I knew was that it didn't have a Starbucks, and I was in dire need of some caffeine.

Lake Henryetta had no shoreline—only trees circling the reservoir. About a mile from the north-eastern edge of the water, I made a turn onto Juniper Road—a winding, two-lane county highway that led me past trees and more trees, until I finally stopped at a house sitting far back from the road. I turned in blind faith, trusting the car's satnav wouldn't lead me astray.

Finally, I spied a log home sitting on a summit, looking down over the trees to the lake below. Not a new, fancy log cabin either. This thing could have been built by the Sooners themselves.

An old woman waited on the porch. Wrapped in a chunky sweater, she wore a black broomstick skirt and a pair of cowboy boots that were so shabby, I knew they must be comfortable.

With my trusty umbrella protecting me from the rain, I walked to the bottom porch step and took her in. Time and life had carved deep crevices into her tanned skin, crisscrossing at points near her eyes, on her cheeks and chin. Her lips puckered inward, as though she'd been sucking on something sour for the last fifty years. Thick, white hair fell past her waist in a braid. As we stood there, she took my measure, too.

"So, you're the fancy null that's costing me a fortune." She talked through her nose in a scratchy voice that reminded me of tree branches scraping a tin roof.

"Yes, ma'am."

"Don't ma'am me. Call me Mary, if you need to call me anything at all. My spells ain't working right. C'mon in." She turned and stomped to the screen door, then disappeared inside the house.

I've never understood the appeal of log cabins. So much wood everywhere—ceilings, walls, floors. Although Mary had added touches of color by throwing patchwork quilts over every available surface and covering the floor with handmade rag rugs. The tiny space seemed homey.

She stood at the small kitchen stove with her back to me. "Want some coffee?"

"I'm fine, thanks." She ignored me and thrust a chipped mug into my hands. As I peered into the cup, I noted a lack of cream. I took a sip and nearly sputtered. What had she used instead of coffee beans—ashes?

"Too strong for you, girlie?" She wheezed out a laugh and took a seat in the rocking chair near a wood burning stove. "Sit down, already."

I wasn't up for a social visit. I still had one other client in town. Plus, the cabin smelled strongly of frankincense and eucalyptus. Probably some concoction she'd mixed up for arthritis. I'd never been a fan of either scent.

"Would you mind telling me what happened to your spells?" I kept hold of the mug and parked myself on the green, threadbare velveteen chair.

"Had to light the fire myself this morning. The spell I used last night didn't work." She rocked back and forth, staring at me with clear, brown eyes.

"And you didn't perform a new spell to fix it?"

She huffed out a breath. "If the first spell didn't work, why would the second one? Besides, I can feel a shift. Something's changed." She swiped her tongue across one bony fingertip then held it up, as if to sense which direction the wind was blowing. "There's an imbalance." With that one finger still in the air, she sipped her coffee, but her gaze remained on me. "I heard about you from some folks up in Tulsa. Figured you could fix my problem."

"Well, all of your spells are nullified, but you won't be able to use your magic until the Council gives the okay. You're right. Something is infecting magic, and even I can't fix that."

"Maybe you're not supposed to." She set down her mug and leaned forward, placing her hands on her knees. "Anyway, girlie, the Council don't have no authority over me. I'm not just a witch, I'm the daughter of a medicine woman. I'll know when my magic is working again."

"Cherokee?"

She nodded. "Kituwah clan on my mother's side. My father was an earth witch. He came to the New World before the rest of 'em." New World? This woman sitting before me was possibly several hundred years old. My null mind couldn't fathom it, living that long, trying to keep pace with all the changes. Maybe that's why she stayed in an ancient log cabin. At least it was familiar.

"Have you ever encountered anything like this—magic mutating, spells backfiring?"

"My people have many stories of magic turning on itself. Are they true—who knows? I ain't never encountered nothing like this myself, though. But nothing is new. All that happens now has happened before. That, too, is the way it should be." She leaned back, her shoulders falling as she rocked in the chair.

Okay, then. I stood and placed my mug on a rickety side table. "Well, nice meeting you. Take care."

She didn't stand as I made my way to the door. Before I walked out, she called to me. "Girlie. I saw you in my dream. What you're looking for—only you can find it. Oh, and watch out for wild animals. They wear two faces." She started laughing again, that wheezing sound like air seeping out of an inner tube.

Not helpful, but then the old ones often weren't. So many memories, so much history to retain—it could drive a person a little batty.

"Thanks."

My next stop was an apartment complex close to an independent coffee shop. I grabbed a macchiato and let it cool in the car while I met with my client, a fairly weak diviner. When he tried to scry for his missing car keys this morning, his crystal took on a life of its own. His face looked like it had gotten into a fight with a feral cat—and lost. Scratches and gouges dotted his cheeks and forehead.

It took me longer to explain why he needed to refrain from using any magic than it took me to walk up the three flights of stairs to his apartment.

"I don't understand."

"Just don't use magic until you hear from the Council."

"But…"

I flew out the door before he could ask any more questions. Not only was I tired of giving the same speech, I didn't have any answers. I had no idea why everyone's spells backfired. And why in Henryetta all of the sudden? Was the infection spreading? If the murder had been the catalyst, how did that explain the model homes or the soybean farm? What was the link between these places? Maybe if I could figure that out, I could stop it from spreading further.

I headed back to Tulsa, and along the way, stopped at a convenience store to grab a map of Oklahoma. Then I headed for the office.

When I entered, I nearly tripped over another five-gallon bucket near the door. "Sunny."

She stopped typing and glanced up at me. "What?"

"How many leaks do we currently have?"

"Eight if we count the toilet."

"Why wouldn't we count that one?" I sidestepped the bucket and propped my umbrella against the wall.

"Because it's leaking from the bottom. I think there's a broken gasket."

"So, there's water all over the bathroom floor?"

"I've put down paper towels to soak it up. But you'll have to use the facilities at Bill's office, next door."

I stared at her for a full thirty seconds, my mouth wide open. Then I snapped, "Are you shitting me right now? This is not acceptable."

"Language."

Language my ass. She was more stubborn than I was. Sunny would rather drown in here than admit I might be right, that we needed a new place. "Has Dean Wyler called with any office listings?"

"No. He said he'll discuss listings at the cocktail party tonight."

Oh, God. I'd forgotten about that. Before I could come up with an excuse to get out of it, she held up one hand.

"Don't even start. I'll look at offices with you, but in return, you have to go to the party with me."

I blew out a breath, my shoulders hunching forward as I angled my chin toward the ceiling. The water-stained, moldy ceiling. "Fine. But I'm not sitting in this cesspit one more minute. Get your stuff. We'll go to my house. But it's only temporary. Got it?"

#

I taped the map to the wall in the entryway. Sunny sat in the kitchen, doing whatever it was that required so much typing. I took out a red pen and circled the towns of Leonard, Eufaula, Midnight Cove, and Henryetta, finding no discernable pattern. With the exception of Leonard, they were all close to large bodies of water.

Leonard was nothing but farmland. But it did sit smack dab in between the Arkansas River and Bixhoma Lake, only half an hour's car ride from each. If the Wylers had their way, soybeans and corn would give way to mini mansions and strip malls, making Leonard one of the swankiest bedroom communities near Tulsa. But as of now—farmland.

All of the sites were within an hour or two of Tulsa. I stared at the map, hoping to get a spark of inspiration, but nothing came to me. It was pretty damned frustrating.

I gave up on the map and fired up my laptop instead, intent on searching for tattoo girl. According to the Google gods, there were twenty-five known tattoo shops in Tulsa and neighboring towns. I started in alphabetical order, and after I called two shops it was clear I'd have to take a field trip.

Surprisingly, it was only two in the afternoon. If Sunny and I split up, each taking half the shops, it might be doable.

I poked my head in the kitchen. "You up for a road trip?"

She'd made herself at home on the kitchen island, her laptop open to a spreadsheet. "No. I'm busy."

"Haven't you ever wanted to see the inside of a tattoo parlor?"

She turned to look at me over her shoulder. "It's never crossed my mind."

Changing the subject, I asked, "What are you wearing to the Wylers' shindig tonight?"

Her eyes flared wide. "What do you mean? What's wrong with what I have on?"

So, so many things. I didn't even know where to start. "Um…I probably have something you can borrow. Something a little, you know…" I wiggled my fingers.

"No, I don't know," she said, her spine stiffening.

"Something less"—my hands fluttered over my body—"nun like?"

Her face brightened, flushing red all the way to the tips of her ears. "There's nothing wrong with my clothes."

"If you say so. I just thought since Dean Wyler was going to be there, you'd want to make an effort to jazz things up a little."

Her eyes twitched and narrowed, scaring me a little. "An effort?" she bit out the words. "You mean conform to current fashions, promoted by companies which make their money by chipping away at women's self-esteem? The same people who design garments created for obsolescence, not only pressuring women to keep up with the latest trends, but also needlessly destroying our environment in the process? Is that the effort you're talking about?" She was now standing, her hands in fists at her sides, panting with righteous indignation.

"That's a hard no, then? Okay. I'm going tattoo shopping." I backed up all the way to the front door, her eyes still searing through me. I grabbed my purse, coat, and umbrella, then slammed out the front door.

Jeez. I'd only asked a simple question.

After I shrugged into my coat and flicked open my umbrella, I hauled ass out to the car. Four tattoo shops were within a six-mile radius of my house. Who knew?

I headed to Inktastic first. Three artists—all men and all heavily tatted—sat in the shop. Only one worked on a client. I showed them the picture from my notebook, the one I'd doodled earlier at Dr. Fishbein's. None of them recognized it.

I headed to the next place. And the next. After number seven, I started to grow a little weary. Since I hadn't stopped to eat all day, my stomach wasn't very happy either.

I grabbed sandwiches from a deli, feeling defeated. What had I accomplished today? I'd discovered a woman might have had a hand tattoo that matched a symbol on Jane Doe. And I'd made Sunny froth at the mouth. Not many checks in the success column.

By the time I got home, it was close to five in the afternoon. The gray clouds brought on an early dusk, filling my living room with shadows. The only light came from the kitchen, where Sunny worked.

I dropped a turkey and cheddar on whole wheat in front of her as a peace offering. "Thought you might be hungry."

She didn't look at me as she unwrapped her sandwich. I grabbed plates, napkins and bottles of water from the fridge. I set a bag of chips on the island next to her computer.

"I didn't mean anything earlier, Sunny. I'm sorry if I hurt your feelings."

"I may have overreacted—a bit." With her head down, she flashed a glance at me and shoved a piece of bread in her mouth. Then she mumbled something unintelligible.

"What about a donkey burro?"

She sighed, wiping her hands on a paper napkin. "Do you have a dress I can borrow?" She kept her eyes glued to her sandwich. "Nothing flashy, just…"

I was so surprised, I nearly fell off my stool. And though part of me—okay, most of me—wanted to tease her, I refrained. "Of course. You can go through my closet after we eat."

My stomach let out a protracted growl as I took a bite of ham and Swiss. Then the doorbell rang. With my mouth full, I jogged to the door and glanced out the peephole.

Standing on my porch was Abby. The perky vampire.

CHAPTER NINETEEN

With her hands full of shopping bags, she threw herself at me—wrapping her arms around my neck, knocking me in the head with a Forever 21 sack. "Holly! I've missed you, girl." She sauntered into the living room, tossing her purchases onto the sofa.

She peeked in the kitchen. "Hey, I remember you. It's Stormy, right?"

"Not even close," Sunny said.

"Damn. I'm really bad at names." Abby turned back to me. "I'm loving this weather. I don't have to wait until full dark to come out and play."

I stood at the open door, hoping Abby would take a hint. I liked her well enough—for a leech—but now was a bad time. "Abs, what are you doing here?"

"Huh. Isn't it obvious?" She plucked a red dress from one of her sacks and held it in front of her. "Do you know how long it's been since I could try on clothes and actually see how they fit? I mean, to see my own reflection is, like, beyond. You know?"

Before her transition to an undead life of blood sucking, Abby had been a sorority girl. With long, straight blonde hair, a shiny smile, and a pair of knockers as big as her grin, she looked every bit the stereotype.

Since baking in the sun was no longer an option, Abby opted for a spray tan, and she liked to show it off by wearing as little fabric as possible. Even though the weather had dipped to the freezing point, she didn't wear a coat over her short, tight blue knit dress that, in reality, was probably a sweater. The V-neck showcased her boobs and the hem barely covered her biscuit. She paired it with a pair of black thigh high boots.

Sunny stood in the kitchen doorway, arms crossed, her brows so low they disappeared behind her frames. "We're kind of busy. It's not a good time for a visit."

Abby blinked rapidly and stuck out her lower lip. "Oh. Okay." She slowly gathered up her bags leaning over the sofa, and in the process, mooned Sunny and me. When she straightened, she pulled her bags to her chest. "Sorry I bothered you."

"Wait." It was out of my mouth before I could think twice. "You can stay." Besides, now might be a perfect time to quiz Abby about why Master Sebastian kept hounding me. While she was distracted, staring at herself in the mirror, I could subtly ask questions.

Sunny just glowered. If she kept pulling that face, she was going to get premature wrinkles. Though knowing her stance on the cosmetic industry, she wouldn't care.

"Actually," I said "we're going to a cocktail party tonight. Sunny needs to try on dresses, too. We could always use a second opinion."

"I don't need another opinion, thank you very much."

My eyes widened and darted to Abby. "Go look through my closet. Find something and try it on." Sunny must have gotten the message because she flung her arms to her sides like a surly teenager and stalked down the hallway.

Once she left, Abby grabbed a bottle of wine from her leather hobo bag. "She's not a people person, is she?"

"She's more of a money person."

Abby held up the bottle. "Drinks are on me." I remembered the brand from high school. Strawberry wine that tasted like Kool-Aid. Abby really was perpetually locked in post-adolescence. "Glasses?"

"Sure." I dodged into the kitchen and grabbed a couple of water tumblers. Strawberry alcohol wasn't worthy of anything with a stem. "If you want to use the bathroom to change, go ahead." I returned to the living room to find Abby standing naked, pawing through a pile of clothes.

I glanced away. "Okay. You're good with just putting it out there, huh?"

From the corner of my eye, I watched her shimmy into a dress. "Listen, when you become a vampire you don't just go on a liquid diet. Everything changes. I was never shy to begin with, but when I turned, I became free of, you know, morals and stuff. You can look now."

I glanced over. The red dress was what I could only describe as ho-rific. The plunging V-neck barely covered her tits, and the slit up the side revealed her hipbone.

"Yikes, Abs. Do you want to get arrested for indecent exposure?"

She laughed, a girlish giggle with an edge. "This gets me noticed."

"I'll bet it does. I'm sure you'll find lots of victims wearing that." Vamps were only supposed to take from willing donors. But because they could mind fuck a Norm with one glance, consent was dubious.

"Yeah, but most of the men who want this, aren't victims." She ran a hand over the side of her breast, down to her hip. "A lot of the people I meet are pretty cruel. Because I dress like this, men think they can do whatever they want to me. I get off on showing them how wrong they are." Her smile was straight up menacing. Combined with the frightening intensity in her cold blue eyes, I finally saw the truth of who she was. I kind of wished I hadn't.

I'd been clinging to the illusion that because I nullified Abby, she was harmless. But she was used to blood and violence. The sorority girl veneer made me forget that.

Then I thought back to Cade's murder victim. Some sicko had done whatever he wanted with Jane Doe, assaulting her, ripping her heart from her chest. The world was full of predators. And one of them was standing in my living room, flashing her tits at me that very moment.

"What's wrong, Holly?"

I blinked, pulled my gaze away from her outfit. "Where do you meet these cruel people?"

She sank into the chair across from me and poured wine into both glasses, handing me one. "Everywhere. Could be the nice man who goes to church every Sunday but likes to cruise the streets on Saturday nights. Or the boring college kid behind me at the coffee shop at two in the morning. He won't stop staring at my tits and he doesn't mind that his boner is on display. He wants me to notice."

I digested that for a minute. "How do you know he'd hurt you, and he's not just a creeper?"

"I can tell the difference. It's in their eyes." She tilted her head to the side, appearing far older and wiser than a college-aged girl. "Guys think I'm a hooker, and hookers are little more than sex dolls. Some of these guys I meet in clubs…like, I can't tell you the number of times an asshole has tried to slip a drug in my drink. Fortunately, I can smell that shit. Hey, why do you want to know so much about my food all of a sudden?"

"Just curious. Wondering how many freaks are lurking on the streets of Tulsa."

"More than there should be." She took a long sip of wine, then set her glass on the coffee table. "I'm going to check out this outfit. Bathroom's down the hall?"

"Yeah." I curled up in a chintz chair near the fireplace and sipped the wine, wincing. God, that was disgusting. I set it aside and went to the bedroom to check on Sunny. I knocked on the door and slipped inside.

"Hey!" She held a dress in front of her in an attempt to cover up her white bra and panties. "Turn around."

I gave her my back and rolled my eyes. Sunny thought she was a virgin from the 1800s, and Abby acted like a stripper in dire need of a pole. In my opinion, they both should meet somewhere in the middle.

"Did you find anything you like?" I asked.

"Maybe. Zip me up."

"You mean, I get to peek at your bra strap? I don't know if I can stand the excitement."

"Shut up."

I turned around and zipped her into a simple black sheath dress. "Spin. Let me see the front."

Looking uncomfortable in her own skin, she slowly turned. The dress had a high collar but was sleeveless. Since Sunny was a few inches taller than me, the hem hit her at mid-thigh. I stared for a moment, made a twirling gesture with my finger. She slowly spun around.

"That looks really nice, Sunny."

She peered over her shoulder. "It's not too revealing?"

"Well, I can see your elbows, you dirty little slut." I moved toward her. "What about your hair? Going to leave it in a ponytail?"

One brow shot upward. "What is wrong with my hair the way it is?"

I held up both of my hands. "It was just a question. Stop snapping at me."

"Sorry. Why did you let Abby stay?" she whispered. "Are you hoping she'll talk about Master Sebastian?"

"Naturally."

Abby called through the door, "Knock, knock." Then she strode into the room, wearing a tight black halter top. The leather booty shorts didn't begin to cover her ass. "What do you think?"

"Those shorts are about two sizes too small for that butt," I said.

"Perfect!" Abby straightened, and tilting her head, glanced at Sunny. "That looks good. But you need to lose the underwear. Visible panty lines, girlfriend."

Sunny's face turned the color of the strawberry wine I'd tried to drink. "I'm not going anywhere without underwear."

Abby sighed. "Can't you wear a thong or something? I just bought a couple. Let me grab one."

Sunny opened her mouth to protest, but Abby had already left the room. So she turned on me. "I'm not wearing it!"

I shrugged. "Wear what you want." I left the room, shutting the door behind me and met Abby in the hallway. She held up a lacy G-string.

"I don't think she'll wear it."

Abby shrugged, moved past me to open the bedroom door, and threw them inside—like a zookeeper would throw raw meat into a tiger's cage.

"Stay out," Sunny yelled.

Back in the living room, Abby sorted through her clothes. "I love being able to see myself. I totally forget how hot I really am. We should do this once a month."

"Sure."

She glanced up at me, her pale brows raised. "Really?"

"Why not?" It was two hours or so out of my life and staring at her own reflection made Abby happy.

"Awesome." She grinned and sorted through the mound of clothes, picking out a scrap of material in Barbie pink.

"Hey, Abs. What does Sebastian want with me?"

Then the smile slowly fell from her lips. "I don't know." When she noted my expression of disbelief, she shook her head. "That's the honest truth, Holly. But I will tell you this: you can't put him off forever. He always gets what he wants. And he wants you." She shoved her pile of clothes out of the way and sat down on the sofa. "Things are a lot different now that he's in charge."

"How so?"

"We always called Monty Triple M—middle management material. He didn't have any kind of vision. He basically kept things running from day to day. The Master has plans. He doesn't share them with anyone, but it's obvious, you know? Like, he's ambitious."

Monty Ridgecliff had been Master Sebastian's personal assistant. He'd also killed his fellow vamps and used their blood in a spell to keep Sebastian in a mystical coma for years. The vamps thought the Master was aloof, a loner who'd isolated himself. A myth Monty encouraged. In reality, Ridgecliff had staged a coup. He couldn't take Sebastian's territory on his own, so he stole it.

When I nullified the spell that kept Master Sebastian contained, Monty had warned me that I'd unleashed an unspeakable evil on the world. Had Monty been telling the truth? Maybe Sebastian was a threat to us all.

"The Master has started a bunch of new businesses, giving us jobs and a new purpose," Abby said.

"Legit businesses?"

"Some are more legit than others." She tossed a blonde strand of hair over her shoulder. "A lot of sex stuff. He's opening a strip club next month. Guess who's going to be manager?" She raised her hand. "And he's got a webcam business up and running. He's bought property to set up bars and clubs—stuff like that."

"Webcam business?"

"Sex cam work. You strip down, touch yourself, talk to the loser on the other end of the computer. Easy money. Only one drawback."

"What's that?"

"You can't tap blood from a computer. That's why I like the other businesses. The strip club will be like a fast food buffet. We're all totally looking forward to it."

It was as repellent as it was brilliant. The blood bags, aka customers, would come to vamps willingly and pay for the privilege. The Norms would get their rocks off, the vamps would get dinner for the night.

"Well, congratulations. I guess."

Sunny walked into the room. She wore her usual white blouse and long black skirt. "You must have some idea why Sebastian is obsessed with Holly. If not you personally, then someone in the Master's inner circle. You could find out for us." She perched on the arm of the sofa, her gaze penetrating as she stared at Abby.

Abby waved both hands. "Forget it. I really like you, Holly, but I'm not going to go around sticking my tits in where they don't belong. Everyone is treading very lightly. The Master cleaned house when he came back. Anyone who wasn't completely loyal was killed. He's not exactly trusting after what happened with Monty."

"Monty told me that setting Sebastian free was a mistake," I said. "What do you think?"

"Hmm." Her lips twisted to one side. "He's powerful. And charismatic. He's forced all of us to take part in a blood rite, binding us to him. We're all…united now, in a way we weren't before, you know? As to his motives with you—maybe the Master's just grateful you set him free."

"And maybe he's curious about what else she can do with her power?" Sunny asked. When the chips were down, she always had my back. If that didn't make us friends, it at least made us allies, and I was grateful for her support.

"That's a possibility," Abby conceded.

That's what I'd figured. Sebastian wanted to use me or my blood in his ambitious plans. Well, forget it.

Then a thought occurred to me. "Did he send you here tonight, Abby?"

She licked her lips and stood, began shoving all of her clothes back in the shopping bags. "He suggested I make contact with you." She stopped and glanced at me. "He just wants to talk."

Sure he did. And brownies were harmless fae who only wanted to help with household chores, not feed on human souls. Uh huh.

"I'm not interested, Abs. Not even a little."

"I figured you'd say that."

"Will the Master be angry that Holly turned down his offer to meet?" Sunny asked.

"Well, he's not going to be happy about it." Abby plucked up her hobo bag, holding it in the crook of her arm.

"Is my refusal going to get you in trouble?" I stood, shoved my hands into my jeans pockets. I wasn't thrilled that she'd come here under false pretenses. In fact, I felt like an idiot for believing she wanted to spend a little girl time with me. But I still didn't want her to be punished for my decision.

"He knew the chances of you accepting were slim. But the two of you will have a meeting, Holly. Whether you want it or not."

"Thanks for the warning. And next time, you don't have to bullshit me. Just deliver the message without all the rest."

"I wasn't bullshitting. I like you, Holly. I think in another life, we could have been friends." She gave me one last look under her lashes. "I'm sorry."

CHAPTER TWENTY

When Abby had left, Sunny and I talked about the vampire situation. She agreed with Cade—that the Master vampire was probably interested in using me as a weapon against his enemies—whomever they may be.

Then I'd casually asked if she wanted me to straighten her hair, hoping she wouldn't rip off my head and piss down my neck for even suggesting it. To my utter shock, she agreed. She even let me add a little hint of blush to her cheeks. A day for the record books.

Sunny sat on my bed while I got ready in the master bathroom. We actually chatted like two pals getting ready for a night out. I'm not going to lie—it was a little weird. But nice, too.

"She hurt your feelings, didn't she?"

She was referring to Abby. "Stupid of me, right? Thinking she wanted to come over and do girly things. I should have known better."

"Yes, you should have. You forgot what she is. A user. A liar. She drains people to survive, for goodness' sake."

I reminded myself of that very thing when Abby and I had been chatting in the living room. And I still liked her enough to overlook her true nature. "I guess so." I swiped on a smoky gray eye shadow and blended.

"You, of all people, should remember what she is. What she's capable of, even if you did nullify her. It's not like vampires have a conscience or anything."

Sunny was preaching to the choir. Yet I had brushed off Abby's more deadly traits. She'd been right beside me as I hunted down the Black Magic Murderer. Yes, she'd done so for her own reasons, but I thought it'd bonded us in a way. The truth was, we were two different species, each with our own agenda. I wouldn't forget that again.

After Sunny and I finished getting ready, I offered to drive to the restaurant. She refused and insisted we take her car instead. The problem was she drove like an old lady on her way to Sunday school. An old lady with cataracts.

"What's he like?" she asked, zipping along at fifteen miles under the speed limit.

"Who?"

"Dean Wyler. He sounded very nice when I spoke to him earlier."

"He's okay." I scrolled through my phone as I answered her, hoping Cade had sent a text. Unfortunately, he hadn't.

Sunny took her eyes from the road long enough to shoot me a glance. "Look, I know you didn't want to come tonight, but it will be good for business. Besides, we can always charge Norms more since they're so clueless."

"You're an extortionist, you know that? By the way, you'd better have my back tonight. The Wylers think I'm a psychic energy reader. I guess that means I can dispel bad juju?"

"No problem. I'll spread the word. I have a handful of business cards in my purse."

As she drove—ever so slowly—my thoughts turned back to the murder. Sunny didn't have many friends. Hell, I didn't either, but if one of us went missing, someone would notice, right? "Cade's murder victim is a Jane Doe."

"Uh huh."

"I'm just thinking out loud here, but why hasn't anyone reported her missing? A friend, a relative, a landlord? Even if she was a runaway or a prostitute, which is what I'm thinking is probably the case, she had to have at least one person who cared about her."

"They're called sex workers."

"When did you get so politically correct?"

"The title encompasses a wide range of activities," she said. "Educate yourself." Well, snap.

"All right, if she was a sex worker, the killer could have paid her to show up for his little party, but instead drugged and killed her. Herb Novak found ketamine in her system."

Sunny turned on her blinker two miles before our exit. "How did she die anyway?"

"If I tell you, you have to swear—"

"Please. Anything you tell me in confidence, I'll keep to myself. We are partners, after all. So, how did she die?"

"The killer performed some kind of ritual. Then he cut her open and ripped out her heart."

Even in the darkness, I watched as Sunny paled. "That's... Holy cow. Does this have anything to do with Moonlight Cove?"

"I don't know. But Jane Doe belonged somewhere. She had a family, even if she was estranged from them."

"Ah. You're equating this girl to your mother." She said it matter-of-factly, without any emotion, in her typical blunt, Sunny fashion.

I turned and looked out the window as she exited the freeway. "Yeah." Jane Doe wasn't disposable. She'd been a person who had feelings and thoughts and troubles, just like the rest of us.

The key was finding the girl with the symbol tattooed on her palm. I was certain of it. Tomorrow, I'd hit the rest of the tattoo parlors.

Sunny parked close to the Asian fusion restaurant downtown. The raining frogs hadn't made it to the Blue Dome District. I was glad I didn't have to see their tiny flat corpses again.

Inside the restaurant, the smell of garlic and curry hit my nose. We gave the maître d' our names and he smiled, then herded us to the coat check. Apparently, the Wylers had rented out the restaurant for the evening.

As we walked deeper into the room, candles glowed softly from every surface and vases of blue and purple flowers decorated the tall, round tables. Waiters circulated, carrying trays of hors d'ouvres. Another offered us flutes of champagne.

Sunny took one without a murmur. And she wasn't a drinker, so she really must have been nervous.

"Swanky," I whispered.

"Well, Dean Wyler is one of the top ten realtors in the state. He's number six, actually. Of course it's swanky."

I was beginning to suspect Sunny might have more than a little crush. Either that, or she really admired his business acumen. Perhaps for her it was one and the same. Dean Wyler made his money by working hard for it, which Sunny appreciated more than any other quality.

Groups of people clustered around the tables, quietly talking. The only person I recognized was Stan McNeil, the Glen Falls developer. He stood across the room chatting with a woman in red. I wondered if she was his wife. I cast my mind back. He hadn't been wearing a wedding ring the other day, but then neither had Aaron. Men on construction sites often didn't. In a suit and tie, Stan looked different tonight, handsome almost.

Sunny and I stood near the entrance. I sipped my champs, and she clung to her flute with a death grip. Eventually, Amanda and Aaron Wyler approached from the back of the room and made their way toward us.

Amanda had smoothed her hair back on the either side of her head and fluffed it up on the top. Her makeup looked darker, more dramatic than the day I met her. She wore a white silk blouse and a full skirt of black taffeta. Très chic. Aaron was dapper in an expensive suit, and while it looked good on him, he seemed more comfortable in faded flannel.

"Holly!" Amanda said, a huge smile on her pretty face. "I'm so glad you could make it." She gave my cheek an air kiss, as though we were old friends.

"Amanda, this is my business partner, Sunny Carmichael. Sunny, Amanda and Aaron Wyler."

"Lovely to meet you, Sunny." Amanda turned to me, placing her hand on my elbow and steered me toward the nearest group of people. "Everyone's been dying to meet you. I've told them all about your gift."

Okay. No pressure.

Amanda introduced me to the first table. I couldn't remember names, and I probably wouldn't remember most of their faces after tonight, either.

"Nice to meet you." I tried for the serene smile of a woman who waved sage sticks all day.

Sunny stood behind me, peeking over her shoulder, no doubt hoping to catch sight of dreamy Dean. She was supposed to be my stalwart companion this evening, swayed by nothing but the smell of a client's desperation. But as Amanda and I moved on to the next group of people, Sunny didn't follow. I was on my own with this crew.

A heavy woman to my left, wearing a silky shawl over her jacket, asked about chakras. One of hers was blocked, apparently. She placed a hand near her diaphragm, and everyone around the table stared at me, waiting.

Shit. I didn't know jack about chakras. They could ask me about herbs or wood sprites or why you should always leave a saucer of milk in a newly planted garden. Pixies loved it and would add their blessing to the crops. But chakras? Ugh.

I set my glass down, and winging it, covered the hand on her belly with my own. "Most of the time our chakras are blocked because of stress, fear, or pain." Seemed like as good a guess as any. I lowered my voice and used a soothing tone I heard so many times from Dr. Fishbein, but I felt like an ass with each word. "What is causing your block isn't from the outside. It's from the inside. You're blocking yourself." I looked deep into her eyes. "Stop reacting out of fear."

She gasped. "I can't believe you just said that. You're absolutely right. I've been so wound up in fear that it's paralyzing me. Thank you, Holly."

I removed my hand and gave her what I hoped was a reassuring smile. "Of course." I tried to sip my champagne, when I really wanted to drain the glass and grab another.

Talk around the table resumed, mostly about their various work situations. I tuned it out and checked for Sunny. She stood on the fringes of the room, stroking her hair. A moment later, Dean walked by. He turned that megawatt smile in her direction, and I swear, Sunny actually blushed.

I refocused on Amanda as she ushered me to an attractive woman in her fifties—the lady in red Stan had been talking to earlier. Senator Barbara Tate held court in the far corner of the room. I didn't know who she was until Amanda whispered her name and title with the same reverence I reserved for people like Michael Kors or Tory Burch. When there was a lull in the conversation, Amanda introduced us. "Holly, this is State Senator Barbara Tate. Barb, this is Holly Black. She's a psychic."

Barbara's eyes widened. She looked every bit the seasoned politician: straight brown hair with tasteful caramel highlights, tailored red suit, subtle makeup. The only thing that stood out was her large-ish nose. "Really? A psychic? How terribly interesting. So, tell me, Holly. Am I going to win my next race?"

I smiled politely, even though her tone was a little derisive. "I think you'll do just fine."

"You are registered to vote, aren't you?" Everyone around her politely laughed. Then she dismissed me, her interest focusing on someone new.

After about an hour of mind-numbing chitchat, I wound up passing out a few cards, and completely lost sight of Sunny.

Finally, Aaron and Amanda came together in the center of the room. Aaron clinked his glass to get everyone's attention. "Thank you all for coming tonight." He glanced down at Amanda with pride. "We have an important announcement to make."

"You're pregnant," a woman yelled from the other side of the room.

Amanda smiled and held up her glass of champagne. "No, thank God." She shook her head, her diamond earrings sparkling in the candlelight. "As you all know, work has been booming this year. Well, I recently took a call from the Hearth and Home Network. After several screen tests and focus groups...they're giving me my own show." She waited until the applause died down. "It's only for eight weeks, but if I receive good audience response, they'll pick it up for a regular season."

As everyone around me cheered, I tried to remember what the hell Amanda did for a living. I thought back to our first meeting in the model home. Dean had said something about staging the houses and antiques. I remembered now, something about a sideboard. Right, she refurbished antiques.

Aaron raised his glass. "Here's to my wife. She makes the world a more beautiful place—in every way."

We all toasted, and as I glanced around the room, I noted Dean's grim expression. For once, he wasn't smiling. Maybe he thought Amanda's new job would take focus away from the family business. Or maybe he wished he had his own show, instead of weekly installments on the local morning news?

After another round of speeches and toasts from all of Amanda's friends, I excused myself and went to find the restroom, but Dean stepped in my path. For once, Sunny wasn't next to him.

"Holly, how are you? Good of you to come tonight. I know it was short notice." The smile was back in place. Like that bleak expression I'd witnessed had never crossed his face.

"Thank you for having me. So, how are the model homes?"

"We're in the process of fixing them. Whatever you did worked. We haven't had any more strange activity."

"I'm glad."

"How…how did you know what to do?"

"Since no one in my family has my gift, I had to read everything I could on the occult and ghost energy, how to break it and keep it from harming people." I clutched my purse as I spit out the lie, hoping it sounded plausible.

"You know, I've experienced some very weird stuff in my life. After a while, you either decide you're crazy or you start to believe. I'm not crazy. And I think you have a gift, Holly. The atmosphere in those homes changed after you'd been there. I could feel it. Sometimes I just wish I could see it with my own eyes."

If he really could sense ghosts, then Dean may have a little bit of magic in him. Not unheard of. Others and Norms had been known to knock boots every once in a while. Sunny's immune status was a prime example. But not all offspring from such unions inherited magic. Some had muted powers. Sometimes, those powers trickled down through the generations.

"Be careful what you wish for, Dean. There are scarier things than ghosts. If you go looking, you might find trouble. The kind that won't leave you alone." That was the most honest thing I'd said all night.

I patted his shoulder as I walked past and headed down a long hallway to the ladies' room, where I checked my phone in vain. Still no message from Cade. I was starting to get worried.

After I washed my hands and touched up my lipstick, I left the room and almost ran smack dab into one of the three or four doctors I'd met this evening. I remembered this one because he was a rare breed—a plastic surgeon whose face appeared natural. Well, a little better than natural, actually. I couldn't tell his age. Thirties? Forties? His skin didn't look puffy from fillers or taut from being stretched. A few gray strands sifted the edges of his thick, dark hair. He'd brushed it away from his face, letting it flow back. Not too fussy, not too casual.

Dr. What's-his-name was a walking advertisement for his brand. Just one thing seemed out of place. His eyes.

I knew a predator when I saw one. And Dr. Plastic betrayed himself. Eyes so dark blue they were almost black. Like a photo taken of space, that vast endless wasteland of distant icy stars—that's what his eyes reminded me of. Cold. Unearthly.

"Miss James. I was hoping to speak with you." He didn't wait for me to answer, but instead, took my arm and guided me to the bar at the back of the room. "Let me get you a drink." He waited until I hopped up on a stool, then took a seat next to mine, his jacket sleeve brushing my arm.

I ordered a sparkling water with lemon. He ordered whiskey—top shelf.

While we waited for our drinks, I studied him from the corner of my eye. He obviously wanted something. Still, I felt the need to fill the awkward silence.

"So, how do you know the Wylers?"

"Through Amanda. She's decorated all my homes, my office, too. According to her, it's all still a work in progress. She's always tinkering with different pieces, swapping out older furniture for something new."

The bartender placed our drinks in front of us and moved on. As Dr. Plastic tapped his glass against mine, I said, "I'm sorry. I've forgotten your name."

He smiled. It didn't reach those cold, distant eyes. "I imagine so. Together, we're all a bit much. I'm Dr. Peter Everett."

"My apologies, Dr. Everett."

"No apologies needed. Call me Peter. I'll call you Holly. See how friendly we can be?" What an odd thing to say.

He looked me straight in the eye. "I heard about you through a friend. I'm the one who recommended you to the Wylers. It is real, what you do. Isn't it?"

I needed clarification on what he was asking. "Clearing bad energy?" I took a sip of water.

"No. Banishing ghosts."

I did, technically. "Yes, it's real."

"How do you do it?" He squinted, as if trying to work out whether I was a fraud or the real thing.

"I just...set them free." Also true. "They don't want to be here, not really. They're trapped, unable to move on."

"But why?" He leaned toward me. "Why do some linger?" I wondered if he were asking for personal reasons or if this was merely an academic exercise.

"I'm not sure, but I think it has to do with their emotional state when they pass. People who are emotionally tethered to this world tend to stay." At least that was my theory. "Why? Do you have a ghost in your life?"

He leaned back and took a long drink as he traced his finger over the woodgrain on the bar. "We all have ghosts of some kind, don't you agree?" He didn't wait for my answer before carrying on. "Where do they go, once you've freed them?"

"I don't know, Dr. Everett. There are some answers I don't have."

"Peter," he corrected. He exhaled slowly, then drained his glass before glancing at me once more. "This has been very interesting. I'm sure we'll see each other again." He slid off his stool and whipped out his wallet, leaving a fifty on the bar. "I appreciate your talking to me."

Then he walked away, leaving me alone with my own thoughts for a few minutes. Out of all the exchanges I'd had tonight, that had to be the strangest. I wondered who might be haunting the emotionally cold doctor. He didn't ask for a card, so I doubted I'd ever see him again, and that was all right with me. He was kind of off-putting, even a little scary—for a Norm.

CHAPTER TWENTY-ONE

I rejoined everyone in the main room and suffered through more small talk. Across from me, Sunny stuck to Dean Wyler like a barnacle. After another half hour, I finally approached her.

"Do you want me to grab an Uber home?"

"Um…no." Sunny slid a strand of hair behind one ear.

Dean placed his hand on her arm. "I've monopolized you all night. Sorry about that."

"I've enjoyed talking to you. The real estate business is really fascinating." Again, color stained her cheeks a pretty pink, and her eyes sparkled as she gazed up at him. It was sort of sweet.

Sunny nodded at me. "I'm ready to go."

Dean walked us to the coat check, helped Sunny into her jacket. He turned to help me, but I was already buttoning up my wool coat, ready to get the hell out of here.

After we said our goodbyes to the group, Aaron waved and Amanda delivered more air kisses. "Thank you for coming."

We left the warmth of the restaurant, walking out into a handful of snowflakes drifting from the overcast black sky. I dreaded snow, but at least it wasn't frogs.

"What was he like?" I asked, repeating her question to me earlier.

"Dean?"

"No, the waiter. Yes, Dean. You two were glued to each other most of the night."

"I was simply learning about the housing market," she said with a sniff. "He's very knowledgeable, you know."

"That's it?"

"He asked me about my role in the business. And if I was dating anyone."

We reached her car. As Sunny hit the fob, unlocking the doors, I looked at her over the hood. She had a glow about her. I couldn't describe it, but she seemed almost…happy. I'd never seen her like this. It was nice.

"Did he ask you out?"

She slowly shook her head and hopped behind the wheel. "He was just being polite, Holly. We're two professionals who discussed business."

"You like him," I taunted, unable to keep the twelve-year-old girl inside of me quiet.

"Shut up or you can walk."

I didn't say another word.

#

When I got home, Cade was still MIA. All this time I'd wondered how we'd get along, living under the same roof for a few weeks. Now I was wondering if I'd see him at all.

I dressed in a pair of flannel pajama pants and an oversized sweatshirt, made myself a cup of tea, and called Gran. I told her about my night and meeting a snooty state senator.

"Well, look at you, running with the big dogs," she teased.

"Right. They think I'm a mystic who can dispel bad energy and unblock chakras."

She chuckled, then immediately sobered. "Well, I prefer you doing that to dealing with the Council. But enough about that. Did you find anything on those symbols?"

"No, but I did meet someone interesting today." I told Gran about Mary, the daughter of a medicine woman. "She thinks this has all happened before, and she spoke about an imbalance. What do you think that means?"

"No idea. Sometimes the old ones like to hear themselves talk. They sound cleverer than they really are." I didn't think Mary fell into that category but kept it to myself.

I signed off with Gran, finished my tea, and crawled into bed. I leaned over and pressed my nose to the pillow Cade had used the night before. Closing my eyes, I took a deep breath, could smell that spicy, unidentifiable scent that was his alone. It was almost worse that he was here in town, so close, but still unavailable.

Feeling restless, I grabbed the small notebook from my purse, along with my tablet and took them back to bed. Reading over my notes about Moonlight Cove and everything I knew about the murder, I still didn't see how it all tied together.

Perhaps I was looking at two completely unrelated events. Just like the model homes and the people in Henryetta were also individual cases. Something was causing the infection, yes, but maybe it was random. I didn't want to believe it, but it could be possible.

Next, I did a computer search on sacrifices—specifically the offering of a human heart. As expected, there was a ton of stuff on Aztec and Mayan culture. A recent discovery in Peru theorized forty-seven people, including children, had their hearts ripped out in a mass sacrifice. But on the whole, it seemed to be a Mesoamerican thing.

Next, I did a search on blackbirds. What significance did the killer see in placing a feather inside the chest of Jane Doe? I got hits all over the board on this one. Some considered blackbirds a bad omen. Some said the feathers repelled evil or were a warning. Perhaps this was simply another bullshit ritual the killer pulled out of his ass. It sounded cool and symbolic but held no true significance for anyone but him.

And the rock in Jane Doe's mouth? Well, according to the webosphere, other than a rare instance in eighth century Ireland, it meant nothing.

Unless the killer was following some archaic rules that no one else in the world knew about, he had to be making this stuff up. Even if I knew why, it probably wouldn't make a difference.

Next, I decided to try and find out what I could on the symbols. I used an app that allowed me to draw pictures. It took another ten minutes to find the stylus I never used, and then I recreated the palm symbol as best as I could. I'd start with that and work my way through the rest.

Why were the symbols placed on those specific areas of the body—the lower back, the abdomen, the sole of the left foot, and the right palm? What was the significance? I couldn't find anything special about their placement, and after trying to faithfully draw three of the symbols, I came up with nothing. I wasn't surprised, but I was sure as hell disappointed.

I still hadn't heard from Cade. I was itching to question the other tattoo parlors. And I couldn't help but wonder if Master Sebastian knew Jane Doe. He ran a sex cam business. Maybe he was a pimp, too.

So many theories, so little evidence. It frustrated me to no end.

Before calling it a night, I drew the final symbol—the one on Jane Doe's lower back. And I got a hit.

I told myself not to get my hopes up, but I sat a little straighter in bed, plumped the pillows behind me, and read an article by Dr. Albert Schumer, Professor of Anthropology at a Texas university I'd never heard of—Scientia Antiquis. He claimed that a fabled ancient manuscript contained the symbol. According to Dr. Schumer, the manuscript had been lost years ago—if it ever existed. After all, history was riddled with these mythical esoteric writings that would reveal the secrets of alchemy or creation or total knowledge. If only they could be found.

Schumer cited other ancients who'd heard about the manuscript in second and third-hand accounts. The article focused on the manuscript rather than the symbol itself.

Could the killer have found this very article and used the symbol in his own ritual? Stranger things had happened.

I jotted everything down in my notes, and hoped I'd be able to talk to Cade about it in the morning. In the meantime,

I shot off an email to Dr. Schumer. I gave him my name and phone number, explaining that I was interested in ancient religious practices, and asked him to get in touch.

I tempered my expectations. He must be a busy man, writing articles on fictitious manuscripts and all, but it was worth a shot.

I turned off the light and quickly fell asleep, only to dream of Moonlight Cove. I walked through the town, staring at each empty house and all those corn dollies attached to the front doors. For once it wasn't raining, though the heavy, gray clouds remained and my footsteps echoed through the abandoned streets.

As I made my way toward the edge of town, I stood at the top of a hill and spied something in the lake. Curious, I walked down the grassy bank and onto the rocky shore. The dead girl—Jane Doe—floated past me, her chest cut open, her body pale, palms upward. The symbol on her right hand glowed with a red light, as if lit from within. Then her bloated face morphed into my mother's.

Brianna's eyes flashed open, and she turned her head looking directly at me. Her lips moved, but she made no sound.

I stepped into the lake. It was surprisingly warm, like bath water. The rocks were rough against the bottom of my feet, but the water felt soothing. The waves gently lapped against my thighs and hips as I moved closer.

"Mom?"

Her hand snaked out, latching onto my wrist. The brand from her palm burned my skin, branding me, as well. "Find me," she mouthed.

That's when I realized I wasn't standing in water. I was wading in blood. As far as I could see, red liquid, smelling of copper and something else I couldn't identify, surrounded me. Thunder rumbled, and the gray clouds turned dark and angry. A blackbird flew in circles overhead.

My mother started sinking, slowly, bit by bit, until the blood covered her ripped torso. Only her head remained afloat, and finally that became submerged, too. All the while, her grip on me tightened.

I tried to pull away, tried wrenching my wrist from her clutched hand, but she wouldn't let go. She was too strong. She pulled me down with her. Lower and lower I sank. Soon, the thick, sticky blood covered my head. I plunged down further, deeper, knowing I was going to die.

I gasped as I awoke, feeling Cade's arms around me. He jerked me off the bed, and my legs tangled with the blankets. I realized the entire house was shaking.

"Earthquake," I muttered, still half asleep.

Cade threw the blankets from my legs and carried me to the bedroom doorway. He held me tight in his arms as everything around us rattled and shook. I clung to him, to his warm, naked torso, gripping his back tight with my hands.

As a lamp fell off the bedside table, my tablet went skidding across the floor. Lightening flared up outside, so bright it was almost blinding. The blinds rattled against the windows, as though shaken by unseen hands. A loud explosion of thunder boomed close to the house, sounding a hell of a lot like a bomb.

Throughout the rest of the house, cabinet doors banged open and closed. Glass smashed onto the kitchen floor. Another shock of lightening brightened the sky, and the accompanying thunder rattled the windows so hard, I thought they might implode.

After several minutes, the earth stopped trembling, but the rain continued. It poured from the sky in heavy sheets and pounded against the house. Outside, the trees bent to the gusts of wind and cast eerie shadows across the walls.

I clung to Cade, resting my forehead against his chest. "What is happening?"

"I wish I knew."

That wasn't the reassuring answer I'd been looking for.

#

Cade held me until I stopped shaking. He petted my hair and muttered calming words in that deep, gruff voice of his.

Between the disturbing nightmare and the shock of the earthquake, it took several minutes for my heart to slow and my hands to steady.

When I finally flipped on the bedroom light an assessed the damage, I noted only the lamp's lightbulb was broken. Cade jerked on his jeans and boots. I slipped on my tennis shoes before cleaning up the glass and righting the lamp.

In the master bath, my moisturizers, facial cleansers, hair products, and birth control pills fell in the sink or scattered to the tile floor. But no damage. Too bad I couldn't say that about the rest of the house.

All that commotion we'd heard in the kitchen turned out to be the better part of my dishes and wine glasses. Three coffee mugs were toast, as well. I grabbed a broom and started to sweep, while Cade tackled the living room. I had several framed photos of Gran and me on side tables. Only one broke, the rest just fell. But the flat screen TV hanging over the mantle crashed and broke. The white bookshelves on either side of the hearth flipped over, too.

"You're going to need some earthquake straps, so this won't happen again," he said.

We were used to frequent tremors in Oklahoma. Some blamed it on the fracking, others claimed it was waste water due to oil wells. I blamed this one on the strange thing infecting magic.

"We've had earthquakes before, Cade. Plenty of them. They've never been this severe. You don't think this has something to do with the frogs?"

He hefted the first bookcase off the ground and pushed it back in place. "What frogs?"

Right. Cade had been in Arkansas part of the day. I explained the frogs and the black and gray jumble surrounding them as I continued to sweep. Neither of us said much, each lost in our own thoughts.

After another hour, Cade and I had the house to rights. I straightened up the main bathroom. In the spare bedroom, I lined my purses back onto the shelves where they lived. They made it through unscathed.

Cade replaced my books and threw away the broken knickknacks in the living room. Then he tidied the laundry room. Unfortunately, the iron had flown into the far wall near the washing machine and made a huge dent in the drywall.

"I'll take care of that as soon as this case is wrapped up," he promised.

"Thanks." God, I was tired. Bone weary, but I wasn't sure I could go back to sleep. That dream stuck with me as I'd cleaned. My mom's face sinking into the blood. Find me.

I desperately wanted to find her. But Gran had spent a fortune on psychics, trackers, and mediums. When she'd exhausted every magical avenue, she'd hired private detectives. No one found a trace of Brianna. Not one single sighting or credit card receipt. When she left Gran's house, it was if she'd vanished.

I rubbed my gritty eyes and grabbed a couple of bottles of water from the fridge before trudging back to the bedroom. After replacing the broken lightbulb in the lamp, I toed off my shoes.

Cade pulled a piece of paper from his back pocket and tossed it on the bed. "That's for you. From that little girl, Annabelle. The one who came in on the stretcher? She's only seven." I remembered. The little girl who couldn't stop running.

I grabbed the paper and unfolded it. She drew well, for a seven-year-old. The picture showed a detailed drawing of the café. Couples sat at the tables drinking coffee, eating pancakes, and reading over the menu. The menu board above the cash register read: #1 Coffee 198. I held it out to Cade. "Look at this. Number two toast is two-hundred-forty-nine. Is that dollars? Maybe that's where the coven gets all their money—a high markup on breakfast." Number three—eggs—were one-hundred-sixty-seven, and good old number four was two-hundred-fourteen. That muffin better be made of edible gold.

Cade glanced at it before handing it back. "She's a cute kid. Feeling like her old self, her mom said."

"Good. Did you find out where the coven is keeping the list of norms who stay during the summer?"

"No." He shucked his clothes and fell onto the bed. "Didn't learn a goddamn thing." He flipped off the lamp, leaving the room in darkness.

Rain continued to pound against the house as I cuddled up next to him. I only wore a tank top and panties, because his body was so hot. I entwined my legs with his, stroked his calf with the side of my foot. "There might be aftershocks from the earthquake."

He threw an arm around my waist. "I'm here. I've got you." When I was wrapped in Cade's embrace, I felt safe in a way I never had before. Protected, somehow.

"Missed you today," I said.

"Me, too. I got your message about meeting Mick. How did that go?"

I leaned up on one elbow. "Who are you? You're not the Cade McAllister I know. He'd lecture me, like I just got caught smoking beneath the bleachers." I deepened my voice. "Smoking is bad. Besides, lung cancer. Grumble, grumble, grumble."

"Huh. I do not sound like that."

"Yeah, you do."

"In what world do I sound like a cartoon character?"

I laughed, then quickly told him about my day, starting with group therapy, the mystery girl with the symbol tattooed on her hand. "Mick said he'd try to find her, and I've hit a third of the tattoo parlors in town. I'll go to the rest tomorrow. Also, I emailed a professor from Scientia Antiquis University. He apparently thinks one of the symbols on Jane Doe came from an ancient manuscript."

Cade's body stilled. I could have sworn he stopped breathing for a few seconds. "Dr. Schumer?"

CHAPTER TWENTY-TWO

"Yeah. Do you know him?"

"He was my professor. He encouraged me to apply to graduate school but I enrolled in the Council Training Division instead."

I peered down at him as I tried to read his expression in the dark. His entire body strained, his bicep grew taut beneath my fingers. "What aren't you telling me?"

"It's a very small university, for Others only. Most delve into history. Some become official record keepers."

"But you wanted to be an archaeologist? Why didn't you follow through?" This was what he refused to talk about the other day. I wasn't expecting him to reveal all his secrets tonight, not when he was so tired and working on such a stressful case. So when he answered, it caught me off guard.

"My parents' death was ruled as a murder suicide. Shayna was in her first year at a regular college with Norms, having the time of her life. I was preparing to start graduate school when we got the call. Mom was dead. Dad had shot her, then himself. No magic to trace."

I didn't know what to say. I wanted to wrap my arms around him, hold him tight, the way he'd held me during the earthquake. But I knew he wouldn't want that.

"I'm sorry, Cade. Do you know...why?"

"It was a lie, Holly. My dad worshipped my mom. They were crazy about each other. Couldn't keep their hands to themselves. It was embarrassing. You've been to the house, seen how small it is. They were very happy—at least three times a week kind of happy. My dad didn't have a temper. Now my mom, she would flare up when Shayna or I got out of line, give us a look that said we'd better straighten up. But my dad was a marshmallow. It's fucking ridiculous to think he'd shoot her."

I sat up, shaken to the core by his story. And I believed him, every word.

I stroked his arm. He'd lost so much. First his parents to a violent death, then his sister to a pyromaniac. No wonder he carried such an enormous chip on his shoulder. "Is that why you became an Investigator? Have you been trying to find out what really happened to them?"

"Of course I have." He felt even hotter than normal, as if dredging up all these memories had stoked a fire inside him.

"What have you found?"

"Nothing. All their friends say the same thing. My parents were happy. They never argued. No one saw it coming."

"What do you think happened? Did they have enemies? Did someone do this to target you or to keep them quiet?"

He sat up, leaned against the headboard. "I've asked all those questions and more. I've dedicated my fucking life to finding out what really happened, but so far, I've come up empty."

"I know that feeling." I crawled onto his lap and looped my arms around his neck. I needed comfort just as much as he did. "I'm so sorry." I kissed the side of his neck, lapping at his skin. My lips hovered over his earlobe and I tugged it between my teeth.

Suddenly, I found myself on my back with Cade's hips settled between my legs. When he kissed me, there was no tenderness, no consideration. He took what he wanted. He wasn't searching for understanding or gentle compassion. He wanted to fuck, to feel something—anything—that would make the pain go away. That was the only consolation he'd take.

I scraped my nails down his back, clutching his ass as he roughly plundered my mouth. I ground my hips against his cock, hard and heavy at my core.

He didn't even bother to undress me, just pulled the edge of my panties aside. He thrust himself into me, filled me up, stretched me. I pulled my mouth from his, arching my neck. His teeth found my good shoulder. He pounded into me, hard and fast, and I absorbed it all.

Cade took everything I had to offer, but he gave me something in return. Comfort from that terrible nightmare. Comfort in the connection he and I shared. We'd both been robbed of parents, and we yearned to find out why.

I came quickly, clutching the blanket in my fist as Cade continued to piston his hips. He was holding out, trying to last, but after a few more thrusts, he buried his head in my neck and groaned against my skin.

It'd been a fast, hard ride. Exactly what both of us needed at that moment.

Afterward, we held each other as our breathing slowly returned to normal. He rubbed his thumb along the edge of my breast, down to the curve of my waist, and over my hip. Then he reversed the path, stroking me with the tenderness that had been missing earlier.

"Too rough?" he finally asked.

I ran my hand over his head, feeling the stubble of his cropped hair against my palm. "You know I like it that way."

"Mmm. Now, tell me about Reece."

I recited, without emotion, everything that happened in college. I kept my voice level, not allowing my feelings, my pain, to color the words. I just gave him the facts.

"Why didn't you want to tell me earlier?"

"I don't like to talk about it."

"That's not the whole story."

I pushed at his chest, willing him to move but he stayed right where he was. On top of me, staring down in the darkness. Even then, I felt he could truly see me, and it made me vulnerable in a way that sex never did. "Let me up, Cade."

"You didn't run. You didn't cower. You could have left school, but that's not who you are. And you learned to take care of yourself, didn't you?"

I stopped pushing against him, letting my hands rest on his shoulders.

"I've underestimated you, haven't I?" he continued. "I have this urge to lock you up, to keep you safe. All this time you've been telling me you can take care of yourself. I didn't listen."

I let out a deep breath and my muscles relaxed. "You didn't understand."

"You could have explained it to me. I've never seen you as weak."

"You called me a liability." I punched his arm, still pissed over the comment he'd made when we first met.

"And I was wrong." He leaned down until our breaths mingled. He ghosted his lips over mine, across my chin, my cheeks, my ear. "Enjoy that admission, because I won't say it often." He grinned against my jawline.

"You're an arrogant bastard."

"I know." He rolled over until I was on top of him. "But you love me anyway."

"I do."

#

I woke to gray light, the sound of rain pattering against the roof, and a soreness between my thighs.

"Wake up, baby. We've got to go." Cade handed me a cup of coffee with extra creamer.

"Where?"

"Back out to the holding cell. I want you to talk to Reece, find out what she's hiding."

I sat up, clutching the sheet to my bare breasts. Not because I was shy, but because I was cold without Cade in bed with me. I took a sip of coffee and glared at him over the rim of the cup. "Why do you think the bitch will tell me anything? She hates me."

He wore only his boxer briefs and, as he walked toward the bathroom, he stopped to take them off. It was a nice view, that naked ass first thing in the morning. What would it be like having Cade around all the time?

He turned back to me with a rare smile. "Because, and I'm saying this as a compliment, you're the most annoying, determined person I've ever met. She'll tell you whatever you want to know just to shut you up."

I shrugged. "But first, tattoo parlors. If we find this girl with the tattooed hand, we might have a lead on the killer."

He paused, his brows tightening over his nose. "Mick didn't have any idea at all?"

"No. He doesn't keep video footage for longer than a week. One of the servers remembered her but didn't get a name. Did you know he hires Norms?" My gaze dipped from his chest to his shapely V-cut, to his hardening dick.

"Can we not talk about Raven?"

I stood from the bed and wiggled out of my panties. "Would you rather talk about shower sex? Because it's on the table, McAllister."

"I'm going to be spoiled by the time I go back out on the road."

In the shower, with warm water cascading over us, Cade rubbed my shower gel between his hands. Then he washed my body, covering every inch of skin. He took his time, playing with me. He worked me into a frenzy and I was pleading with him by the time he finally bent me over and slid inside me.

When we climbed out of the shower, the water had chilled. But I felt warm and tingly inside. Yeah, I could definitely get used to this, waking up to Cade every morning, going to bed with him every night. A voice in my head warned caution, but I put that voice on mute, ignoring it. I could deal with reality later. Right then, I wanted to feel good, just a little while longer.

Cade was dressed in minutes, but I had to dry my hair and put on makeup. Also, I chose to switch purses. I swapped everything into a Burberry cross-body bag. Then I grabbed the picture little Annabelle had drawn and stuck it on the fridge using a magnet from the local pizza place before snagging the last package of Pop Tarts.

"How much longer, Little Null? Don't have all day, you know."

"Hey, you have no one but yourself to blame, McAllister. You distracted me with sex. I'd be ready by now if it weren't for you and your peen."

His eyes warmed and his scowl dropped a degree. "Worth it."

I grabbed my stolen umbrella and he opened the front door to find Sunny standing on my porch. She brushed against me and headed toward the kitchen.

"Figured I'd set up here again since you have a working toilet. Did you feel that earthquake last night? Six-point-two."

I stared after her, watching as she popped open her laptop and settled onto a stool. "You have coffee, yes?"

"Made a fresh pot this morning," Cade said. "Good to see you, Sunny."

"Uh huh. Do you have time for any clients today? Clients who pay up front and should be your first priority? Because I have a dozen more calls about spells that have gone awry."

"No, but send me their addresses, would you?" I still wanted to track them, see if I could find a pattern to all this madness.

She just sighed. "Also, Dean texted this morning. He's pulled some properties he wants us to see."

If I didn't have time to meet with clients, I sure as hell didn't have time to stop and look at offices. And I really, really wanted to. "Can we postpone it?"

"You're the one who says we need a new office ASAP." She sighed dramatically. "I guess I'll just have to make time to go, even though I'm just as overloaded as you are."

Being alone with Dean? Yeah, I was certain that'd be a real hardship, but she played it like a martyr.

Cade walked toward Sunny. "Don't think that's a good idea. I checked that other developer you told me about, the one with mob ties." He glanced at his phone. "Liam Snyder. No known links to Others. I'm having someone look into the

Wylers, too. I don't want either of you alone with him until I clear it."

Sunny sat up a little straighter, shooting daggers at Cade. "Since when do you call the shots?" Her glare slid my way. "Does Cade get a say in how we conduct our business?"

"No. But since we're investigating a murder and the infection spread to the Wyler property, it might be a good idea to clear Dean. Just to be on the safe side."

She rolled her eyes. "He's not your killer."

"How do you know that, Sunny?" Cade lowered his chin, crossed his arms.

"Fine. Check him out, if it makes you happy." She turned her back on him and flipped on her computer.

I tugged on Cade's arm. "We've been dismissed."

Once we hopped in the truck, Cade turned to me, sneering. "Sunny actually likes that toothy guy?"

I handed him a strawberry Pop Tart. "Yep." I explained about the cocktail party from the night before. "And Amanda's getting her own TV show."

"Huh. Good for her, I guess."

After glancing at my list of tattoo shops, Cade pulled into the nearest one, off Yale Avenue. Inksation. What was with all the cutesy names? I expected something more…hardcore, like Badass Biker Tats.

"Where did you get your tattoo done?" I unbuckled my seatbelt and hopped out of the truck with my umbrella.

Cade met me on the sidewalk in front of the shop, droplets of water coating his short hair. "An enchanter did it for me." He walked toward the door, but I tugged on his hand, stopping him.

"What?"

"I got it after Shayna. The dragon was so that I'd never forget how she died." By fire. The man punished himself at every turn. "And because of the enchanted ink, the dragon heated, alerting me to unseen dangers."

My heart plunged to my stomach. "And I nullified it."

"Yeah, but it's fine." He pulled on my hand, beckoning me to go inside. I still didn't move.

"Cade, we need to talk about this. We never do because you're always on the go, but at some point we're going to have to."

His eyes held mine. "It's not a choice. I can have both you and magic." But he couldn't. Not on a full-time basis. And maybe that was enough for him, seeing me every few weeks, being satisfied with stolen moments. For right now, it was enough for me, too. But ultimately, I'd want more.

"Not today," I said. "But soon." I finally let him pull me inside.

We didn't get any information on our tattoo girl. So, we stopped by the next place. And the next.

It was mid-morning when we decided to get some real food, but before we could argue over where to eat, Cade's phone rang.

"Well, shit." He hung up and turned to me, his eyes frigid and slightly terrifying as they met mine. "We've got another murder on our hands."

CHAPTER TWENTY-THREE

I had to reassure Cade that I wanted to go with him to see the victim in person. My voice may have been firm, but my stomach felt like watery Jell-O. I'd seen dead bodies before, and it was never a good experience.

"What are the details?"

Cade took I-75 south. "They're texting me the address. Somewhere in Henryetta."

"I should have known." I explained my two recent experiences in Henryetta. "And according to Sunny, more people need their spells nullified." I glanced at her list of addresses she'd texted earlier, then I pulled up a map. "Most are between Henryetta and Eufaula, but not all of them." I glanced at his rigid profile. He was working the muscle in his jaw like it was his job. "Do you think the infection could be spreading?"

"I don't know anything for sure. But we'd better start getting some breaks in this case."

Cade made it to Henryetta a lot faster than I had. The rain abated a bit, and he drove fifteen miles over the speed limit. But once he started navigating curvy country roads, he slowed down.

He parked on the edge of a gravel path, and from there it was a hike to get to the edge of Lake Henryetta. The latest body had been pulled from the water earlier this morning.

"Who found it?" I asked.

"A woman lost her dog through the woods. She found it on the banks of the lake, barking at the dead body. In spite of the rain, the lake lost water last night from the earthquake. We think that's why the body surfaced so quickly. Herb doesn't believe she's been in the drink for long."

He left me in the truck to assess the situation, make sure he couldn't detect any signatures other than the gray and black jumble that accompanied a contaminated zone.

He returned within ten minutes. "The body is infected. There's nothing we can do, magic-wise."

I hopped out of the car and followed him through the wet grass. A white tent had been set up near the edge of the lake. Cade held up the flap for me.

"Ms. James," Herb said with a wide smile. "I'm glad you're joining us on this one." He turned to Cade. "Our null has a unique perspective."

I wasn't paying attention to Herb. I was too busy staring at the victim. There's a total lack of privacy in death. You become a body to be handled. Even if you die at home in bed at the age of one hundred and three, strangers put their hands all over you, drain you of fluids, pump you full of poison to slow down deterioration. You become a thing. A shell.

"Any ID?" I wanted to know her name, wanted to give her that much dignity, at least. And as my stomach clenched, I forced myself to focus on the woman, to look for signs of who she'd been, not just what had been done to her.

"Not yet," Cade said. He stepped forward to inspect her.

My gaze barely skimmed her naked torso and the gaping hole beneath her breasts. It felt like too much of an intrusion to focus on that. So, instead I paid attention to other facts. Unlike our original Jane Doe, Jane Two had dark hair. Obviously, hair color wasn't important to the killer. Not part of his ritual. Her ears were pierced, but she wore no earrings. She had a small tattoo, badly done, of two tiny stars on her right ankle. A distinctive mark.

I approached from the other side, across from Herb. Jane Two was bloated and blue. "How long has she been in the water?"

"Again," Herb said, "it's hard to tell, but maybe a day or less. She's still in rigor." He used his gloved hand to point to the vertical slit in her torso. "Again, I suspect the heart has been removed. I'll know for certain once I get back to the lab." Her right palm faced upward—baring another symbol along with the one on her abdomen.

The markings glowed bright red against her deadly pallor. The skin was puffy where the killer had carved them into her.

I glanced over her abdomen. "Is that an appendix scar?"

"Mmm hmm." Herb felt along the back of her skull, checking for damage.

As I stared at her, her gaunt features told me something else. I glanced up to find Cade watching me.

"What do you see?"

I glanced again at her face. "She looks like an addict to me."

"No track marks." He nodded at her arms.

I shrugged. "I could be wrong." But I didn't think so. I'd seen enough inner-city junkies and back country meth heads as I traveled around the county, and they all start to take on the same characteristics. Their faces were thin, haggard, showing signs of acne and a certain lack of self-care.

"I don't think you're wrong," Cade said.

Herb pulled back her upper lip, as though she were a horse he was looking to buy. "Bad teeth, another sign. I'm sure you're correct, Ms. James. I'll find what was swimming in her system."

Cade moved to the tent flap. "Keep us informed, Herb. Chances are good her fingerprints are on file." He jerked his head toward me.

I said a quick prayer for Jane Two, even though I didn't believe it would do her much good.

Cade and I slogged through the grass back to his truck. He held the door, helped me inside, took my umbrella and stuck it in the back seat. Then he reached out and cupped my cheek.

"I know it's hard, looking at death. But you always hold up." He leaned forward, kissed my forehead.

We drove toward town, neither of us saying much. One thought kept running through my mind: both Janes had to be prostitutes. Sex workers. Whatever you wanted to call it. So, where did our killer find his victims? From the street? A website?

"Where do you go to hire a prostitute?" I glanced over at Cade, found him stroking that scar on his cheek with a deep furrow between his brows.

"You can pick one up downtown. Cruise around the streets, and they're standing around. Almost all of them are on drugs, and it shows. That's why they're out on the street in the first place."

"Back in college, Reece put my name and number up on several escort sites. Maybe that's how the killer found our victims."

"You might be right about the first Jane Doe. No signs of drug use, no distinguishing features. He could have picked her out of an online catalog, like ordering takeout. I think he wanted someone who was clean, young, no existing marks or scars. But he fucked up with the second Jane. Which means he was desperate and not as picky the second time. He might have found her on the streets."

"Why was he so desperate?"

He turned to me, his eyes iced with anger. "That's a damned good question. I think it must suggest a need on his part. Why did he need to kill again so quickly? Because he was driven to it, or for another reason?"

"Maybe the killing urge was strong? He did it once and couldn't wait to do it again."

Cade shook his head. "I don't think so. This ritual of his takes time, planning. I think the girl with the symbol was a test run. And that was a few weeks ago. Maybe he performed the ritual without killing her, but it wasn't as satisfying."

"I have another question," I said, glancing at him. "Can we agree that whoever is doing this is an Other? I mean, the gray and black jumble of magic. That means something, doesn't it? Maybe he's so mentally ill, he's corrupting magic with these kills."

"I go back and forth. Why can't you nullify the contaminated areas? What besides magic corrupts magic?"

I told him about Mary, the Cherokee woman in the log cabin. "She said things are out of balance. You've got dead frogs, two headed cattle, and warped magic. Maybe something in the very nature of…well, nature is messed up."

"Now, there's a thought. But if that was the case, I'm not sure how we fix Mother Nature. You said you had some nullifying to do, right? At least a dozen more clients. Let's take care of them. You nullify, I'll question."

I glanced through the client addresses Sunny had sent and Cade and I planned our route. Almost all were in Eufaula or Henryetta but three were just north, between Okmulgee and Winchester.

I thought about the locations of corrupted magic. Jane Doe—so close to Midnight Cove. Jane Two—in Henryetta. But there was no murder at the Glen Falls model homes, yet they'd been infected.

"Do you think our tattoo girl could have been taken somewhere near the model homes? They performed the ritual without taking her heart. Maybe having sex and starting the ritual was enough to screw up magic at the subdivision."

"That's not a bad idea. I texted the guys in my office, told them to do a background check on the Wylers. If anything pops up, he'll let me know."

We stopped and grabbed a bite to eat before we met with my clients. I wasn't really hungry, after viewing Jane Two's body, but Cade still had an appetite.

Once he was done eating, I called my clients before we descended on them. We started with an earth witch in Eufaula. Cade questioned her as I walked through the home, nullifying her kids. She'd spelled them to sit down and be quiet, so naturally, they were stuck on the ceiling, spread eagle, unable to move. Fortunately, mom scattered pillows beneath them, so when I entered the house they didn't hurt themselves.

Once we left, I asked Cade if he'd learned anything new.

"Her spells started going haywire early this morning."

"Why not on Sunday night, when it happened at Midnight Cove? This place is only about ten or fifteen miles from the coven."

"This witch isn't powerful. Maybe the concentration of magic in the coven had something to do with it?"

So many variables and unanswered questions. I had so many ideas swirling around in my head, it was like a bunch of rabid squirrels chasing each other.

We methodically made our way through the other eleven clients. Four more witches, two psychics, one medium, a metalmancer, a diviner, and two shifters who couldn't change into their animal selves. Cade didn't get any information out of them, and when he warned them not to attempt magic until the Council sanctioned it, they were all pissed to varying degrees.

By the time we were done, we were forty minutes outside of Tulsa. Darkness had fallen, the rain continued, and the temperature seemed to have dropped even further.

My shoulder was screaming at me. I'd forgotten to use the salve Gran had given me. The scratch was feeling hot and itchy—which worried me slightly. I figured once I got home, I'd clean the wound and apply her garlic-goldenseal treatment.

"We're not going to make it to the holding cell tonight," Cade said.

"Isn't that a lower priority? The murders need to take precedence, don't they?"

He turned his head toward me and lifted a strand of my hair, smoothing it back behind my ear. "What if one of the coven's spells did this? They're lying about something, but we don't know what it is. They may not have killed the Janes, but they could still have set off the catalyst that's causing the infection."

"Fine."

"We'll plan on it tomorrow. Right now, I'll drop you off, then I need to go see Herb. He has some thoughts on Jane Two."

"And I can't come?"

"You'll nullify his entire lab."

Right. "Follow up with the Wylers, would you?"

"Will do."

On the way home, I texted Gran, letting her know I was all right. She texted back that she'd been looking for the symbols in more of her books. She'd come up with nothing.

I was beginning to feel a little hopeless, to tell you the truth. Cade and I kept striking out, over and over. We'd find one small lead, and then land on our asses.

"Is this how all your cases go? One step forward, three steps back?"

"Not all of them, but yeah, it happens. To be a good investigator, you have to keep asking questions, which you're good at, by the way. And you have to be as tenacious as a pit bull."

By the time Cade dropped me off at home, I was starving. I went to give him a quick kiss goodbye, but he prolonged it. Cupping my face, his thumbs glided along my jaw and cheeks.

"I enjoyed spending the day with you."

"Back atcha, Sorcerer. Try and make it home sometime tonight?"

"Yes, ma'am."

#

After scavenging the kitchen cabinets and the fridge, I came up with crumbs from the bottom of a cereal box and an empty carton of milk. We'd eaten the last of the Pop Tarts that morning.

I had no choice but to go to the grocery store.

I thrust my arms back into my coat, grabbed my Burberry, and headed out the door. The security lights flickered on as I walked to the Honda parked in the driveway. As I opened the driver side door to get in, something heavy landed on my back.

As soon as I smelled the combination of sloppy joes and dust, I knew Matilda the Goblin had gotten the jump on me. Her momentum lurched us forward and I knocked my forehead onto the hood of the car. That blow stunned me, but as soon as she pulled my hair, I snapped to.

Adrenaline and anger spiked through me. Don't panic. My old self-defense coach pounded that into my head. In college, that became my mantra whenever I encountered Others. But she'd taken me by surprise, making me forget everything I intuitively knew—how to fight back.

I struggled to stay on my feet. The bitch was heavy. Her grip on my hair tightened and she used her free hand to slash through the front of my coat. She sliced right through my Burberry purse strap, and my bag fell to the ground.

Damn, my gun was in my purse. But I realized I still had my keys in my hands. I reached back over my shoulder and shoved them into her, not knowing where I hit. Not caring. She let out a screech and loosened her hold on my hair. I used that to my advantage. I spun, slamming her back into the car as hard as I could.

Her soft grunt told me I hadn't done enough damage, so I rocked forward, then shoved myself backward once again, slamming her spine into the car. I did it over and over.

Eventually she let go of my hair, but only to wrap her arm around my neck, choking me. "Where's my magic? Answer meeeeee!" She yelled in my ear, that high pitched voice piercing through my skull like a drill.

I used my keys to stab at her arm, puncturing the skin, making small wounds. Her blood coated my hand. I pivoted to the side, to try and ram her into the car from a different angle. I didn't have much time, because black spots dotted my vision. Her arm tightened around my neck, cutting off all oxygen.

And then suddenly, she was off my back. I could breathe again. I took gulps of cold, damp air into my lungs. It stung, but I was too grateful to care.

Holding onto my throat, I turned to see why she had let go.

"'Ello, love." James Sharpe, the sadistic asshole vampire stood right behind me, an unconscious goblin at his feet.

CHAPTER TWENTY-FOUR

"What are you doing here," I croaked.

"Saving your bacon, by the looks of it." His British working-class accent always threw me off. While Sharpe's suits were every bit as expensive as Mick Raven's, he didn't care if they were tailored to perfection. His dark waves were a tad too long and shaggy, making him flip the hair out of his eyes every now and again. Large diamond studs glinted from both ears. He must have been turned in his late twenties, early thirties, but I had a feeling he was very, very old.

"Yeah, thanks for that." My throat still hurt, but I was starting to feel better, not so woozy. "So, you just stopped by to help me out in a goblin fight?"

He kicked Matilda in the head with the toe of his Louis Vuitton loafers. "Well, that's not the only reason, of course. Master wants to see you, yeah?"

Now my heart started kicking into panic mode once more, thumping painfully. Abby had said it was only a matter of time before this happened, before Sebastian would demand a meeting. I didn't imagine it would be so soon.

"I can't." I backed up, only to run into the still open driver side door. "I'm on the way to the grocery store." That sounded inane even as it tumbled out of my mouth.

Sharpe stared at me with those golden eyes, the color of honey. Honey that had frozen and crystalized. "Doesn't work that way, love."

Swallowing hurt, but I did it almost compulsively as I thought about running. Or grabbing my purse from the ground and pulling out my gun. Shooting him would be a very satisfying experience. But once I bolted, he'd heal. Then he'd come after me.

As if he could read my mind, he lowered his head, his gaze still intent upon me. "Don't. Don't make me chase you. Besides, I like it when they run," he whispered.

A cold sweat broke out all over my body. I started shaking. The thought of going with James, getting trapped in the Master's lair terrified me.

"I'll see Sebastian first thing in the morning. I'll bring Cade with me," I said in a bid to make a deal.

"You'll come with me. Now. Easy way or hard way, doesn't matter to me, love."

"And what's the hard way? Are you going to knock me out like you did with her?" I pointed toward the goblin.

"Nah, I'll just stuff you in the boot of the car. I don't want to hurt you, right? Just talk."

My time was up. I knew I had to meet the Master tonight, and there was no getting out of it. "Fine, but I'm going to call Cade and let him know where I'm going."

"Well, I'm not giving you the Master's address, now am I?"

There was no way Sharpe would reveal Master Sebastian's resting place. That would be high treason. "I'm telling him that I'm with you. So if anything happens to me, he'll know who to kill." I wasn't kidding. Cade would rip this vamp apart if I got hurt tonight. He wouldn't give a damn if it started a war. Cade was old school in a lot of ways I didn't appreciate, but this wasn't one of them.

"He's not alone in that, is he? Mick Raven would do the same." He cocked his head to the side, his gaze assessing as he looked me over slowly, from head to toe. "Don't get me wrong, you're a decent looking bird, but I'm not sure you're worth all the fuss."

"I'm not either, to be honest."

He laughed at that. His smile made him look not younger, but lighter somehow. "I do like you, Holly. You've got spirit."

I tucked my keys into my coat pocket and bent down to grab my bag, keeping my eye on Sharpe the whole time. I pulled out my phone and hit speed dial, smudging my screen with the goblin blood still coating my hand. Unfortunately, I got Cade's voice mail.

"Hey. When I got home, James Sharpe was waiting for me. Master Sebastian is demanding a meeting tonight. I don't have a choice. I have to go. Hopefully, I'll be home before you will. But I wanted you to know where I was. Love you."

When I ended the call, James batted his lashes dramatically. "Look at you, all in lurve. And wif a sorcerer. How bloody delicious is that? Now, let's shake a leg."

I had no reason to trust James. We'd met under difficult circumstances, and I thought he might be more than a little psycho. Even Abby was terrified of him. But I owed Sharpe two favors, no questions asked, no offer refused. It was a long story.

I swallowed again, then forced myself to stand a little straighter. "Fine, but this will cost you, James. You're using up one of your favors."

His expression didn't change, but I got the sense that I'd seriously pissed him off. The hairs on the back of my neck stood on end. That fight or flight instinct took hold. This was the sensation the experts warned you not to ignore. That feeling of being in a dangerous situation. Trust your gut, they said. Listen to your intuition. My gut was telling me to get the hell out of here, to hop in the car and lock the doors. To drive away and not look back.

Then like a balloon slowly losing its air, the tension between us deflated. He grinned, flashing his fangs at me. "All right, then. You still owe me one favor. And darlin', it will be a big one."

"Agreed." I hated being in his debt. He could ask me to do anything, and I'd be obliged. It was a bad position to be in, but what choice did I have?

Mama Goblin groaned, rubbed the side of her large head. Then she gazed up at me. "You. You stole my magic." She rolled to her feet, much more gracefully than I would have expected. She started to charge at me again, but Sharpe grabbed her by her huge, pointy ears, stopping her in her tracks.

"No, you don't. You're not going to bother Holly again."

She winced and tried to swat at his hands with her claw-tipped nails. "She stole my magic."

Sharpe glanced at me, his brows raised.

I sighed. Deeply. I had to tell her how to get her magic back, or she'd never leave me alone. "Take a bath. A long one. Scrub every inch of yourself."

Her frown was almost comical. Her yellow eyes narrowed. "What are you talking about, null?" Her fleshy upper lip curled on the last word.

"I told you how to fix it. Do it or not."

"I just have to bathe?"

"Thoroughly. With rose-scented soap." I wasn't above dealing out a little payback. I really hoped she hated the smell of flowers.

Sharpe let her go and produced a handkerchief from his pocket. He wiped his fingers and glared down at her with distaste. "And by the looks of you, you may have to wash yourself several times to cut through all that grime."

She peered up, pointing one bony finger at him. "I'll remember you, vampire."

"Good, because next time I won't pull any punches, and the null won't be here to fuck with my mojo. Go on with you."

She gave me one last glare before loping off down the street.

"Now it's your turn." He led the way to the curb, where his fancy black vampire-mobile sprawled low to the ground. I was surprised when he opened the passenger door for me, because Sharpe wasn't a gentleman. But then he plucked a black eye mask from his jacket pocket, and it all made sense.

"Put this on."

I grabbed it from his hand. "I don't trust you, James."

He sighed, glancing up at the sky as it spit rain on his face, dampening his hair. "Well, that's a sign of your intelligence, innit? Would you rather go in the boot? C'mon, now. Make up your mind, Holly, love, because I don't have all bloody night, now do I?"

I settled back into the plush leather seat and slipped the mask over my face, feeling every muscle in my body tighten like a bowstring. My stomach knotted, all thoughts of dinner long gone.

Sharpe slammed the door, then came around and climbed in beside me. The car smelled of his expensive aftershave.

He started driving, but to my irritation instead of being silent, he insisted on talking about Cade. "What's it like, him being wif a null? Doesn't he resent you for stealing his powers? And yet you risked your life to save his. Fucking foolish of you, if you don't mind my saying so."

I dug my fingers into the buttery soft leather seat, hoping my nails might make a hole. "Why is the Master desperate for this sudden meeting? He's waited months, and now he needs to see me tonight?"

"That's for him to tell, not me. So, what do you and the sorcerer do, besides shag, I mean? It's not like he can take you round to see his mates. Like a real couple."

A real couple. That echoed through my head. The fact that Cade had no friends—at least none that I knew of—barely mattered. But what if he did? What if he had a whole group of Others he liked to hang out with on the rare day off? Was he avoiding them on account of me?

When I realized what I was doing, playing into Sharpe's hands, letting all the worries and fears about my relationship with Cade come flooding to the surface, I put a stop to it. This manipulative son-of-a-bitch was not going to get in my head.

"What happened to Monty?" I asked. When the Master found out his personal assistant had betrayed him, he'd disemboweled Monty in front of me. Then he'd taken him home to heal. I shuddered again.

"Cold?" He turned up the heater and the small space flooded with warm air. It didn't help. I was so frozen, my bones shivered. "Monty. Yeah, I'll let Master Sebastian answer that one, too."

The eye mask was starting to make me feel claustrophobic—and I needed to scratch my cheek. When I lifted my hand, Sharpe batted at my wrist.

"None of that. Put your hand down and keep it down."

"It must be a change for all of you. Monty let you do what you wanted, as long as it didn't bounce back on him. The Master seems much more...formidable."

"I don't mind following a leader who knows his onions. Used to be a soldier, you know."

"What war?" I asked.

"Crusades. Those were the days. All the raping and pillaging and burning with no consequences. Now, they put you on trial for that sort of thing."

"Stupid justice. Am I right?"

"Mock all you want, but things were a lot simpler back then."

"For rich white guys who had weapons and power, I'm sure things were great. For everyone else, life was probably a little tougher."

"You sound like one of 'em snowflakes, you do." He fell silent after that, and I'd run out of questions. We drove in silence for maybe forty minutes, possibly an hour. I had no way of judging the time. Every other second was measured in the click of the windshield wipers, but I'd lost count along the way. Eventually, Sharpe slowed down and made a few tight turns.

"Look, don't be nervous," he said. "Just show the Master deference and you'll be all right."

Was he trying to comfort me? I'd have said that was thoughtful—if I didn't know him.

He slowed the car and pulled to a stop. "You can take off the blindfold."

I ripped off the mask and blinked a few times against the bright lights. We were inside a large space—like a warehouse. Maybe an airplane hangar? Expensive, shiny sports cars surrounded me. Red and black and white and blue, with sleek designs. There were a couple of SUVs, too.

"What is this place?"

"The Master's stable. He's traded horses for horsepower."

I followed Sharpe as he got out of the car and walked to an elevator at the end of the building. "Are we above ground?" There were no windows in this place, but huge ventilation tubes running across the ceiling made me think we must be subterranean.

"So many questions."

I handed him the eye mask as we stepped onto the elevator. Sharpe hit the button for the first floor. There were ten in all. I didn't like being this far underground. We didn't have basements in Tulsa for a reason.

When the elevator stopped, the doors slid open revealing a tiled wall. Humidity filled the air and moistened my skin. I detected no hint of chlorine, but it did smell of salt water, reminding me of when Gran and I took a trip to Florida when I was ten. We spent a day at the ocean, playing in the surf and collecting sea shells.

I followed Sharpe down the tiled hallway—intricate mosaic patterns covered the wall from the floor to the ceiling, telling stories of Greek gods and goddesses. I recognized some of them. Sisyphus rolling a stone up a hill. Actaeon turning into a stag.

Sharpe buttoned his jacket as we turned a corner, and there, standing in an enormous saltwater pool was Master Sebastian. His dark eyes drank me in and he wore a triumphant expression.

Sharpe bowed his head. "Master, the null is here."

"Finally, Holly, we meet again. Welcome."

Sebastian was a huge man, easily seven feet tall. The last time I'd seen him, his long dark hair had been a tangle down his back. His beard had been nearly as long. Now, his wet hair hit him above the shoulders, with reddish highlights gleaming through it. His beard had been trimmed close to his face. I was almost certain he was naked under the water, which hit him at his waist. Copper colored skin covered the massive muscles of his arms and chest. He was handsome in a scary, brutish way.

Though he now spoke without accent or inflection, when he'd first awakened he uttered words in a language I didn't recognize. I wondered where he came from, originally. How old was he? Hundreds of years, at least. Maybe thousands.

Sharpe patted my shoulder before he disappeared, and I was left alone with the most powerful vampire in Oklahoma.

CHAPTER TWENTY-FIVE

The heat was starting to get to me, even though my hands and feet were still freezing. Sweat dotted my forehead and upper lip as Sebastian and I simply stood and stared at each other.

After a few long, silent minutes, he said, "You didn't like my gifts. I sent so many."

I summoned my most diplomatic response. "They were lovely. I just didn't feel right keeping them."

He regarded me with those eyes, glittering dark, like onyx stones. "Why not?"

I took a deep breath and tried to find the right words. He must have seen my hesitation.

"Let's have honesty between us, hmm? You saved me, Holly, and I'm most eager to show my gratitude."

"Do you really want honesty? Sharpe said I should show you deference."

He grinned a flash of white teeth, contrasting with his skin and beard. "Can you not do both at once?"

I lifted one shoulder, the sore one. "I'm not sure I can."

He laughed a rich, throaty chuckle that suddenly made him seem less Other and more human. "Then just be honest. You didn't like my gifts."

"They made me uncomfortable."

He cocked one brow. "How so?"

The diamond ring had been as big as a quarter. When I sent it back, he sent me a sapphire to take its place. It was even larger than the diamond. "They were too expensive, for one thing." I was bone weary and walked over to a teak bench tucked into a tiled niche. I plopped onto it and leaned back, finally relaxing. The vampire was going to do whatever he wanted, but in the meantime, why shouldn't I get comfortable? My muscles were tired from being so tense during the long drive.

He turned his head to watch me. "What else?"

He asked for the truth, so I gave it to him. "I thought there were strings attached, and I don't want to be in your debt."

"But I am in your debt."

He moved smoothly to the side of the pool and crossed his arms on the flat rim, studying me. Even his hands were enormous. His beard trapped beads of water and they glowed in the soft light, just like the diamond he'd given me. "In my very long life, you're the first null that I've met. I find it...strange. I barely remember being human. To have to breathe again, it's like I've stepped down several rungs on the evolutionary ladder."

It shouldn't surprise me that he saw himself superior to humans. After all, he was at the top of the food chain. "Monty liked it. He liked the feel of his heart beating."

"He would. Monty has always been weak."

"And yet you trusted him as your second in command?" When I realized how confrontational the question really sounded, I immediately apologized. "I'm sorry. That's none of my business."

"No, it's not. But I'll answer. Monty was an efficient little prick. So good at all the social niceties that I despise. He's still alive. Would you like to see him?" A smirk graced his mouth, and I had no doubt that whatever state Monty Ridgecliff was in, I didn't want to see it.

"No, thank you." And since when did vampires need social niceties? They sipped blood the same way I drank a glass of milk—without any thought to the cow that provided it. But maybe vamps had all sorts of customs that I wasn't privy to. Perhaps they were forced to be nice to one another?

"Your face is like a book," he said. "Every thought flashes across your features. I find it charming. Come."

The next thing I knew, the vampire was hauling himself out of the pool. Water slid down his back and over his full, tight ass. So awkward. As he strode toward a rack of white towels, I turned away and glanced at the ceiling, spanning a good fifteen feet over my head. That's when I noticed the constellations set in tile. It bore an amazing resemblance to the real sky. I hunted for the North Star and ignored Sebastian until he spoke again.

"I wanted to thank you in person, Holly James." His voice was closer than before, and my name rolled off his tongue as if he was tasting it, savoring it.

My gaze darted up to see him standing a foot away, a white towel wrapped around his waist. Steam wafted from the pool, swirling in the air and covering him in a layer of fragrant mist.

This guy wasn't just a blood sucker, he was a Master. I didn't know what true powers he might hold, though unlike other vampires, masters could tolerate sunlight. They were few and far between—I wasn't sure what made a master's magic stronger, what separated them from the rest, but it must be significant.

I pasted a smile on my face. "You're most welcome. Now, if you don't mind, it's late and I need to get home."

Those eyes remained fixed on me. "I do apologize for any inconvenience." He didn't sound the least bit sincere. "But now that I have you here, I'd like to talk. As...friends."

"But we're not friends." The words slipped out before I could stop them.

"Would you rather us be enemies?"

"No. I'd rather us be amiable strangers."

He laughed, his firm pecs and chiseled abs flexing with the movement. Then he quickly sobered. "No. I want to be friends."

His long stride carried him across the tiled floor and out the door. I stood and scrambled after him. He stalked down a wide hallway with heavy wooden doors closed on either side. He turned the corner and disappeared into a room on the right.

I peeked in cautiously before following. It was some sort of ornate sitting room. Opulent silks in colors of scarlet and tangerine and cobalt covered the furniture. Rich looking pillows in velvet were carelessly flung on the sofas and the white marble floor. The walls appeared to be papered in gold leaf. Overhead, crystal chandeliers bathed the room in soft light.

Sebastian strode to the center of the room where a woman in a navy housekeeper's uniform waited, holding out a blue silk bathrobe. He whipped off the towel, and before I could lower my head, he faced me, naked and nonchalant. He slid his arms into the robe and tied the belt.

Yeah, I took a peek, and yeah, it was big. Just like the rest of him.

The woman disappeared and Sebastian settled on to a low sofa, gesturing that I sit across from him. With a sigh, I walked forward and fell down onto the tangerine sofa. I leaned back, letting the soft material cradle me.

The maid returned in a jiff, this time with a silver tray. She poured thick, dark sludge into espresso cups from a copper jug with a long handle. She handed the first to Sebastian, the second to me. Then she disappeared by the side door once again. During the entire exchange, Sebastian didn't acknowledge her in any way.

I took a small sniff from the cup. I was pretty sure it was coffee of some kind.

"Turkish," he said.

"Is that where you're from?" I didn't expect him to answer me, and I wasn't disappointed.

"Drink it. It's delicious."

I made sure he sipped before I did. He simply gave me a mocking grin and drank. Then I did, too, forcing myself to swallow it down. Tasted like ashes mixed with mud.

I tried to school my face, but Sebastian's dark eyes twinkled. "It's an acquired taste."

"If you say so. Well, I'm here, so what did you want to talk about?"

"So impatient." He tsked at me and sipped more of that awful brew.

I waited, saying nothing. He'd wrangled me into this meeting, now he wanted to act civil. But he wasn't civil, and this faux show of hospitality was bullshit.

After he finished his coffee, he wiped his mouth with the little white cloth napkin the maid had provided with our cups. "Tell me about yourself, your powers," he said at last.

Ah. Now we were getting down to it. "Are you going to share, too? I'd love to know what powers you possess." Yes, I was still quaking in my boots, but I'd been playing nice with him for months. Now he'd forced my hand, and I wasn't going to sit here like some meek little rabbit. I had to respect him, as Sharpe suggested, but I wasn't going to cower.

He placed his cup on a black enameled table next to him. "You are bold. But I realized that the night we met. Such a fierce loyalty to your sorcerer. An unusual choice, if you don't mind my saying."

I did mind, actually, but I kept my lips zipped and waited him out. This was his show.

"Your powers fascinate me, Holly. Your blood nullifies, too, doesn't it?"

"You know it does." Tired of games, I scooted to the edge of the sofa and placed my cup on the round, tufted purple ottoman between us. "Is that why I'm here? Because you want my blood?"

"Would you give it to me if I did?" He lifted his brows in question.

"No. You'd have to take it from me. Is that what you plan on doing?"

"Let me understand, just to be clear. You hire yourself out to any Other willing to pay for your services." He made me sound like a whore. "And yet you won't sell your blood? Where is the sense in that?"

I could see where this was going. He was old and cunning. He'd twist my words and have me agreeing with him in no time if I didn't keep my wits about me. No magic required. Just an ancient manipulative mind at work.

"It's mine to sell or not. I don't have to justify it to you, and I think you understand that my time and my blood are not remotely the same thing."

"Aren't they? Your blood is your very essence. The thing that keeps life pumping inside of you. It controls your time here on this earth. What is the difference?"

"I control how I spend my time. If I give my blood to you, I'm no longer in control."

He leaned back, spreading one arm along the back of the sofa, widening the edges of his robe and flashing glimpses of his bare chest. "Control is important to you?"

Was he trying to psychoanalyze me now? "No more than it is to you, I think. Being a Master means having control of an entire territory."

"All right, if your blood is off the table for now—"

"It's off the table forever."

"Forever is a very long time, Holly James. Don't make declarations you may not be able to keep. You'll only look foolish in the end."

I narrowed my eyes at him. "Are you threatening me? And here I thought we were being friendly."

He leaned toward me—only a few inches—but I got the full effect of his charisma, his intensity. Then he grinned without showing fang. That took practice. "I'm not threatening you. I'm merely stating that life is unexpected. Sometimes we make compromises along the way." He leaned back, continuing to study me, my reactions.

"I understand you're on retainer to a few of your clients. I'd like to hire you in that capacity."

"I'm sorry, but I'll have to decline."

His face became still, impassive. I had that same feeling I'd had with Sharpe—that I was on thin ice. My refusal irritated him. But his anger wasn't as intense as it had been with Sharpe. Was that because the Master was holding himself in check or had he expected my refusal all along?

"I'm very busy at the moment. More clients than I can handle."

Another beat passed before his taut features relaxed a bit. "And you have that murder investigation. Strange that. You working with a sorcerer."

"I suppose it is." It didn't surprise me that he knew about the murder. Sebastian probably had spies everywhere.

"Why do you do it?"

"Why wouldn't I want to get a killer off the streets?"

"Ah, a warrior." He gazed at me with those obsidian eyes, as though he could see clear through to my soul. It was uncomfortable, and I tried hard not to squirm.

"I don't know about that."

"I do. You have the heart of one. A champion for the dead, hmm? That's how you see yourself."

Yeah, that would be a good, if not pompous, description. I wanted to give those dead women a voice. I wanted the killer punished for what he'd done to them. If that made me a warrior for justice, then I'd take it. But it squicked me out that Sebastian could read me so easily. Like my mind was an open book. He could thumb through the pages and learn all my secrets.

"And what of the anomaly where magic is concerned? Why is that happening, do you think?"

"I have no idea. Do you?" I asked.

He tipped his head back and bit his lip in thought. "I remember something like this happening once before." He lowered his chin and looked me in the eye. "Pompeii. It wasn't just a volcano. It was a magical blackout."

I scooted even further on the edge of my seat. "What caused it?"

"I couldn't say."

Couldn't or wouldn't? Was he deliberately leading me down a rabbit hole? "What stopped the blackout?"

He shrugged one massive shoulder. "I wasn't in the area at the time." Again with the evasive answers.

I brushed my hands over my thighs. "Thank you for the coffee, but I really need to get home."

"So soon? I was hoping we might discuss the dead girl."

I almost slipped and asked which one. "I can't discuss anything about the case."

"I heard about the strange symbols carved into her hands."

Carved into one of her hands. So, he didn't have all of his facts correct. "Sounds like you're very familiar with the murder. Why is that?"

"I had nothing to do with it, if that's what you're asking." He gave me a tiny smirk. "Rituals, despite Monty's strange proclivity for them, are not something we subscribe to."

So, he knew about the ritualistic aspect, but not everything. Maybe this was a fishing expedition for him. But why would the Master want info on the murders? Did he suspect one of his own of carrying them out?

"Where are you getting your information?"

"I have eyes and ears all over this city."

"What about the marks? Do you know what they mean?" I asked.

"No, but I would hazard to guess that you have more than one death on your hands. And the toll will rise."

"Why do you think that?"

"Ask yourself, what is the killer gaining from the death of this girl?"

"It's a power trip. He's living out his fantasy," I guessed.

"Perhaps. But the reasons for murder are usually very simple, though the means may not be."

"Serial killers have their own sick reasons for doing it. It's a compulsion."

"But why? Power, as you stated, yes? Or it could be revenge. Jealousy. Greed. These are still the petty motives that drive humans to commit crime."

He didn't have much respect for his food source. "I'm sure the same can be said for vampires."

"Touché. Do you know the girl's identity yet?"

Cade was going to be pissed that I discussed the case, but the Master seemed to have some information already, so I decided to be honest. "No."

"The Italian might be able to help you with that."

"The Italian?"

He stood then, wrapping his robe tighter and retying the sash. "I enjoyed our talk, Holly. We'll have to do this again. Very soon." Then he left through the door the maid had used.

All righty, then. Good talk. And if I had my way, we'd never do this again.

I wandered back into the hallway where Sharpe waited for me. He pushed off the wall when he saw me coming.

"How did it go?"

"Who's the Italian?"

"Fabrizio Buratti."

"And?"

"And, he's a man of secrets. If the Master sent you to him, he'll have information you might want. Come along, then." He began sauntering down the hallway, hands in his pockets. "We should get you back to your sorcerer."

I followed him around the corner, and came to a stop when the man I'd spoken with the night before appeared. The plastic surgeon, the one who'd cornered me at the cocktail party. Dr. Peter Everett.

"What are you doing here?" I asked.

CHAPTER TWENTY-SIX

Peter smiled. "I told you I'd be seeing you again. I work for the Master."

Sharpe cast a scrutinizing eye over the doctor. "How did you two meet?"

"He introduced himself at a cocktail party last night." Had Sebastian sent the doctor to spy on me?

"Really?" Sharpe asked. "How interesting." He didn't sound interested. He sounded as suspicious as I was.

Peter gazed at Sharpe. "I asked about ghosts. She was at the party as a psychic energy reader." He used finger quotes around the title. "I wondered if that was true." He peered down at me. "Can you banish them or were you just sticking to the script?"

"That's what I do, Dr. Everett. I'm a null."

This time when he smiled, it wasn't quite so bright. "Peter, remember?" He patted my sore shoulder, and I flinched away.

"What's wrong?"

"It's nothing." I glanced up at Sharpe. "I'm ready to go home."

"It's not nothing. I saw that look of pain. Let's go to my office." Peter strode down another corridor, not waiting to see if we followed.

"What's up wif the shoulder, love?" Sharpe asked, leaning toward me, keeping his voice pitched low. "Wouldn't have something to do wif that goblin bitch having your blood on her, now would it?"

"Maybe."

"Let's go." He took my elbow and steered me down the hallway where the doctor had disappeared.

Sharpe led me to a white room that contained three hospital beds. Peter patted one of them. "Hop up. Let's take a look."

Sharpe slouched elegantly against the wall, watching as I shrugged off my torn jacket and my thick navy fisherman's sweater. I pulled down the collar of my long-sleeved T-shirt and bra strap to show him the gash.

Peter donned a pair of gloves, then poked and prodded the wound. "Looks like it's getting infected. What happened?"

"Just a scratch."

He leaned his head back to get a look at my face. "From what?"

"Crazy goblin bitch took a swipe at our null, didn't she, love?"

I glared at Sharpe.

"Hmm. Never met a goblin," Peter said.

"They're disgusting creatures." Sharpe studied his own manicured nails.

Peter prodded the scratch once more, making me scrunch my face in pain. "Let's get some antibiotics into you." He crossed to a cabinet and opened a door that contained a small pharmacy. He searched through several bottles until he found what he was looking for. "Not allergic to anything, are you?"

"No."

He handed me a bottle. "Cipro. Take it twice a day for ten days. When did you have your last tetanus shot?"

"A couple of years ago."

"Good." He grabbed a fresh tube of ointment and spread some on a long Q-tip, dabbing it on my shoulder. "Put this on twice a day, as well." He patched me up with a small gauze bandage. "And you should be good to go." He snapped off his gloves, threw them away, and then reached in his pocket and handed me a business card. "Call if it doesn't start clearing up in a few days. I'll get you into the office."

I fingered the edge of the card. "And this is what you do for the Master? You patch up his blood bags?"

Peter shot a glance at Sharpe. "We prefer the term donor."

No wonder he looked so youthful. He was probably partaking of the world's best anti-aging serum: vampire blood. As a blood slave, he would get a taste of vamp blood every now and then. A little go-go juice to make him appear younger and boost his immune system. From what I'd heard, it was every bit as addictive as heroine or meth.

I slipped my bra and shirt up over my shoulder. "Thanks."

"No problem. Good to see you again."

Even though he'd helped me, I couldn't say the same. The guy made me uneasy.

#

When Sharpe pulled into my driveway, Cade stood in the open doorway. Light from the house cast him in silhouette. As soon as the car stopped, Cade flew across the yard and had my door yanked open before I could unlatch my seatbelt.

He helped me from the car, then gently gripped my hands as he looked me over by the glow of the security lights. "Are you all right?" He was keeping that temper leashed, but I could feel it swirling through him, almost tangible, definitely combustible.

"I'm fine. And we have a lot to talk about."

He dipped his chin. "Yes."

Sharpe emerged from the driver side, and stood with his arm propped on the open door. "She's fine, mate. Didn't harm a hair on her lovely head."

Cade let go of me as he looked over the roof at Sharpe. Then he practically leapt over the hood, and had Sharpe's throat in one hand. He used the other to punch the vamp's face, each jab lightning fast and full of raw rage.

"You fucker." Another punch to Sharpe's nose. "You sick asshole." Two more jabs to Sharpe's eye.

I walked toward them. All that adrenaline from earlier left me feeling drained. I placed my hand on Cade's arm. "Enough. I'm going inside. Come with me."

Cade paused, his arm still cocked for yet another blow to Sharpe's bloody face.

"He's not fighting back, Cade." I jerked my head toward the vampire. He'd stood there and taken every punch without even raising his hand in defense.

Cade's arm slowly dropped, then he let go of Sharpe's throat, and took a step backward. "You touch her again, I'll kill you for real."

Blood ran down Sharpe's face—from the corner of his eye, his nose, and his mouth. He pushed out his tongue, testing his lower lip. "She came wif me to pay off a favor owed. But I don't blame you for taking it badly. Any bloke put his hands on my woman, I'd do the same." He touched the corner of his eye and winced.

"Get the hell out of here," Cade said, his voice icy calm. Scary as hell.

Sharpe climbed behind the wheel, and tore out of my driveway like a bat out of hell.

Cade put his arm around me, pulled me close. He kissed the top of my head as we walked toward the house.

Once inside, Cade insisted I sit on the sofa while he washed his hands of Sharpe's blood. Then, as though I had the flu, he wrapped a fuzzy ivory blanket around my legs. "I'll make you some tea."

"How about a glass of wine. No, wait. I need to take an antibiotic, so I should probably stick to the tea. Damn." I could really use a drink after the last couple of days I'd had.

Cade held his questions until he had brewed a cup of Gran's concoction for relaxation. I tasted Valerian root and citrus. Cade had added a nice dollop of honey, just the way I liked it.

He settled next to me on the sofa, placing his arm along the back, twisting his body to face me. "When did you have time to go to the doctor?"

"I saw Master Sebastian's doc. I met him last night, actually, at the Wyler's party."

"What does he have to do with the Wylers?"

"Amanda's his interior designer." I shrugged.

"And you trust his judgement?"

"About my shoulder, yeah. He gave me some pills and some cream to put on the scratch. Mama Goblin came back tonight and tried to finish what she'd started. She jumped me from behind."

He closed his eyes, his nostrils flaring slightly as he took a deep breath. "Did she hurt you again?" When he opened his eyes, they were dark with anger.

"Worse." I held up my busted purse. "She broke my Burberry. I bought it secondhand, but damn, I love this bag." I wondered if I could take it somewhere and get a new strap. Still, it wouldn't be the same.

Cade coughed out a rough chuckle and covered his eyes with one hand. "You are a piece of work." He smoothed his hand over his head, and sighed.

"Sharpe pulled her off me. And he knocked her upside the head. She was out for three or four minutes."

"I'm not forgetting what else he did, dragging you off to see Sebastian without me. That was a bitch move."

"He does what Sebastian tells him to do. By the way, Sebastian wanted me on retainer, but I turned him down."

"Good. But he'll keep asking. Until he demands your help. Did he mention your blood?"

I nodded and sipped my tea. "He also seemed to be interested in the murder investigation. Claimed he had nothing to do with it. Said he'd heard about the magical infection before. When Pompeii blew, which might strengthen my theory about nature itself being all jacked up. And he said The Italian might know the identity of our Jane Doe."

Cade's brows skyrocketed. "Shit."

"Why? Who is this Italian character?"

"A badalisc. He feeds off secrets, then uses them as leverage, and he can tell if you're lying. I try to avoid him. He's slimy. And a pimp, so it would make sense that he might know our Jane Doe. By the way, Jane Two's fingerprints were on file. She'd been arrested for soliciting and drug charges. Her name was April Walsh."

I leaned my head back, sighing in relief. "Halleluiah. At least we have one lead we can follow."

"And my people said the Wylers are squeaky clean. They donate time and money to charity. They're politically active. And they're self-made."

"Good for them."

I took my first pill with a sip of tea, and as we sat on the sofa, I told Cade about my night at Master Sebastian's lair. Every detail I could remember.

"Bastard made sure you saw him in the raw, huh?"

"Yep, I caught the full package."

A glint came into his eyes. "How do I measure up?"

I set my cup on the coffee table and stroked his whiskered cheek. "No comparison, McAllister. You always come out on top."

He smiled, picked me up, and carried me off to bed. By the time we were both undressed, I was nearly asleep. He tucked me into his warmth and stroked my hair. In seconds, I was out.

#

I woke up a couple of hours later, my mind whirring. Everything that had been going on from the mystery at Moonlight Cove to the dead girls to Master Sebastian ran through my head in a kind of disjointed freeform, jumping from one problem to the next.

I climbed out of bed, careful not to disturb Cade, and padded into the living room. I realized I was hungry, and I still hadn't gone to the store. I opened the refrigerator door, as though it might have magically been filled with food in my absence. It hadn't.

I made another cup of tea and pulled out my notebook, jotting down everything that ran through my head. It wasn't coherent, some of it didn't make sense, but I got it all down—my fear of Master Sebastian, my concern about never finding the girl with the symbol on her hand, my frustration at my grandfather, Wallace, and his broken promise of finding my mom. Once I finished, I felt better, more centered.

Then I grabbed my tablet and looked up Fabrizio Buratti, the Italian. I found nothing on my local badalisc. Not one damned thing. But I found some information on badaliscs in general. In certain parts of Italy, a Norm would don a muppet-like costume and play the role of the badalisc. He'd give a prediction for the year to come, then let the locals chase him out of town.

Eventually, I found the true nature of the badalisc on a site run by an occult academic. As I glanced through his list of paranormal creatures, I realized this guy knew his shit. He gave honest and accurate definitions of Others, not the video game version or a TV show depiction, making me wonder how he obtained all this information in the first place. Anyway, according to him, a badalisc fed on secrets. Literally, the juicier and nastier, the better. As some creatures feed from the soul or from a person's life force, the badalisc grew stronger, more powerful in his magic as he devoured more and more private information. Once he knew his victim's deepest and darkest, he could easily blackmail them. He also doled out information, too, in exchange for money or more secrets. Like a barter system. And this was the man we were going to meet in the morning. Lovely.

I must have dozed at some point, because when my phone rang, I jerked upright and experienced a moment of confusion, not remembering why I lay slumped over on the sofa.

I blinked a couple of times before glancing at my phone. "Mick, what time is it?"

"Almost three, darling. Sorry to wake you, but I have something you want."

For a second, I thought he was propositioning me. Then I remembered tattoo girl. "You found her?"

"I've detained her. She's here at the club, if you still want to talk to her."

"I do. I'll be right there."

I tossed the blanket aside and softly walked to the bedroom. Cade slept on his back, his face angled toward the window, painting his harsh angles in light and shadow. Before waking him, I quickly threw on a pair of jeans and pulled on a sweater.

I reached out and stroked his arm. "McAllister."

His eyelids fluttered, then he popped up, instantly alert. "What's wrong?"

"Mick called. He has our girl. The tattoo girl."

Without hesitation, he stood and grabbed a fresh set of clothes from the top of the dresser, his movements swift. "You've had a hell of a night, why don't you stay here?"

"Nice try. Let me get my boots on and I'll be ready to go."

We didn't speak on the way to the truck. Rain poured down, gushing like a creek along the curb. As we drove, the streets were empty, but the rain was so heavy it obscured visibility, causing Cade to slow to a crawl at times. Some of the side streets contained standing water. Much more of this and we'd have a serious flood problem on our hands.

It seemed to take forever to make it to The Raven but it was only half an hour. I might be tired but my mind remained active, thinking about all the things I'd been wanting to ask this girl. And for once, I'd better get some answers. I was tired of hitting dead ends.

With the exception of Mick's SUV and one other car, the lot was empty. We were only a few feet from the entrance but I was glad I wore boots, because it was impossible to avoid deep puddles of water. Cade opened the door for me but I spun around, my gaze roaming over the parking lot. No stacked-up frogs in sight. I wondered what Mick had done with them.

I walked into the club. Unlike the other morning, the place smelled of booze and perfume and sin. Mick waited for us at the bottom of the stairway. I was surprised he'd opened for business, knowing no spells or incantations could be used on the premises. Not with the magical infection looming over the club.

"Ah, you brought your guard dog, I see." Mick's dark eyes locked onto Cade.

McAllister said nothing, just glared back, his scowl firmly in place. "Where's the girl?"

"Good to see you, too." He turned toward the bar, where Titus wiped down glasses. "We'll be in room three."

"Understood." Titus flung the white towel he'd been using over his shoulder, his gaze flitting between Cade and me. I read the curiosity on his face. He probably had the same questions everyone else had. A sorcerer with a null?

Mick started up the stairs. Cade and I followed as he sauntered past the tables, through the maze of black hallways until he reached a door to a room I'd never been in, one with a keypad mounted next to it on the wall. Mick pressed in a code and the door clicked. He held it open and jerked his head, indicating Cade and I should enter first.

I walked into a windowless room of startling white. Quite a contrast from the dark hallway behind me. White tiled walls met white tiled floors, and it smelled faintly of bleach. A drain sat in the middle of the room. Except for a small counter with a sink, the room was empty. Well, except for the girl handcuffed to a metal chair, which was bolted to the floor.

CHAPTER TWENTY-SEVEN

It took a second for my mind to realize what this was: a torture room. One that would be easy to clean. Bile rose in my throat. Why did Mick have this in his club?

The girl's eyes were glazed over, her head bent to one side.

"She's high," Cade said.

"I slipped her a valium."

I swung my head back toward Mick. "Was this necessary? We just need to ask her a few questions."

Cade and Mick stood on either side of me. Mick crossed his arms, and that cruel countenance I sometimes glimpsed rode his features. His full lips twisted in a cruel smile. "You keep forgetting this is my house. Besides, she didn't want to talk. And since I couldn't use magic to force her, this seemed to be the only solution." He looked down at me, his tone haughty, his dark eyes glimmering in the bright light. "I thought you'd be pleased, darling."

"That's enough, you prick." Cade's voice rumbled, bouncing off the tiles, echoing slightly. "Call her that one more time. I dare you."

"I'll call her what I like. You're here as a courtesy. One that can be revoked at any time."

Cade and Mick glared at each other over my head. The energy in the room expanded. They'd come to blows before, but I wouldn't put up with that shit tonight.

A knock on the door broke some of the tension. Mick turned and opened it, revealing Titus.

"I'm headed out, boss."

"Fine. Don't bother with the alarm. I'll take care of it."

Titus turned away, seemingly undisturbed that a human girl was being kept chained in this room, which made me wonder how often it happened. Every night? Once a week? And why, for God's sake?

Cade approached the girl. "What's her name?"

"Dena Talbot."

Cade hunkered down before her, lightly tapping her face. "Dena. You with us?"

It took a while for her glazed eyes to focus on Cade. "Who are you?" Her words were slurred.

"How much did you give her?" I asked.

Mick's chin tilted as he gazed down at me. "One pill. I have no idea what else she might have taken through the night, though."

My eyes drifted closed. This was fucked up. It wasn't that I didn't want to talk to this girl, but drugging her, detaining her—it seemed like overkill.

"Who are you?" she mumbled. "Just let me go." She lazily pulled at the handcuffs. "Let me go." She shook her head, dark blonde hair spilling over her face as she slurred the words.

"I want you to answer a few questions for me and then I'll take you home, okay? Dena?" Cade rarely had patience with anyone, but he was speaking very softly to this girl in an effort to keep her calm.

"M'kay." She sniffed and flung her head, trying to get the hair out of her eyes.

Cade reached toward her and smoothed her hair back. "You had a symbol tattooed on your hand."

"No." She leaned her head back, taking deep breaths. "Why is it so bright in here? God." She looked up at the ceiling, squinting at the fluorescent tubes.

Cade reached for her right hand, turning it over. No tattoo. No symbol.

I cut Mick a sharp look. "Are you sure this is the right girl?"

"Positive."

"Did you have a symbol on your hand, Dena?" Cade asked.

"Henna."

Okay, now that made sense. A henna tattoo would fade in a few weeks.

"Why did you have the symbol?"

She tilted her head, looked at Cade with her lids half closed. "You're not as hot as the other one. But you're okay."

"The symbol, Dena. Why did you have the symbol?"

"That's what he wanted. But he wanted…real…thing." We were losing her. In another minute, she'd be unconscious.

"Who wanted you to get a tattoo?" Cade lightly tapped her cheek. "What's his name?"

She pulled a breath and her eyes scanned me for the first time since I entered the room. "Who are you?"

"Holly."

"Holly. Holly jolly." Then she lightly laughed until her chin fell to her chest. She let out a soft snore.

"Now what?" I muttered.

Mick pulled a bottle of pills from his pocket and snagged the bottle of water sitting on the counter.

Cade glanced at the bottle before shaking out a pill. He lifted Dena's head, placed it on her tongue, and held the bottle to her mouth. Tipping her head back, he forced the water down her throat. She swallowed, then sputtered and coughed, but she was awake again. Groggy, but her eyes were open.

"What was that?" I asked.

"Just something to counteract the effects of the valium," Mick said. "She'll be more alert in moments. Far less pleasant, but more alert."

I turned to him. "You do this on a regular basis?"

"If you don't like my tactics, I suggest you stop coming to me for help."

Cade stalked over to where Mick and I stood. He tossed the pills back to Mick and turned to me. "Maybe she'll talk to you. Give it a try."

After ten minutes or so, Dena became far more alert. And more hostile. She jerked at the handcuffs chaining her. "Let me out of here. Now!" She glanced at all of us, her teeth gritted in anger. "You have no right to keep me here."

I approached her. "Answer our questions and you're free to go."

"Fuck you!" She jerked her body, but the chair didn't budge. "Fuck all of you," she screamed.

I tucked my hands in my pockets. "You're making this harder than it has to be, Dena."

She leaned forward. "You want something from me bitch, you have to pay for it. Just like everyone else. I don't give away anything for free."

"Good to know. So how much did you charge to get the henna tattoo?"

She pressed her back into the chair and stared at me.

"You want out of here? Start talking. Because that one?" I pointed at Mick. "He's going to keep you here, drugged and docile. And that one." I nodded at Cade. "He's going to lose his temper sooner rather than later." Then I leaned toward her. "You will tell us everything, Dena. You can do it the easy way or the hard way." God, I sounded just like Sharpe. I was threatening her to get what I wanted, and I didn't really care how Dena felt about it. The ends justified the means if it meant finding a killer.

But what did that make me? Was I becoming one of the monsters?

I believed I was dancing dangerously close to the line.

"I don't have to tell you a goddamn thing," she said. "And when I go to the police, they're going to have all sorts of questions about this room." She glared at Mick. "How many other people have you tortured here? This is what gets you off, drugging women and tying them up? Makes you feel like a big man? You're pathetic."

Mick strode forward, his face cold, impassive. "I have not tortured you. Yet." He whipped out his wallet and pulled out a handful of bills. "I was willing to pay two thousand for any information you may have. But with every nasty word, you're losing money."

She pursed her lips, staring at the wad of cash. Then she jerked once more against the handcuffs. "Go to hell."

Mick peeled off a twenty and stuck it in the pocket of his trousers. "Shall we try again?"

I glanced back at Cade. With his arms crossed, I wondered what was going through his head. But he stood back and let Mick have the floor.

"What's the name of the man who wanted you to get the tattoo?" I asked.

"Seriously? You think they give their real names? Just how stupid are you, bitch?"

Mick stuck another twenty in his pocket. Dena watched, her jaw clenched. The money angle was getting to her.

"How did he find you?"

She turned her attention back to me. "Website. His user name is Likes It Nasty 13."

"And he paid you to get the tattoo?"

"Yes." She blew out a breath and bumped the back of her head against the chair.

Cade strode forward. "You didn't get permanent ink, and you pocketed the cash."

"Yes." She kept banging her head. Harder and harder.

"Did you have one symbol or were there more?"

"More. I had henna tattoos on my foot, my spine, my stomach."

"And then you met with him," Cade said.

"Yes." Thump, thump, thump.

My head ached in sympathy just watching her. "What does he look like?"

"I don't know." She stopped the head banging when Mick plucked another twenty from the stack. "I'm serious. I don't know what he looked like. I...I can't remember."

Mick put the twenty back in the pile.

"Why not?" I asked.

"Because he drugged me."

"It's all fuzzy. I don't remember details." She swallowed. "I met Likes It Nasty at a hotel bar."

"Which one?" Cade asked.

"The Marriott downtown. It's safe there. We sat at a table, had a drink, and the next thing I knew, I think I was in the woods, but I'm not sure. I remember the sky, the stars." Her gaze remained fixed on the white wall, but I had a feeling she was reliving everything that happened to her that night—everything she could remember, at any rate.

"The next morning, I had rope burns on my wrists. I kept thinking about animal faces but I don't know why."

She blinked, took a deep breath. Glancing at all of us, her eyes narrowed. "I was drugged. I'm sure I was raped more than once. Or at least it felt that way."

Now I felt like shit. She'd been drugged and bound. Just like we'd done to her tonight. I understood her rage then. She must feel completely out of control like this, at the mercy of strangers who could do what they wanted, taking away her right to say no.

"What about the animal faces?" Cade asked. "Was there a picture or painting of animals?"

"I don't remember anything else."

"Where did you wake up?" I asked.

She said nothing for a full minute, then in a small, shaky voice she said, "In my own bed. He knows where I live."

Cade shifted. "We can protect you, get you to a safe house for a few weeks until we find this guy."

"And why would I trust you? Any of you?" she bit out.

Mick pulled the keys from his jacket pocket, tossed them to Cade, who unlocked the handcuffs. Then he bent down and used his pocket knife to cut through the zip ties binding her ankles together.

Mick pulled the other twenties from his pocket, added them back to the pile, and handed her the cash. "Do you want a ride home?"

"Fuck you." She folded the bills, stuck them down her bra, and left the room, slamming the door behind her.

"Charming girl," Mick said.

"You don't think she'll go to the police, tell them about this?" I asked.

"No. If she were going to report anything to the police, she'd have turned in Likes It Nasty."

I turned, facing both of them. "Speaking of that perv, we still don't know who he is. Or what he looks like." And what was with the animal faces?

I thought back to Mary, the Cherokee woman in the log cabin. She'd told me that animals had two faces. Had she been referring to the killer?

Cade and I left The Raven. Mick walked us to the door so that he could reset the alarm. None of us said a word. Not even goodbye.

It was still dark out, but the rain slowed for now. As Cade drove, I thought about the brain dump I'd written in my notebook from earlier and began musing out loud. "I guess I'd been hoping the murder took place at Moonlight Cove, but that doesn't seem likely."

"No, it doesn't," Cade said. "We've been over every inch of that town. If they killed Jane Doe there, I'd have found some evidence of it. And since it sounds like the coven was in chaos early Sunday morning, it hardly seems likely they'd have their wits about them to mop up every drop of blood."

"And you're sure she was killed near the lake, right?" I was still trying to figure out these strange no magic zones. Blackouts, Sebastian had called them.

"Most likely. You don't drive miles to dump a body. You do it as quickly and efficiently as possible."

"Unless you kill someone in the city and want to cover your tracks by dumping the body in the middle of the country, when vacation season is long over. The area where the model homes are being built hasn't been completely cleared yet. Lots of wooded acres surrounding Glen Falls."

He took his eyes from the road to glance at me. "You think Jane Doe was killed near Glen Falls, then driven over an hour out of town to be dumped in Lake Eufaula?"

"I don't know. Like I said, it's just a thought. I have tons of them, most leading nowhere. But I do wonder how, of all places, the model home became a zone. Unless, like you said, Dena was a test run. The symbols were tattooed rather than carved into her skin. She was drugged and raped, but not killed. Maybe the killer didn't have the courage to go through with it the first time. But after the trial run, he fantasized about it, wanted to take it a step further."

"Now that's a theory I can get behind. Wish to hell we could find the kill site."

"I've been thinking about that. I know this sounds crazy—"

"As opposed to all your other ideas?" He reached out and squeezed my knee.

"Very funny. But listen, I know that werewolves can't change in a contaminated zone, but they're still good at tracking, better than most Others. Why don't you call Dawson Nash, see if his people will search the wooded area around Glen Falls." Dawson was the alpha for eastern Oklahoma. He was a decent guy. For an Other.

"That doesn't sound crazy at all, Little Null. That's a brilliant idea." He pulled into my driveway and cut the engine. "Now, why don't you try and get a few hours of sleep. You look like you're running on empty."

We walked to the house and I unlocked the door, turning to him as he stood on the porch. "Will you join me? I'll sleep better if you're there."

His eyes softened as he leaned down and kissed me. "Of course."

When we broke apart, I still didn't move to enter the house. "Why does Mick have that room?"

Cade's expression turned grim. "Mick isn't my concern."

"And you don't care that he's torturing people?"

"He does what he has to do to keep everyone in line. That doesn't match up with the suave image he's shown you, but that's who he is, baby. He's ruthless."

I'd always known Mick had a fierce reputation, and I assumed it was well earned, but to see what he was capable of up close, it gave me a whole new appreciation for just how dangerous he really was.

CHAPTER TWENTY-EIGHT

When I awakened, Cade wasn't beside me. Dull gray light seeped into the room, and when I glanced at the clock, I was surprised to see I'd slept until nine.

I threw on a pair of pajama pants and walked to the kitchen. Cade was MIA, but the coffee was hot. I poured a cup and stood at the window above the sink. The clouds were strange and ominous this morning, like thick smoky swirls hanging low in the sky.

As I took my coffee to the living room, intent on texting Cade, I glanced at the fridge. My picture was missing. The one Annabelle had drawn. Had he taken it for some reason?

I was fairly certain he wouldn't go sleuthing without me, but he may have decided I needed sleep. When I glanced at my phone, he'd already left a message: Picking up breakfast. Be back soon. Thank God, I was starving.

Next, I texted Sunny. She'd shown up yesterday morning, and she usually got into the office by eight-thirty. Where are you?

She texted back that unless I had evidence Dean Wyler was a psychotic killer, she planned on going to see offices with him today. I wished her luck and instructed her to send me pics of anything that looked promising.

I grabbed my broken Burberry and pulled out the notes I'd made the night before. Mostly questions or theories I'd jotted down in an exhausted frenzy. Half of them didn't make sense, but some might have legs.

Cade arrived about ten minutes later with two bags of food. Though he'd shaved, he still appeared rugged and sexy. He wore tight jeans that cupped him in all the right places. His black T-shirt had faded to dark gray. The cuffs of his olive-green coat were frayed and a tiny stress hole appeared at the edge of one pocket. In other words, casually perfect.

He scowled at me. "What's wrong?" Holding the bags aloft, he glanced down at his shirt, then his gaze flickered over my face. "You're looking at me funny."

"I'm glad you're here. That's all."

His face heated, his eyes taking on a predatory gleam. "Baby."

I grinned. "Don't get excited. I was just appreciating the scenery. I need to eat before I collapse."

"Appreciating the scenery? I can live with that." He walked to the kitchen, dropped the bags, and began rumbling through the cabinet. "Better come and eat before it's all gone."

I wearily climbed to my feet, coffee cup in hand, and refilled it before sitting down to takeout from Tally's. Cade seemed to have bought a little bit of everything—eggs, sausage, biscuits, gravy, and their legendary cinnamon rolls.

"I called Dawson this morning. He and his pack are checking out the woods near Glen Falls."

"Good," I said around a mouthful of eggs. I ate so fast, I barely tasted it. Once my stomach was full, I watched him methodically plow through a mound of food.

I waved my notebook at him. "I have some thoughts."

"Course you do." He took a large bite from his cinnamon roll.

"Why was Master Sebastian so eager to give me The Italian's name? The vamp said he had nothing to do with the crime, but he employs prostitutes and has his own webcam girls. Maybe he's misdirecting me, because he's really the killer."

"Do you seriously believe that?" Cade asked, wiping his mouth on a napkin.

Deflated, I slumped forward, resting my elbow on the island. "No, not really."

"Listen, I'm going to file a formal complaint against Sebastian with the Council. Sharpe, too. It will carry even more weight since you were working for the Council when he kidnapped you."

Even though I felt better after eating, I still didn't have enough energy to fight about this right now. "I don't want you to do that, Cade."

"I'm not arguing about this, Holly. Those assholes crossed a line."

"A line I knew Sebastian would eventually cross. And so did you. You warned me. What will the Council do, anyway, send him a formal letter of complaint? That's a weak move, worse than doing nothing at all. It has no teeth. Last night? That was his version of friendly."

Cade rubbed his forehead with one hand, then stared at me with bleary eyes. "Have you thought about shutting down the business, just for a while until things cool down?"

"When will they ever cool down? And what am I supposed to do in the meantime? Get a desk job? I'd die of boredom. Following Others around isn't always a thrill, but it pays well. Very well. And I have Sunny to think of, too."

Before he could argue further, I continued thinking out loud. "Sebastian talked about motives last night. He thought money, power, or fame might be a reason to kill these women."

"How could the killer gain any of that by murdering prostitutes?"

"Maybe the ritual brings him luck? Or he believes it does. Because that's what rituals do, right? They either appease a deity or you sacrifice to get something in return."

"Why was Sebastian so damn curious about this case?" Cade asked, then sipped at his coffee.

"Maybe because I'm involved? He pointed me toward The Italian, so now he thinks we're even? I nullified his mystical coma, and he helped me in this murder investigation. But whoever has been feeding him information got some things wrong. He didn't know about the second body, and he thought Jane Doe had marks on both of her hands. He claimed not to know what the symbols were about." I plunked my forehead on the island. "Ugh, all these thought loops are exhausting."

"Want to leave The Italian to me? You could get some more rest."

I lifted my head, glaring at him. "Have we met? Of course I'm not letting you go alone. I want to see this badalisc, get a read on him. Are we going to April's place first?" I'd finally stopped referring to her as Jane Two in my mind and called her by her given name.

"Yeah, I thought we should. Get a look at her digs, see if we can find out who she met with the night she died. We have a last known address for her. A motel." Cade wadded up his napkin and tossed it in the Styrofoam container. "I still think we should at least report Sebastian to the Council, so there's a paper trail."

"We both know they won't do jack shit, so why bother? I get how you're feeling. If someone took you, I'd tear the earth apart to get you back."

"You did that once. I don't want you to ever put yourself in danger for me again." His eyes darkened as he reached out and took my hand, entwining his fingers with mine.

"Even though you'd do the same?"

"Even though." He leaned down and kissed my fingers.

"Look McAllister, there are times when I need you to have my back, like last night when you went after Sharpe. That sent a message. This Council paperwork is nonsense. You just want to do something, anything to keep me safe, and I get it. But let me have my own back on this one?"

His eyes fell closed for a minute, then he opened them and nodded. "All right."

#

April Walsh lived in a cheap, roadside motel on the east side of Tulsa. I noted the shabby condition of the chipped paint and rusted iron railings. It reeked of smoke and pot, with a little kick of urine thrown in for fun. The cars in the lot were older and tired, like the motel itself.

There was no sign of life stirring, even at ten a.m. We bypassed the office and headed up the cement stairs to the second story. Cade stopped at room two-oh-three and knocked. When no one answered, I asked if he wanted me to back up, allowing him to perform an opening spell.

"No need." He pulled out his wallet and grabbed a credit card. "The locks here are a joke." He wiggled the card between the door and the jamb, then jerked the handle a couple of times until the door sprang open.

"Nice trick, Sorcerer."

"I have a few up my sleeve."

He darted inside, and I trailed after him, shutting the door behind me. The curtains were closed, so I flipped on the light. If I'd thought the outside was sad and decrepit, it was nothing compared to the interior.

The place reeked of stale cigarettes, despite the No Smoking sign posted on the door. The bedspread used to be white, maybe ten years ago. Now it was gray with yellow stains and black burn marks. The tiled floor was dirty, littered not only with clothing, but with hair and ashes.

"Not exactly a glamorous lifestyle." I peeked inside the trashcan and spotted several used condoms, empty baggies, and some napkins. Diet Coke cans covered the small bedside table. Her room hadn't been cleaned since her death. I had a feeling that housekeeping wasn't exactly a priority here.

Cade kicked aside a pile of clothes on the floor, then started rifling through the dresser drawers, while I checked out the bathroom. The blue toilet and matching bathtub hadn't been updated since the sixties, maybe early seventies. It matched the cracked linoleum.

I poked through April's toiletries scattered around the tiny sink. Nothing unusual. The toilet was a tankless model, so no hiding spot there.

"Find anything?" Cade asked, coming to stand in the doorway.

"No, you?"

He held up a burner phone. "Kleenex box."

"You really are full of tricks."

"That's not all." He pulled a piece of paper from his jeans pocket.

"What's that?"

"A pawn ticket for a laptop. And there's a pawn shop right across the street."

"Perfect. Want to stop by the office and ask the manager a few questions? I'll stay out of the way, let you do that mind voodoo you do so well." I wiggled my fingers at him.

"Yeah, sounds good."

"Go ahead. I'll double check everything in here. Make sure I didn't overlook anything."

"I'll meet you at the truck in five."

When he left, I ripped through all of April's makeup, but came up empty. I flipped the lid off of her stick deodorant, turned the tube upside down, and rolled it upward until the deodorant itself fell out. A tiny bag of pills had been wedged inside the plastic holder.

I wasn't after April's stash, so I tossed the pills in the toilet and watched them swirl away.

Before leaving the room, I glanced over my shoulder. April's life had led her to this pathetic, desperate existence. I remembered her bloated body stretched out along the edge of Lake Henryetta, and my heart hurt for this woman I'd never know. Hopefully, she'd find some rest in the world beyond this one.

I shut the door, making sure it was locked. As I turned toward the stairs, the door to room two-oh-two opened a crack. My gaze met a pair of bloodshot blue eyes.

"Good morning," I said.

"What are you doing in April's room?" The woman opened the door a bit further and looked me up and down. "Who are you?" she whispered.

I pulled a business card from my coat pocket. "Here." She hesitated before snagging the card from my hand. "Do you know how April met her clients?"

"Who are you?" she repeated.

I decided to be honest for once. I was too tired to think of a clever lie. "My name's Holly. Your friend April is dead. If you have any information to help me find the person who did it, call that number." I started walking away.

"Wait." She glanced back in the room, then stepped out onto the walkway, quietly shutting the door behind her. She wore faded jeans and an oversized yellow sweatshirt. Three inches of dark roots sprung from her scalp, proving she wasn't a natural blonde. Red spots and scratches dotted her pale face. I figured she and April were in the same line of work and shared the same substance abuse problems.

"How do you know she's dead?" She stared down at my card. "This says you're a consultant."

"I am. What's your name?"

She glanced up at me, her eyes wary. "Why do you care?"

Suspicious of everyone and everything. I supposed she had to be, given this lifestyle. She probably had to be on guard twenty-four-seven.

"I saw her dead body. When was the last time you saw her?"

"We walked over to Taco Bueno and grabbed a burrito on Wednesday afternoon. She had a date who wanted to pay for an all-nighter. She was charging him five hundred bucks. I told her not to trust it, but she wanted to get her computer out of hock and score."

"Score what?"

"Meth."

"I didn't see needle marks on her body, and there weren't any syringes in her room."

The woman folded her arms and hunched in on herself as the wind picked up to a light gale, whipping her hair around her head. "She was terrified of needles. She snorted." She cast a glance over her shoulder, then backed up toward her door. "I have to go."

"Wait. We found a burner phone. Why would she hide it? Did she have another phone that she carried with her?"

"The burner was for her dealers. She carried a regular phone for her clients."

"Thank y—"

She'd already eased back into her motel room before I could finish speaking.

#

"What's up?" Cade asked, sitting in the truck, a Journey tune playing low on the radio. McAllister loved him some oldies.

"A neighbor confirmed the last time she'd seen April was on Wednesday afternoon. She said April had a date that night. The client wanted her to spend all night with him and was paying five hundred."

"The manager confirmed that. She told him she'd have a week's worth of rent the next day."

"He still hasn't touched her stuff, though." I buckled my seatbelt, even though we were only driving across the street.

"He said she'd been living here a year, mostly paid on time so he was giving her a few extra days."

Cade crossed the four-lane highway and parked in front of a dumpy looking little pawn shop. "Want to wait in the truck? Shouldn't take but a few minutes."

"Sure."

While he was gone, I switched to a country station and zoned out, thinking about poor April. When my phone rang, I didn't recognize the number, but that didn't mean much considering I'd been doling out business cards like a blackjack dealer for the past few days.

"This is Holly James."

"Ms. James, this is Dr. Albert Schumer." His accent contained elongated New England vowels and slurry r's. "You emailed a few days ago."

The professor from Cade's alma mater. "Thanks for getting back to me." I glanced up, frantically hoping Cade would pop out of the pawn shop. No such luck.

"How can I help you?" he asked.

"I'm working a murder investigation with one of your former students, Cade McAllister."

He paused. "Cade. How is he?" He sounded as though he really cared about the answer.

"He's…" Angry at times. Impatient. Full of self-recriminations about saving his sister. "He's okay. He's an amazing Investigator."

"I have no doubt. He was one of my more brilliant students. Whatever he chose to do with his life, he'd do it well."

It twisted something inside of me when I realized that for years, Cade hadn't had anyone in his corner. Since Shayna's death, he'd had no one rooting for him, no one he could really trust.

"Tell him I said hello?"

"I will, thank you."

"Now," he said, "you wanted to talk about the Perdidit in Codice."

I felt like the dumbest kid in class. "You'll have to enlighten me. I'm not up on my Latin."

"Ah, sorry. It means The Lost Code. Not its true name, of course, but we have to call it something."

"Okay, and what is in this lost code?"

"Well, assuming it really exists—"

"For the sake of our discussion, let's assume just that."

"All right, but you understand this supposed manuscript hasn't been seen in centuries, and even if it was found, one would need the linguistic skills to translate the ancient Sumerian and Akkadian languages."

"Let's push all rational thinking to the side for a second." I ignored his laughter. "What does the manuscript say?"

He took a deep breath. "It tells how to summon demons."

That actually made sense. Power, wealth, or fame. "Summoning is done all the time." Maybe not all the time, but it wasn't unheard of. Still, summoning demons was tricky business. Keeping them from running amok and focused on the task at hand wasn't easy. And of course, they could always turn on the one who summoned them. Precautions had to be in place to prevent that from happening—salt, binding spells, and talismans to call the demon back to the protection circle.

"These aren't just any demons, Ms. James. These are the highest-ranking generals and commanders who rule Hell itself.

If one is successful, those who summoned the demon will receive a boon."

Boons here, there, and everywhere. "What kind of boon?"

"The usual. Untold wealth, esoteric knowledge, etc."

"And how does the symbol fit in?"

"It's part of the invocation, inviting the demon to surface."

As my stomach plummeted, I had a feeling I finally had the answer I'd been searching for. The why of it all.

CHAPTER TWENTY-NINE

Dr. Schumer continued speaking, but I was too freaked out to listen. I jumped when Cade opened the truck and climbed inside. I stared at him as he plugged the laptop into the truck's USB port.

When the professor finally took a breath, I jumped in. "What about removing a heart from the victim, Dr. Schumer?"

McAllister lifted his head, his eyes wide. I pointed to the phone, silently asking if he wanted to speak to his old professor. He shook his head and used his hotspot to get online, then started scrolling through the laptop.

"Removing the heart?" Dr. Schumer echoed. "I don't know anything about that. But it would make sense, I suppose, if one were trying to get the attention of a powerful demon. A serious offering on the part of the supplicant. This is much more than a mere summoning. It's more like an act of worship. Listen, Ms. James, I don't think you'll ever find evidence of this alleged manuscript, but if you do I'd like to study it."

"That would be up to the Council."

He sighed. "Yes, of course."

I hung up and turned to look at Cade. "Why didn't you want to talk to him?"

"No reason to." He didn't want to discuss it, and I didn't want to push him. "The computer was still in pawn, so it has all of April's files on here."

"Finally, a little bit of luck."

He found her history, then pulled up a page. "Look here." He flipped the computer so that I could see the screen. "A website."

I took the computer from him to get a closer look. A selfie of April in lingerie, showing off her assets, stated she was willing to offer companionship for fifty "roses." Code, I guessed, for dollars. There was a number to call, so I dialed it, but the burner we'd found didn't ring. The call took me to voicemail and I hung up.

"You think the killer kept her phone or is it at the bottom of Lake Henryetta?" I asked.

"If he was smart, he got rid of it. Wish to hell I could use my powers to check the Lake, see what else we could find." The contaminated zone prevented that.

"Let's look at the burner," I said.

He plucked it from his pocket and flipped it open. He pressed buttons and the last few incoming calls popped up. "This number called four times. I'll have to take this to Herb's, get one of the tech guys to go through it."

He grabbed a plastic evidence bag from the storage box in the center console, placed the burner inside it, then put it back in his coat pocket. I handed him the computer, which he stuck in his messenger bag.

"What did Dr. Schumer say?"

I relayed everything the professor and I talked about. "Mighty demons who will grant a boon for being worshipped and summoned."

"Fuck." His hands clenched the steering wheel, his knuckles turning white. "Who would be stupid enough to summon the generals of Hell?"

"I don't know. And it still doesn't explain why spells are rebounding."

He pulled out of the parking lot, his expression grim. "No, it doesn't."

#

Cade pointed the truck toward downtown and made his way through the city. Across the street from the historic

Wright building, in an old brick six-story, an Italian restaurant commandeered the first two floors. Though Bella Roma didn't open until noon, Cade had contacted the manager this morning. The manager was the badalisc's version of Sunny. Any meetings were set up through this guy, and he coordinated The Italian's commitments.

"I didn't know what a badalisc was until I looked it up. Are they rare?" I asked as Cade parallel parked on the street.

"Don't see many of them outside major cities, that's for sure. Usually, they stick to New York, Miami, Chicago. Most of them tend to stay in Italy and Europe, though."

Not rare, but not all that common either. I packed that tidbit away in my brain file.

"Why is one here in Tulsa? Seems out of place."

"Don't know. Never asked. Asking questions denotes interest, and I have none. I've only talked to this guy a couple of times and I don't particularly want to do it again. Doing business with him is dangerous. While he's a good source of information, I don't trust him."

"You think he'd lie to you?"

"No. I think he'd tell me non-important information in order to get a bigger bite out of me. I told you he feeds on intel."

"Secrets."

Cade turned and glanced at me. "That's another way of putting it. I know it's hard, but try to keep your face blank. Don't give him anything. In fact, let me do the talking."

I thought about Sebastian saying all my thoughts showed clearly on my face. I wasn't sure I could pull off a blank expression, but I'd do my best. And if Cade wanted to take lead on this guy, I'd gladly sit back and observe.

"This place was his first restaurant." Cade climbed out of the truck. "He now has dozens of places throughout the city. But this is where he likes to do business."

I hopped out of the truck's cab and stood next to Cade on the sidewalk in front of the restaurant. The wind whipped my ponytail in my face, piercing through my jacket and sweater, making me shiver.

"You said you've dealt with The Italian before. Did you have to tell him your secrets?"

"Some."

Uh oh. Cade didn't like talking about himself. Not even with me. Spilling info to the badalisc must have chapped his hide.

"And he knows I'm with you today, right?"

"Nope." Cade smiled then. A cold, cynical twisting of his lips. "Thought we might surprise him."

Cade moved to the door, but I stayed glued in place. "He probably won't like that. And since we're trying to get information out of him, maybe we shouldn't piss him off?"

"I'll take my chances."

Inside the restaurant, a dozen square tables crowded the center of the room. Overstuffed blue booths lined two walls. A sleek wooden bar stood at one end of the room. Standing opposite was a pair of double doors, made of wood and covered in hammered copper.

A lean man with short brown hair, who appeared to be in his early forties, emerged from the kitchen area near the bar. Suited and booted to impress, he wore a blue checked jacket and matching vest with skinny navy slacks. He moved toward us, his hand outstretched to Cade.

"Inspector. Good to see you again."

Cade briefly shook. "Brakeman. This is Holly James."

"Ah, yes. Mr. Buratti has been expecting you. Both of you." We weren't taking the badalisc by surprise at all. I wondered what else The Italian knew? And who might be feeding him the intel.

Brakeman strode toward the closed doors, grabbed the enormous handle, and pulled it open. "Right this way."

Cade placed his hand on my lower back but remained close as we walked into a private dining area. A table that could easily fit fourteen people sat under a half a dozen crystal chandeliers.

A man sat at the head of the table. He puffed on a fat, smelly cigar, with an espresso cup at his elbow. His button-down shirt was expensive, silk maybe, and a deep wine color. No tie. He reached for his cup with long, knobby fingers.

"McAllister," he said, but his eyes widened when they fixed on me. "And the null. How delightful." His accent was charming and light. He was a handsome man with thick dark hair and steely blue eyes. They were cold and assessing, cataloging me from head to toe.

"Brakeman, fetch coffee for my guests."

"Yes, sir." I glanced back at him, and he actually made a little bow before turning and letting the heavy door close.

"Come and sit." The Italian didn't stand, but rather gestured toward the table with his cigar.

Cade pulled a chair out for me, then took the seat on Buratti's right."

"I've heard much about you, Ms. James. You're not quite what I imagined."

"Oh?" I kept my teal Coach bag on my lap and placed my forearms on the table. "I don't live up to the hype?"

He puffed on the cigar. Through the hazy cloud of smoke, his eyes narrowed as he scrutinized me. "You're much more delicate than I'd have guessed."

"Huh."

Brakeman returned with two tiny cups, then left without a word. I'd had my fill of extra strong coffee lately. I'd do just about anything for one of these guys to offer me a caramel macchiato. Cade didn't touch his cup, either.

"Let's cut to the chase, Buratti," he said. "We believe you have information regarding our murder victim." Cade slipped his hand into his jacket and pulled out a five by seven photo of Jane Doe, then slid it toward The Italian.

Buratti refused to glance at it. "Who told you to seek me out?"

Cade said nothing, so I followed suit.

"Ah, Inspector. We must have some give and take, between us. You know how I operate." He continued to puff away, filling the room with blue-gray smoke.

Buratti smiled. His teeth were slightly uneven, but like the dimple in his left cheek, it was kind of charming—if you didn't know what he was. A parasite, sucking the marrow out of people's most personal information, feeding off it, and then using it against them whenever it suited him.

"Tell me who threw out my name, and then I will tell you if I recognize this girl."

I glanced at Cade from the corner of my eye. His jaw twitched twice. "Master Sebastian," he said.

"Really? How interesting." He stubbed out his cigar and looked down at the photo of our dead Jane Doe, her eyes closed, her skin mottled. "Yes, this one looks familiar."

"Was she one of your girls?" Cade asked.

The Italian turned his gaze on me. "What did you think of Master Sebastian?"

Whew. The badalisc knew a hell of a lot—about me, about my comings and goings. Again, I wondered what else he knew. That I'd become an object of interest to this guy was scary.

Cade started to say something, but Buratti held up his forefinger. "I want to know what she really thought. Then I will answer your question."

"You're not getting fed today," I said. "Why not just tell us what we want to know? If she was one of yours, you didn't protect her. Is that how you run your business?"

A smile hovered over his lips. "I don't tell you how to run your business, do I, Ms. James? Provide me the same courtesy. And no, with your presence, I'm not feeding on these secrets, but everything has a price. Especially information. Your boyfriend knows that very well, don't you, Inspector?" His gaze slipped to Cade, and he was looking far too smug for my liking. I wondered again what Cade had revealed to the badalisc.

Under the table, Cade reached out and squeezed my leg. Comfort or a signal telling me to be quiet? We'd been running blind these last few days. I was tired of it, tired of the games these Others liked to play. The Italian wanted the truth? I'd give it to him.

"Fine," I said, ignoring the tightening of Cade's hand on my thigh. "I found the Master intimidating."

"In spite of the fact that you nullified him?"

"Is this your girl?" I nodded toward the picture.

"You're getting the hang of this, Ms. James. Yes she's mine." He didn't bother glancing at the picture again. My guess—he'd known she was dead since she went missing. And he didn't care enough to alert the Council or file a missing person report with the Norms. Asshole.

"I hear Mick Raven is quite taken with you," Buratti said.

Cade's grip was now like a vice. I placed my hand on his, stroking his fingers, and he relaxed a bit.

"I'm sorry," I said with a faux frown, "is that a question?"

Those blue eyes grew a little harder at my sarcasm. "No. But this is: do you find Mick Raven as attractive as Inspector McAllister?"

I couldn't help it—I started laughing. He reminded me of the little old ladies standing in the aisle of the local Piggly Wiggly, trying to get dirt on their neighbors.

Buratti's eyes were now angry, flashing with fire as if lit from within. "You find that question amusing?"

The laughter bubbling out of me died as quickly as it had risen. "Which would you like me to answer? Because I want her name, her given Christian name in return."

"Why were you laughing?"

"Because it was a question a gossiping old woman would ask."

The Italian and I locked gazes. He was pissed that I hadn't shown him the proper amount of respect. I was pissed that he hadn't respected the dead girl who'd sold her body and gave him part of the profits. I had the moral high ground here.

I felt Cade relax. He slid his hand from my leg and settled back in his chair, arms crossed, watching the show.

"Cassandra Duncan," Buratti said.

We still stared at each other, neither one blinking. I had a feeling he was dying to ask me something, but now he was second-guessing himself. Maybe I shouldn't have laughed, because he'd been throwing softballs until now.

Then he shifted in his seat, lowered his gaze, and drained his espresso cup. "I hear your mother has been missing for years. Do you think she left because of what you are?"

Cade's arms slammed down on the table. "That's out of line."

"I don't know," I said, answering honestly. "When did Cassandra go missing?"

"October fifteenth." Saturday night, right before all the trouble started at Moonlight Cove. "What else would you like to know, Ms. James?"

"The name of the person who hired her the day she went missing."

He breathed a sigh through his nose. "I want a secret, one you've never told anyone."

I thought about it for a moment, then said, "In the second grade, I stole a girl's necklace. A little heart locket, with her initial etched on it." My hand drifted to my throat. "The clasp broke and the necklace dropped while we were sitting in story time. I put my hand over it and looked around the room. No one noticed, so I slipped it in my pocket."

"Cassandra didn't have a booked client the day she went missing."

Was she secretly hooking up with her own clients? Or had she gone out on a real date?

"Did you keep the locket or not?" he asked, sounding bored.

"For about a month. It had a little picture of her dog inside. I was so ashamed, I threw it away."

Cade's hand returned to my thigh.

"That is a pathetic secret, Null." Buratti stared at me with contempt.

"But it's still a secret," Cade said. "Now it's your turn. Was Cassandra seeing clients on the side, cutting you out of the equation?"

"Yes, but of course I knew about it."

Then why had he let it continue? He didn't seem like a man who'd let that kind of thing go. Had The Italian killed Jane—Cassandra—as payback for betraying him? Or maybe as a warning to the rest of the girls?

No, that didn't seem likely. The ritual aspect, the demon summoning—that was far too elaborate for a warning.

Cade pushed back from the table. "We're done."

Buratti raised one dark brow. "What a pity. I was hoping your paramour might tell me about the time she stole a pack of gum when she was six. You're quite rebellious, Ms. James." I wasn't the only one adept at sarcasm.

We rose to leave, and as Cade opened the copper door, The Italian got in one parting shot.

"Tell your grandfather hello for me. Councilman Dumahl is such an interesting man."

CHAPTER THIRTY

Cade and I sat in the truck, the windshield wipers slapping away fat snowflakes that had accumulated in the half hour we'd been inside the restaurant. First all that rain, now snow. The bad weather only added to my irritation.

"How the hell did Buratti know that Wallace is my grandfather?"

Cade rubbed a hand over my cold cheek. "He likes to create doubt, while giving away as little information as possible. He wanted to get under your skin. Don't let him."

I tried not to, but it was hard. "Do we believe him, that he doesn't know the name of Cassandra's last client?"

"Maybe. Or he might be hedging the truth. Let me make a call, see if we can get a bead on Cassandra's address."

While he did that, I checked my phone. No messages from Sunny.

When Cade finished with his call, he settled both hands on the steering wheel, staring at the snow swirling around the truck. "Cassandra Duncan, aged twenty-two, lived in a condo about ten blocks from here. Let's go check it out."

Twenty-two. Too young to die, but to die the way she had, being raped and tortured… And for what? A boon from an evil demon? It was too sick to contemplate.

I hoped The Italian hadn't misled us. My patience was running thin. If Cassandra and Jane Doe weren't the same person, I'd come back and eat dinner here every night for the next month, just to screw with him.

As Cade drove over the snow-covered roads, he laid his hand on my knee. "You did a great job back there, except when you laughed in his face."

"Couldn't help it. He knew all about me anyway."

"That locket story was a lie. If he had his powers, he'd have called you on it."

I grinned. Sometimes being a null wasn't too terrible.

"You almost had me convinced. I might teach you to play poker after all."

Cade and I exited the car, and that's when I noticed a silver Hummer idling across the street. If I never saw another goblin as long as I lived, I'd be okay with that.

"Hang tight." I walked across the street and the Hummer's window rolled down.

"G-Dog."

"Hey, null. Heard you and my moms got in a bust-up. Her magic be working now, though."

"I'm beyond delighted. Listen, don't you have better things to do than stalk me?"

He scoffed and rolled his yellow eyes. "Course I do. But I need you to tell me your boon. Like now. The suspense is making me crazy, yo."

"Go home." I glanced around at the snow piling up. "It's a nasty day. Go count your gold and stay warm."

I walked back across the street to where Cade stood waiting. The sidewalks were starting to become slick, so I was glad when Cade reached out and latched onto my hand.

Fortunately for us, there was no doorman on duty, and according to the sign, the entrance would remain open until nine p.m. The small lobby did its best to keep up with the art deco motif that was so prevalent in many buildings downtown, but it was a poor imitation of the real thing.

We slid into the elevators without meeting anyone and stepped out on the fourth floor. At unit four-twenty-three, Cade dug in his pocket for a small pen knife and popped the lock.

"How did you learn breaking and entering the Norm way?"

"YouTube videos, mostly. Figured that since we're together, I won't always be able to rely on magic. I may need to improvise." He leaned down, his nose grazing my cheek. "It's coming in handy."

Mixed emotions—pleasure and guilt—warred inside me. I was glad Cade thought about our future, but stealing his magic still weighed on me.

When we entered Cassandra's condo, a smell of stale air hit my nose. Cade flipped on an overhead light and proceeded into the living room.

The unit was pretty generic with gray carpeting and white walls. Cassandra had jazzed it up with deep purple drapes and a plum colored sofa.

In the entryway, I picked up a framed photo of Cassandra and another woman with their arms around each other. To see Cassandra smiling, full of life made my stomach hurt. I pulled the back of the frame apart and took the picture, sticking it in my purse. I wasn't even sure why.

Cade searched the living room while I took the kitchen. It was small, but nice. White cabinets and gray quartz countertops made the space seem bigger. A couple of dishes crusted with what appeared to be cereal, sat in the sink. Cassandra used inexpensive white stoneware, so I guessed she wasn't much of a cook.

I opened all the cabinets, which were bare except for two boxes of Special K. The fridge contained a bottle of wine and an expired carton of skim milk. Her trashcan was empty, not even containing a liner.

I stood in the hallway, peeking into the bedroom as Cade searched her dresser drawers. "Anything?"

"No paper, no mail, no bills. No purse or phone."

I checked the bathroom. Nothing but girly stuff and one of those European washer-dryer combos. Again, the trash bin was empty. "Think the killer came back here and cleaned up after the murder?"

Cade stood at the foot of Cassandra's bed, hands on his hips. He swung his head left and right, taking in the room as I glanced through her closet.

"That's a possibility," he said, "but she must have gotten some mail in the last few days. I'll check out her mailbox when we leave."

This had been a useless exercise. We'd found the name of our Jane Doe, but she didn't have one bit of information that would lead us to who might have killed her. We didn't even find anything that told us who she was as a person.

I slipped out the door and into the hallway with Cade right behind me. "I'll meet you at the truck."

"What are you going to do?"

"Talk to some neighbors."

"Yeah. I'll see you downstairs."

He bent to give me a swift, warm kiss then strode off down the hallway.

I knocked on the door directly across from Cassandra's. I heard someone moving around in there, and after a moment, the door opened a crack. A woman in her sixties peered out. Her short hair was cut in a flattering way and streaked with honey blonde to offset the gray.

"Can I help you, hon?"

"I'm a friend of Cassandra's, from Arkansas." I added a little sugar to my accent to make it sound more believable. "She was supposed to meet me here, show me the town this weekend, but I haven't been able to get ahold of her. I'm starting to worry."

She opened the door wider. "Oh, hon. Come on in and have a cup of coffee. I'm Vera Nolan."

I smiled a thanks as I entered. Where Cassandra's condo showed very little of her personality, this woman had an overload on display. Pictures and little figurines and silk flower arrangements filled every nook and cranny.

"Sit down. Do you take cream or sugar?"

"Both, please."

She returned with a mug covered in hearts and roses. I took a sip and closed my eyes. Heaven.

"Have you seen Cassandra lately?" I asked.

She sat in a floral-patterned chair and waved me off. "No, but that girl comes and goes at all hours. Not that she's noisy or anything. She's always very respectful." She probably met her clients at another location then, not at home. Like Dena said, hotels were supposedly a safe place. Not that it helped either one of them in this instance.

"What did you say your name was?" Vera asked.

"Holly James. So, when was the last time you saw her?"

She rolled her eyes toward the window, her brows puckered in thought. "Saturday or Sunday? She'd picked up her laundry—fluff and fold. I chatted with her for a minute in the elevator."

"Did she say who she might be seeing that night? Any plans for the weekend?"

"No. But as a pharmaceutical rep, she was always in and out of town. I tried to get samples from her once, for my hip. Arthritis. She said it was against the rules. They have a very tight control on those samples, you know."

Pharma rep. Well, that was as good a cover as any. Gone at odd times, getting home late. Which also told me she didn't dress like a hooker, but as a business professional. The few clothes Cade had found in the closet reinforced that idea.

"You know," she said, "it's strange that you're meeting her this week."

"Why is that?"

"Her uncle dropped by on..." She placed a finger next to her lips and glanced up at the ceiling. "Wednesday, I think it was. Anyway, he came over to check the condo. He said she'd be gone for a few weeks and he wanted to water her plants. Very nice man." Cassandra didn't have plants. And I was betting she didn't have a thoughtful uncle, either.

"Which uncle, I wonder." I tried to keep my voice from squeaking with excitement. "What did he look like?"

"He was very average looking, to be honest. I don't know if I could place him again."

I pulled out my phone and pretended to look at my calendar. "Vera, you're not going to believe this. I have the wrong date. I'm supposed to meet Cassandra next week." I slapped my forehead. "What an idiot I am."

"Oh, hon. That's terrible. And you picked such a bad week to visit. The weather's been simply awful."

I thanked her for the coffee and scooted back to the truck, where Cade waited with mail.

"Gimme, gimme." I slammed the truck door, held out my hands and explained what I'd learned from Vera.

Cade and I divvied up the envelopes, and together, committed a felony as we opened Cassandra's mail. I had her phone bill. I wondered if any of the numbers matched up with calls from April Walsh's burner phone.

"What did you find?" I asked.

"She spent a lot on clothes and makeup, according to her American Express card."

"Well, I could have told you that. She favored Ann Taylor casual wear. That shit isn't cheap."

When Cade's phone rang, he glanced at the screen. "It's Dawson Nash." He answered, listened, and then started the engine before hanging up.

"I take it the werewolves have good news?"

"I'd say so. They found an altar."

#

Most small towns looked the same to me. A few fast food places, a feed store, some boarded up buildings that the town no longer needed, and tall grain silos within close proximity to railroad tracks. Homes built anywhere from the turn of the twentieth century through the forties populated the downtown area. Churches. Lots of churches on every street corner. But that wasn't the case with Leonard, Oklahoma.

Leonard was too small to have a main drag. It contained farmland, a post office, and a liquor store-gas station combo. There was a small deli, if you needed milk or bread in a hurry, but for anything else you had to haul ass to either Bixby or Coweta.

Cade exited Highway 64 and turned down a lane hugging a densely wooded area. The snow, two or three inches now, covered the field on the other side of the road. That's not much to people who are used to shoveling all winter, but down here it was a real showstopper.

He hooked a right onto a narrow service road and drove five or six miles, until we finally caught sight of Dawson Nash standing next to one of three trucks. He waved as we approached.

"Sorry you have to get out in this mess," Cade said, and shut off the ignition.

"I'm not sugar." I smiled. "I won't melt."

"True. You're more spicy than sweet." He climbed out of the cab before I could slap his arm. He trotted around to my side and helped me from the truck. Together, we made our way to where Dawson stood.

When I picture an alpha werewolf in my head, I picture the exact opposite of Dawson Nash. Yes, he's tall and muscular. I was reasonably certain he could use those big hands to pound someone into the ground, even without his shifter strength. But his relaxed attitude was so deceptive, it was hard to reconcile that with a big, bad wolf. Until you saw him in action. Even as a human, when he decided to flip his alpha switch, watch out. Underestimate that wolf at your peril.

Normally, his chin-length hair was perfectly rumpled, but today it was damp, turning it a few shades darker than its normal wheat blond. His face was a thing of beauty with a strong, angled chin, a wide forehead and sharp cheekbones. A male model who surfed in his spare time. Or vice versa.

I figured he purchased his entire wardrobe at a thrift store. Every item of clothing I'd seen him wear was either faded or ripped or in serious distress, and if he owned an iron, he sure as hell didn't know what to do with it.

Now Dawson slouched casually against the truck, hands shoved in the pockets of his ratty jeans. Even in my wool coat, I was freezing. But the alpha only wore a long-sleeved, black T-shirt bearing the name of a band I'd never heard of. When the snow hit him, it immediately melted upon contact.

As soon as we approached, Dawson held his hand out to Cade. "Hey, man. Good to see you." His blue eyes were flecked with light brown. He turned them on me, and in a move that surprised me, he reached out and pulled me into a hug.

I didn't know we were at the hugging stage, so I awkwardly patted his shoulder until he let go.

"Hey, Holly. You good?"

"Yeah, you?"

"Can't complain. Some of my people have been affected by this weird magic thing, though. I hear it's spreading. Is that true?" He glanced from me to Cade.

"I think so," I said. "Are your people all right?"

"Yeah. A few of them were unable to change all the way back to human form. I knew immediately they were in trouble, but as soon as we moved them to a different area, they were fine. It was pretty scary for a hot minute, I'm not going to lie. Shifting is painful enough. Being stuck in a partial shift is even worse."

"How many were affected?" Cade asked.

"Ten so far."

"Send me their addresses. We're trying to track locations and see if there's a pattern." Cade glanced over at the line of trees hugging the road. "What have you got?"

"Come this way."

"Let me go first, Holly, see if I can detect anything magically, pick up a signature. I won't be long." He slid his hand down my arm before trekking into the woods.

I waited next to Dawson and his enforcer, Nick Alpert, who stood a few feet away giving me the stink eye. Nick didn't like me. Probably because I'd suspected him of killing his girlfriend. He turned out to be innocent, but he still resented my accusations. It wasn't personal on my end, but it was obvious Nick still carried a grudge.

I nudged Dawson's arm. "Nick seems thrilled to see me."

"He'll get over it. Or maybe he won't. You did what you had to do. Granted, you could have done it with a little more tact, but…"

"Yeah, because Others have always been so gracious and tactful around me."

He peered down at me with those strange colored eyes. "Give me a list of names. I'll kick their asses for you."

I laughed and shook my head. "The list is too long."

"My memaw always told me that what other people think of you is none of your darned business." He leaned back against the truck and crossed his arms.

"Well, if your memaw said it, it must be true."

I turned to Dawson, taking in his strong profile. "You said you knew your wolves were in trouble. How, exactly?"

He bunched his wide shoulders. "The magic that links us, it's like a psychic connection. I know where all my wolves are." He pointed to his head. "In here, they're all accounted for. If one is missing, I feel it. And when they need help, I feel that, too."

I'd picked up a lot of knowledge about shifters over the years. Mostly from sitting in on their events and keeping quiet. People, even Others, revealed themselves if you remained unobtrusive. I knew that they were all linked somehow, but I didn't know to what extent.

"What about their emotions?" I asked.

"Yeah, if they're strong enough I can feel it. The daily shit, troubles at work, family fights, stuff like that I block out."

Yeah, I could understand where that would be a good trick to have. Who would want to feel every single emotion running through the pack?

Nick, his massive arms crossed over his chest, stared a little harder. "You writing a book or something? Why are you interested in wolves all the sudden?"

"Just curious as to how the wolves contacted the alpha if they'd partially shifted. You can't pick up a cell phone with a paw, now can you?"

Dawson chuckled. "My sister tried more than once."

I finally caught a glimpse of Cade striding through the trees, moving toward us. He stopped in front of me, his breath coming in steady streams of fog with every exhalation.

"The same chaotic pattern as before. Not as severe as with the murder victims, but it's covering the woods. And since Glen Falls lies that way"—he pointed to a spot over my shoulder—"I'd say we found our reason why the model homes were affected."

A link to the other murders. Finally.

"Come and have a look at the scene. Nash, thanks for everything. I appreciate your help."

Dawson tipped his head back and smiled. "Sorry McAllister, you're not getting rid of us that easily. This magical thing is a danger to my people. We're not leaving."

Cade shook his head. "There's nothing else you can do. I can't have civilians knowing the details of my case. Sorry."

Uncrossing his arms, Dawson straightened to his full height. With his shoulders back, his chin tilted upward, a serious expression crossed his face—this was his no-nonsense alpha mode. "Fine. I'll send my people home with strict instructions to keep what they saw today to themselves. But Nick and I, we're staying. We found your altar, so we have that right."

Cade propped his hands on his hips and worked his jaw from side to side. He was gearing up for a fight.

"What could it hurt?" I asked. "He's already seen the altar."

"Fine." Cade's lips tightened. "You did me a solid, Nash, but I want your word that none of this information will get out."

Dawson leveled his cool gaze on Cade. "You have my word." Not as binding as a vow, but I'd trust anything that came out of Dawson's mouth. He was a straight shooter.

Cade turned back to the woods, and this time I followed. Nash moved in line behind me, and Nick Alpert played the caboose in our little group.

We moved through snow-covered trees, stepped over fallen branches. When the terrain got a little too rough, Cade gave me his hand, offering assistance. What surprised me was that the snow wasn't silent. It hit the tree branches arching above us with soft pings and fell to the earth with small, wet plops. But once we reached a circular clearing, the branches provided some cover for the area.

Four people stood in front of the clearing and Dawson introduced us. "Holly, this is Rachel, Andrew, Tomas, and Steve. Y'all have already met McAllister."

They nodded at me, their faces far from friendly. I nodded back.

The woman, Rachel, looked me in the eye. "I remember you. You came to our territory and accused Nick of murder."

"Yes, that would be me." I glanced back at Nick. "But we're good friends now, aren't we?" When he didn't respond, I said, "Well, you're on my Christmas card list."

Tomas moved aside. "This is what we found."

CHAPTER THIRTY-ONE

That's when I saw the birds. Blackbirds, dead and stiff, lay just inside the clearing in a perfect circular pattern. All evenly spaced.

Dawson stepped forward. "Y'all head back now. Nick and I will hang here in case they need anything else."

If they were angry about being dismissed, it didn't show. They simply obeyed without a murmur and disappeared through the woods. A few minutes later, I heard an engine roar to life and tires crunching over snow.

I'd make a terrible werewolf. I couldn't blindly follow an order like that. It would make my skin crawl to do anyone's bidding without a peep.

Cade moved to the center of the clearing but turned back to the two wolves. "Stay back, please. I need Holly to come and take a look. The fewer people traipsing through here, the better."

I stepped over a dead bird and crossed to where Cade hunkered down next to a long, thin board, barely wider than a plank. It could hold a person, if the person were a small female. Dena fit that description. The edges had been sanded smooth, and carved into the four corners were the four symbols we'd seen on the victims. At the head and foot of the board, a metal stake had been screwed into the ground. A triangular hook protruded from the patchy snow.

"She was tied to this?" I asked, reaching out to touch the cold metal. Cade caught my hand before I made contact.

"I'm going to get Herb out here to take fingerprints."

"What's the deal with the altar?" Dawson asked.

While Cade rose and gave him a quick rundown of the murders and the magical hotspots, I grabbed a stick and walked from the altar to the fire pit, ringed with large stones. I poked in it, looking for something, anything that might provide a clue. Sadly, I found nothing but ashes. But it did make me wonder what the killers did with the hearts they'd taken. Did they keep it as a trophy, burn it up in the fire, or toss it in the lake with the victim?

When Cade finished speaking, I asked, "Do you think this was where Dena was taken as a test run?"

"I'd say so." Cade knelt down and examined the altar once more. "No blood. And while the chaotic signature is here, it's less tangled than it was at Midnight Cove or the other places we've been."

I took out my phone and snapped some pictures of the altar and the symbols. I captured the fire pit and the birds, as well.

"Were the birds killed and placed here?"

Dawson bent down and examined one. "Looks like the neck was snapped, so I'd say your killer set the stage."

And that's where they got the feathers to stick in the torso of the victims.

I glanced at the wooden board once more. Every good altar required a few things: fire, water, earth, and air elements, along with a items of supplication. Gran used oil and herbs in the summer, gourds in the fall. During the winter, she added a bough of holly. Always something earth-related. A water witch might use shells or a jar of water from the nearby lake or ocean. Air witches used feathers, birds' eggs, things like that. And fire witches used coal, wood, anything flammable.

Then it hit me. "The rock and the feather, the ones found inside the victim. They must represent earth and air. Maybe the branding represents fire. The killer dumped them in the water. Bingo. All the elements."

Cade nodded. "But the water should be present when the offering is made."

"Unless the killer doesn't know what the hell he's doing."

Cade's eyes met mine. "Are you saying we're looking for a Norm?"

I turned it over in my brain. It would make sense. Pulling out the heart, using esoteric symbols from a lost manuscript—symbols no Other seemed to recognize—all pointed in that direction. Along with the weird weather patterns, the frogs and strange animal births. Like Mary, the Cherokee woman said, there was an imbalance.

"What if the manuscript is real?" I asked. "What if a Norm found it and has been using it to summon a demon? Couldn't that kick the natural world out of balance? And it might explain why magic itself has become warped."

"What manuscript?" Dawson asked.

"A Norm is doing this?" Nick chimed in. "They're the ones messing with our magic?"

"That's a big jump." Cade thrust his hands in the pockets of his jacket and waited me out.

I explained the manuscript to the wolves. "It's the only reference we have of the strange symbol. If a human managed to get ahold of a summoning spell, he'd been using bastardized magic. Magic no mundane human was ever meant to access, and it's thrown nature out of whack."

Dawson nodded slowly. "That's a damn good theory."

"The Ars Geotia," Cade said. "It lists the seventy-two demons. Supposedly, Solomon bound them and forced them into service for God. But the directions for summoning are sketchy at best, and there's no mention of human sacrifice at all."

"That's not what Dr. Schumer called it. He said it was The Lost Code."

Cade and I locked gazes. "Perdidit in Codice?"

I snapped my fingers. "That's the one."

"I'll get Herb out here and I'm going to the library to do a little reading."

I frowned. "What library?"

"The Council has an extensive one. Maybe I can turn up something more concrete that will give us a direction."

"I'll work on the map and see if the hotspots are growing," I said. "Also, if you give me the burner, I'll go through the phone and search the incoming and outgoing numbers."

Cade's scowl grew. I sensed his hesitation, but eventually he nodded. "Yeah. It needs to be done. Let me call Herb, get him out here to secure this scene."

"What can we do to help?" Dawson asked.

"Why don't you send them to Longtown, Cade? They've found one altar, maybe they can find a kill site, too."

"It's a hell of a big area to cover. With the snow, it'll be even tougher."

Dawson shrugged. "Let us try. We'll get all our people on it, fan out. We'll be respectful of your crime site."

"I know it physically pains you to outsource, Sorcerer," I said, "but we need all hands on deck."

Cade nodded. "Yeah, okay." He grabbed his phone, pulled up a set of coordinates, and texted them to Dawson. "This is where the body was found in Lake Eufaula."

"We're on it."

"Holly, I'm going to wait here for Herb. Why don't you get a ride home with Nash?" He pulled the burner out of his pocket. "I'm trusting you with this."

He sounded like a dad handing over the car keys for the first time. "I'll be very careful. I promise not to fuck with the evidence." That was rule number one on Cade's very long list.

#

The ride back to the city was one filled with tense silence. Dawson concentrated on driving, since the roads had become something of a slick mess. Nick Alpert, the enforcer sat behind him, his brooding silence and hostility palpable.

I stared out the window, my mind turning over all the evidence. And then I spied a twister moving in from the east. A wide funnel, making its way across the snow-filled sky like an atom bomb. I'd never seen one up close before.

"Dawson." I punched my finger against the glass. "Tornado."

"Shit," Nick bit out. "It's headed our way."

Dawson ducked his head and peered through the passenger window. "Okay, hold tight. We're going to gun it."

I watched in terror as the twister rose and fell, now just half a mile away. Up and down, like a kid's twirly top it circled and dipped, touching the ground before arching back up into the sky.

I held my breath as Dawson floored the gas. The truck spun out, skidding on the highway before he could course correct.

My gaze flickered between the rising speedometer and the whirling tornado. I offered up a quick prayer for mercy to whomever might be listening and kept a death grip on the armrest.

"It's getting closer," Nick warned.

"There's a bridge up ahead." Dawson gunned the truck once more.

"No," I yelled. "Overpasses are the worst place to ride out a tornado."

"Unless you have a better idea, I'm going for it."

I didn't. I was out of ideas.

The snow kept piling up as the twister dipped and hit a gulch on the side of the road. I held my breath as it darted closer. Dawson barely managed to pull under the overpass just as the twister hit the road directly behind us. Then it jerked up to cross the highway.

I turned in my seat and stared out the back window. The twister played tag with farmland for the next three or four minutes, until it finally rose back toward the sky and dissipated.

I blew out a trapped breath. "That was too close."

Dawson spun in his seat and glanced at me. "Yeah, but it's a hell of a tale." Then he calmly drove me the rest of the way home at a reasonable speed.

When he pulled into my driveway a half hour later, I was still reeling. On shaky legs, I hopped out of the truck and onto the slick driveway. "Thanks."

"Anytime. Good to see you, Holly." He winked and waved goodbye as I slammed the door.

Freaking weirdo.

#

After making a cup of hot tea, I realized I still didn't have food in the house. Damn it.

I dug through all the cabinets and the small pantry, reaching all the way into the back. I came up with a can of chicken noodle soup I had no memory of purchasing. It expired three years ago. Not willing to risk it, I called for pizza and offered a fifty-dollar tip if they got here within the hour.

In the meantime, I sipped my tea and Sharpied new dots onto my map, filling in all the places where Dawson's pack had trouble shifting. It looked as if the infection was indeed spreading northward, from Leonard to Bixby and even into the southern border of Tulsa itself.

That wasn't a good sign. If what I suspected was true, a Norm had stolen magic, perverted it, and was screwing up the natural order of things. The elements themselves were in rebellion.

I stood back and stared at the map. I had only one question. How did we get the earth back into balance?

Master Sebastian said the last time this happened was when Pompeii blew. Would it take a disaster like that for nature to reset itself? God, I hoped not. For all our sakes. That snow-nado that almost wiped out Dawson's truck was natural disaster enough for me, thank you.

When my pizza arrived, I found I didn't have a lot of appetite, but I forked over the hefty tip and made myself eat a slice. Then I grabbed the burner phone from my coat pocket. Since the battery was running low, I plugged it into my charger.

There were no voicemail messages, so I started by listing all the incoming numbers. The same five people called April over and over. I made a note of them and looked them up on my laptop. They were all unlisted, leading me to believe that they may be linked to burners, too.

Her outgoing list was a little more varied, with short names to identify the callers. But Mustache, Golden Shower, and Minute Man didn't lead me anywhere useful.

I began plugging those into my computer as well, to see if I could match any names to the numbers. I ran into a few more unlisted, then caught a few hits. Sam Keith. Robert Jackson.

Peter Everett.

Dr. Peter Everett?

I looked up his website. His office number matched the one in April's burner. This was too much of a coincidence.

But before getting too excited, I snatched the phone bill we'd stolen from Cassandra Duncan and quickly glanced through the numbers. And there it was. Two calls from Dr. Peter Everett, the last being Saturday at seven p.m. Mere hours before everything went nuts at Moonlight Cove.

With my hands shaking like a hyper chihuahua, I glanced at April's burner once more and scrolled through all those incoming numbers. Everett had called April once, the day she went missing. Wednesday.

Could he be the killer? I could buy that, but he'd been at the cocktail party. When did he have time to casually meet April, drive her to the middle of nowhere, and ritualistically kill her—then go to work the next day like nothing happened?

You don't know that he went to work the next day.

But I saw him the next evening, at Master Sebastian's lair. He seemed completely calm, totally in charge. But then, psychos were like that, right? Everyone thinks they're the nicest neighbor on the planet, until the cops dig up a graveyard full of corpses in the crawlspace.

I immediately called Cade. For once, he actually answered his damned phone.

"What's up?"

"Dr. Peter Everett. The doctor who treats Master Sebastian's blood bags. He called April on the day she went missing and the same with Cassandra."

"Shit."

"And I've been taking those pills he prescribed. What the hell?" My stomach soured, the muscles in my abdomen clenching into a knot. I didn't think they were anything other than antibiotics, but they could have been.

"Okay, listen," Cade said. "This has to be handled correctly. I want to go to the Council, make my case in person. We're talking about arresting one of the Master's people, and that requires an extra layer of proof. We'll have to inform Sebastian of what we're doing. I don't need some kind of territorial shit show on my hands.

"He has access to ketamine, Cade. He obviously wants power, otherwise he wouldn't be donating for a vamp. He's a successful surgeon, so it would be easy for him to remove the heart."

I thought about Herb's autopsy notes. "But Herb said that the incision on Cassandra seemed hesitant, as if the killer wasn't used to cutting into a body."

"Everett could have been doped up, too. Or maybe the fact that he was killing for the first time made him hesitate. Either way, I'm going to search his house and office. I just want to have all my i's dotted and my t's crossed with the Council first."

"You'd better not leave me out of this. I want to be there for the search."

"No way. You've done a great job on all this."

"Thanks, Sorcerer." A little burst of pride shot through me. "When will you be home?"

"Huh. The Council loves to hear itself talk. If I had to guess, sometime tomorrow. But I'll keep you posted."

Before I hung up, I told him about the contaminated zones spreading northward into Tulsa.

"The news just keeps getting better and better, doesn't it? Look, Hols, there's nothing you can do right now. Why don't you try and get some rest?"

We said our goodbyes, and I decided Cade's idea was sound. I could use a good night's sleep. But it was only five o'clock.

I tried to turn my brain off as I took a hot shower. But it was impossible.

I got out, dried off, put on some fleece pajamas, and refilled my teacup. I glanced out at my darkened back yard.

The snow had slowed considerably. It was kind of pretty, if you didn't have to drive in it. Or try to outrun a snow-nado.

I grabbed my tablet and my cup, then climbed into bed. Cade had mentioned Ars Goetia earlier. It took me awhile to figure out the spelling, but once I did, I found all sorts of hits. The translation was available online, but as I glanced at it, I didn't think this was the template for the ritual. The directions for summoning demons were short, abrupt, and full of specific speeches.

Whatever directions Peter Everett followed, this was far too simplistic.

I still read through the various demon entities. According to those listed, they could make men wise, rich, popular, mathematically inclined—and all without any downside. How super-duper convenient. Real magic wasn't like that. Blood rituals, black magic, always had a downside.

I also didn't believe Everett was following his own ritual, as we'd first suspected in this case. Somehow, he'd found a copy of The Lost Code. A translated copy at that.

Where had Everett found something so archaic? Did Master Sebastian have a copy in his possession, and the doctor stumbled across it?

I continued glancing through the list of demons until one jumped out at me. Camio, sometimes called Caim. The Great President of Hell itself.

What struck me about this character was that he took on two forms: one as a man with a sword, and the other a blackbird. According to the Ars Goetia, he gave men understanding of birds, dogs, and answers about the future. I suspected that was an incomplete list of what Camio could do. According to Dr. Schumer, he'd offer his summoner a boon.

Peter Everett was handsome, successful, rich, and a doctor for Master Sebastian's blood bags. How much more powerful could he be? What could he want? Immortality? In a few more years, the vamps would probably make him one of their own. He had money. What was left—fame? Not exactly helpful when working with vamps. They liked their anonymity.

My tea was cold, and I'd managed to fritter away two hours. I hadn't gone to bed at seven o'clock in twenty years but I was doing it tonight.

CHAPTER THIRTY-TWO

I still couldn't get to sleep right away, so I let my mind wander. For some reason, the thought of Peter Everett as the killer didn't sit right with me. But the two dead women had received calls from his office.

His office. Why from his office and not his cell phone?

My eyes started closing. My breathing evened out. I must have dozed for a few minutes.

When my eyes snapped open an hour later, I realized the answer had been in front of me the whole time. Amanda Wyler.

I sat up in bed but kept the light off. She must have found a copy of The Lost Code in an old piece of furniture. How had I missed that? Everett said she was constantly changing his furniture, trying out new pieces. She must have used the phone in his office to call April and Cassandra.

But no, that wasn't exactly right, either. Both prostitutes planned on meeting men. Dena met the killer through her website and met up with him at the hotel. And Vera, Cassandra's sweet neighbor, told me an uncle had come by, saying she'd be gone for a week.

Maybe Peter was the killer. Perhaps he was the one who found The Lost Code in a drawer, one overlooked by Amanda?

I fell back against the pillow, feeling frustrated. The only way to solve this would be to interrogate Peter. And Cade may have to use his mind mojo to get anything out of the doctor.

Slowly, my body relaxed, and I once more drifted to sleep.

When I felt a sharp prick on my arm, I awoke briefly. A figure loomed over me—the blurry figure of a man. Then darkness, thick and heavy, sucked me down into unconsciousness.

#

My eyelids were heavy. Too heavy to lift, but I needed to open them. I just couldn't remember why.

I heard voices. They seemed to be coming from far away, the words gibberish.

Sleep tugged me back, pulling me under, where it was warm and comfortable. *You have to stay awake, Holly.*

But why? I was so tired.

#

"Put another drop cloth down."

"I've put two down already."

"Adding another won't hurt."

They wouldn't stop talking. I wished they'd shut up, so that I could go back to sleep.

"I don't want blood on this floor." A man's voice. I'd heard it before. Couldn't remember where.

"We're getting a new floor next week, so what the hell's the difference?"

A different voice, this one deeper.

"This is all wrong. I think we need to go back outside. Do it at the altar. We've had success because we're following the rules. We shouldn't veer from that." A woman's voice.

I tried to remember something from earlier. Something important about a woman, but it slipped through my grasp as I fell back into unconsciousness.

#

Cold. So cold.

I struggled to open my eyes, but my lids were too heavy. It was impossible to keep them open.

After several attempts, I barely managed to peek between the lashes of my left eye—the right one refused to cooperate—but it was enough to get a sense of my surroundings.

A large fire burned near me, bright orange tongues of flame licked at the darkness. The scent of wood smoke curled around me. Despite the heat it gave off, I shivered.

As I lay there, trying to figure out where the hell I was, I realized it was still snowing. Small, cold, flakes peppered my face and forehead, which shouldn't have hurt but did. Each one a tiny burn on my sensitive skin.

Everything that happened tonight was foggy and my head hurt. Tentacles of pain spread outward, across my forehead, down my nape, wrapping around my skull. I wanted to go back to sleep. Sleep would dull the pain.

I tried to lower my arms, but couldn't. I couldn't just roll over and retreat into sleep because I couldn't use my arms.

I blinked, opening my eyes a little wider. They burned and felt gritty.

Voices rose around me. Not a conversation. Voices singing. No, that wasn't right. Chanting. They were chanting.

How many of them? I tried to count, but what little vision I had doubled, wavered. Goddamn, they were loud. Chanting in monotone, they repeated words I didn't recognize. Ancient words too evil to be uttered filled my head, making it throb in time to their tuneless drone.

I tried to move my arms again. Why couldn't I move?

My breath started coming in pants, filling the air with fog. I struggled to lower my arms, once more, and that's when I realized my hands were tied.

I attempted to move my legs. My ankles were constricted as well.

In that moment, I realized a few things. Unable to move, unable to speak because of the rough, foul-tasting rope shoved in my mouth, I wasn't just helpless. I was utterly powerless. And I was naked.

No amount of target practice or self-defense tactics could have prepared me for this. I realized at that moment how truly weak I was. It burned like acid in my gut, got mixed up with the fear and made my stomach churn. I swallowed convulsively, afraid that if I puked, I'd asphyxiate.

Absolute terror finally surfaced. That terror bypassed the pain in my head, shoved past the drugs flooding my system, and squeezed my heart in its painful grip. I couldn't take a deep breath. Panic took over, squeezing my stomach.

I arched my back and twisted my head in an effort to get a look at the killers. Two men, one woman. They wore red capes and as they moved, I caught flashes of naked skin beneath. Animal masks covered their faces—the old Cherokee woman's warning. This was what she'd meant.

The cow was Amanda, clearly. I could tell by her short, dark hair and red nails. The tallest man, the pig—firelight captured glints of flaxen in his short blond hair. His long, lean body towered over the other two. This was Aaron. And the shorter man in the sheep mask…was that Stan, the developer? I blinked, then took in his hairy, big barreled chest.

A trio of demon summoners. That's probably how Amanda got her new television show, by summoning Camio or another powerful demon like him.

And now they were going to kill me.

A fresh wave of nausea roiled through as I realized I was never going to see Gran again. I loved her more than anything, and now she'd never know what happened to me. A case of history repeating itself. Just like my mother. Would Gran spend the rest of her life searching for me, or would she just give up altogether?

And Cade. After the death of his family, he was all alone. He'd blame himself for my disappearance. None of this was his fault, but that wouldn't matter. He'd shoulder it, just like he did the deaths of his parents and his sister.

In anger, I bucked against the ropes, harder this time. With the same results.

The three dip shits kept chanting as they circled to my right, blocking the firelight from view. I watched them, my mind less fuzzy now.

There was no way out of this. I was going to die tonight. Not a quick, painless death. That would defeat their purpose.

No, they'd drag this out, torturing and abusing me to the very end. They were going to rip the beating heart out of my body.

The more I thought about it, the angrier I became. Hot tears burned my eyes, blurring my vision even further. And stupidly, childishly, I cursed at the unfairness of it all. Whatever these psychos had planned, whatever power they thought my sacrifice might bring, they were wrong.

They didn't know who I was.

I wouldn't usher in power.

I'd annihilate it.

I didn't know how long they kept at it, repeating the same words, the same syllables. They circled around me so many times, I lost count.

While they chanted, I yanked at the ropes binding my wrists, but it was no use. The ones at my feet barely allowed my legs any movement at all.

Was this the same fate that befell my mother? All this time, that had been my true fear. Not that she left me for good but that she'd been kidnapped and killed.

I wondered if I'd ever see her again, if not in this life then the next.

When they stopped chanting, another shaft of fear scorched through my body. The fire crackled and popped. When the snow hit the hot stones, it softly sizzled.

They stood there silently, the three of them. Amanda at my head, Stan on my right, and Aaron at my feet. In their animal masks, they ghoulishly grinned down, those cartoon faces smiling as though this were all some funny joke.

As if my life meant nothing.

I bit the rope, not caring that the stiff cords rubbed painfully against my tongue. I'd never thought much about death. I'd been too busy working and thinking about my next designer handbag. But my time had run out. Would they carve symbols into my body or rape me first?

Goosebumps broke out over my cold skin. I wished they'd pumped more drugs into my system. I didn't want to be conscious for this part.

I wasn't brave enough to face what they had in store for me. I'd always thought of myself as strong, but if I could, I'd have begged for my life right then, promised them anything if they'd just let me go.

Aaron the pig stepped closer, mocking me with that vile mask. My scream was muffled, as I watched him draw nearer. I wanted to demand he take off the mask, let me see the real monster behind it.

He untied his cape and flung it to the ground, baring his naked body. A slick sheen of sweat coated his torso. His dick was hard, and he was panting now, betraying his excitement. He got off on this, hurting women. On fucking them, then killing them. Sick, demented Norm asshole.

"Shhh," he whispered. "This is your sacrifice. You'll be a part of something bigger, Holly." He lowered his knee onto the plank near my feet and placed a hand on my outer thigh. I bucked and tried in vain to twist my body and avoid his touch.

But it was no use. This was going to happen. As his warm, clammy hand slid upward, grazing my hipbone, my eyes burned. Tears rolled down my cheeks as he hovered over my body.

"Yo, is it too late to join the party?" G-Dog strutted into the clearing, his rope chain dangling around his neck. The fire bounced off his gold medallion. "Somebody's got a boon coming."

Aaron spun his head around as Amanda let out a sharp gasp.

Relief and gratitude hit me hard. I'd never been happier to see that damned goblin.

Amanda lifted a hand and raised it toward him. "You're the one we've summoned. You've finally graced us with your presence. Thank you, Dark One."

These dumbasses thought the goblin was the demon they'd been summoning. He must not have shown up in person the three previous times, but somehow, they'd received their boon anyway.

"Ain't nobody summoning me, woman." G-Dog leaned past Aaron to stare at me, his medallion swinging back and forth. "Figured now might be a good time for us to talk."

I nodded. And that's when I noted the long, sturdy branch in his hand.

Aaron moved off me to kneel in the snow, his head bowed in subservience. "We're not worthy, Dark One."

"Huh. Ain't that the truth?" Gordon whacked the top of Aaron's head with the branch. The sound made a sickening thud before the naked man slumped over in the snow, staining it red from the bleeding gash.

Stan remained still for a moment, then he must have finally realized G-Dog wasn't here for adulation. He was here to take them out, one by one. Stan charged the little goblin.

Gordon simply sidestepped the masked man and used the branch like a baseball bat, hitting Stan in the gut first. "That was a double." Stan let out a moan and doubled over. "Now let's try for a homerun." He lifted the branch and clobbered Stan on the back of the head. The sound echoed through the woods.

Amanda covered her mouth with one hand. "What are you doing? We're here to serve you."

"Not me you're serving, mama." Gordon spun on her.

Amanda's eyes grew huge as she pivoted before dashing through the woods. I realized then she wasn't completely naked. She wore snow boots, which apparently weren't made for running.

G-Dog took after her, catching up to her in three strides. He swung the branch against her spine, causing her to fall to her knees. Then he clubbed her over the head, too.

I glanced at each of them, hoping they'd all stay down. I finally took a deep breath once I saw the blood surrounding each of them.

Gordon turned and swaggered back to me, tossing the branch aside. "My moms is still wicked pissed at you." He kicked Aaron in the ribs before he began untying my ankles. "She smells like flowers or something. My pops won't go near her. Says she stinks like a Norm." He laughed, a raspy chuckle, as he stood and moved to my hands.

I wasn't going to die. The reality finally settled in, making me shiver. Tears flowed freely from my eyes. Snot ran down my nose as I rotated my feet. They tingled as blood started circulating back into my toes.

When my hands were free, G-Dog worked on the rope in my mouth. I flexed my hands, then rubbed the skin at my face. I moved to sit up, but a wave of dizziness overwhelmed me.

G-Dog eased me back down into a prone position. "Give it a minute, mama."

I stared up into those big yellow eyes. "Thank you, Gor…G-Dog. You're my hero."

He shrugged, but his cheeks flushed and the tips of his pointed ears turned purple. "No big. You could have taken everything I have, but you were, like, cool and all. You ready to sit up again?"

"Yeah. I want to get these assholes tied up before they regain consciousness."

"Not likely. I hit 'em but good. Probably all concussed and whatnot." He held my hand and gently pulled me into a sitting position.

My head was still woozy, but it was better than before. He helped me stand, and the snow was so cold my toes curled inward. "Can I have Amanda's boots?"

"Yeah, yeah. Hang on." I climbed onto the wooden altar to keep from getting frostbite while he walked back and stripped Amanda of her boots and cape. He brought them to me and helped me shove my frozen feet inside. Then in a gallant move that surprised me, G-Dog stepped behind me and draped the cape over my shoulders. "That should keep you from freezing."

Ignoring the fact that we were both naked, I threw my arms around his neck. "Thank you."

He quickly pulled away, acting embarrassed as he plucked at his chain. "None of that, mama."

He loped over to each of the killers, yanking their hands behind them and securely bound them with the rope. "You good to walk?"

"Yeah, I think so."

"Should we leave them out here, let your man come and pick 'em up?"

I thought for a second. "No. I don't want to risk them waking up and running. I have something better in mind."

Since I'd been here earlier today, I knew it was about a half a mile to the road. I could make that. Hell, I was alive and conscious and had Amanda's boots. I felt almost invincible in that moment.

"I'll help you to the Hummer, then come back and get them."

I didn't thank him again, but every cell in my body was grateful to the goblin. He kept hold of my elbow and assisted me in slogging through the woods. The woolen cape helped protect me from the snow, but I was still freezing and weary. Four or five times I had to stop and lean against a tree to catch my breath.

The drugs may not have knocked me out, but they zapped me of energy. Plus, my head still hurt.

When I finally spied the road through the trees, I nearly fell to my knees and kissed the ground. The Hummer sat there like a silver chariot, waiting to carry me to safety.

Gordon opened the passenger door and helped me inside. Then he started the car, cranking up the heater. "I followed them to a house before they brought you here. I got your clothes and shit." He reached into the back seat and handed me the bundle.

Snippets of the night flashed in my mind. The plastic tarp. Someone saying they didn't want blood on the floor. Right. That had been in the first model home. They'd talked about killing me there.

"Get dressed," Gordon said. "I'll go back for the Norms."

"You can't use your magic. The woods are contaminated."

"I don't need my powers to haul them. I got innate strength." No lie. His mom had moves like a professional wrestler. I'd hate to see what she was capable of with her powers.

While Gordon disappeared into the forest, I shed the cape. I sat in the front seat and struggled into my clothes. My fingers fumbled with the button on my jeans, but I finally got it.

Gordon returned with Aaron and Amanda first. I didn't know how he managed with both of them, and I didn't ask. He folded down the back seats and tossed them in. Then he was gone again.

Aaron gave a little moan, and my heart fluttered in fear. I glanced down at the floor, where my Coach bag sat at my feet. I grabbed it and pulled out my gun. No, I didn't shoot Aaron. But I did coldcock him with the hot pink butt of my gun. He didn't make a peep after that.

G-Dog returned minutes later with Stan. He tossed him on top of Amanda, then slid behind the wheel. "Where to, mama?"

"The Raven."

CHAPTER THIRTY-THREE

Once more, Mick stood at the door waiting this time with his bodyguard and right-hand man, Jasper. Except for the size of his muscles, Jasper's looks were unexceptional. Medium height, medium brown hair, and forgettable features.

Mick's dark gaze traced my frame, lingering on my face. "Are you all right?" His smooth voice was low, tight. Not the melodious accent I'd grown used to.

"I am, thanks to G-Dog. He literally saved my life."

Mick glanced down at Gordon. "I'll not forget this, goblin."

Gordon nodded. "Cool."

I stood in the club while Jasper, Mick, and Gordon pulled the trio from the Hummer into the club, dumping their bodies on the floor by the entrance.

Mick shook Gordon's hand. "Again, you have my gratitude." Then he ushered the goblin to the door.

G-Dog glanced back at me. "Take care, mama."

"You, too." I waved until the door closed behind him.

Mick turned to Jasper. "Take them up to room three. I'll meet you there momentarily." Then Mick escorted me up the stairs to his office.

I fell onto the sofa, my head still pounding—a side effect from the ketamine, most likely. Mick propped his hip against his desk and stared at me from across the room.

"So, now that you need me, I'm no longer horrible. You find it acceptable that I have a room for which I detain people?"

"And torture them."

"Yes. Sometimes that is what happens."

"I still don't approve. Not when you do it to people like Dena. She was harmless. And she's probably been a victim all her life." My own words ate at me. I was just as guilty as Mick. I'd questioned her as she'd been tied up and drugged. The ends justify the means, remember?

Hell, I didn't know what to think anymore.

Mick's dark eyes narrowed. "When it's someone who harmed you, then a little rough treatment is all right. But when someone has harmed me, I'm supposed to what, turn the other cheek?"

I rubbed my forehead. "I don't have the strength for a philosophical debate right now, Mick. I don't know the details of what you do in that room, and I don't want to know. If that makes me a hypocrite—"

"It does."

"Then I can live with that. Will you hold them until Cade can take them into custody?"

He stood and tucked his hands in his pockets. "Yes, of course. Go up to the green room and get some rest. I'll let Cade know where to find you."

I just stared at him, his cold features, his rigid posture. "You're mad at me, aren't you?"

"No. I'm glad you're alive. Goodnight, Holly." He strode to the door.

"You're angry. I saw another side to you, one I don't approve of, and that pissed you off."

He gripped the doorknob as he tipped his head to one side. "Why do you care if I'm angry?"

I wasn't sure. I shouldn't care how Mick felt, but I did.

When I didn't answer, he nodded. "That's what I thought."

Then he slammed out of the room, leaving me alone for the first time since I woke up in the woods.

The horror of the night sank in. All the fear and stress and panic I'd gone through. The aftershocks rocked through me, and I burst into tears. Curling up on the couch I cried until my eyes were swollen. Until I didn't have any tears left.

# #

Cade found me in the green room, so named for its green walls. He eased into the dark, treading silently to the bed. I rolled over and reached for him.

"I'm not asleep."

He settled on the mattress next to me and pulled me to him. "I wasn't there for you." He buried his face in my hair, his scent surrounding me, comforting me.

"I should have figured it out sooner," I said. "Amanda, the TV show, the antique furniture. That's how she found The Lost Code."

"Not the whole manuscript. Just a few translated pages that had been copied. I turned them over to the Council."

I turned in his arms, facing him. "You interrogated her?"

"No, Gordon hit her so hard, she's in a coma. Stan told me how it happened. They were all jealous of the attention Dean received. They wanted their share of fame, and they decided to perform the ceremony. They saw a little bit of success after their trial run with Dena, and they talked one another into killing Cassandra. She was a prostitute with no criminal background. Who would miss her? But a few days ago, their good luck shorted out."

"Because they met me."

"Right. They understood their good fortune had come to an end, but they didn't know why. So, they quickly found April and killed her, too. Then they got greedy, figured if they killed a psychic, they'd get a double boon from the demon."

Mary, the old witch, had been right. It was all about balance. Parts of Oklahoma were out of balance because those Norms had found a summoning spell they had no business using. "They killed two girls and fucked up the elements with their rituals."

"They have at that." He rubbed his warm hand up and down my spine. "I shouldn't have left you tonight. It's my fault you were taken."

"Stop right now, Cade McAllister. How could you have known what was going to happen? You're not psychic, you know. And you can't take responsibility for everything. It's kind of egotistical."

He didn't laugh. "If I hadn't given you the Council's offer, you wouldn't have been on the case in the first place."

"Bullshit. The Wylers were already my clients."

He blew out a breath, blowing a strand of my hair in the process. "I can't keep you safe."

"No, you can't. And what's hard for me to acknowledge is that I can't always keep myself safe." That truth scared the bejeezus out of me. If I couldn't fight back, how was I supposed to protect myself?

#

I awoke to Sunny's muffled ringtone. Dark gray filtered into the room. I lay there, trying to get my bearings when everything came rushing back to me. Getting taken from my bed by the Wylers and Stan. Almost getting raped, being tied to an altar. G-Dog rescuing me.

When I sat up, the phone stopped ringing. Cade was gone, his spot in the bed cold.

I brushed back my hair, then grabbed my purse off the floor. I dug out my phone and called Sunny.

"How are you?" she asked.

Cade must have filled her in on what happened the night before. Otherwise, she'd have been barking orders instead of inquiring after my wellbeing. "All right, I guess. All things considered, I'm doing pretty well."

"Take a day to rest up. We have a lot of people calling, wanting you to nullify their misfired spells."

"A whole day, huh? Very generous of you."

She paused. "You know I'm not good at this type of thing. Sympathy. I'm more a pull-yourself-up-by-your-bootstraps-and-get-on-with-it type of person."

"I know who you are, Sunny. It's okay. I'll call you tomorrow."

"Wait. Don't hang up. I took that picture on your fridge."

"Annabelle's drawing?"

"Didn't you notice the numbers?"

"The cost of toast and stuff? Yeah."

Sunny gave a prolonged, longsuffering sigh. It was all very dramatic. "Those weren't prices. It was a DynDNS."

"Okay, sure." No clue what she was talking about.

"It's a secure website. A private one that requires a username and password. I got in and found a list of all the parents who've used Moonlight Cove to get pregnant. It's basically a testimonial site and tells what happens during the ceremony."

Ha! I was right, and Reece Tolliver was still a weasel. "I knew they were up to something. Wait, what ceremony?"

"Sabbats and solstice. They allow the Norms to participate in fertility rites, and several have ended up pregnant. But it's not cheap. It's fifty-thousand-dollars for a one week stay at Moonlight Cove. No guarantees of a baby, but lots of hopefuls pay anyway. And if they do get pregnant, they pay a tithe to the coven in perpetuity."

"Whoa." I couldn't even begin to count how much money that added up to over the years. Then a thought occurred to me. "You're right. We haven't been charging enough. Fifty-thousand for one week?"

"That's exactly what I've been trying to tell you.

"How did you know the password, anyway?"

When she didn't answer, my eyes grew wide. "Sunny, did you hack into their system or something?"

"I don't care for that word. I may have prodded and poked a bit. Nothing wrong with that."

"Um, I'm pretty sure it's illegal. But I'm not busting your balls for it. Good work."

"Watch your language. Anyway, I sent everything to Cade in an email. Did he get it?"

"No idea. I'll call you later."

I tidied up and used the restroom, then went to find Cade. I also needed to talk to Mick but was dreading it at the same time. He'd been angry with me the night before, and I felt as if I'd let him down, not the other way around.

Hey, I didn't have an easy-to-clean torture chamber in my house. I wasn't in the wrong here.

I exited the room with my bag and coat and headed down to the stairs to the darkened bar. It was empty.

I was just about to text Cade when he blew through the entrance. "You're awake."

"What time is it?"

"Eight. The snow finally stopped, but it's an ice rink out there."

"Did you get Sunny's email?"

His lips tilted slightly. "Sure did. That was pretty damned smart, adding the code to the kid's picture like that. Never would have looked for it myself. We're fining the coven and putting a halt to their little baby making enterprise."

Good. I hoped Reece got kicked out for bringing the idea to the coven in the first place. But the town itself—it was home to two-hundred people. "They still get to keep their land, right?"

Cade approached me. "Of course. Though I'm not sure why you care."

"Because of the other witches who rely on it for their livelihood."

He reached out and rubbed my shoulder. For once, it didn't flare up in pain. Maybe I was finally on the mend.

"What about the Wylers and Stan McNeil? What happens to them?"

Cade's Adam's apple bobbed as he swallowed. "I'd have liked to kill them with my bare hands, but the Board nixed that idea." The Board of Twelve was the real power behind the Council. They decided who lived and who died. If an Other seriously stepped out of line, they didn't get a jury or a fair hearing. The Board decided their fate. "I hate those fuckers for what they were going to do to you."

I placed my hand over his. "I do, too. So…what's going to happen?"

"The Board ruled that their deaths should look like an accident. Since we kept the murder of those girls out of the Norm news, it had to appear that way or the family would get suspicious. Officially, the Wylers' SUV crashed late last night. Stan was in the backseat. The slick roads and bad weather caused the car to flip off an overpass. They didn't make it." His eyes darkened as he rattled off the story.

"And in reality?"

"A telepath caused the SUV to crash. Right now, the Council is concerned with getting the elements back in alignment, so that our magic starts working again."

"If I were you, I'd call on Mary, the old lady in Henryetta. She seemed to know a thing or two about a thing or two." Cade nearly smiled at my use of the old phrase.

"I'll let them know, and speaking of the Council, they'd kind of like you to get out of town for a couple of weeks while they try to get things back to normal. They're concerned that your presence might interfere with their efforts."

"No problem."

His brows shot up. "What, I don't get an argument about this?"

"Nope. I was going to take a few days off anyway."

"Well, you deserve it." He caught both of my hands in his. "Wherever you go, I'm riding shotgun." His eyes were serious as they met mine.

"Don't you need to stay and help make things right? The Council needs you."

"Fuck the Council. I need you." He tugged me close and placed his arms around my waist. "Don't care if the whole goddamned world falls apart. I want some time alone with you. So, what were you thinking? The Bahamas? London? Australia? Name it, and we'll go."

"Alabama."

"Shit." Cade's head dropped back and he groaned. "You're going to confront your grandfather, aren't you?"

"Yeah. Wallace swore an oath to me. And I want to meet my family. I don't imagine they'll be happy to see me, but that's what I need."

He sighed and rested his chin on the top of my head. "Alabama it is."

"Well, isn't this cozy?" Mick's sarcasm hit me like a tidal wave, dousing me with his anger. He glided the rest of the way down the stairs and stood with one hand on the railing.

Cade's arms tensed around me, but he didn't pull away. "Mick. Thanks for taking care of last night's issue."

"Of course. That's what I'm here for. Not to run a business, surely, but to play Watson to your Sherlock."

Cade looked down at me, his eyes narrowed. "Let's go home and pack."

"Can you wait for me in the car? I want to chat with Mick for a minute."

His lips pressed together. I could literally hear him grind his teeth.

"You trust me, remember?"

His head dipped in agreement. He squeezed my waist and left the club without another word.

I turned on Mick.

"You've got him trained, darling. Never thought I'd see the day when Cade McAllister reacted like a whipped puppy."

"Stop it."

He raised one brow. He hadn't shaved this morning. I'd never seen him with dark stubble covering his face. Made him look more villainous than ever. "Stop what?"

"I don't approve of your room."

He pulled his hand out of his pocket and studied his nails, as though he were bored stiff. "Yes, we've been over this. You made your position quite clear."

"But that doesn't mean we're not friends. I may not like everything you do, and that's okay. I still like you."

"You can't possibly be that naïve." He dropped his hand and walked toward me at a slow and steady pace. His nostrils flared slightly and his dark eyes glimmered in the dim light. "I am many things, Holly, but I am not your friend." He came to a stop when only inches separated us.

I carried on as if he hadn't spoken. "And I think you're Cade's friend. He's punished himself all these years. And he's borne your punishment as well. He misses her, too, Mick. You need to forgive him."

Fury sparked behind his eyes, but his expression became even more remote. "Do I? Perhaps I should simply destroy him, take away the only thing that's important to him. Then we'd be even."

I reached up and pressed my palm to his cheek. He didn't run as hot as Cade, but he was warm all the same. "If you think that would make you feel better, then you're not as smart as I thought you were." I dropped my hand and walked to the door. I glanced back, and what I saw on his face nearly broke my heart. I'd never seen anyone look so lonely, so hopeless. He masked it in an instant, but that raw, pained expression had been there.

"Goodbye, Mick."

Thank you

Thanks so much for reading Disheartened. I hope you enjoyed Holly's story, and there's more to come in the Null for Hire series. If you'd take the time to leave an honest review on your favorite site, I'd greatly appreciate it.

I love to hear from readers. Contact me at **TerriLAustin.com** and sign up for my newsletter while you're there.

Diners, Dives & Dead Ends

As a struggling waitress and part-time college student, Rose Strickland's life is stalled in the slow lane. But when her close friend, Axton, disappears, Rose suddenly finds herself serving up more than hot coffee and flapjacks. Now she's hashing it out with sexy bad guys and scrambling to find clues in a race to save Axton before his time runs out. With her anime-loving bestie, her septuagenarian boss, and pair of IT wise men along for the ride, Rose discovers political corruption, illegal gambling, and shady corporations. She's gone from zero to sixty and learns when you're speeding down the fast lane, it's easy to crash and burn.

Praise for Diners, Dives & Dead Ends

"Austin's debut kicks off her planned series by introducing a quirky, feisty heroine and a great supporting cast of characters and putting them through quite a number of interesting twists." – *Kirkus Reviews*

"I predict this will be a long and successful series...I strongly recommend picking a copy up to read this summer. I know I am looking forward to reading more books by this author. FIVE STARS OUT OF FIVE." – *Lynn Farris, National Mystery Review Examiner at Examiner.com*

"What a blast! Diners, Dives & Dead Ends is a fast-paced mystery loaded with wonderful wit and humor that had me laughing and loving every page. Terri Austin will hook you right away and keep you riveted until The End. I want more!" – *Ann Charles, Award-Winning Author of the Bestselling Deadwood Mystery Series*

His Every Need

Allie Campbell is determined to take care of her family, no matter the cost. But when her father loses their home to British tycoon Trevor Blake, Allie finds herself forced to plead for more time to pay off the loan...and if she has to use her own body as collateral, then so be it.

Trevor isn't moved by Allie's story. But when Allie impulsively offers to do anything to keep the house, he's intrigued enough to raise the stakes: for the next two months, she must cater to his every need, no matter how depraved. To his amazement, she agrees.

Allie has no intention of enjoying her time with the arrogant, domineering Brit, but it doesn't take long before he's got her aching for his touch—and he'll do whatever it takes to make her beg...

Praise for His Every Need:

"I was so into it... I read it all in one night – so I think that means it's a winner." – *Diary of an Eager Reader*

"Is it possible to give a book more than five stars? If so, this book would be at the top of the list to deserve those extra stars... It's a wonderful story, full of surprises and love." – *One Final Word*

"Easily one of the best books I've read this year and possibly ever. The characters are brilliant and the love story is extraordinary; truly a whimsical modern day Beauty and the Beast tale testing the bonds of family and the fragility of love... I've been irrevocably enchanted." – *Expressions of a Hopeful Romantic*

"From nicknames to bizarre wedding plans, this is a story that will stimulate your funny bone...in between moments of extreme heat." – *Romancing the Book*

Printed in Dunstable, United Kingdom